A FROLIC IN THE SNOW

Whup!

The snowball hit with unexpected force, causing Justin to stagger as he dropped the hatchet. He spun around, glancing about for his assailant, and took another snowball directly in the face. Seeing Amanda taking aim for a third shot, he hunched his shoulders and rushed toward her, a wicked grin making his intentions all too obvious.

At the sight of her victim turned aggressor, Amanda dropped her snowball, a shriek of laughter bursting from her lips as she turned to flee. She didn't make it very far before Justin brought her down with a tackle.

"Monster!" she cried, laughing as she fought to free herself from beneath his oppressive weight. "Hinting that I am such a milk and water miss that I can't be trusted to chop down a simple tree! Now, kindly let me up; this ground is cold."

"Is it?" he asked, his tone teasing. "Perhaps that is something you should have considered before attacking me." He settled his weight more evenly over her.

Amanda's smile vanished at the intimate touch. She was suddenly aware of Justin in a way that made the blood run wild in her veins. . . .

THE BEST OF REGENCY ROMANCES

A Christmas Affair

JOAN OVERFIELD

ZEBRA BOOKS
KENSINGTON PUBLISHING CORP.

For my editor Wendy McCurdy, for her patience and encouragement. Merry Christmas!

ZEBRA BOOKS

are published by

Kensington Publishing Corp.
475 Park Avenue South
New York, NY 10016

Second printing: September, 1992

Printed in the United States of America

 *Prologue*

Vitoria Spain, June 1813

"Do you think this storm will hold off?" Colonel Justin Stockton's sherry-colored eyes narrowed as he studied the battle maps spread out before him on the rickety camp table. "I'd hate to lead my men into a sea of mud and that is precisely what that valley will become should it start raining."

"Aye, but you know Wellington," General Hardgrave responded with a rueful grin. "Old Nosey believes 'tis best to seek the high ground and let the enemy bring the battle to us. Are the men all in place?"

"Yes, sir," Justin responded indicating various marks on the first map. "The artillery is stationed here and here, along the upper ridges and I have the cavalry held here in reserve. We will have need of them in the final attack."

The general grunted his agreement of the plan. "And your own men? I suppose you will be leading them out to face the enemy?"

"Yes, General." Justin thrust an impatient hand through his midnight-black hair as he pulled the second map toward him. "Our intelligence report puts the forward column of Jourdan's army here"—he made a slashing mark—"and I plan to lead a company of Light Infantry out to engage them, and with any luck cut them off from the main body of the army."

"That would put you directly between our guns and theirs," the general replied after a moment. "Dashed uncomfortable place to be. The grapeshot will be thick as snowflakes in January."

"I'm aware of that sir"—Justin met his commander's eyes—"but it can't be helped. We must hold the French off until we are better entrenched. This action will buy us the time we need."

General Hardgrave didn't answer, his pale blue eyes assessing as he studied the young colonel standing before him. Although Stockton was scarcely four and thirty, he was one of the general's most capable officers, leading his men to victory with raw courage and sheer determination. That determination was evident in the harsh lines carved deep in his lean cheeks and the hard thrust of his firm jaw. He knew without questioning the matter that Stockton would either achieve his objective or die in the attempt. A pity more of his officers didn't share those same sterling qualities, he thought, turning his attention back to the maps.

"Very well, Colonel Stockton" he said after examining the maps, "I approve of your plan. Hold those Frog bastards off and we'll do the rest. Now, go and have a word with your men. They're bound to be a might fearful and it will do them good to see their commanding officer. Go," and he waved the colonel toward the door.

"Yes, General." Justin snapped a smart salute and then hurried out into the cool Spanish night. He stood outside the small cottage that had been pressed into use as company headquarters his head tilted to one side as he listened to familiar sounds of soldiers preparing for battle. The ringing of the blacksmith's hammer almost drowned out the neighing of the horses and the rattle of swords and bayonets as the men saw to their weapons.

All around him the lights from hundreds of campfires twinkled in the velvet darkness and the shapes of his men could be faintly seen in their flickering light. Justin paused, drinking in the momentary peace as he fought to master his own fears and trepidations before facing his men. Even if his assessment of the French position was right, many of them would die. And if he was wrong. . . . He pushed the thought firmly aside, tugging his greatcoat about his shoulders as he struck out in the direction of the nearest campfire.

The first camp he came to was surrounded mostly by his junior officers, who were lounging on the ground, laughing in appreciation as a young lieutenant read aloud from the letter in his hands. When another officer saw him standing at the edge of their small circle, he called out a warning, and they all leapt to their feet, snapping to attention with well-trained discipline.

"As you were, gentlemen." Justin gave the young officers a set smile, limping slightly as he took his place beside the other men. "What is that you were reading, Lieutenant Lawrence? It sounds most interesting."

"Just a letter from my sister, Colonel," Daniel Lawrence replied his lean cheeks coloring in embarrassment. This was only the third time he'd spoken with his formidable commanding officer, and he was still in awe of him.

"Indeed? And what has she to say?" Justin asked, stretching his booted feet toward the sullenly smoking fire. The chilly wind was making the wound in his thigh ache like the very devil, and he needed something to take his mind off the pain. Perhaps hearing a bit of gossip would prove an effective panacea, he thought, striving to look more interested. "How are things in . . . Surrey isn't it?"

"Yes, sir." Daniel was pleased the colonel had remembered his place of birth. Given all the men under his command, he was certain that was significant. He picked up the letter and found the paragraph he'd been reading when Colonel Stockton had arrived. "My eldest sister, Amanda, was describing an assembly she and my younger sister,

7

Amelia, attended." He cleared his throat and then continued reading:

> *"The good vicar was so taken at the sight of Lady P's pulchritude, generously displayed in a French-cut gown of cream sarsanet, that he quite lost his step and fell head-long into the punch bowl, emerging with his dignity in tatters, his best neckcloth stained, and an orange slice draped coquettishly above one eye. The ladies present must have thought the new style most fetching, for within the week several bonnets of a similar design were to be found adorning the heads of various members of the congregation."*

Roars of masculine laughter drowned out the rest of the passage as the battle-weary soldiers doubled over in merriment. Justin joined in, grateful the others could find something to laugh about so close to the coming fight. How far away from the genteel world of vicars and country assemblies this all seemed, he thought wearily, casting a knowing look at the laughing faces of his men. Tomorrow these same soldiers would be locked in deadly combat, killing and dying for reasons most couldn't even comprehend, and yet tonight they could delight in the actions of a bumbling country cleric.

"This Lady P sounds most delightful," he drawled once the chuckling had subsided. "Although I fear the same can not be said of your sister. What a cutting wit she must have."

"Aye, that's Amanda." Daniel chuckled at the thought of his fearsome older sister. "She's a regular tartar, with a tongue like a cat-o'nine-tails and a temper that would put a Top Sergeant to the blush. You should have heard the dust she kicked up when I said I wanted to enlist in the Light Infantry! Boney's guns are a lark's song compared to that," and he shuddered in remembrance.

Justin's smile widened as he envisioned a sour-faced old

8

harridan ringing a peal over his junior officer. "Where were your parents while she was screeching at you? Hiding out in the cellars until it was safe to come out?"

"Both dead, sir," Daniel replied with a casual shrug. "My father died when I was but a lad, and my mother and stepfather were killed in a coach accident some six years ago, leaving Mandy to rule the roost, although she was scarce out of the schoolroom. Not that she's a complete quiz, mind," he added, not wishing to give Colonel Stockton the wrong impression of his sister. "But she does like her own way."

"She sounds the sort of managing female that makes a confirmed bachelor like me quake in his boots," Justin said, rising to his feet. He still had a dozen or more camps to visit before seeking his own bedroll, and the sooner he was about his business, the better.

He bid the young officers a good night, reminding them they would be marching out at first light, and then turned to leave. He'd barely taken a few steps when Lieutenant Lawrence called out to him. "Colonel, I should like a word with you, if you please."

"Of course, Lieutenant," Justin returned coolly, waiting patiently as the young officer made his way to his side. "What can I do for you?"

Daniel blushed at the colonel's polite words. "Well, I was wondering if you might hold this for me." He thrust a packet into Justin's hand. "It's just some letters and a portrait of my mother," he continued, his words tumbling out in an embarrassed rush. "I also included a few pounds from my salary and some money I won gaming. If . . . if anything should happen, could you see that my sister gets them?"

Justin gazed into the lieutenant's anxious face, his heart turning over in his chest as he took in the younger man's bright red hair and freckled cheeks. God, the lad was scarcely twenty-one, he thought with grim despair. He should be getting into trouble for gambling and chasing light skirts, not standing in the darkness of a Spanish night facing the prospect of his probable death. His gloved hands closed spasmodically around the packet of papers.

"It will be done," he said, his fierce eyes meeting Lawrence's. "You have my word on it."

"Thank you, sir." Daniel sighed in relief. "I'm the eldest son, you see, and they do depend upon me . . . even though Mandy would die sooner than admit as much." He added this last part with a whimsical smile.

"Ah yes, the martinet in petticoats." Justin returned the lieutenant's smile. "Well, hopefully we shan't have occasion to meet, but should we, sir, you may rely upon me to give a good accounting of myself."

"I daresay you will, Colonel." Daniel's hazel eyes began to dance with boyish laughter. "I should enjoy seeing it; the pair of you would be at daggers drawn within ten minutes of clapping eyes on each other."

"In that case, Lieutenant, then I very much hope we shall not meet." Justin tucked the letters in his inner pocket and began moving away. "A female who would incite me to violence is not at all to my liking. Good evening to you then. Mind you get a good night's sleep. You will have need of it come the morrow."

Shells exploded all around Justin, filling the air with choking smoke and the screams of the wounded and dying. He fought on desperately, ignoring the pain in his arm and shoulder as he ran his sword through the blue-coated grenadier who had cut him off from his men. He saw the life flicker and die in the man's dark eyes, and then turned to meet the rush of another French soldier.

Another shell screamed past him, and Justin felt a burning pain as a piece of shrapnel tore into his leg. The impact threw him to the ground, knocking his sword from his hand. The French soldier he had been fighting was also wounded, and blood flowed from his left side; but he retained his weapon. Triumph glittered in his eyes, and Justin glared up at him defiantly as the man raised his bayoneted rifle high above his head to deliver the death blow.

"Colonel, look out!" Daniel exclaimed, interposing himself between Justin and the French soldier, giving him time to drag himself to safety. Justin scooped up a rifle dropped by a fallen cavalry officer and rolled to one side, firing a single bullet into the French soldier's chest. The man staggered and fell, and a grinning Daniel leaned down to offer Justin his hand.

"That was a clean shot, sir," he said wiping the dust and blood from his cheeks. "You got him right through the—" a volley of fire cut off his words of praise, and a sudden look of faint surprise crossed his face. "I say, I do believe I've been shot," he said, and then tumbled forward into Justin's arms.

Cursing softly, Justin rolled him over onto his back, his curses growing in volume and intensity at the sight of the blood staining the front of the lieutenant's jacket. He tore open the jacket, his breath catching in his throat at what he saw.

"Gut shot, ain't I?" Daniel asked, his face paling with pain and shock. "Guess that tears it for me, sir."

"Nonsense, Lieutenant." Justin pulled a bandage from the kit at his side and began dabbing at the steady flow of blood. "I'll have you at the hospital tent in no time at all."

"No." Daniel shook his head weakly. "Too late. Besides I'd rather die here than let one of those drunken sawbones have at me." He blanched at the pain and the bitter chill he felt creeping over him. He grabbed instinctively for the colonel's hand. "Colonel!"

"Yes?" Justin abandoned his efforts, knowing they were useless. His hand closed protectively over Lawrence's, and he was not ashamed at the tears that were burning in his eyes.

"You won't tell my sister, will you? About the gaming, I mean?" His bloodless lips parted in a rueful smile. "Mandy don't approve of it, you see, and she'd kick up a devil of a dust if she was to know."

"It will be a secret between us," Justin promised, his voice hoarse with grief. He had seen death so many times he thought he was inured to it, but this was almost more than he could bear. God damn Napoleon Bonaparte, he cursed silently, knowing full well that the carnage about him was the direct result of that madman's dreams of glory.

"And you'll see she gets the letters?" Daniel could no longer see, and his voice was already beginning to fade.

"I'll deliver them myself," Justin vowed. "Upon my honor, I'll place them in her hands myself."

"Thank you, sir," Daniel managed another smile. "And you'll have a care of them won't you? Never mind what Mandy says . . . tell them I'm sorry. . . ." And in the next instant he was gone, leaving an anguished Justin to weep in bitter fury as the battle raged around him.

 *Chapter One*

Surrey, December 1813

"It is not that I am ungrateful, Amelia," Miss Amanda Lawrence began, her velvet-dark eyes snapping with vexation as she glared out at the thick curtain of snow falling beyond the snug confines of the parlor. "Indeed, I consider myself the most fortunate of females, being blessed as I have with a loving family and a situation that is far more agreeable than most of my countrymen. But even you must admit that the prospect of being snowed in while Aunt Elizabeth is in residence is beyond all enduring. I vow, I can think of nothing we might have done to warrant so harsh a punishment!"

"I am sure God doesn't look upon a visit by our only surviving relation as a punishment, dearest," Miss Amelia Lawrence replied, her smile gentle as she added another stitch to the shirt she was mending. Accustomed as she was to her elder sister's fiery temper, she knew Amanda meant only half of what she said, and so was able to meet the pronouncement with some show of equanimity.

"That is because God doesn't know her as well as I do," Amanda retorted, picking up her own sewing and jabbing the needle through the worn cambric. "She is an avaricious, interfering, impossible, old harridan, and I shall consider it one of the wonders of the world if I don't throttle her before the fortnight is out! Why did she have to pick Christmas to descend upon us like a blight?"

"Because we are all that she has," Amelia answered serenely. "Where else would she pass the holidays if not with us?"

Several locations occurred to Amanda, but out of respect for Amelia's tender feelings, she grudgingly held her tongue. Her sister's disposition was almost as angelic as her blond, blue-eyed appearance, and she had no wish to upset her. Still, the thought of her tedious aunt intruding upon them made her lips thin with displeasure. Try as she might, she found it impossible to warm to her late father's younger sister, and it was not, as Daniel had once teasingly suggested, because no home could endure two tyrants. *She* was not in the least bit tyrannical.

The thought of her beloved brother intensified the frown puckering her copper-colored brows. It had been over five months since they had last heard from Daniel, and that letter was more than a month in reaching them. She knew his regiment had fought in the Battle of Vitoria that drove Napoleon's brother from Spain, but she'd been unable to learn anything else. Her entreaties to the War Office had gone unanswered, and as the weeks passed, she was beginning to fear the worst.

"Well, at least Aunt has brought the latest gazettes with her," Amelia said with forced cheerfulness. She sensed Amanda's disquiet and was anxious to tease her into a more gentle humor. "I haven't seen a copy of *La Belle Assemblie* since her last visit, and I wouldn't want Charles to think me unfashionable when he comes home for the holidays."

"Yes, we wouldn't want to give him a horror of you," Amanda replied, shaking off her melancholy at the warm glow in her sister's eyes. Amelia had been in love with the neighbor's eldest son since the pair of them were in leading strings, and although nothing had been said, there was an understanding that they would marry once Charles had fulfilled his obligation to his king.

"Perhaps you might want to study the gazettes as well," the younger girl ventured, casting Amanda a hopeful look. "It's been years since you've had a new gown, and I'm certain that you'll want to look your best for the Harmiston's Christmas ball. I heard it from Lavinia Whitehead that her cousin Eustace will be in attendance." This last bit of information was offered with a sly look that brought a reluctant smile to Amanda's face.

"If you mean that as some sort of inducement, Amelia, I fear you are far off the mark," she said with a chuckle. "Eustace Whitehead is an odious prig who told me that he considers redheaded women to be, and I quote, 'inherently forward.' "

"He could never have said anything so thick-skulled!" Amelia was clearly horrified.

"Ah, but he did," Amanda assured her, her dimples flashing at the memory. It had been at the squire's last rout, and the pompous young clergyman had cornered her out on the terrace, his beefy hands clutching his lapels as he offered his opinion on everything from how the war was being fought, to the wanton conduct of females with "hair too colorful to be pleasing."

"What did you say?"

"Only that I could quite understand how he felt, as I had often regarded men with double chins to be prosy, self-indulgent bores," Amanda replied sweetly, tucking a flame-colored tendril back into place. As usual her thick hair was bound up in a tidy bun, a few wisps escaping confinement to curl about her neck and ears. The style was better suited to a woman twice her tender years, but Amanda liked its ease and practicality. Besides, as she had once told her younger brother, an old maid such as herself ought to dress the part.

"You didn't," Amelia gasped, her cheeks burning with embarrassment. But even as she made the demand, she already knew the answer. Amanda, with sufficient provocation, would say whatever crossed her mind.

An arch smile was the only reply as Amanda turned her attention to the mending on her lap. Tuesday was the day she and Amelia set aside to catch up on the family's sewing, and with four growing children, there seemed to be an unending supply of it. The shift she was now hemming had once belonged to Amelia, and she was cutting it down for Belinda. She was only happy that the lively eight-year-old was so indifferent to the vagaries of fashion, for there was no way the family coffers could extend to a new wardrobe this year.

They were just finishing up the last of the mending when the door to the parlor opened, and an elderly lady dressed in black merino entered the parlor, her sallow face pinched with displeasure. "Really, Amanda," she began in the hectoring tones that Amanda was growing to hate, "I can not think why you insist upon keeping that cook in your employ. She is too forward by half, and her breads leave a great deal to be desired. You really must replace her."

Amanda bristled in instant defense of the cook, her dark eyes narrowing as her aunt took her chair before the fire. Mrs. Hatcher had been with them since before her father's death, and she had proven a loving and loyal friend over the years. She opened her lips to administer a sharp retort when she caught Amelia's eye. At the gentle shake of the younger girl's head, she reluctantly amended her speech. "I shall have a word with her, Aunt," she managed, gritting her teeth with determination.

"See that you do," Mrs. Elizabeth Herrick sniffed, settling her starched mobcap on her thin and graying locks. "And while you're about it, you might also have a word with the butler. I distinctly smelled spirits on him last night. A proper household manager would never tolerate a servant who imbibes."

Amanda clenched her hands into tight fists. "Yes, Aunt" she said, fighting the urge to toss the disagreeable old woman into the nearest snowbank. Relative or nay, she fumed silently, there was only so much she was willing to tolerate in the name of familial obligation.

"And I think it time you were dismissing the maids as well." Mrs. Herrick began helping herself to the meager tea the girls had been sharing prior to her arrival. "You pay them far too much to my way of thinking, and in any case it will do you girls no harm to help earn your keep. You do little enough as it is."

This was too much for Amanda, and she leapt to her feet, the trousers she'd just finished mending tumbling to the floor. "How dare you, ma'am!" she cried, her thin face flushing with fury. "This is my brother's house, and I will thank you to remember that fact!"

"Indeed?" Rather than taking offense, the older woman looked faintly amused. "I shouldn't be so certain of that, missy."

"What is that supposed to mean?"

"Merely that I would have a word with your guardian if I were you," Mrs. Herrick said, taking a greedy bite of a fruit tart. "This house belonged to my grandfather, and should anything happen to Daniel, I will be next to inherit. It has been what . . . six months since you've had news of him? And anything can happen in wartime. Who knows"—she sent both girls a poisonous smile—"he could well be lying dead even as we speak."

"Why you hateful old—" Amanda began hotly, only to be interrupted by a horrified cry from Amelia.

"No! No, Daniel is not dead! He's not . . . is he Amanda?" She turned to her older sister, seeking comfort and reassurance as she had always done.

Amanda's heart broke at the frightened look on Amelia's face. She longed to tell her that all was well, but there was

17

no denying that the long silence was ominous. Tamping down her own fears, she turned a look of such fury on Mrs. Herrick that the woman shrank back in her chair. Amanda paid her no mind but rushed to her sister's side.

"Hush, my dear," she soothed, slipping a comforting arm about Amelia's shoulders as she helped her to her feet. "We mustn't even think such things. Come now, let me help you to your room," and she guided her gently toward the door. When they reached their destination, she turned to cast a final, glaring look at her aunt.

"I shall speak with our guardian," she said, her voice cold with menace. "In the meanwhile, if you dare repeat such things in front of the other children, I vow I'll have you thrown out into the snow. Do you understand me?"

"Really!" Mrs. Herrick was shaken but still determined. "You can not take that tone with me! I am your aunt, and—"

"Do you understand me?" The words were all the more threatening because of the soft manner in which they were spoken.

Mrs. Herrick's cheeks paled, and she averted her head from Amanda's piercing gaze. "I understand," she muttered crossly.

"See that you do," Amanda said, turning back toward Amelia, who was crying into her handkerchief. "And understand something else as well; there is nothing I won't do to protect my family. Nothing." And with that final threat she closed the door quietly behind her.

"Why didn't you tell me?" Amanda demanded some three hours later, her eyes dark with fury as she confronted the elderly solicitor who had been appointed her guardian shortly before her stepfather's death. "Didn't you think I'd want to know?"

"Of course, my dear, of course," Mr. Elias Stranton stammered, mopping his perspiring brow with a snowy handkerchief. "But there didn't seem to be any need for it. Daniel's a young lad, after all, with the whole of his life yet before him. I made sure he would survive Mrs. Herrick by a good five decades, if not more."

Amanda raised her eyes to the ceiling, mentally calling upon divine help in controlling her temper. "But Daniel is a soldier now," she reminded him through gritted teeth. "A rather hazardous occupation for a man, don't you agree?"

"Perhaps," the older man conceded reluctantly. "But there is every hope that he will make it through the wars unscathed. Why, my own brother fought the French for ten years or more without so much as a scratch to show for all of it. You worry too much, my dear; it is the way with you ladies," and he gave her hand a pat.

That same hand closed in a fist to resist the urge to land a stinging blow to the solicitor's ears. It took a great deal of effort, but she managed to resist the impulse. "Did Daniel know of this proviso before he enlisted?" she asked, her voice low with controlled anger.

"We spoke of it," Mr. Stranton answered with a vague shrug. "That is to say, I told him that should he die without male issue your father's inheritance would then pass to your aunt according to the terms of your grandfather's will. It was but a mere formality, you see, and as I told him he—"

"But did he know about the house? That it would pass on to Aunt Elizabeth?" Amanda pressed, determined to get to the truth before her temper exploded. She'd left the house without lunch, scarcely bothering to change her clothes before setting out for the village. Her aunt's taunting words had filled her with such apprehension that she knew she couldn't rest a single moment until she'd spoken with her guardian.

"As to that I can not say, Miss Lawrence," came the cautious reply. "We never specifically discussed the matter, but it stands to reason that the manor house is the most significant part of the inheritance. May I ask you why you are suddenly so interested?" he asked, shooting her a worried look. "You've not received any unhappy news, have you?"

"No." On this point at least she could reassure him. "But neither have I had any good news. I suppose I was just curious." Despite her extreme dislike of her aunt, Amanda didn't wish to discuss their falling out with anyone, especially Mr. Stranton, whom she knew to be an inveterate gossip.

To her surprise the solicitor gave an approving nod. "A wise move, Miss Lawrence, especially in light of your situation. If you like, I can go over your finances with you. I fear they are not as good as one might hope."

Amanda felt her heart plummet to the soles of her wet pattens. "What do you mean?" she asked, nervously running her tongue over her lips. "I know we are not wealthy, but what of the portion left me by my mother? Surely that is enough to keep us in some comfort?"

"For a while, if you practice every economy," he agreed, perching his glasses on the edge of his nose as he went over the figures detailed on the papers spread out before him. "Your step-father left a small sum for the care of your half brothers and half sister, but it is not what I would call a large amount. And of course there are the jewels and other items not detailed in your grandfather's will that will go to you on your brother's death. But other than that I fear there is nothing else."

"But how—how shall we live?" Amanda asked fighting against the sudden urge to burst into tears. She was seldom given to such displays of feminine weakness, but the prospect of losing the only home she had ever known was more than she could bear.

"Oh, I am sure you and your aunt will soon come to terms," he said, peering at her over the edge of his glasses. "Family and all that. And if one of you was to make an advantageous marriage, well, that would be of great help would it not?"

Amanda could find no breath to answer. The Maxfields, although comfortably situated, were hardly wealthy enough to settle a large portion on Charles once he and Amelia wed. Even if they did, she and the others could hardly descend upon the newlyweds en masse.

And that was another thing, she realized with mounting alarm. What about Amelia's bridal portion? Her own had gone to purchase Daniel's commission, lest he enlist as a common foot soldier as he had threatened to do. She didn't think Charles' family would cry off when it became known she was virtually destitute, but what if they did? And what of Stephen and the twins? They would soon be old enough to send off to school; however would she pay for their tuition and lodging?

"There, there, Miss Lawrence." Mr. Stranton was patting her hand again, thoroughly alarmed at the bleak expression on her face. "No need to be looking like that, no need at all. It'll all come about in the end, you'll see."

Amanda stared up at his bland, helpful countenance, wishing he was somebody of strength, someone she could lean upon, if only for a moment. She'd been standing alone for years, and she longed for the comfort of supporting arms. . . .

In the next moment she was shaking off the unfamiliar sensations, her chin coming up with determined pride. "Of course you are right, Mr. Stranton," she said, infusing more confidence than she felt into her soft voice. She needed no one to help her, she told herself firmly. She had been caring for her large family since she was barely twenty, and she would go on caring for them for as long as necessary.

The next morning found Amanda hard at work poring over the household accounts. In light of her conversation with Mr. Stranton, she decided it was time to make some more cuts in her already pared-down budget. There would be no more talk of new gowns, of course, and the trip to Bath Amelia had been hinting for would have to be put off. They still employed two footmen and three maids in addition to the butler and cook, but she thought with a little effort they could dispense with the service of at least two of them. But which two, she wondered glumly.

She was no closer to solving this dilemma when the door to her study burst open and twin whirlwinds came rushing in, their voices raised in acrimonious dissent.

"Is not!"

"Is too!"

"Is not!"

"Is too! Even Belinda knows 'tis the grenadiers that wear white plumes in their shakos, cloth head!" Jeremey Blanchford announced in the superior tones that only a twelve-year-old boy could achieve. "The colonel's in the Light Infantry, I tell you, just like Daniel. Tell him Mandy!" And he turned indignant blue eyes upon his sister, clearly confident of her support.

"I should be more than happy to do so, sir, if you'd only tell me who it is you are discussing in such an unpleasant manner," she replied with the calm of one accustomed to such displays of sibling disharmony. Usually the twins were the best of friends, but as both were cursed with the same stubborn nature as she, disagreements often arose between them. She'd learned at an early age that if they were left to their own devices they would soon forget the source of contention and return to their play.

"The colonel, of course!" Jeremey shot her a look that indicated he considered her sadly backward in the matter. "Joss would have it that he is in the grenadiers because of his epaulets. But I say he is in the Light Infantry. His plume is green and—"

"What colonel are you talking about?" Amanda interrupted, her brow wrinkling in thought. She was well acquainted with most of her neighbors, and knew none of them had ever managed to rise above the rank of major. It was conceivable that with Christmas so close at hand an officer might be paying his family a visit, but she felt she would have heard if such were the case. Almost every family in the county had some relation or other in uniform, and any such information was eagerly shared.

"The one in the parlor." Jocelyn's impatient look matched that of his twin. "He just arrived and was asking for you, so I told Linsley we'd fetch you. Do hurry!" and he began tugging her to her feet.

"*What?*" Amanda collapsed back on her chair staring at the twins in disbelief.

"He's a bang-up looking fellow," Jeremey offered. "He limps a bit and has a scar on his left cheek. Do you think he got them in battle?" His eyes began gleaming with incipient hero-worship.

" 'Tis possible, I suppose," Amanda replied smiling at the boy's enthusiasm. "Now kindly go and tell our guest that I will be with him once I have made myself presentable. I certainly can't greet him looking like this," and she cast a rueful look at the rumpled skirts of her gown.

"But what if he leaves?" Jeremey wailed, dancing impatiently from one foot to the other. "Joss and I have dozens of questions we want to ask him!"

"He will wait," Amanda assured him, ruffling his light brown hair with an affectionate hand. "Now hurry, we wouldn't want him to think we have abandoned him, would we?"

The twins' eyes widened in horror at such a possibility, and they dashed from the study, leaving a worried Amanda behind to speculate about their mysterious visitor. If the colonel was in the Light Infantry, then there was every chance he was bringing them news of Daniel. But was it good news or bad? Her heart began pounding with anxious fear, and as she made her way up to her rooms, Amanda found herself sending a silent prayer winging heavenward. God help them all if anything had happened to Daniel.

In the small parlor to which the aging butler had guided him, Justin waited for his hostess with increasing impatience. He'd finally managed to rid himself of the two younger boys who had been pestering him with questions, and his head was aching almost as much as his shoulder. He'd been travelling almost non-stop since his arrival in Portsmouth some two days earlier, and he was weak with pain and exhaustion. The ship's surgeon had tried talking him into going directly to London, but he'd curtly refused, determined to fulfill his promise to the dying young officer.

His light brown eyes moved restlessly about the small parlor, taking in its tidy appearance with cool interest. The rug and furnishings were worn with age, and the heavy velvet drapes covering the mullioned windows, once a brilliant blue, had faded from years of exposure to the sun. He ran a hand over the back of a chair, a tanned finger touching the lace doily that had been placed there to hide a stain. Evidently the Lawrences weren't as wealthy as the large manor house would lead one to believe, he thought, his dark brows gathering in a worried frown. How would Lawrence's death affect them?

The door to the parlor creaked open, and Justin turned just as a tall woman with bright red hair hurried toward him. "How do you do, sir," she said, smiling as she held her hand out to him. "I am Miss Amanda Lawrence. My brothers say you wish to speak with me?"

Justin accepted her slender hand, his lips twitching with the need to smile. So this was the martinet in petticoats young Lawrence had warned him of, he thought, his eyes moving over her in discreet perusal. He could well believe it. Despite the demure gown of yellow merino trimmed at the high waist with a dark green riband she was currently wearing, there was something in the tilt of her small chin and the sparkle in her deep brown eyes that spoke of a fiery temperament held carefully in check. Justin prayed she was every bit as strong as her brother had claimed she was, for she would soon have need of that strength.

"Miss Lawrence," he murmured, his eyes meeting hers with cool politeness. "I am Colonel Justin Stockton of the 55th Light Infantry. Perhaps you have heard of me?"

Amanda's heart turned to stone in her chest. That was the name of Daniel's commanding officer. In his last letter home he had been generous in his praise, describing him as a man as hard as steel and twice as deadly. Gazing up into his hard face, she could well believe that assessment of him, and a fine tremor shook her as she contemplated the reason behind his unexpected appearance.

"Of course, Colonel Stockton, Daniel has written of you." She withdrew her hand from his, her legs trembling as she turned toward the armchairs set before the fireplace. "But pray, will you not be seated? I am sure you must be feeling quite exhausted after your long journey. Did you come from London?"

"From Portsmouth," Justin answered, his eyes never leaving her face. Although she appeared outwardly calm, he could detect the strain about her full mouth, and his heart moved with pity. He'd had to break the news of an officer's death to an anxious relative before, but never had it seemed more difficult.

"I . . . I see," Amanda stammered, her heart growing dry at his curt reply. If he had travelled from Portsmouth, then it was likely he had only just returned to England. She clenched her hands together in her lap, knowing she could no longer avoid the inevitable. Steeling herself as best as she could, she drew back her shoulders and met his stare.

"What news have you of my brother, sir?" she asked, willing her voice to remain even. "Is he well?"

Justin held her unwavering regard, not knowing that the

compassion gleaming deep in his golden eyes gave her the answer long before he spoke. "I regret to inform you, Miss Lawrence, that your brother is dead. He fell at the Battle of Vitoria six months ago. I am very sorry."

 *Chapter Two*

"Dead?" Amanda repeated dully, wanting to scream a denial of that awful word. She had thought herself prepared to hear it, but nothing, she realized, could have prepared her for the terrible finality of it all. Daniel was dead. She would never see him again. Never hear him laugh, or watch him grow to manhood and claim his inheritance. . . . She swayed on her chair.

Justin was at her side in a moment, ready to catch her should she swoon. He'd seen her creamy complexion pale to purest ivory and knew she was in shock. He reached out to take her hand in his and was stunned by its iciness.

"Miss Lawrence?" he asked, his tone gentle as he chafed her small hand between his. "Are you all right? Is there someone I can send for? Your maid perhaps, or your sister?" He recalled Lawrence had said something of a younger sister. . . .

Amanda stared at him uncomprehendingly. As if from a great distance, she could hear the ticking of the clock on the mantle and the snap and pop of the fire blazing cheerfully in the hearth. She blinked at the man bending solicitously over her hand and realized he had spoken.

"I . . . I beg your pardon, sir," she said her voice sounding oddly weak. "What was it you said?"

Justin stared down at her, fully alarmed. This stunned,

helpless creature was hardly the virago of Lawrence's description, and he wondered if he had erred in coming to her as he had. Perhaps it would have been better to have the news broken to her through the dispatches, rather than personally attending to the matter himself. Then he remembered his promise to the dying officer and mentally steeled himself for the hysterics he was certain were to follow.

"I asked if you wished me to ring for the maid," he said, his voice brisk. "You are rather faint, and I —"

"I have never fainted in my life, sir." Amanda was glad she could still feel annoyance, and she seized on to the emotion as if to a lifeline. "I own I am shocked, but you needn't fear that I will dissolve into a watering pot."

"I didn't mean to imply that you would," he answered, relieved but puzzled by her sudden show of spirit. Perhaps she was growing hysterical after all, he thought, wondering if he'd be required to administer a sharp slap to her cheek to return her to her senses.

"Well, I shan't," she declared, her tone sharper than she intended. Now that the initial shock had worn off, she was aware of a devouring pain that was tearing at her soul, and she sternly thrust it aside. Later, she promised herself, she would collapse into hysterics later. In the meanwhile there was much that required her attention, beginning with her brother's commanding officer.

"It was kind of you to bring me the news yourself, Colonel," she said, raising her chin with unconscious pride. "Thank you."

"You are welcome, Miss Lawrence," he answered, moving slowly away from her. The long carriage ride had irritated the old sword wound in his thigh, and he was grateful to resume his seat again. Lord, but they kept it warm in these rooms, he thought, running a shaking hand across his forehead.

"I — how did it happen?" she asked, her voice trembling despite her resolve. She hated the necessity for such a question, but knew the others would want to know. Especially the twins; they had been so proud of their older brother. . . .

"It was in close combat," Justin began, feeling a trifle awkward. He'd never had to go into detail before, and he was uncertain how much he should tell her. But he did want her and the others to know of their brother's bravery, and so he forced himself to continue. "We'd ridden out to engage the enemy at some distance from our camp, and we got pinned down by artillery fire. We were attempting to fight our way back when a company of grenadiers attacked our flank. I was knocked down by shrapnel from a one-pounder and would have been killed if it hadn't been for Daniel. He saved my life."

Amanda flinched, envisioning the terrible scene. "Did . . . did he suffer?" she asked, praying for the strength to listen.

"No." Justin saw no reason why he should be completely honest in the matter. "It was over very quickly, and afterward I . . . I was able to see he received a proper burial. I want you to know that."

"Thank you," Amanda replied, blinking back tears. She'd heard how a fallen soldier's body was often left to rot where he lay, while grave robbers and other scavengers picked at the remains. At least Daniel had been spared that final indignation.

"There are some of his personal belongings that I have brought with me," he continued, relieved by her calm acceptance. "They are out in my carriage and I'll have my footman fetch them in if you'd like. He also left me this and asked that I give it to you." He withdrew the packet of letters that he hadn't let out of his possession in six months and handed it to her. "I gave him my most solemn word that I would give them to you myself."

She accepted the packet silently, her fingers trembling as she untied the faded ribbon holding the contents together. A sad smile touched her lips as she recognized the letters she and the other children had sent him. They were wrinkled and somewhat worn, as if the recipient had read them over and over again. The sight of the miniature of their mother made her eyes swim with tears, but she wouldn't let them fall. She briefly examined the rest of the items, stopping only when she came to the money that had been carefully wrapped in a stained piece of cloth.

"His salary and some other money he . . . er . . . acquired," Justin explained at her puzzled look. "He wanted you to have it."

"But where could he have gotten it?" Amanda asked, counting the money in mounting confusion. "There is over a hundred pounds here!"

She made it sound as if it was a huge amount, and then he realized that perhaps to her it was. He cast another look about the parlor, wondering again what impact the lieutenant's death would have on his family.

"I am not at liberty to tell you," he said in answer to her question. "I can only assure you that it is his, and that he wanted you to have it."

"He was gaming," she guessed, rewrapping the money with loving hands. "And after he solemnly gave me his word he would not."

Justin smiled at her words, recognizing the love behind the scolding tones. "Yes, he told me you would not approve," he said, his eyes warming with laughter. "In fact, he seemed most particularly anxious that you not find out."

"Our stepfather gamed, and it cost us dearly." Amanda set the packet aside and gave the colonel a shy smile. Now that her emotions were under some semblance of control, she was feeling more the thing, and for the first time she began to notice the tall man sitting opposite her.

He was much younger than she thought a colonel should be, and she put his age as somewhere in his late thirties. His hair was coal-black and worn slightly longer than current fashion dictated, curling over the collar of his uniform jacket. Beneath his slashing eyebrows his eyes were the color of a deepest amber, and they stared out at her with sharp intelligence.

He was a handsome man, she decided objectively. But the small crescent-shaped scar and the deep lines grooving his face saved him from the charge of being *too* handsome, a sobriquet instinct told her he would find annoying. His complexion was darker than most of the men she was accustomed to seeing, although not quite as dark as one would expect from a man returning after several months on the Peninsula. In fact, she frowned suddenly, in fact now that she thought of it, the colonel was looking decidedly gray.

"Colonel, are you feeling quite the thing?" As usual she spoke without thought, studying him worriedly. "You will forgive my saying so, but you look rather done in."

"I found the journey here somewhat longer than I had anticipated," Justin returned coolly, annoyed by her acuity. He disliked being weak as a damned kitten and was unwilling to admit to being less than totally fit.

"But of course, you said you had been wounded!" Amanda leapt to her feet, her hand reaching automatically for the rope pull. "What a terrible hostess you must think me," she cried, focusing her attention on the mundane requirements of proper hospitality. "Not to offer you so much as a cup of tea, and after all you have done for us!"

"That is perfectly all right, Miss Lawrence," he began, anxious to be on his way now that he had fulfilled his obligation. He was beginning to shake and realized he was about to succumb to the fever he had picked up in the field hospital. The thought of being reduced to such a state was an anathema to him, and he struggled to rise from his chair.

"There is no need, I promise you. It is already grown rather late, and I must be on my way if I am to make the inn by—"

"Nonsense!" She cast him an indignant scowl. "I won't

hear of you staying anywhere but with us. We have plenty of rooms available, which is more than can be said of The Hare and Hound."

"The Hare and Hound?" Justin repeated weakly.

"The nearest inn. It is in the village some two miles from here, and I doubt you'll be successful in finding lodging. 'Tis but two weeks before Christmas, you know, and there's not a room to be let."

He'd forgotten it was so close to the holidays. Blast it, Justin cursed silently. The wench was right; he would be lucky if there was a private room to be found between here and London. In the next moment he was shaking off the very notion of defeat. His pockets were deep enough to insure the cooperation of even the most harried of innkeepers, and if worse came to worst, he could spread out his blanket before the inn's fireplace. God knew he'd slept in even worse places over the last three years.

"That is very kind of you, Miss Lawrence," he said, his voice firm with resolution. "But I really must be on my way. I am expected at my brother's home in London and I—"

"Ah, there you are, Linsley." Amanda ignored his protestations as she smiled at the elderly butler who had come in response to her summons. "Kindly have Cook prepare the colonel and I a nice tea, and then have the footman prepare rooms for our guest and his servants. They will be passing the night with us."

"Miss Lawrence," Justin tried again, this time using the same sharp tones he used to scold his troops, "I have told you, there is no need. Edward is expecting me, and I—"

"The Red Room, Miss," Linsley suggested, paying the stern-faced colonel no mind. He knew his mistress too well to be of a mind to ignore her orders. " 'Tis not as large as the old master's rooms, but it's a dashed sight warmer."

"Excellent, Linsley, thank you." She nodded her approval. "You might also inform Cook to move dinner back one hour, I . . . I have some news I must share with my family."

Linsley's face puckered. "The . . . the young master, miss?" he asked, his voice quavering slightly.

"Yes." Amanda had to steel herself to say the words. "Colonel Stockton has just informed me that Daniel has fallen in the Battle of Vitoria. He . . . he is dead."

The old butler made a choking sound and then drew back his frail shoulders. "Shall I tell the other servants?"

"If you would be so kind." Amanda knew the duty should fall to her, but it was more than she could bear. "I would also appreciate it if you would have one of the footmen fetch the vicar."

"Yes miss." Linsley inclined his head and then quietly withdrew, his gait shuffling and tired as he closed the door behind him.

Justin stared after him for a few moments and then turned to Miss Lawrence. "Are you certain you wish me to remain here?" he asked, crossing the room to take her hand. "You and your family should be alone in your grief; I will only be in the way."

"No, never think that," Amanda replied quickly, her smile brightly determined as she faced him. "Besides, Daniel would want you here. Please? If only for this night," she added when it looked as if he would refuse.

Justin hesitated, torn between his need to get away and the appeal in Miss Lawrence's deep brown eyes. In the space of the half hour or so they had spent in each other's company, he felt he had grown to know her rather well, and he could imagine how much it vexed a woman of her obvious pride and temperament to beg a favor of any man.

"Very well, Miss Lawrence," he capitulated, deciding it would do him no harm to grant her this one request. "For the one night, then. But on the morrow I really must be on my way."

"Thank you, Colonel." Amanda's shoulders slumped in relief. She wasn't certain why she was so determined the colonel remain; she only knew that she was. "Now, if you will pardon me, I must go and speak with the others. Would you like tea served here or in your room?"

"My room, if you please" Justin answered, deciding it might be prudent to lie down for a bit. The room was beginning to sway and dip in a most alarming manner, and he knew the sooner he was abed, the better. He only prayed his valet still had some of the medicine the doctor had prescribed from his last attack. Army doctors were bad enough, but he'd be damned if he'd have a country physician quacking him.

"Very well, Colonel." Amanda gave him a gracious smile. "We dine at seven. Until then, sir, I bid you *adieu.*"

"Amelia?" Amanda poked her head into her sister's room some six hours later, her expression anxious when she saw the small figure huddled on the bed. "Dearest, aren't you dressed yet? 'Tis almost seven o'clock."

"Oh, Amanda, how can I even think of eating when Daniel is dead?" Amelia sobbed, dabbing at her swollen eyes with a crumpled handkerchief. "I . . . I vow my heart is breaking!" And a fresh stream of tears flowed from her eyes.

Amanda bit back a sigh and made her way to her sister's bed. As she expected, the overly sensitive girl had taken Daniel's death the hardest of all. She had broken down completely upon hearing the news, carrying on in such a manner that Amanda had been forced to give her a mild dose of laudanum.

The twins had also been deeply affected, their identical blue eyes filling with tears as they struggled manfully not to cry. Little Belinda, God bless her, had taken the news best of all, crying only a little when Amanda had told her.

"But he is with Mama and Papa now," she said, wiping the tears from her cheeks with a chubby fist. "And so I know that he is safe."

Aunt Elizabeth, of course, had said nothing when

Amanda told her. She'd merely inclined her head; but Amanda had seen the smug sparkle in her malevolent dark eyes, and she had longed to shake her.

"I know you are upset, Amelia," Amanda said, rubbing a gentle hand down the younger girl's back. "But we must be brave now. We have a guest, remember? And after all his kindness, it would not do for us to shirk our duties."

"I suppose so," Amelia said after a few moments, delicately blowing her nose into her handkerchief. "And . . . and it is what Daniel would expect of us, isn't it?"

"Yes, it is precisely what Daniel would expect of us." Amanda's voice was husky. "The colonel was his commanding officer, remember? Daniel would expect us to show him every courtesy."

That was all it took to bring Amelia to her feet. Her sense of duty, while nowhere as extreme as her beloved elder sister's, was still deeply ingrained, and she didn't want to disgrace her brother in any fashion. She crossed the room to sit before her tiered mirror, sniffing in dismay at the sight of her blotched face.

"Oh, dear, I do look a fright," she said, picking up her brush and running it through the tangled gold of her curls. "The colonel will think me a quiz if I meet him looking like this."

"Try splashing cold water on your face," Amanda advised, hiding a relieved smile as she watched Amelia arrange her hair. Her sister wasn't vain by any means, but she did take shy pride in her appearance. The fact that she could worry over her looks meant that she was slowly recovering from the terrible shock of Daniel's death.

"What . . . what do you think I should wear?" The younger girl shot her a worried look. "I don't have any black gowns, and my purple gown is much too gay for mourning."

"I'm sure the colonel won't expect to see us rigged out in full black" came the reply as Amanda investigated the contents of her sister's wardrobe. She shoved aside several dresses as unsuitable before extracting a simple gown of midnight-blue silk. "Wear this," she said, handing it to Amelia. " 'Tis a trifle out of fashion, but I am sure our guest is too well-bred to comment on it. At least, I pray that he is." And she glanced down at her own gown, last worn while in mourning for her mother and stepfather some six years earlier.

The subject of mourning and how she would outfit her family was much on Amanda's mind as she made her way to the dining room. The vicar agreed with her request for a simple memorial ceremony in the village church, so at least she didn't have the expense of the funeral costumes; but that still left the rest of the proper year of mourning to worry about.

Amanda acknowledged that in the light of the more serious problems facing her family, these concerns could at best be described as petty. But she could do nothing about the future or what would become of them should Aunt Elizabeth throw them out, and she could do something about this. And she needed to do something, she realized with growing desperation. The others depended upon her to take care of them, and she was determined to do just that. No matter what happened she *would* take care of her family; on that one point she was resolved.

Halfway through the simple dinner of roast beef and capons Justin realized he had committed a tactical error in leaving his room. The heavy sleep he had enjoyed earlier in the afternoon only served to heighten the effects of the fever, and he was now suffering the full-blown symptoms of the virulent disease. His head ached, his stomach churned with nausea, and he felt as if he were being slowly roasted alive. But worst of all was the increasing sense of weakness that grew ever more debilitating as the meal progressed.

"Well, at least we shall be able to enjoy one meal in uninterrupted peace," Mrs. Herrick opined as she helped herself to a second helping of the Stilton cheese Cook had served in lieu of dessert. "I can not imagine why you insist upon having those loud children present at mealtimes, Amanda. It simply is not done in proper households. Is that not so, Colonel Stockton?" She flashed him a coquettish smile.

Upon learning their visitor was brother to the current duke of Stonebridge, the elderly lady had gone out of her way to converse with the colonel. Had she been a few decades younger, Amanda would have suspected her of having set her cap at him, and as it was she could only blush at her aunt's forward behavior.

Justin shared his hostess's aversion to the old woman's marked preference for his company, but he was far too well-bred to show it. He hid his impatience behind a carefully blank facade, replying to her question with a coolness that was just this side of polite. "I would not know how it is done in other households, Mrs. Herrick, but for myself I see nothing wrong with sharing the meal with the young ones. They are, after all, part of the family." He turned a much warmer look upon Amanda.

He noted she had changed from the yellow gown she'd been wearing earlier that afternoon into a severely cut gown of black bombazine. The unfashionably high waistline and puff sleeves betrayed the garment's age, as did the worn, black velvet ribbons that served as the gown's only decoration. He also noticed she had rearranged her fiery hair into a stately coronet of braids, and his gaze lingered admiringly on the curve of her cheekbones.

Aware he'd been staring at her like a moonling, he stirred himself and said, "I hope, ma'am, that you haven't banished your brothers to their rooms on my account. I have no objections to their chatter, I promise you."

"That is very kind of you, Colonel," Amanda replied, grateful for his unexpected support in this. "But in lieu of

. . . everything, I thought it best that the twins and Belinda take their meals in their rooms."

"Belinda?"

"My youngest sister, and a most engaging scamp she is too," Amanda answered, her expression softening at the thought of the little girl. She'd been but a few months above her second birthday when the coach accident claimed her mother's life, and Amanda had raised her more as a daughter than a sister.

"I see," Justin said, frowning as he realized how little he really knew of the Lawrence family's situation. "Have you any other brothers or sisters I know not of? I only heard Daniel speak of you and Miss Amelia, of course." He sent the sad-eyed blonde sitting at his left—an encouraging smile.

Amelia blushed at the smile, feeling slightly flustered by the colonel's polite attentions. He had discarded his uniform for an evening coat of black velvet and a pair of cream-colored breeches, but he was still very much the officer, she thought. "Our younger brother, Stephen, is away at school," she answered in a shy voice, not meeting his piercing gaze. "But we have sent for him."

"Your half brother is what you mean," Mrs. Herrick interjected with an indignant scowl. *"He* is not a Lawrence."

"No, but he is our brother in every way that matters, and we are all very proud of him," Amanda replied, furious that her aunt should air their family's differences before their guest. She knew full well what the old lady was really saying, and it was all she could do not to upend the coffeepot over her black turban.

"What school does he attend?" Justin may not have been in full possession of his faculties, but he could still sense the underlying hostility in the small room.

"Exter." Amanda was more than happy to turn her shoulder on her quarrelsome relation. "He is top in his forum in Greek and mathematics. And what of you, sir? What school did you attend?"

"Eton, of course." He pretended to be affronted "Is there any other?"

Following dinner they retired to the parlor for a glass of sherry. Amanda noted the colonel was imbibing rather freely, and if his flushed cheeks and overly bright eyes were any indication, he was well on his way to becoming foxed. She frowned at the realization, disliking the notion that he should be so lax in his personal habits. She cast about in her mind for some topic that might distract him.

"Tell me more of your plans for the holidays, Colonel," she said, giving him an inquiring look. "You mentioned your brother was expecting you; will you be spending Christmas together?"

Justin paused in the act of raising the brandy glass to his lips and blinked at her sleepily. He seldom drank so deeply, but the fever in him had made him thirsty enough to forget his usual discretion. "I shouldn't think so Miss Lawrence," he answered, unaware he was slurring his words. "His Grace prefers the lights of London, while I am more partial to the country. Like as not I'll pass the holiday at Stonebridge Hall."

"Alone?" The question was out before Amanda could help herself, and she immediately colored with mortification. She prayed the colonel didn't think she was attempting to learn his marital status, as Aunt Elizabeth had been doing earlier.

"Except for the servants." Justin shrugged his shoulders carelessly. The effects of the spirits he had inadvisedly consumed were beginning to make his head swim almost as badly as the fever, and he wondered if he would be able to make it to his room before disgracing himself in front of the ladies. He set his half-empty glass on the table beside his chair and rose somewhat unsteadily to his feet.

"If you ladies will pardon me, I believe I shall retire now," he said, knowing better than to attempt a bow. "Thank you for your kind hospitality, Miss Lawrence. I only wish we might have met under more felicitous circumstances."

"As do I, Colonel Stockton." Amanda was hard-pressed not to laugh at the preciseness with which he enunciated each word. He was obviously very much in his cups.

Justin blinked down at her, suspecting that beneath her prim smile the little minx was laughing at him. Ah well, there was nothing he could do about it now. The most vital thing at the moment was that he make it to his room.

"I'll have the footman assist you, sir." Amanda took pity on him-and rose belatedly to her feet. Even though she disapproved of heavy drinking, the colonel was still her guest, and it would not do to leave him to stumble to his room on his own.

"That is quite all right, ma'am." Justin's flush intensified. "I am perfectly capable of—"

"Nonsense, sir," she overrode his objection with her usual firm sense of command. "The hallways are not as well lit as they should be, and I wouldn't want you to become lost. Come," and she laid a firm hand on his arm ,determined to guide him from the room.

The moment her flesh touched his, she was aware of having made a terrible error. The colonel wasn't bosky, she realized with horror; he was burning up with fever! She no sooner reached this conclusion when he gave a low groan, collapsing at her feet with a loud thud.

 *Chapter Three*

"Well!" Mrs. Herrick exclaimed, shooting the fallen man a disapproving frown. "This is a fine way for a guest to conduct himself, I must say! But then, what else can one expect of a soldier?"

"He isn't drunk, Aunt," Amanda replied impatiently as she bent over him. She laid a hand against his throat, her alarm growing at the threadiness of his pulse. "He has the fever."

"The jug fever, mayhap," Mrs. Herrick grumbled, taking another sip of sherry. "My late husband was oft given to heavy drinking, and I daresay I can tell when a gentleman has distinguished himself."

Amanda withheld comment, turning to her younger sister, who had joined her beside the colonel. "Have Linsley send one of the footmen for Dr. McNeil," she instructed in gentle, but firm tones. "And then have him fetch Colonel Stockton's valet. I'm sure he will know what to do."

After her sister had dashed off to do her bidding, she turned her attention back to her patient. The colonel still hadn't regained consciousness, and she winced at the fever she could feel blazing in him. She stared down into his flushed features, and after a moment's hesitation her fingers went to the starched cravat knotted beneath his chin.

"What do you think you are doing?" her aunt demanded in outraged accents. "Amanda, you scarce know this man!"

"What has that to do with anything?" Amanda asked, continuing to unravel the cravat. When it was loosened she pulled it away from his throat, praying it would help his breathing. The wide chest beneath the proper black evening jacket was rising and falling in an uneven rhythm, and she wondered if she should remove the jacket as well. She was debating how best to accomplish this when Aunt Elizabeth gave a choked cry.

"What do you mean what has that to do with anything?" she exclaimed clasping her hands to her bosom. "It has everything to do with it, you ninnyhammer! Only a . . . a Jezebel would calmly strip a strange man of his garments in so brazen a manner!"

"Then, I would suppose that makes me a Jezebel," Amanda replied without even looking up. She decided against removing the tight-fitting jacket, fearing it would do more harm than good, and turned her attention instead to his waistcoat of rose and silver brocade. She was reaching for the buttons when Amelia returned, Linsley and the colonel's valet in tow.

The squat man knelt beside Amanda, unceremoniously nudging her aside as he examined his employer. "It be the fever, all right," he said when he had finished. "We'd best be gettin' him to his rooms."

"Is it serious?" Amanda asked, biting her lip as she studied Colonel Stockton's still form. He hadn't moved so much as a muscle since his collapse and she was beginning to fear for his life.

"Serious enough" came the terse reply as the valet motioned the remaining footmen to step forward. "He all but died of it in Spain. I told him 'twas folly to travel so soon after our return, but he'd not listen to me."

Between the four men they managed to carry the colonel up the narrow stairs. Amanda stayed below long enough to instruct her sister to wait for the doctor's arrival and then dashed up the stairs, ignoring her aunt's indignant cries that she remain. They'd already removed Colonel Stockton's outer clothes and were putting a nightshirt on him when she strode boldly into the room.

"This be no place for a lady, miss," the valet said, pausing in his ministrations long enough to shoot her a warning look. "I've nursed him through this before, and I can tell you 'tis not a pretty sight."

"I didn't expect that it would be," Amanda replied calmly, elbowing the footman to one side as she stood over the bed. "But nonetheless I will remain."

The valet's sharp blue eyes moved over her resolute features, and then a slow smile stole across his wrinkled face. "Aye, miss," he said at last, "I can see that you will."

The footman fetched them basins of cool water, and while the valet, whose name proved to be Williams, saw to the colonel's more personal needs, Amanda carefully bathed his hands and face. They were repeating the process for what seemed the dozenth time when Linsley arrived with the doctor.

If he was surprised to see Amanda tending her guest in such a fashion, the young doctor was too polite to show it, concentrating instead on his patient. He felt the colonel's pulse, listened to his heart through a tube, and then turned to Amanda.

"I am afraid I must ask you to step out in the hall, Miss Lawrence," he said with no trace of the usual deference he showed her. "I must examine Colonel Stockton in greater detail, and I can not do that with you in the room."

She opened her mouth to refute his request, and then decided she was being foolish. The colonel's health was the main issue here, not her own willful nature. Besides, she thought with a smug grin, she could always return once the doctor had concluded his examination.

"Very well, Doctor," she said, inclining her head coolly. "I shall be in the parlor. Please let me know the moment you have finished your examination," and she departed from the room, her small chin held high in the air.

Amelia and Aunt Elizabeth were waiting in the parlor when she returned, and it soon became obvious that the elderly lady had worked herself into an agitated state during her brief absence. "This is beyond the outside of enough!" she began before Amanda had even taken her seat. "Bringing a diseased person into the household when you must know that I am susceptible to fevers! How can you be so selfish?"

"With a great deal of practice, ma'am," Amanda replied, her lips curling in a mocking smile as she gazed at her aunt. She was not the most tolerant of persons to begin with, and she'd been through too much this evening to endure the older woman's catty remarks.

Mrs. Herrick's mouth opened and closed several times before she managed a strangled "How dare you!"

"Again, ma'am, with a great deal of practice," Amanda returned, clearly unrepentant. "This is still my home, and until such time as you claim it, I will say and do as I please. A fact you would do well to remember." She added this last part by way of warning, knowing her aunt's vicious ways all too well.

"And if you don't mind your manners, missy, that time will come sooner than you think!" Mrs. Herrick retorted, rising to her feet in majestic rage. "A fact *you* would do well to remember!" And she stalked out of the parlor, calling for her maid in strident tones.

"Oh, Amanda, must you always be pulling caps with her?" Amelia sighed, shaking her head at her older sister. "You must know that it only makes her worse!"

"I know." The sudden burst of defiance had faded, leaving Amanda feeling curiously drained. "And I don't mean to; it is just that she is so vexing sometimes."

"I know." Amelia's smile was loving as she squeezed Amanda's hand. "And you do seem to rise to her taunts like a trout to a fly."

Amanda smiled at the image her sister's words invoked; but before she could reply, there was a tap on the door, and the butler stuck his head inside.

"The doctor's finished now, miss," he said his weathered face lined with anxiety. "He asks that you come at once."

Amanda murmured a quick apology to Amelia and then hurried from the room, her heart pounding with trepidation as she mounted the stairs. The room Colonel Stockton had been assigned was in the newer part of the house, removed from the family quarters by a broad hallway. She paused outside the door, gathering her courage to face whatever lay beyond.

"Come in, Miss Lawrence," Dr. McNeil greeted her as she walked quietly toward the tester bed. There was a fire burning low in the grate, casting a reddish glow about the room. A brace of candles stood by the bed, and their flickering flames revealed the doctor's drawn features as she approached him.

"How is he?" she asked, her eyes going automatically to the colonel's face. He seemed much paler than he had before, and his chest rose and fell with each labored breath.

"Not well." Dr. McNeil's voice was soft with regret as he studied Amanda's face. "He is running a dangerously high fever, and if it doesn't break soon, I fear for the worst."

"Do you mean he may die?" Amanda's voice shook despite her determination that it not do so.

"Unless we can break the fever," the physician answered, keeping nothing from her. "His man tells me he has some sort of Spanish potion he feels may be of help, and has

45

gone to fetch it. But I must warn you that I don't put much stock in it."

Amanda considered the doctor's oblique warning. He was telling her not to hope, she realized with growing annoyance. He was telling her Colonel Stockton was already as good as dead. Well, they would just see about that, she decided, her dark eyes beginning to dance with a martial light. She had already lost her brother and her home; she'd be damned if she would lose anything else. Even if she had to wrestle old Nick himself, she would not allow him to die. She would not.

The long hours of the night passed with painful monotony, broken only by the arrival and departure of footmen bearing fresh basins of water. Amanda had grown accustomed to Williams' silences, and the two shared their watch like old friends. Toward morning Justin, as she now privately thought of him, began to grow restive, his head thrashing about on the pillow.

"This could be it, miss," Williams said, dipping the cloth in the cooling water and applying it to his employer's feverish skin. "I seen him like this in that hospital in Spain; he's fightin' the fever now."

Amanda knelt over the bed, her hand closing on Justin's twitching arm. "That's it," she urged softly. "Fight for your life. Don't surrender now."

Justin's eyes flew open suddenly, the pupils glazed with fever as he glared at her. "No surrender, damn your eyes," he muttered, his dazed mind grasping on to the one word he had understood. "No surrender. Fight on."

Amanda blinked down at him and then realized what was happening. He was hallucinating, his mind back on that battlefield. She tightened her fingers around his arm. "It's all right, Colonel," she soothed, seeking to reassure

46

him. "You're safe now. You were wounded and you must rest now. We'll take care of you."

Justin's eyes grew cloudy. He saw not Miss Lawrence's lovely features, but the sweat-stained, blood-spattered countenance of the field doctor as he bent over his pallet, his voice lacking all emotion as he called for the tourniquet and saw.

"No, you black-hearted bastard, you'll not take my arm," he snarled, his good hand flashing up like a snake to close about the doctor's throat. "I'll kill you before I'll let you do that to me."

Amanda gasped painfully as the colonel's fingers dug into the soft flesh of her throat. She pulled at his hand, attempting to pry it away before he succeeded in throttling her. Williams rushed to her assistance, grabbing his employer by the shoulder and pressing him back against the pillows.

"Take it easy now, Colonel," he implored. "You're at home now, sir, and—"

Justin threw him off with a strength born of desperation and delerium. "No amputation!" he shouted, his fingers tightening about the doctor's throat with deadly intent. "Do you hear me, you damned leech? Call off your orderly, or I'll snap your neck in half."

Amanda knew then that he was beyond all reason, lost in the terror of his memories. "No . . . no amputation," she gasped, praying he wasn't so far gone that he couldn't understand. "My word to you, sir. I won't hurt you."

Justin continued glaring up at the face above his. It was growing fuzzy and indistinct, fading in and out with his consciousness. Even the voice was different; it sounded softer somehow, the rough tones giving way to gentle inflections. He loosened his grip slightly, too weary to go on fighting. In his mind he could still hear the screams of the wounded around him, and his stomach rolled at the stench of blood and sweat that filled his nostrils.

"No amputation," he repeated, his voice slurring as his arm dropped uselessly to his side. "If I die, I die a whole man. No . . ." his voice trailed off as he fell into a deep, dreamless sleep.

"Are you all right, miss?" Williams had picked himself up from the floor and was hovering behind her anxiously. "The colonel didn't hurt you, did he? He didn't mean it, you know, he—"

"I know," Amanda interrupted, her voice somewhat hoarse as she rubbed her aching throat. The imprints left by Justin's fingers stood out like a brand on her pale skin, and she knew they would doubtlessly bruise.

"Poor lad." Williams' voice was also decidedly husky as he began bathing his employer's face again. "Must have thought he was back in that hellish hospital after Vitoria. Those damned sawbones would as soon cut off a man's arm as try to heal it, beggin' your pardon, miss." He flushed for using such strong talk in a lady's presence.

"No, I understand," she said, forgetting her own discomfort as she gazed down at Justin. His features were more relaxed, and he looked as if he was merely sleeping. "I weep when I think of how he must have suffered," she added, reaching out to brush back a lock of dark hair that had fallen across his broad forehead.

"Aye, that he did," Williams confirmed, his face growing grim as he remembered his frantic search for the colonel through the carnage of the battlefield. "By the time I found him in that filthy hospital tent, they had him half tied down, and he was holding them off with a knife. He threatened to . . . er . . . do the doctor an injury if the drunken fool didn't back away. I got him out of there quick as I could, I can promise you."

"The physician was drunk?" Amanda was appalled.

"No more than usual." Williams shrugged his shoulders.

"Happens sometimes. Army's glad to take what they can get, even if it's a broken-down old sot."

Amanda muttered a few choice words beneath her breath. Oh, to be a man, she thought with mounting indignation. If she were a man, she'd stand for Parliament, and once there she'd make quite sure her country's soldiers received the care they deserved. How could a nation treat its heroes so? It was a disgrace.

The candles beside the bed burned low in their holders, the flames fluttering and waving in the long hours that followed. Amanda changed positions with Williams, wiping Justin's face, throat and hands with the damp cloth. She was dipping the cloth in the water when she noted the sweat beading his upper lip and forehead.

Her hand shook with trepidation as she reached out to touch his face. The flesh beneath her fingertips was faintly damp with perspiration, and it was noticeably cooler than it had been only minutes before. Tears filled her eyes, and she allowed them to fall, so weak with relief that she was almost giddy. She must have made some sort of noise, for Williams gave a low cry of distress and bent closer.

"The colonel!" he moaned in horror. "He's not—"

"No, no." Amanda shook her head at him, her smile widening with sheer happiness. "But the fever has broken. We did it, Williams; we did it!"

"I would like a word with you, Amanda."

Amanda glanced up from her account books, her heart sinking at the sight of her aunt standing in the doorway. She'd come to the study directly from Justin's room and was hoping to review the books before confronting her aunt. She'd even been nursing the faint possibility the other woman would have the decency to wait until after Daniel's funeral before making her demands known. Ap-

49

parently she'd given the disagreeable creature more credit than she deserved.

"Of course, Aunt Elizabeth," she said, carefully masking her emotions as she closed the book and pushed it away from her. "Pray, will you not be seated?"

Mrs. Herrick gave a loud sniff before stepping forward to take the chair Amanda had indicated. "I hear the colonel's condition is much improved," she said folding her thin hands in her lap. "And I must say I am relieved. It would have been most awkward if the fellow had died while our guest."

"Awkward for the colonel, certainly," Amanda retorted, then bit her tongue. She'd promised herself only that morning that she would mind her manners in regards to her aunt. "But you are right; he is doing much better this morning," she rushed on, anxious to avoid an unnecessary exchange of unpleasantries. "The fever broke late last night, and his valet expects that he should awaken sometime this afternoon."

"Excellent." Mrs. Herrick nodded, as if giving her approval. "As I said, it would have been most awkward had he not recovered. His brother would be certain to take offense, and it never does to annoy a duke."

There seemed to be no polite response to this, and so Amanda remained silent. Instinct warned her she would soon have need of all her wits, a premonition that was borne out by her aunt's next words.

"I have decided to return to London after Daniel's services," she began without preamble. "I need to speak with my solicitor, and naturally I'll need time to make all the proper arrangements. With luck, I should return by the end of January. Will that give you enough time, do you think?"

"Enough time for what?"

"Why, for removing yourself and your family from La-

50

wrence Hall, of course," Mrs. Herrick responded, her eyes glittering with malicious delight at the stunned look on Amanda's face. "Surely you didn't expect to stay on indefinitely?"

Amanda could not answer. She had expected this, knew it was only a matter of time, but the pain of it quite took her breath away. For a moment the panic she had been keeping successfully at bay threatened to overwhelm her, and she feared bursting into tears. Only the knowledge that such actions would give her aunt pleasure kept her from doing just that, and she sternly suppressed her emotions.

"Not indefinitely, ma'am, but I had hoped you would show us some Christian charity," she said, her chin coming up with pride as she faced her aunt. "I should have known better."

Her aunt's sallow cheeks reddened at Amanda's cutting words. "I should mind my tongue if I were you," she snapped, pulling her shawl closer about her. "You are my dependent now, and—"

"I am no one's dependent, ma'am," Amanda interrupted, her voice glacial with fury. "And I pray God I never shall be. You needn't worry that either my family or I will impose upon your kind generosity. We will be gone before your return; that much I can promise you."

Mrs. Herrick shifted uneasily beneath her niece's cold stare. She'd been planning to keep the defiant little minx firmly under her thumb, and she could not like the thought of her escaping. "You needn't be as hasty as all that," she said, pinning a smile to her thin lips. "I am sure we shall be able to come to some kind of understanding."

"What kind of understanding?" Amanda asked suspiciously. Much as she would have liked to throw her aunt's offer back in her face, she knew she didn't have the luxury of such an action. For her family's sake, she would hear the old tartar out before making any decision.

"Well, naturally I shouldn't be so lacking in familial responsibilities as to deny my nieces the only home they have known," Mrs. Herrick rushed on. "Indeed, I should never be half so cruel! And I suppose some provision might be made for the others. The military for the boys, perhaps, and a nice charitable school for the girl. Mrs. McAbernathy's establishment in Kent has a very good reputation, and the child would receive training as a governess so we needn't fear she would become a burden to us."

"Belinda would never be a burden to me," Amanda retorted, her eyes almost black with fury. "And as for Stephen and the twins, they remain with me. We are a family, ma'am. A family."

"Brave words, my dear," Mrs. Herrick scoffed, still refusing to believe she had lost. "But how do you propose to support this *family* of yours? That handsome wastrel your mother so foolishly married—quite against my advice, I might add—left you without a feather to fly with! You've been scraping along until now, but without your brother's inheritance I think you will find things far more difficult. With me, at least, you will have a home."

"With you, Aunt, I would have a prison," Amanda replied, rising proudly to her feet. "And I would as lief starve as be beholden to you for so much as a bread crust! Leave my study."

"Why, you insolent little hoyden! Who do you think you are talking to?" Mrs. Herrick stumbled to her feet, her chest rising and falling in her agitation. "This is my house now, and—"

"No." Amanda's proud words cut into her aunt's tirade. "It is *my* house, and for the moment at least, I have final say as to whom I choose to shelter here. I do not choose to shelter you."

Mrs. Herrick was almost apoplectic she was so furious. "You . . . you baggage!" she shrieked pointing a shaking finger at Amanda. "I won't be spoken to like this! I am your aunt, missy, and you will regret this! You will regret this!"

The door to the study flew open at the sound of raised voices, and the butler and one of the footmen stood in the doorway, gaping at the two combatants with undisguised interest. Amanda drew an uneven breath for control and then turned to the elderly butler.

"Aunt Elizabeth will be leaving, Linsley," she said, her soft voice firm despite the fact her legs were trembling with reaction. "Kindly see that her bags are packed and that she is driven into the village."

"Y-yes, Miss Lawrence," he stammered, watery eyes flickering toward Mrs. Herrick. "Ma'am?"

For a moment Amanda thought her aunt would succumb to the vapors, but in the end, breeding won out. "Very well, *Miss Lawrence*"—she spat out the name as if it were an epithet—"you win . . . for now. But when I return, you may be quite sure I shall make you pay for such insolence. All of you." Her eyes flashed meaningfully in Linsley's direction before she brushed past them, her nose held high in the air as she stalked up the stairs.

Amanda collapsed against the door, her defiance melting like the morning dew under a summer sun. She closed her eyes briefly and then opened them to send Linsley an apologetic smile. "I am sorry, Linsley," she said with a heavy sigh. "I hadn't meant to include you in all this."

"Nonsense, miss." The old man drew himself up proudly. "As butler, 'tis my duty to show undesirable persons the door. And in the case of your esteemed aunt, 'twas also my pleasure."

53

Amanda's smile softened and then disappeared. "She is the new owner of Lawrence Hall."

"I know, miss."

Of course he knew, she thought, turning back toward the parlor; Linsley knew everything. The man was a veritable fount of information, and the oddest thing was that he had never once been caught listening at keyholes. She closed the door quietly behind her, Linsley's acuity forgotten as she resumed her seat. What was she going to do?

It was the middle of December, and if Aunt Elizabeth adhered to her promise to return at the end of January, that left her less than seven weeks to find a new home for her family. She'd contact the solicitor at once, of course. She'd sent him a note inviting him to Daniel's memorial service, so he already knew the worst.

Perhaps he might know of some house she might hire, she thought hopefully. It needn't be anything grand, just clean and sturdy, with enough room for the children and perhaps a few of the servants as well. She doubted any of them would wish to remain in her aunt's employ, even if the old harridan would have them. And perhaps they might even arrange to sell the horses and ancient carriage sitting in the stables. They'd belonged to her stepfather and so were not entailed with the house.

Then there was the money Daniel had given them. One hundred pounds, if spent judiciously, could last months, longer even, if she practiced every economy. The thought spurred her on, and she grabbed a piece of paper, adding figures in a desperate attempt to solve her family's current dilemma. But no matter how often she added them, or how many items she subtracted as unnecessary, the result was always the same. Two hundred and fifty pounds per anum was simply not enough to keep so large a family in anything approaching style.

Tears gathered in her eyes as she stared down at the

last column of figures. Stephen would be arriving home tomorrow; how was she to tell him there was no money for him to return to his beloved school? Thank heavens Christmas was so close. School would be closed for the holiday and she could. . . .

Christmas. She groaned, covering her face with her hands. What was she going to do about Christmas? Naturally with Daniel's death they wouldn't entertain as lavishly as they usually did, but the children, especially the younger ones, would still be expecting the usual trimmings. Presents, a fine dinner, and the *tannenbaum* that was part of the family tradition. How could she deny her family these things?

Suddenly Amelia knew that she could not. This could well be their last holiday as a family, and she was determined it would be the best they had ever known. She thought of the one hundred pounds that was Daniel's last gift to his family, and a slow smile spread across her face. Foolish or not, she knew what she was going to do.

 *Chapter Four*

"Shhh! You'll wake him!"

"Will not, you old bossy! I just want to look at him."

The quarrelsome voices edged into the thick mists filling Justin's head, drawing him slowly out of the darkness. The speakers were young, male, and he was vaguely aware that he knew them. He frowned, trying to think of any drummer boy or powder monkey in his regiment daring enough to slip into his tent. Most of them seemed terrified of him, although God only knew why; he'd never spoken so much as a cross word to one of them. Before he could puzzle the matter any further, the voices drew closer and increasingly strident.

"Stop pushing! You almost made me spill it."

"I'm telling Mandy! You know she said we wasn't to come in here."

"Well, since you're in here with me, you'll be in just as much trouble, so you'd best keep your tongue between your teeth. Now, you hold his nose and I'll stick the spoon in his mouth."

Seconds later Justin felt his nose being tentatively pinched, and then a spoon was thrust between his lips. At the sharp bite of raw spirits in his throat, he gave a choking gasp, sputtering indignantly as his eyes flew open to focus on the two wide-eyed youngsters standing beside his bed.

At first he thought he was seeing double, for the two were virtually mirror images of each other. He blinked his eyes to clear his vision, but both boys remained where they were, their expressions avid with curiosity as they gazed at him. They were twins, he realized with mounting confusion. What on earth . . . and then he remembered.

"Hello, Colonel Stockton," the boy standing nearest the bed spoke first, taking a cautious step to bring him closer. "How are you feeling, sir? I trust you are more the thing?"

"Indeed," Justin answered, sizing up the lad with a judicious eye. Unless he was much mistaken, he knew who had forced the foul medicine down his throat. His eyes flicked from the boy's face to the brown bottle sitting on the bedside table, and a reluctant smile touched his mouth. Much as he disliked the notion of being drugged against his will, he couldn't help but admire the imp's pluck.

"Have I the honor of addressing Mr. Jeremey Lawrence, or Mr. Jocelyn Lawrence?" he asked, settling back more comfortably against his pillows.

"I am Jeremey; I'm the oldest." Jeremey snapped to attention, preening with self-importance. "This is Jocelyn." His brother was indicated with a casual wave of his hand. "But our last name isn't Lawrence, sir, it's Blanchford. Daniel was our half brother."

"My apologies," Justin murmured, recalling that Lawrence had said something about his mother remarrying. And last night at dinner hadn't that disagreeable old witch made some mention of the matter? At least, he thought it was last night. His brows gathered together as he realized he had no idea what day it was or how long he had lain ill.

"Are you really better now?" Jocelyn crowded in beside his brother, his light blue eyes resting on Justin's face. "Ain't going to stick your spoon in the wall, are you?"

"I am completely recovered, Master Jocelyn, I promise you." His mouth quirked in amusement at the lad's suspicious regard. "The . . . er . . . medicine you gave me seems to have done the trick, thank you. May I ask how long I have been here?"

"Just one day," Jeremey answered for his brother. "You was sick as a cat last night, but Mandy sent for the doctor and he dosed you."

Justin had no recall of the doctor's visit, but there was a vague memory of a soft voice and the soothing touch of a feminine hand stroking his face. Miss Lawrence? Or was it just a trick of the fever? He remembered the nightmares he'd had and without conscious thought his right hand reached out to touch his left arm. Still there, thank God.

"Will you be attending Daniel's services, sir?" Jocelyn prattled on, unaware of the colonel's dark thoughts. "It's to be held in two days' time, and Jeremy and I think it would be most splendid if you was to come."

"And wear your uniform," Jeremey added, his eyes sparkling with enthusiasm. "That would be ever so grand!"

Justin's chest tightened at the boys' eagerness. The bout of fever must have left him weaker than he realized, for he found himself blinking back tears at their earnest expressions. Had he ever been that young, he wondered, striving to control his voice.

"It would be my honor, gentlemen," he said, clearing his throat. "Thank you for the kind invitation."

The twins beamed at his acceptance and drew closer, their wariness forgotten as they began quizzing him. Justin answered their questions with an openness quite unlike his usually reticent nature, enjoying the demands of the lads' bright conversation. He had just launched into a description of the siege of Cuiad Rodrigues when there was a loud gasp from the doorway.

"Joss! Jeremey!" Miss Amanda Lawrence stood in the doorway to his room, her hands on her hips and an aggrieved expression on her face. "Just what are you two doing in here?" she demanded, her brown eyes flashing as she advanced toward the boys. "I thought I had made it clear you were not to disturb the colonel."

"We wasn't disturbing him, Mandy!" Jeremey denied, and Justin had to hide a smile at the look of angelic innocence that flashed across the lad's face. "We were giving him medicine."

"What medicine?" Amanda knew her younger brother too well to be taken in by his sophistry. Jeremey was aware of the fact too and hopped off Justin's bed (where he had been sitting for the last quarter hour), obediently retrieving the bottle from the table and handing it to his sister.

She opened the bottle curiously, her nose wrinkling in distaste at the strong smell of spirits. "Where did you get this?" she asked, returning the stopper to the bottle.

"From Linsley's room," Joss volunteered manfully assuming his share of guilt. "It was in his cupboard, but we was able to reach it by standing on a chair."

"I see." Amanda was aware of the colonel's amused stare, and she was determined not to crack so much as a smile. She repressed her natural inclination to laugh at the twins' antics, and fixed them instead with her most reproving look. "And did Linsley give you leave to enter his room and ferret through his belongings?" she asked her slippered feet tapping out an impatient tattoo as she awaited their answer.

Twin blond heads were hung in shame. "No, ma'am."

"I thought not. Well then, you may return Linsley's medicine to his room, and then you are to go and apologize to him for trespassing on his privacy."

But, Mandy—"

"And once that is done, you are to go to your rooms and remain there until dinner." she continued, ignoring their cries for clemency. "Am I understood?"

Jeremey and Joss exchanged speaking glances with one another before shuffling away with a muttered "Yes,

Amanda."

She waited until the door had closed behind them before turning a knowing smile on Colonel Stockton. "My true name, you will note," she said, advancing into the room and settling on the chair beside his bed. "Now I know I am in their black books. I hope they haven't been pestering you. They are the dearest boys alive, but quite mad when it comes to the army."

"Not at all, Miss Lawrence. In fact, I found them quite charming. A family trait, it would appear," Justin answered, eyeing her with cool skepticism. He was unaccustomed to the presence of a lady—at least, a respectable lady—in his bed chamber and could only wonder at her lack of propriety. For a brief moment he wondered if she was attempting to compromise him.

"Cut line, sir!" Amanda laughed at his flattering words. "I saw your expression when I was giving those scamps the dressing down they deserved. You looked as if you thought me the cruelest sister alive!"

Her words reassured Justin to such a degree that he felt a smile tugging at the corners of his mouth. "Well," he conceded with a wry drawl, "perhaps I did think you a trifle hard on them. No man likes having a peal rung over him in the presence of other men, you know, especially by an older sister. And they really weren't bothering me."

"Perhaps not, but I left strict instructions that you were not to be disturbed, and like all good commanders, I expect my orders to be carried out without question," Amanda answered with a ready smile. She was usually not so bold with men, but for some inexplicable reason, she found herself able to relax in his presence. Perhaps it had to do with the fact she had helped nurse him, she decided with a sudden flash of intuition. It was really rather hard to be intimidated by a man after one had spent several hours bathing his fevered brow.

She was aware that her remaining in a bachelor's bed-chamber would doubtlessly shock the local gentry senseless, but she didn't care for what they thought. Propriety, while it was something she always tried to instill in her recalcitrant family, was something she seldom troubled herself with. Why should she? At six and twenty she was an acknowledged spinster and, as such, safely immune from the strictures that applied to marriageable females.

"But enough of that, sir," Amanda continued briskly, aware of the silence that had fallen between them. "How are you feeling? You're looking much better, I must say."

"I'm feeling much better, thank you, ma'am," he replied, feeling a sudden awkwardness. He had a faint memory of collapsing in the parlor room and was mortified by his lack of control. He shifted restlessly on the bed forcing himself to meet her velvet brown gaze.

"I hope you will accept my apologies for causing you such inconvenience," he said, his voice stiff with formality. "It was not my intention to land myself on you when I arrived, I promise you."

"I'm sure it was not." Amanda had to hide a laugh at his rigid expression and the hard line of his mouth as he offered the oh-so-proper apology. Heavens, what a prig he was, she mused, although she was careful to keep such thoughts to herself. She remembered how unbearably prim Daniel had been after returning home from his first posting, and how she and the others had teased him out of what they called his starched collar period.

"You have only yourself to blame for it," she admonished in a rallying tone, waggling her finger at his recumbent form. "Williams told me the ship's surgeon warned you against undertaking so arduous a journey."

Rather than responding to her teasing scold with a smile as Daniel would have done, Justin's brows rose haughtily. "That was quite impossible, Miss Lawrence," he informed her in his most superior tones. "I had given your brother my most solemn vow that I would deliver that packet to you, and a Stockton always keeps his word."

"That may as be, sir," Amanda continued, still hopeful of jollying him out of his present mood, "but after so long a time, a delay of a few more days would not matter. Williams told me you were badly wounded at Vitoria and have only now recovered from those injuries."

"Williams seems to have told you a great deal," Justin responded coldly, annoyed by his valet's loquaciousness. "Which reminds me, where is he? 'Tis not like him to be so derelict in his duties."

Her willingness to tolerate his poor humor vanished at these words. "I sent him to bed, Colonel," she replied, her tones every bit as crisp as his. "We were up half the night nursing you, and the poor man was quite fagged. If you require any assistance, you have only to ring for the footman."

Justin ignored her cool offer, his brows gathering at what he considered to be the most pertinent piece of information. " 'We were up,' " he repeated, his expression darkening as he glared at her. "Am I to understand that *you* helped care for me?"

"Well, you needn't look so outraged, sir!" Amanda snapped indignantly. "I am your hostess, and it was my duty to see that you received every care. One of the servants was always present, so there was nothing in the least bit untoward about the situation if that is what you are so concerned about."

"I wasn't questioning the propriety of it all," he gritted, feeling faintly harassed by her bellicose manners. "But I can not help but wonder at your lack of sensibility! Did it never occur to you that no man would wish his hostess to see him in such a state?"

"Stuff!" Amanda retorted, tossing her head back defiantly.

"For your information, Colonel, I have nursed my mother my brothers and sisters, and any number of neighbors and acquaintances through a variety of diseases, and I still hold each of them in the highest regard! Although," she added, as her temper gave way to impishness, "you are the first of my patients to have attacked me."

Justin's face paled with shock. "What the devil are you talking about?" he demanded, a feeling of horror washing over him as a particularly vivid memory flashed in his mind.

"Nothing," she denied quickly, embarrassed that her teasing words caused him such distress. "I-I was only funning you."

"No." He moved his dark head restlessly on the pillow, recalling the dream where he had been back in that damned hospital in Spain. The doctors had him tied down and they were going to . . . He shook off the sickening memory, his gaze fastening to her face with a burning intensity. "What happened?"

In the light of his stark plea there was naught she could do but give him the truth he demanded. "You were hallucinating," she said quietly, tearing her eyes away from his molten gold gaze. "You thought I was going to hurt you, and you grabbed me 'round the throat. That's all."

Justin's eyes closed briefly, and when he opened them they held an anguish that made Amanda want to cry out in pain. "Did I hurt you?" he asked, his voice strained.

"Of course not! I told you, it was noth—"

"Take off your scarf."

Amanda blinked at the terse command. "I beg your pardon?"

"I said, take off your scarf," he repeated, infusing every ounce of his considerable will into the command. He had noted the paisley scarf tied around her throat the moment she had entered the room, but other than wondering why she wore it in such an odd fashion, he hadn't given it another thought.

"Really, Colonel Stockton, you forget yourself!" She bristled, embarrassed and annoyed by his clipped order. "I shall do no such thing."

"If you don't, I will" he threatened, his voice soft with menace. "I may be incapacitated, Miss Lawrence, but I'm far from helpless."

And so he was, curse him, Amanda thought, glaring at him with mounting indignation. She could see the power and determination reflected in the amber depths of his eyes and knew that he wouldn't hesitate acting on his threat. Telling herself that she was only humoring a sick and sulky guest, she untied the scarf, exposing her throat to his intense scrutiny.

"Oh, God." Justin's stomach lurched at the sight of the bruises marring her soft, alabaster skin. He reached out a tentative hand, wanting to smooth away the marks his fingers had left, but there was nothing he could do. His hand fell to his side, curling into a tight fist.

"I'm sorry."

Amanda's anger evaporated at his hoarse apology. "Don't be absurd," she said softly, retying the scarf about her neck. "You thought I was about to cut off your arm; how could you do other than defend yourself? Believe me, had I been in your place, you may be quite sure I would have fought like the very devil."

"I make no doubt of it, ma'am," Justin replied, grateful for her wry humor. "You struck me as a most formidable woman from the first moment I clapped eyes on you."

"Ah yes, the veriest virago, or so Daniel always called me." Amanda laughed, her face softening at the thought of her younger brother's relentless teasing. Then another thought came to mind, and her smile faded as she met Justin's eyes. "He . . . he wasn't operated on, was he?" she asked, her voice shaking with horror. "Williams described those dreadful hospitals in Spain, and I have been picturing him—"

"No," Justin interrupted, and this time when he reached out a hand, it closed comfortingly around hers. "No," he repeated gently, his eyes gazing deeply into hers. "He died on the battlefield. He was at peace, and his last thoughts were of you."

Speech was impossible just then, and so Amanda simply returned the pressure of his warm hand, blinking rapidly against the tears that scalded her eyes.

"Jeremey tells me Daniel's services are to be held on Thursday," Justin continued, wisely giving Amanda time to compose herself. At her silent nod he added, "Here?"

"At Godstone." Amanda found her voice at last. "It is the nearest village."

"I had thought to leave on the morrow," he continued, rapidly adjusting his schedule in light of his promise to the boys. "But I suppose 'tis possible to delay my departure for a few days, provided the weather is cooperative," he added, recalling the heavy snows that had made his journey from Portsmouth so difficult.

"Leave?" Amanda cried, staring at him as if he had taken leave of his senses. "Are you mad? You were all but at death's door yesterday! Surely you can not be so foolhardy as to risk a relapse? I forbid it."

Now it was Justin's turn to gape at her. "I beg your pardon?" he said weakly.

"I forbid you to leave," she said, her voice unconsciously taking on the same hectoring tone she used toward her brothers. "You are still in a weakened state, and I will not have you racketing about the countryside."

Justin's first impulse was to tell her to go to the devil, but since he had never spoken to a lady in such blunt terms, he quickly restrained himself. Instead, he fixed her with a

65

quelling look that had been known to make even the most battle-hardened troops quail in fear. "Your concern for my welfare does you proud, Miss Lawrence," he said, his soft voice in direct contrast to the fury blazing inside him. "But you are far off the mark if you think I will tolerate such insolent familiarity. I am not one of your brothers to be bullied and ordered about, and I will do as I see fit. I trust I have made myself clear?"

The sight of those perfectly shaped, dark eyebrows arching in haughty condescension made Amanda's temper flare, and her eyes rested wistfully on the carafe of water sitting on the table. No, she decided unhappily, it would not be at all the thing. Instead she drew herself upright, folding her arms across her chest and bending her most intimidating scowl on him. "You may not be so young as Jeremey and Jocelyn," she told him coolly, "but you are every bit as foolish! Why can you not accept the simple fact that you are ill? You can not go."

"And you can not make me stay." As a retort, it left much to be desired, but it was all Justin could muster at the moment.

Amanda's eyes took on a dangerous glow. "Can I not?" she challenged softly. "I shouldn't be so certain of that."

"You are a hell-cat without equal!" he fairly shouted, losing all semblance of control. "I don't doubt that you are unmarried; what man with any wit would have you?"

"And you are an arrogant poppinjay whose foolishness is only surpassed by his opinion of himself," she returned heatedly. "Is your vanity really so important to you that you would rather court death than do as I am suggesting?"

"You are not suggesting, ma'am," he snarled, a lock of dark hair falling across his brow as he glared up at her. "You are *ordering!*"

"And of course as a colonel of the Regiment it would never do for you to follow another's instructions!" she jibed,

66

shooting him a look of acute dislike. "I suppose it would be another story had I wrapped my wishes in pretty linen, simpering and smiling at you like some foolish Bath miss!"

He returned her look tenfold. "Perhaps it would be," he drawled, his tone both mocking and challenging. "But we'll never know . . . will we?"

Amanda swallowed her ire, knowing he was right. Much as it galled her, she knew that if she wished him to stay, it was up to her to apologize. Pride warred briefly with her innate sense of right and wrong, and pride lost. Drawing a deep breath, she raised her chin and said, "It would please both my family and me if you would do us the honor of spending the holidays with us," she began, meeting his gaze with a quiet dignity. "Please say you will stay."

Justin stared at her in surprise. He had been expecting her to ask him to remain a week, perhaps even a sennight, but until Christmas . . . he should have known to expect the unexpected from her.

"If . . . if you have other plans, I will understand," she said quickly, her cheeks reddening with embarrassment as he remained silent. "You mentioned something about going to your ancestral home for Christmas. . . ."

"Stonebridge," he provided, thinking of the huge, impressive pile of stones that had been home to his family for over a hundred years. With Edward remaining in London for the holiday season, the house would be all but deserted. There would be the servants, of course, but most of them were from the nearby village and home farm, and so had family in the area and would doubtlessly be spending the day with them.

He remembered the last Christmas he'd spent at Stonebridge, shortly before being posted to the Peninsula. He'd spent a lonely Christmas Eve sitting in the family pew of the nearby church, and an even lonelier Christmas day eating his dinner in the solitary splendor of the ancestral dining room. His suggestion that Cook prepare a simple tray for him had been met with cries of horror, and he had a sinking feeling it would be the same this year. It was tradition; just as it was the tradition that the older son become the next duke, while the younger son went into the army.

Tradition. Duty. Honor. These were the bywords by which he lived his life. They gave him a sense of continuity, of belonging, and he hoped he would never do anything to compromise these values that he held so dear. But this once he wanted to do something for himself, and for no other reason than the fact it was what he wanted to do.

"Thank you for your invitation, Miss Lawrence," he said, inclining his head to her with grave courtesy. "It would be my pleasure."

Chapter Five

After spending a restful evening, Justin was up early the next morning. Except for a lingering weakness, he was over the worst effects of the fever, and despite William's vociferous objections, he insisted upon joining his imperious hostess and her charming family for tea. Besides, he was eager to meet with young Stephen, who, according to the twins, had arrived early, that morning on the mail coach. The lad might be only fifteen, he thought, as he added the finishing touches to his cravat; but he was the man of the house now, and it was time he was apprised of his duties.

The family was already sitting in the parlor when Linsley announced his arrival, and Justin quickly motioned for everyone to remain seated as he took his place beside Miss Lawrence.

"Good afternoon, Miss Lawrence, everyone," he said, inclining his head to the others. His eyes rested briefly on the young lad with dark blond hair whom he took to be Stephen. "Sir, I do not believe I have had the pleasure?"

"S-Stephen Blanchford, Colonel Stockton," Stephen stammered, knocking over his chair as he scrambled to his feet. "P-pleased to make your acquaintance, my lord." Then he bowed somewhat awkwardly, hitting the tea table with his outstretched hand and sending a platter of delicacies flying.

"Oh, Stephen, do please sit down before you destroy something," Amanda reproved with a rueful shake of her head. The boy was as awkward as a young colt these days, and when nervous, he was a positive menace. She turned to Justin and was surprised to find him regarding her with a disapproving frown gathering his dark brows together. Good heavens, whatever could have set his back up this time, she wondered, although she was careful to keep her own expression pleasantly polite.

"I am happy that you have joined us, sir," she said smoothly. "I trust this means you are recovered from your illness?"

"Quite recovered, ma'am, and feeling decidedly peckish," he answered, vowing to have a word with her at the earliest opportunity. The dratted female might regard her younger brother as scarcely out of short breeches, but that still did not give her the right to embarrass him in front of company. He turned his attention to the twins, and after greeting them, he glanced next at the two blond chits sitting on the settee and regarding him with wide blue eyes.

The younger girl looked to be seven or eight, and as she shyly returned his smile, Justin noted she was missing a few front teeth. The other girl suffered no such disfigurement. She was, in fact, just as beautiful as he remembered, with a mass of golden ringlets surrounding the perfect oval of her face. If Miss Lawrence's fiery nature was betrayed by her bright red hair and snapping dark eyes, so were her sister's sweetness and gentleness revealed by her dimpled smile and the demure way she lowered her eyes to avoid his.

"Miss Amelia," he murmured, his smile warm as he gazed at her in appreciation. "I am pleased to see you again."

"And I you, Colonel," Amelia answered, feeling somewhat flustered by his admiring look. She was not so lackwitted that she did not know men found her lovely, but she nonetheless found it somewhat disconcerting to be stared at so frankly. As was the case whenever she was nervous, she turned to her elder sister for assistance.

"Have you told the colonel about Daniel's service?" she asked, seizing upon the topic they had just been discussing. "I am sure he will wish to attend."

"Of course he will be attending!" Jeremey said, his voice full of derision as he stuffed another macaroon into his mouth. "I just *told* you as much, didn't I? Females!" He shook his head in obvious disgust.

Amanda opened her mouth to remind the brat to mind his manners when Justin said, "A gentleman, Jeremey, never corrects a lady, especially when there are others present. A courtesy, I regret to say, that is not always returned," and he shot Amanda a meaningful look.

Amanda took his meaning at once, and it was all she could do to hold her tongue. The insufferable prig, she fumed, taking a hasty sip of her tea. He was actually scolding her for rebuking Stephen! That he was perhaps right occurred to her, but she quickly discarded the notion. Stephen was her brother, after all, and it was her place to see that he behaved in a fitting manner. Well, she decided, her eyes flashing with resolve, it was time she reminded her arrogant guest just who was mistress here!

"Ah, but given the male propensity for misbehavior, how can we poor ladies resist?" she retorted, her smile falsely sweet as she set down her teacup with an angry rattle. "We are the natural custodians of society, are we not, and it is our duty to see that you men behave in a civilized manner."

Justin's eyebrows rose at her reply. "An interesting hypothesis, Miss Lawrence," he drawled in a dampening

71

tone, "but not one, I fear, that will prove out. Men make history, and history makes society."

"Men make wars," Amanda replied, meeting Justin's gaze defiantly. "And 'tis left to the women to tend the wounded and bury the dead!"

There was an uncomfortable silence, during which Amanda could have cheerfully bitten off her own tongue. Fortunately Justin recovered faster and turned an inquiring look upon Amelia.

"But where is your good aunt?" he asked, pretending as if nothing was amiss. "Is she in her rooms?"

Amelia gave a guilty start, her creamy cheeks suffusing with color as she cast Amanda a beseeching look.

"She is not here," Amanda answered, her tone every bit as cool as Justin's. "She has returned to London to attend to some pressing business."

"More pressing than her nephew's memorial service?" he asked, wondering if this curst family ever did what was proper.

"Aunt has never been one for ceremony," Amanda replied with an indifferent shrug. "Besides, Daniel would understand." As he would, she thought with a sudden flash of whimsey. Daniel had disliked the old shrew almost as much as she did.

"I see." He didn't, of course, but there was no way he was going to debate the matter with the little she-devil. Justin sought refuge in the plate of food Amelia had pressed upon him, listening half-attentively as the family resumed its conversation.

"I was hoping Charles might be home for the service." Amelia sighed, the corners of her lips drooping unhappily. "But his mama says she does not know how to reach him."

"Never mind, my dear," Amanda said, reaching out to give the younger girl's hand a sympathetic pat. "You will be seeing him in less than a fortnight; you have only to be brave until then."

Justin wondered idly who Charles might be and then dismissed the subject from his mind as he glanced at Stephen. "How are things at Exter?" he asked, polishing off the last of the cakes Amelia had given him. "What are you studying this term?"

"Advanced mathematics and Latin, sir," Stephen replied, grateful for the colonel's attention. "I hope to study medicine."

"An admirable choice," Justin approved. "You must take care that you not fall behind in your studies. Will you be returning to classes after the holidays, or will you be sitting out the rest of the term?"

"This is a topic that is perhaps better left for another time," Amanda said quickly, determined not to display their impoverished state before their haughty guest. "In the meanwhile, sir, perhaps you might tell me if there are any particular customs you would like to observe for the holidays? I am not sure how things are done in Kent, but we in Surrey do like to celebrate our Lord's birth."

Justin stared at her in amazement. It had been so many years since he had truly celebrated the holiday—any holiday—that he was not sure how to answer. He cast about in his mind for some happy memory associated with Christmas, but there were none. Just a few vague images of the yule log burning in Stonebridge Hall's massive fireplace, and a flaming plum pudding one of their cooks had once served. His taciturn father had never been one to engage in such fustain, he recalled bitterly.

"Except for the few years I spent at Oxford, I can not say that I ever participated in any particular ceremony, Miss Lawrence," he answered coolly. "But to the best of my knowledge, we in Kent celebrate the same as folk everywhere. I am sure whatever you arrange will be more than satisfactory."

"Cakes," Belinda announced, speaking for the first time since Justin had entered the room. "Cakes, and candies, and some tarts. Do you like tarts?" She bent a suspicious frown on him.

"I adore tarts," he assured her gravely, although his eyes began to twinkle with laughter. "Do you think you might share some of yours with me?"

Belinda cocked her head to one side and regarded him with solemn blue eyes. "Mandy says I am s'posed to share," she told him in a chiding manner that was reminiscent of her older sister. "And Nanny says it is more blessed to give than to receive, so I s'pose I could give you *one* tart."

"Thank you, ma'am," Justin replied, his entire face lighting with a warm smile of amusement. "That is rare kind of you."

"You are welcome." Belinda inclined her head gracefully, feeling vastly pleased with herself. "You can even play with Phillipa if you want to," she offered in a rare spurt of generosity. "She is my bestest doll, but if you promise to be very careful, you can hold her."

The image of the colonel playing with one of their pesky sister's dolls set the twins to laughing. They were careful not to sneer at her in their idol's presence, however, a marked change in their usual behavior that had Amanda frowning in dismay. Much as she welcomed their new-found restraint, she could not help but feel slightly put out that it had been occasioned by Justin's interference.

The rest of the hour passed in relative harmony as both Amanda and Justin were too busy talking with the others to engage in any further disagreements. They were just finishing their tea when Linsley stepped in to announce Mr. Stranton had arrived and wished to speak with Amanda.

"Alone, miss," he added, his graying eyebrows arching in disapproval. "I have placed him in your study."

"Thank you, Linsley," she replied, setting her napkin to one side and shaking out the crumbs from her skirt as she rose to her feet. "Pray tell him I will be with him momentarily."

After the butler had withdrawn, she turned to the others and began issuing orders. "Stephen, I want you and the boys to show Colonel Stockton about the house. Amelia, dearest, do you think you might watch Belinda? Nanny has been pressed into service in the kitchens and will not be available for the rest of the day."

"Of course, Amanda," Amelia answered sweetly, giving the younger girl's blond hair an affectionate tug. "It will be my pleasure. We shall play dolls, Belinda; how does that sound?"

"Ugh!" Joss's nose wrinkled in masculine disgust. "*We* are going to show the colonel Daniel's room, and then he is going to tell us some fine war stories . . . aren't you, sir?" Pleading blue eyes were raised to his face.

Justin was no proof against such shameless wheedling and gave a low chuckle. "I suppose I might be persuaded to bore you all with a few tales," he murmured, casting Amanda a challenging look. "Provided, of course, that your sister has no objections?"

The very possibility set up such a hue and a cry among her brothers that it was several moments before Amanda was able to make herself heard. "Naturally I have no objections, sir," she said with a strained smile, silently cursing him for the adroit way he had made her the villainess of the piece. "I only hope that the boys won't tire you out."

"I'm sure I'll survive," he replied, acknowledging her unspoken anger with a half-smile. "We soldiers are tough as old boots, you know."

There seemed to be no polite way to answer this, so Amanda excused herself, departing from the parlor before she said something she knew she would later regret. And to think, she brooded unhappily, that she had an entire fortnight of his company to endure. She would have to guard her tongue if she hoped to survive without the two of them coming to blows. Fortunately for him, she was blessed with a strong nature and didn't doubt her ability to control both her temper and her obstreperous guest.

Mr. Stranton was nervously pacing the study when she arrived, and at the sight of her, his lined face broke out in a relieved smile. "Ah, Miss Lawrence," he said, hurrying forward to take her hand in his, "it was good of you to see me on such short notice. I trust I haven't caught you at an inconvenient time?"

"Not at all, Mr. Stranton," she replied, inclining her head graciously and indicating the chair behind him. "But will you not be seated and tell me what has brought you so far from the village and on such a snowy day?"

"Well, naturally I wished to offer you my condolences on your good brother's death," he began, smoothing out the creases in his black kerseymere trousers. "Such a tragic loss. My wife and I extend our most heart-felt sympathies to you and your family, and we want you to know that you are ever in our prayers."

"Thank you, sir," Amanda replied, her brown eyes frankly speculative as she studied the agitated solicitor. "But surely you didn't travel three miles in this weather to tell me that. What else is there you are not telling me?"

The elderly man swallowed audibly, his watery eyes darting away from her face. "How very clever you are, my dear," he said with a nervous laugh. "As I was telling my wife only this morning, that Miss Lawrence is too sharp by half! One would have to keep all one's wits about him if he hoped to—"

"Mr. Stranton, you will forgive me for being so blunt, but would you kindly get to the point?" Amanda interrupted, rubbing a hand across her temples. "You have obviously come out here to tell me something, so please do so." She gave him a knowing look. "Has this anything to do with my aunt?"

The guilty expression on the older man's face was all the confirmation she needed, and Amanda's sigh was decidedly weary as she said, "Does she wish to claim the house sooner than January?"

"She—she did mention taking immediate possession," he replied, relieved that she seemed so calm. "But I was able to convince her 'twould be better to wait until after the New Year. She seemed somewhat . . . er . . . upset."

"I daresay she was," Amanda muttered, remembering the oaths her aunt had shrieked at her as her carriage rolled away. "My aunt and I have never gotten along, and this matter of her inheriting our home has only made matters worse. She offered to allow me to stay, on but I found her conditions completely unacceptable."

"Do you think that advisable?" Mr. Stranton's expression grew grave. "As I have already told you, your financial position is far from strong. If Mrs. Herrick is willing to give you shelter—"

"Mrs. Herrick was willing to keep me as her unpaid lackey," Amanda interrupted, her full lips thinning in remembered anger, "nothing more. She made it quite clear what my position would be, and when she let it be known that there was no room for the others, I asked her to leave. As I told her, sir, we are a family, and so we shall remain. We'll rub along together somehow. Now, was there anything else you wished to discuss with me?"

"Nothing that can not wait until after the holidays," the

solicitor answered, suddenly eager to be gone. He had only come out to warn her of her aunt's intentions, but as she was already aware of the situation, he felt free to leave. "With your permission, I believe I shall be leaving now," he said, rising to his feet. "The snow is deepening, and I really should be on my way. In the meanwhile, should you have need of anything, you have only to send a note to my home, and I shall come out straightaway."

After escorting her visitor to the door, Amanda returned to her study to brood. The solicitor's visit had driven home the grim reality of their future, and she wondered yet again what would come of them. She settled behind her desk and was going over her budget when there was a knock on the door.

"Come in," she called, hastily covering the column of figures she'd been adding. To her surprise Colonel Stockton stood there, his expression grave as he closed the door and advanced towards her.

"Is there anything amiss, Miss Lawrence?" he asked, easing his tall form onto the faded chair facing her desk. "Stephen just informed me that your caller was your solicitor. Is there some problem with Daniel's will?"

"Of course not," Amanda replied swiftly, deciding that she wasn't really lying: The problem lay with her grandfather's will. "Mr. Stranton merely wished to offer me his condolences."

Justin's eyes flicked toward the mullioned windows. "His sense of duty is to be commended," he drawled, his brows lifting at the sight of the thick white snowflakes swirling in the icy wind. "But surely he could have waited until after the service tomorrow to pay his respects."

"He has known Daniel all his life." Amanda defended Mr. Stranton's actions with a challenging lift of her chin. The thought of the colonel learning of their plight was simply too humiliating to bear, and she resolved to keep the truth from him at all cost.

Justin said nothing, although he knew the chit was lying between her pretty teeth. If his years of command had taught him anything, it was to know when someone was being less than honest with him. For some reason she wished to keep the purpose behind the solicitor's visit a secret, and he could not help but wonder what those reasons might be.

"Speaking of tomorrow," he began, deciding it might be wiser to abandon the subject for the moment, "I wanted to ask your advice on something."

"And what might that be?" Amanda didn't trust his air of indifference for a moment. Granted, she did not know the man well, but instinct told her he wasn't the type to give in quite so easily.

"I have already promised the twins I would wear my uniform to the church," he continued, crossing his arms across his chest. "But I thought it might be better to obtain your permission first. I wouldn't wish to upset either you or your sisters by raising unpleasant memories."

Amanda stared at him in surprise. "Why should your wearing your uniform upset me?" she asked in some confusion. "We were all very proud of Daniel!"

"That isn't what he said," Justin replied, recalling the brief conversation he'd had with the young officer so many months ago. "In fact, he said you kicked up a devil of a dust when he first enlisted in the Infantry."

"Only because he was threatening to enlist as a common foot soldier if I didn't buy him a commission!" she protested, blushing to think Daniel had told anyone of their quarrel. "Naturally I was somewhat upset with him at the time. He was my brother, and I feared for his life."

Justin frowned at her words. "*You* bought him a commission?"

Amanda nodded warily. "Most of Daniel's inheritance

79

was entailed and it would have been . . . difficult to arrange for the necessary money to be released. He was determined to join the army and fight for king and country, so there was nothing else I could do." Tears shimmered in her eyes before she added, "At the time I thought I was doing him a service, now I am not so sure."

Justin's heart softened at her obvious distress. "You gave the lad what he wanted most," he said softly. "Never doubt that for a single moment. Your brother knew the risks and chose to take them; don't blame yourself for that."

She bowed her head for a moment, and when she raised her eyes to his face, they were warm with gratitude. How odd that only a short while ago she'd been stiff with resentment toward him, she thought, her mouth relaxing in a hesitant smile. Then she could have happily throttled him, but now she was feeling quite charitably disposed toward him.

"Thank you," she said simply, knowing he would not welcome more effusive expressions of gratitude. "And I do hope that you will wear your uniform. It meant the world to Daniel, and I know it would please him that you should honor him so.

"Then, it is agreed," he said, pleased that things should have been resolved so peacefully. He didn't really think she would oppose him on the matter, but with Miss Lawrence, one could never be certain what she would do. She was every bit as stubborn as Daniel had said she would be, and just as managing.

The thought of her managing ways brought to mind the other reason why he had decided to seek a private audience with her, and he shifted forward in his chair until his arms rested on the polished surface of her desk. "Miss Lawrence," he said, fixing her with a stern look, "I was wondering if I might speak with you regarding your

80

brother."

"Do you mean Daniel?"

He shook his head. "I was referring to Stephen. I realize the lad is still wet behind the ears, but that doesn't give you cause to treat him like a tiresome cub. He is fifteen now, and trapped between adolescence and manhood. I know from my own youth that this is a painful age, and—"

"I beg your pardon, Colonel," Amanda said, her icy words cutting into his admonishing speech, "but my brothers are my responsibility. I thank you for your concern, but—"

"But you'll not countenance any interference," he concluded for her, his golden-brown eyes snapping with anger. "Come, Miss Lawrence, surely you can not be so petty a tyrant as that!"

"And surely you sir, must know that there can be but one commander in any enterprise!" she retorted furious with herself for being taken in by his show of sympathetic understanding. The man was obviously so accustomed to being the superior officer that he couldn't abide the thought of anyone else exerting the smallest amount of authority.

"Blast it, ma'am, I am trying to help!" Justin roared, coming to his feet in an angry rush. He'd meant to discuss her behavior in a cool and rational manner, and instead he found they were once again at daggers drawn. He'd always considered himself to be a man of modest temperament, but Miss Lawrence seemed able to rouse him to fury sooner than any female he'd ever had the misfortune to meet. He shook his head and made an effort to obtain the cool control that had always been his.

"I beg you will pardon me," he said, his voice straining with suppressed emotion. "Naturally, you must do as you see fit. As you have said, they are your brothers, and my opinions are clearly unwanted. Good afternoon." He turned and walked from the room, his back held stiff with pride.

Amanda watched him go, wondering what it was about the colonel that made her admire him one moment and then long to box his ears in the next. All her life she had been the one in control, hiding her emotions behind a brisk, efficient facade. Yet with him she was as much at the mercy of her emotions as any silly female.

Her lips thinned at the realization, and she vowed to keep a tighter rein on herself in the future. With her family's future hanging in the balance, she could ill-afford the distraction of emotion. When next she and Justin met, he would find her as sweetly bidable as a lamb. No matter what, she promised herself, she would not allow him to draw her into another argument. He was naught but a guest here, and with that thought in mind she put her papers aside and set out to speak with Mrs. Hatcher. It was past time she was planning her guest's Christmas dinner.

"A boar's head, miss?" The elderly cook stared at Amanda as if she'd taken leave of her senses. "Whyever would you be wantin' such a heathenish thing?"

"I have told you, Mrs. Hatcher, it is for Colonel Stockton," Amanda repeated in her most cajoling manner. She knew the other lady held a firm distrust of anything "new," and that if she wished her cooperation, she'd have to tread very carefully. "He attended Oxford, you see, and 'tis the tradition there to serve a boar's head at Christmas dinner."

"Well, I've never heard the like," Mrs. Hatcher muttered darkly, "Goose is what we serve of a Christmas Day, and always have to my recollection."

"Nonsense," Amanda countered firmly. "My own father

attended Oxford, and when I was younger I often heard him speak of the ceremony and the speeches that accompanied it."

Mrs. Hatcher looked thoughtful. "Aye," she said reluctantly, "that he did." And in the next moment she was shaking her head, her sharp knife slicing through the pile of currants she'd been chopping when Amanda burst into the kitchens.

"And next I suppose you'll be wantin' those fancy French pastries instead of my plum pudding," she grumbled with the familiarity of an old retainer. "And what of my Christmas cake, eh? 'Tis baked and frosted, and the wee ones are already beggin' for a taste. I'll not be the one to tell them nay." She shot Amanda a disapproving scowl.

"We shall have the Christmas cake, and the plum pudding, and the goose. The boar's head is more for show than anything," Amanda soothed, wishing she had waited until after dinner before approaching Mrs. Hatcher. The good cook was always more amenable after a glass or two of the spicy ale she took with her evening meal.

"A rather dear piece of show if you ask me," she sniffed, but Amanda could tell by her thoughtful expression that she was already more than half won over.

"True, but only think how much the children will enjoy it," she added, deciding she had nothing to lose by playing her trump card. "It will make a lovely memory for them."

"There is that," the cook agreed, her face softening at the thought of the younger members of the household. She set her knife down as she considered the matter. "John Turnbow's oldest has a boar he was talkin' of butcherin'. Mayhap I could have a word with him."

Amanda gave her an impulsive hug. "Thank you, Mrs. Hatcher," she said with a relieved laugh. "I knew I could count upon you."

83

Mrs. Hatcher returned her hug and then quickly pushed her away, her cheeks bright red. "And you'll be havin' one of those infernal trees as well, I don't doubt," she snapped, turning her attention to her work. "Although why anyone should go to all the bother of hangin' that folderol on a tree, I'm sure I don't know!"

"It is called a *tannenbaum*," Amanda corrected, not the least bit taken in by her objections, "and you know that it is a custom my great-grandmother brought with her when she came to this country with one of the Hanoverian princesses. We had them when I was a child, and I seem to recall seeing you admiring them from the servants' hall," she added with a knowing grin.

Mrs. Hatcher gave a loud sniff, refusing to own up to admiring something so decidedly foreign. "The candleholders will be up in the attic with your mother's things," she said briskly. "And it will be left to you and the children to make the other nonsense. Heaven knows I shall have enough to do what with preparin' the funeral meal and then my Christmas bakin' as well."

"That sounds delightful," Amanda replied, thinking of the paper chains and stars she and the children could make. It would help them pass the long evenings until Christmas. Perhaps Colonel Stockton would like to help, she thought, her lips curling in sudden amusement. She was willing to wager he'd never seen a real German tree before.

She remained in the kitchen discussing the buffet that would be served following Daniel's memorial service, and then excused herself, pleased that she had the situation so well in hand. When she was almost to the door, Mrs. Hatcher called out to her.

"The plum pudding will be ready to pour by Monday, Miss. Will you and the children be takin' your turns stirrin' it?"

84

Amanda's pleasure vanished as a wave of pain washed over her. She could remember last year when she and the others had joined in the ancient custom of making a wish as they stirred the Christmas pudding. If only her wish had been granted, she thought, blinking back her tears. If it had, then Daniel would still be alive, and they would not be faced with the loss of their home and their very way of life.

"Of course we will, Mrs. Hatcher," she said firmly, and then hurried away before she could disgrace herself by bursting into noisy tears.

 *Chapter Six*

Tempting as it was to retire to her room and indulge in a strong fit of the vapors, Amanda returned to her study. The door was standing open when she arrived, and the sight of her brother standing beside her desk brought her to an abrupt halt.

"Stephen!" she exclaimed, a pleased smile touching her lips. "What are you doing here? I should think you would be resting after your long journey."

In answer he held up the account sheet she had been laboring over. "What is this?" he asked, his dark blond eyebrows meeting in a worried frown.

Amanda bustled forward, her cheeks flushing with distress. "Really, Stephen," she protested, attempting to snatch the sheets away from him, "I wish you wouldn't snoop in my desk. Those are my private papers."

He easily avoided her, holding the sheets just out of reach. "This looks like a ledger," he said, turning away and hunching his shoulders as he studied them. "And these figures are an account of some kind. What do they mean? What is going on?"

"Nothing!" Amanda ducked under his arm to make another try at the papers. "Stephen, would you just—"

"Blast it all, Mandy, I ain't a child!" he cried suddenly, his eyes bright with emotion as he whirled around to face her.

"Tell me what is going on! Has this anything to do with Mr. Stranton's visit?"

Amanda gazed up at him silently, noting how much he had grown in the months since she'd last seen him. When he'd left for school at the beginning of the fall term, he had been an inch or so shorter than her, now she had to tilt her head back to look at him. Colonel Stockton was right, she thought unhappily; Stephen was a man now, and she was doing him no favors by treating him like an ill-mannered child.

"Not precisely," she said, realizing the time had come to tell him everything. "As I told the colonel, Mr. Stranton was anxious to offer us his condolences, but he also wanted to speak to me about Aunt Elizabeth."

"What about her?" Stephen asked, his frown deepening. "Amelia told me she was here, but that the two of you had had words and the old girl stomped off to London. Can't say as I am sorry," he added with a grimace. "I wasn't relishing the notion of spending my holiday listening to her jaw at me."

"Yes, well, as it happens Aunt Elizabeth is my grandfather's secondary heir, and now that Daniel is dead, she is the new owner of Lawrence Hall," Amanda said quietly, determined to keep nothing from him.

"*What?*" Stephen gasped, his cheeks paling in horror.

Amanda repeated what she had learned from the solicitor, and he began to angrily pace the room.

"But that is infamous!" he cried, his hands clenching into tight fists. "What of you and Amelia? You're Lawrences too . . . aren't you?"

"Yes," she admitted, resuming her seat with an unhappy sigh. "But we are female Lawrences, unfortunately, and by the terms of grandfather's will, that is not quite good enough."

"I don't see why not," Stephen muttered, looking mutinous. "Aunt Elizabeth is a female, and *she's* inheriting everything!"

"Only because her father had the foresight to protect her," Amanda replied bluntly. "But that is neither here nor there, I suppose. The will is valid, and Aunt Elizabeth will be assuming ownership at the end of January."

Stephen uttered an oath which a few short months ago would have earned him a sharp rap across the mouth and gave her a searching look. "Do the others know?"

Amanda shook her head. "I've told Linsley and some of the other servants, but I haven't had the heart to tell the children. They've been so upset about Daniel."

"They'll have to be told."

"I know." Her shoulders drooped in defeat, and she suddenly felt a thousand years old. She glanced at the painting of her father hanging over the fireplace, studying his bright red hair and flashing dark eyes with a wistful expression. Would Aunt Elizabeth leave the portrait where it was, she wondered, or would she consign it to some dark corner of the attic? The older woman had always expressed an acute dislike of it. . . .

Stephen shifted restlessly from one foot to the other at his sister's brooding silence. This was the first time he'd seen her cast so low, and for a moment he was afraid. Then he remembered that he was now the man of the house and resolutely squared his shoulders.

"It won't be so bad," he promised, infusing a note of confidence into his voice. "The twins are a plucky lot, and Belinda won't care where we are so long as she has her cursed dolls. And Amelia, well, she'll soon be marrying Charles, and they'll be living in that crumbling old manor house he inherited from his uncle."

"And what of you?" Amanda asked gently, touched by the way he thought first of the others. "You do know that you won't be able to return to school? At least, not this year," she added, doing some swift calculations in her head.

He shrugged his shoulders. "I was thinking of coming home anyway," he said, manfully swallowing his disappointment at the thought of giving up his beloved studies. "School's a dashed bore."

"Oh, Stephen." She leapt to her feet to give him an impulsive hug. "I do love you!"

He returned her embrace somewhat awkwardly and then stepped back, the tips of his ears reddening with embarrassment. "Come now," he said, loudly clearing his throat, "let's go and tell the others, shall we? And don't worry, Amanda. It will all work out in the end; you'll see. We shall all be together, and in the end, that's all that matters."

The small stone church where five generations of Lawrences had worshipped was filled to overflowing as neighbors and villagers filed in to pay their final respects to Daniel. In celebration of the holidays, the interior had already been hung with festive greenery, but at Amanda's request they had been left up, adding a touch of poignancy to the services. She was aware of a few shocked whispers, but she paid the speakers no mind. Daniel had always loved seeing the church decorated for Christmas, and she knew he would have approved.

On her right she could hear Amelia crying softly into her handkerchief, while Belinda sat on her left, a crooked finger tucked into her mouth as she listened to the vicar's stirring eulogy. Amanda reached out and plucked the girl's finger from between her lips, giving her hand a loving pat before turning her glance toward her brothers.

Stephen sat between Colonel Stockton and Belinda, his thin face rigid as he fought against tears. He was wearing one of Daniel's old jackets, and the black velvet fitted somewhat loosely across his bony shoulders. She couldn't see the twins without leaning forward, but for once she wasn't afraid they would misbehave. She'd overheard the colonel telling them that good soldiers never broke rank, and since then they'd been sitting as still and silent as a pair of statues.

Thoughts of the twins made her remember last evening and the brave way her family had taken the news. Amelia had instantly offered her bridal portion, insisting Charles wouldn't mind. While she was thanking her, the twins disappeared into their rooms, emerging with an old metal box which they promptly placed in her hands.

"It's our treasure," Joss had said, for once speaking before Jeremey could open his mouth. "We was saving it to buy us a ship so we could be pirates, but you can have it."

Even Belinda was eager to contribute to the family coffers, gravely offering to sell her beloved dolls. Amanda had blinked back tears as she refused both the dolls and the twins' treasure—which amounted to almost ten pounds—but she knew she would never forget their unselfish generosity for as long as she lived.

The sound of the vicar offering the eucharist brought Amanda back to the present, and she silently bowed her head. Listening to the soothing words, she knew a sudden lifting of her spirits, and a feeling of peace and contentment washed over her. She could see Daniel's smiling face in her mind's eye, and she felt that if she tried very hard, she would be able to hear him speak. She shut her eyes tightly and concentrated with all her will, and from a great distance she heard a faint and familiar laughter.

"Don't worry, sister, it will be all right. Never you fear, I shall look after you. . . ."

Following the service, the mourners adjourned to Lawrence Hall for a somber repast. Mrs. Hatcher had out-

90

done herself and Amanda was pleased to note that everyone seemed to have more than enough to eat. She moved about the company like a quiet ghost, a set smile pinned to her lips as she accepted the condolences of her friends and neighbors.

From his position in front of the fireplace, Justin watched her progress with narrowed eyes. Her bright hair was scraped back in a bun so tightly not a single curl was allowed to escape, and the fierce temper he associated with her was nowhere in evidence. Not that he expected her to kick up a dust at her brother's memorial service, he thought, his mouth lifting in a grim smile, but with her one could never be certain. Looking at her now, her slender body draped in a simple gown of black silk trimmed with jet beads, he found it hard to believe that she was the same woman who only yesterday had challenged him so defiantly.

The realization made his smile fade as he remembered last evening. She had been subdued, even somber, but he had put her mood down to simple grief. After all, the whole family had been surprisingly restrained—even the twins—and they'd made an early evening of it. Breakfast had been equally as quiet, as had the carriage ride to the church, but he suddenly found himself wondering if perhaps there might be some other explanation for his hostess's lack of spirit.

"Ah, Colonel Stockton." An elderly man paused before Justin, holding out a heavily veined hand in greeting. "I am Mr. Elias Stranton, sir, and I am most happy to make your acquaintance."

"Mr. Stranton." Justin recognized the solicitor's name at once, and he stiffened with interest. Instincts honed by a decade in uniform told him the solicitor's arrival yesterday was connected with Miss Lawrence's behavior, and he was suddenly determined to learn just what had transpired in that little study.

"I am also pleased to meet you, sir," he said, accepting the man's hand with a warm smile. "I apologize for not introducing myself yesterday while you were here, but Miss Lawrence explained you had come on important business."

"Ah yes, the will." Mr. Stranton sighed, pleased the colonel was proving to be so approachable after all. He'd seemed so cold and haughty at the church. "A rum business, that."

Justin's ears pricked at this bit of news. Taking care to hide his interest, he took a casual sip of his punch, allowing a moment or two to pass before he remarked, "Yes, Miss Lawrence remarked that there was some impediment. Nothing too difficult, I trust?"

"Well, I really should not be saying," Mr. Stranton said, licking his lips nervously. It wasn't often he found himself the center of attention, and for a moment a rare sense of discretion warred with his natural inclination to gossip. "Professional confidence and all that," he added, shooting Justin a look that indicated he could easily be persuaded otherwise.

Justin was quick to take the hint. "Come, Mr. Stranton," he said, fixing him with a commanding look, "you can tell me. The lad died taking a musketball meant for me, and I promised him I would have a care for his family. If there is some problem, I insist that you tell me at once!"

That was all it took to loosen the solicitor's tongue as he launched into an eager description not only of the terms of her grandfather's will, but of her precarious financial situation as well. By the time he had finished, Justin was white-faced with fury.

"Do you mean to tell me that they are virtually penniless?" he demanded, his fingers tightening around his cup.

"Well, I would not go so far as to say that, my lord," Mr. Stranton corrected in his pedantic way. "There is some income; two hundred and fifty pounds per anum, not counting the annuities to the younger children and the money Miss Lawrence will inherit from her mother. Their circumstances will be greatly reduced, but they are certainly not destitute."

"But how will they live?" Justin asked feeling a cold wave of horror wash over him. Good God, he thought with growing consternation, he dropped more than that in one night's gaming and never gave the matter another thought.

"I have mentioned the possibility of a marriage of convenience to Miss Lawrence," the older man confided. "It is often the only way in such cases. A well-heeled Cit with more brass than breeding has been the salvation of many a highborn family, and although there is no title, the Lawrences are unmistakably Quality."

"She could never have consented to such a thing!" Justin thundered, shooting Amanda an appalled look.

"No," Mr. Stranton admitted with an indifferent shrug, "but you must agree, 'twould be the best for all concerned."

"I do not," Justin answered tightly, everything in him revolting at the very thought of either Amanda or the beauteous Amelia being reduced to such a choice. It was unthinkable, preposterous, and he for one would not allow it. Clearly something had to be done, and equally as clear, he was the man to do it. He set his punch cup on a nearby tray and turned to the solicitor.

"I would like to meet with you on the morrow, Mr. Stranton," he said, coming to a sudden decision. "Please be here by one o'clock."

The other man blinked at the terse command. "Of course, my lord," he said, looking puzzled. "Er . . . might I ask what this is in reference to?"

"Duty," Justin replied tersely, his jaw hardening with resolve as he studied Amanda. "It seems that I have been remiss in mine."

"As you say, sir," Mr. Stranton replied in a perplexed

tone, his expression clearing as he watched the colonel striding purposefully toward the corner where Miss Lawrence was standing. So it was like that, was it, he thought, his thin lips parting in a pleased smile. Excellent. And on that happy note he went off to explore the delights of the buffet table.

". . . terrible thing," Mrs. Kingsfield concluded dramatically, dabbing at her dark eyes with a lace-edged handkerchief. "My heart quite goes out to you and your precious family."

"That is very good of you, ma'am, thank you," Amanda replied dutifully, casting a surreptitious look at the clock above the mantle. She'd been trapped by her loquacious neighbor for the better part of a quarter hour, and her head was pounding with the effort of being polite. The elderly woman with her affected manners was trying under the best of circumstances, and given the present situation, Amanda was beginning to doubt her ability to remain civil much longer. She was wondering if she should simply slip away while the woman was still talking when she felt a strong hand cup her elbow.

"I want a word with you," Colonel Stockton said, his voice commanding as he bent to whisper in her ear. "Now."

Amanda's first inclination was to ignore his curt demand, but the opportunity to escape from Mrs. Kingsfield was too tempting to resist. After murmuring a polite apology to the older woman, she allowed him to escort her out into the hallway. The moment they were alone, however, she pulled her arm free and turned around to face him.

"Really, sir," she began, her eyes sparkling with a militant light, "I will thank you not to order me about like one of your soldiers!"

"And I will thank you, ma'am, to be honest with me when I ask you something!" Justin retorted, his face darkening with anger. Lawrence was right, he decided, crossing his arms over his chest and meeting her incredulous stare. The minx was a regular tartar, and it hadn't taken but a few minutes to put them at daggers drawn. But he was done with coddling her. He was in command now, and the sooner she realized that, the better.

"I—how dare you accuse me of dishonesty!" Amanda gasped, a flush of indignation adding needed color to her pale cheeks. "When have I ever deceived you?"

The presence of a gawking maid called Justin's attention to their unsecure position and without another word, he grabbed her by the hand and pulled her down the hall and into her study. When the door was closed firmly behind them, he said, "I know about the will, Amanda."

His use of her Christian name was almost as shocking as his admission, and for a moment she could only stare up at him in mute astonishment. In the next she was exploding with fury.

"Mr. Stranton! I might have known that loose-tongued fool was not to be trusted! Why my stepfather saw fit to name him our guardian, I know not! He is the worst gossip in the county, and—"

"He only told me what he thought I had the right to know." Justin's cold voice cut off her tirade as effectively as a knife. "And I did have that right, Amanda, regardless of what you think."

"I don't see why," she muttered ungraciously. "*You* aren't our guardian."

"No, but if it weren't for me, Daniel might still be alive," he said with uncompromising honesty. "Directly or indirectly I am to blame for your financial difficulty, and I mean to set it right."

For a few seconds Amanda was tempted, terribly tempted, to take whatever aid the colonel saw fit to offer. She'd been struggling with the lack of money for so long that the thought of being taken care of was sweet beyond all bearing. But in the end her sense of pride and honesty won out over her weakness.

"Daniel was a soldier, sir, and he knew and accepted the risks he took," she said quietly, her brown eyes serious as she met his gaze. "You aren't to blame for his death, and I can not allow you to accept a responsibility that isn't yours. I appreciate your concern for us, but we will manage."

"How?" Justin demanded, his brows meeting in a fierce scowl. "By making a marriage of convenience? Stranton said you were as good as considering one."

Amanda was hopelessly confused until she remembered the solicitor's innocuous remark about an "advantageous" marriage. She hadn't given the matter another thought since, but now she could see its merits, especially if it would convince the impossible man facing her that they didn't need his help.

"Yes, I suppose a marriage of convenience would solve all of our problems rather nicely," she hedged, mentally crossing her fingers.

Justin uttered a harsh oath under his breath as he stood glaring down at her. She was impossible, he thought savagely—a managing, infuriating scold—and he almost felt sorry for the poor, misguided fool who would offer for her. He would be expecting a lady for a bride, and would get a fishwife instead.

Despite the serious nature of their heated discussion, Amanda suddenly found herself fighting laughter. He looked positively apoplectic, she thought, biting her lips to hold back a smile. Apparently the thought of marrying out of one's station, regardless of the reasons, offended his delicate sensibilities. She might have known he was a snob as well as a tyrant and a prig, she decided, casting about in her mind for a suitably abhorrent candidate for her hand.

"In fact, Colonel," she said, batting her eyelashes and simpering like a schoolgirl, "I have received just such an offer.

But naturally I told Mr. Harper we must wait at least a year until we are out of mourning for Daniel."

"Who the devil is Mr. Harper?" Justin demanded, his fists clenching in anger. "Is he here?"

"He was earlier, but I believe he has left," she answered with another cloying smile. "Business, you know."

"What kind of business?" His tone was frankly suspicious.

"Why, wine, of course," Amanda replied serenely. "He owns one of the largest wine cellars in Surrey, and sells to the best inns in England. He is quite rich, and even though he is almost eighty, I am sure he will make a most admirable husband. He—"

"Eighty!"

"Well"—Amanda wondered if she was overplaying her hand—"perhaps not quite so ancient as all that. It is just he is so dissipated it is rather difficult to tell. He has too much of a fondness for his merchandise, I fear." She sighed heavily, and then brightened as if a sudden thought had occurred to her. "But he has assured me he isn't terribly violent when in his cups, and—"

"And do you mean to tell me you would consider this animal's suit?" Justin interrupted, having heard more than enough. "My God, what of the others? Surely you wouldn't expose Amelia or Belinda to his drunken rages!"

"Oh, but he wouldn't harm them." Amanda was beginning to regret ever having initiated this ridiculous conversation but having come this far, she could see no way to withdraw without admitting to her own duplicity. "I daresay I am painting a blacker picture than the poor man deserves! Really, he is a very pleasant man." She managed a sickly smile.

Justin saw her smile, and his own mood darkened. It was obvious Amanda had settled on her repulsive bridegroom as the only way of providing for her family, but he was damned if he would let her make such a sacrifice. Biting back an angry oath, he turned and stormed from the room.

"Will that be all, Colonel?" Williams asked, surveying his employer's grim countenance with concern. "Some brandy, perhaps?"

Justin stirred himself, raising his eyes from his brooding study of the fire long enough to cast his valet a dismissing smile. "No, Williams, thank you," he said, returning his gaze to the flames. "You may go now."

Williams hesitated, unwilling to leave his master when he was obviously so bedeviled, but equally unwilling to disobey him. He had been in a black mood since returning from the church earlier that afternoon, and it seemed he meant to spend his evening the same way. Ah well, the valet decided with a troubled sigh, let the lad wrestle with his demons; doubtlessly he would eventually work things out.

After the valet had gone, Justin rose to pace impatiently about the room. Blast it all, what the devil was he going to do, he brooded, rubbing the back of his neck with a weary hand. He couldn't allow Amanda to sell herself to some decrepit merchant, and yet how could he stop her? He wasn't her guardian, as she had been at such pains to remind him, and by law she could marry whomever she bloody well pleased.

He had to give the devil her due, he acknowledged with a bitter smile. She'd chosen the one defense he couldn't overcome. Once married, she and the others would fall under her husband's protection, and there was nothing he could do about it. Unless he was to marry her himself, he—

Justin's hand dropped to his side as the realization struck him. Marriage, he thought, allowing the notion to settle in his brain. Of course, why hadn't he thought of that before? Marriage was the perfect solution to all their problems! Not only would it grant him the right to provide for Lawrence's family, but it would also give Amanda the security she seemed to crave. And at least with him, she needn't fear his drunken rages.

He had to marry sometime, he told himself, and it might as well be to Amanda as to anyone else. For all her hoydenish ways, she was still a lady, and a rather attractive lady at that, now that he thought of it. She was difficult, demanding, and much too independent for his tastes, but he knew instinctively he could rely on her to keep his honor.

Yes, he decided, a slow smile lighting his eyes. He *would* offer for the hellcat. Now all that remained was convincing her to accept him. Something told him it would not be an easy task.

 *Chapter Seven*

Over the next few days Justin quietly began setting his plans in motion. He first wrote his brother's solicitor, requesting information on a small property he had inherited from a distant relation. The property included a lovely country house as well as a comfortable living, and he decided it was just the thing to keep his soon-to-be-acquired family in style.

He next wrote his commanding officer, informing him of his coming marriage and dropping a subtle hint that he would soon be available to resume command of his unit. Information from the continent was sketchy, but Justin knew instinctively that Napoleon, while reeling from his defeat at Leipzig, was still a very real threat to England. He had always put his duties as a commander above all else, and he saw no reason why this should change merely because he was about to take a bride.

Upon reflection he also wrote Edward, although he doubted his elder brother would bother attending whatever ceremony he and Amanda decided upon. Although the two of them were close, he frankly found Edward's racketing ways to be vexing. The fool had apparently squandered most of his inheritance on high living and imprudent investments, and was already asking him for "pocket money," as he called it.

Thoughts of his brother were very much on Justin's mind on Sunday as he and the Lawrences spent a quiet afternoon at home. The three girls were sitting before the fire, their heads bent over their sewing while the twins and Stephen were involved in a noisy game of jack straws. Glancing around the shabby parlor, he couldn't help but compare this scene to the cold, sterile memories of his own boyhood. Despite the luxury he had known then, he had never felt the warmth and sense of belonging he experienced now. Amanda was right, he decided, wincing as he stretched his feet toward the fire. They were a family, and it was best for all that they remain that way.

"Are you all right, sir?" Amelia asked unexpectedly, her blue eyes troubled as she studied him. "I noted you seem uncomfortable; is your leg paining you?"

"It is a bit stiff, Miss Amelia, that is all," he replied, grateful for her concern. The girl was an angel, quite unlike her elder sister, he mused, flicking his eyes toward Amanda. As if aware of his scrutiny, she raised her head from her sewing, her dark brown eyes cool as she returned his gaze.

"Are you quite certain, Colonel? We can send for the doctor if you are in any pain," she offered, proud of the lack of heat in her voice. Since their last encounter following Daniel's funeral, she had been at pains to avoid any further confrontations. Of course, the fact that Justin had kept mostly to his rooms during the past few days probably had something to do with the fragile peace, she admitted with a flash of wry humor.

Justin noted the mischievous gleam in her eyes, but prudently decided to ignore it. Like Amanda, he was hopeful of maintaining familial harmony, at least until he had his ring on her finger. Once they were man and wife, however, he would lay down the law in no uncertain terms.

"That is unnecessary, Miss Lawrence, thank you," he murmured, favoring her with a warm smile. "As I told Miss Amelia, 'tis naught but a touch of stiffness. One of the hazards of advancing age, I dare say," he added with a self-deprecatory shrug.

"You aren't old," Stephen protested with an indignant frown. Like the twins, he worshipped Justin, endowing him with all the heroic virtues, and it was obvious he would countenance no slur on his idol.

Justin was aware of the lad's adoration, and while he was touched by it, he didn't allow it to go to his head. He more than anyone knew just how fallible he really was, and he never forgot that fact. "Trust me, Stephen," he said, his expression rueful as he leaned forward in his chair, "there are times when I feel as ancient as Methuselah's grandsire. And I fear today is just such a day. This cold is making my leg stiff as wood."

"The squire's cousin has a wooden leg," Jeremey volunteered, his bright blue eyes glowing with excitement. "If you give him a drink, he'll even take it off and show it to you!"

"Jeremey!" Amanda was appalled by her brother's ghoulish comment. "What a terrible thing to say!"

"Well, he will," Jeremey countered her protest with a defiant toss of his head. "And you needn't glare at me neither, 'cause Mr. Nesmith said he showed it to *you* when you was a gel!"

Everyone burst into laughter, and after a few moments she ruefully joined in. "Hoisted by my own petard, you little imp," she said, reaching out to ruffle his blond hair. "But I still don't feel the conversation at all suitable, and I

102

will thank you, sir, to mind your tongue. Next you will be telling us all about Lord Ethelmeyer's eyepatch, or some equally ghastly thing."

"No use talking about that," Joss offered with an unhappy sigh. "He charges a pence just to raise his patch a bit."

The arrival of Linsley announcing dinner proved a welcome diversion, and Amanda gratefully led the others into the dining room. While they devoured the excellent beef Mrs. Hatcher had prepared, Justin began plotting the best way to present his suit to Amanda.

The romantic approach would never do, he decided as he listened half-attentively to the conversation about him. Not only did he refuse to make a cake out of himself by even hinting he had fallen in love with her, but he strongly suspected she would laugh in his face were he to attempt such a thing. No, the best approach was to be as straight-forward as possible, reminding her of all the advantages marriage to him could bring her. Given the present state of her pocketbook, he did not doubt but that she would accept. Amanda might be a proud and stubborn minx, but she was no fool. With any luck they could be married by special license by the new year, and he could then rejoin his regiment, secure in the knowledge that he had done his duty. Bolstered by this thought, he turned his attention to his food, his eyes gleaming with the smug sense of satisfaction from a job well done.

Amanda devoted the remainder of the afternoon preparing the house for the coming holiday. With the children's assistance, they spent several hours stringing the parlor with greenery, and the old house soon took on a festive aspect. Candles scented with bayberry flickered on the dining table while small bunches of holly decorated every available surface. The boys had discovered some mistletoe growing in the crook of an old elm, and they hung it above doorway with much good-natured giggling.

Amelia and Belinda had made it their special task to see to the holiday baking, and the smell of sugar and spices blended with the pine, creating the unforgettable fragrance that was Christmas. After a hurried family conference, it was decided they give Justin the presents they had originally made for Daniel, knowing it was what he would have wanted.

Amanda also decided to make him something special and after some thought decided upon a new pair of gloves. As she didn't know his glove size, she asked his valet to smuggle her out a pair for sizing, and she was carefully tracing out the pattern when the footman appeared to say the colonel was in the parlor and asking to see her.

She paused long enough to hide the glove from prying eyes, and then hurried to the parlor. As she was still in the same black dress she had worn at luncheon, she was surprised to see that Justin had changed and was looking somewhat formal in a well-cut jacket of topaz velvet, his cravat tied in intricate folds and his muscular legs enclosed in a pair of cream kerseymere trousers. She barely had time to take in his altered appearance before he turned around to face her. Their eyes met, and for the briefest moment she thought he looked anxious. Then the expression was gone, and he was moving forward to greet her with his usual air of cool control.

"Thank you for coming so quickly, Miss Lawrence . . . Amanda," he corrected, guiding her to one of the worn chairs set before the fireplace. "I hope you do not object to my using your Christian name?" he added with a polite smile, settling himself onto the chair facing hers. "I would not wish to give offense."

"Not at all, sir." Amanda wasn't taken in by either the smile or the smooth apology. She knew the colonel well enough to know he wasn't asking her permission to use the informal mode of address. Rather, he was announcing his intention of doing so.

"You are most kind." Justin inclined his head, pleased that things were going so nicely. "And I would that you would also call me by my given name. It is Justin," he provided, thinking that with a bit of luck and a modicum of charm he just might succeed in pulling this thing off after all.

"Justin." Amanda imitated the regal tilt of his head. "And now, Justin, perhaps you might be so good as to tell me why you have asked to see me? The footman made it sound rather important. You're not leaving, are you?" she added as the possibility suddenly occurred to her. "The children will be so disappointed."

"No, no," he assured her, grateful she had mentioned her younger siblings. Her devotion to them was his trump card, and he was anxious to play it as quickly as possible. This proposing business was decidedly hard on a fellow's nerves.

"However," he continued, resisting the urge to clear his throat, "I am glad that you mentioned them as what I have to tell you directly concerns them. And their future."

Amanda's eyebrows arched in interest. "Really?" she asked coolly, wondering what new maggot had crawled into his brain. "How so?"

"Well—" this time he could not help himself and nervously cleared his throat—"the day of Daniel's funeral you indicated that you were seriously considering a marriage of convenience. Might I ask if that is still the case?"

Amanda squirmed uncomfortably in her chair, realizing he had just provided her with the perfect excuse for wiggling out of her outrageous lie. She could say she'd had a change of heart and that she'd decided she and Mr. Harper would not suit. Or she could say that he had withdrawn his offer and was even now making overtures to a titled but impoverished countess. But in the end she knew she would have to tell him the truth, and she lifted her chin to meet his steady gaze.

"Actually, sir, I am afraid that I—"

"I must own that at first I was shocked at the notion of a gently bred young lady selling herself to the highest bidder," he interrupted, anxious to make his offer before she had the chance to say she had already accepted another man. "But now that I have had the time to consider the matter, I have decided that you were right."

She blinked at that. "I am?"

"Yes." He nodded his head gravely, a heavy lock of dark hair falling across his forehead. "A marriage of convenience would solve all of your family's financial difficulties, and I can understand your desire to contract one."

She could only stare at him, piqued that he should decide to sell her off just as she was removing herself from the market . . . so to speak. There was no way she could admit her falsehood now, she realized glumly. Knowing her luck, the cursed man would either take out an advertisement in the *Times* seeking an eligible *parti,* or worse still, offer for her himself. Determined to avoid this ignominious fate, she flashed him a hasty smile.

"That is very kind of you, Justin. I must write Mr.

Harper a note and tell him you have given us your blessing. He will be very pleased, I am sure."

"I haven't given you my blessing!" Justin protested in obvious horror.

"But you just said—"

"I said I understood your desire to provide for your family's security," he said, his brows gathering in a familiar frown as he rose to tower over her. "And so I do. But if you think I'm going to allow you to sacrifice yourself by marrying some jug-bitten fishmonger, you are sadly mistaken!"

"Mr. Harper isn't a fishmonger!" she exclaimed, feeling rather like a character in one of those French farces Papa used to read. "He's a wine merchant, and he didn't—"

"I don't care if he's one of the Royal Dukes, you aren't marrying him!" Justin made this pronouncement with every ounce of command he possessed. "You are marrying me."

Amanda's jaw dropped. Although she'd fully expected him to propose, she'd been foolish enough to think he would have the courtesy to couch his offer in polite terms. That he should *order* her to become his bride was completely unacceptable, and she stumbled to her feet.

"How dare you!" she gasped her eyes bright with indignation. "I am not one of your junior officers to jump at your command! I will not marry you!"

"Yes, you will," Justin replied, crossing his arms over his chest and meeting her glare. He was well aware that he had erred badly in barking out his proposal like that, but he was not about to compound that error by apologizing for it. His safest course was to continue with the battle plan he had meticulously worked out and, if need be, call in the cavalry he had held in reserve.

"Oh, will I?" she snapped, tossing him her most defiant look. "And pray, Colonel, why do you think that?"

"Because if you don't, I shall offer for Amelia in your stead."

Amanda sat back down with an unladylike *plop*. "What?"

"You heard me," he said, feeling pleased he had anticipated her reaction so correctly. He'd known she would reject his offer—if only out of sheer spite—and he'd taken the appropriate steps to circumvent her. It may not have been the most honorable tactic he could have employed; but if her pale cheeks were any indication, it was a successful one, and that was all any commander could expect.

"But . . . but you can't be serious," Amanda managed at last, raising a shaking hand to her forehead. "You don't love Amelia . . . do you?" She shot him an anxious look as if fearing the worst.

"Of course not." His wry denial made her shoulders slump in relief until he added, "I don't love *you* either, although that is neither here nor there. Most married couples of my acquaintance can't abide the sight of each other."

"Then, why are you so determined to marry me?" she cried, clenching her hands in her lap and glaring up at him in impotent fury. "Surely not even you can mean to carry your sense of duty to such ridiculous extremes!"

"Why not?" He eyed her coldly. "That is what you intend to do, is it not? Or do you expect me to believe you would welcome Mr. Harper's suit?"

"But marriage is such a serious step, and such a final one," she said, wisely ignoring his rhetorical question. "There must be some other way."

"Such as?"

"You could establish a trust for the children," Amanda began, eager to accept that which she would have proudly rejected only moments before. "See that the boys receive a proper education and are established in the world. I-I know Stephen has hopes of becoming a physician."

Justin pretended to consider her offer. "What of you and the girls?" he asked, making no move to return to his chair. "I believe you said you used your bridal portion to purchase Daniel's commission?"

"Yes, but you needn't concern yourself with me. And as for Amelia and Belinda, I suppose it wouldn't hurt if you were to provide them with a dowry," she said, swallowing her pride with the greatest difficulty.

"Perhaps," Justin agreed after a thoughtful pause. "But how do I know you won't dash off with your suitor the moment my back is turned? You seem rather anxious to become his bride." He shot her a cutting smile.

"Don't be ridiculous!"

"I'm not being ridiculous; I am merely being prudent, the hallmark of a good officer. Your suggestions, while they may have some merit, still won't serve as they fail to address the key issue."

"What key issue?"

"Survival," Justin replied bluntly, deciding he'd had enough of this verbal fencing. "You can not survive without assistance, Amanda, and it is obvious you know it. Why else would you have agreed to marry Harper?"

"I didn't agree to marry him!" It took all of Amanda's willpower not to run shrieking from the room like a madwoman.

"Perhaps not." He shrugged his shoulders indifferently. "But you're considering his offer, aren't you? Very well, then, you can consider mine as well. God knows I couldn't make you a worse husband than a broken-down Cit."

"Oh, for heaven's sake, there was no offer! I made the entire thing up!" She met his startled gaze with a sullen stare. "There, I hope you are satisfied."

Justin snapped to attention, his golden eyes darkening with anger. "Why you little. . . ." He could think of no epithet suitable for a lady's ears but still strong enough to convey his sentiments. "Why the devil would you do such a thing?"

"To keep you from offering me your charity, for all the good it has done me," she replied with a heavy sigh, wishing for a glass of strong brandy. Lord knew she could use something to soothe her poor nerves.

"It's not charity, damn it!" Justin shouted, bending to grasp her shoulders with his strong hands and drawing her out of her chair. "It's called duty, curse you, and I will do my duty by your family, no matter how hard you may fight me! The choice is yours, Amanda, will you become my bride, or must I offer for Amelia?"

For a moment Amanda almost said yes, if only to spare her sister from Justin's insulting proposal. Then another thought occurred to her.

"What . . . what if Amelia will not have you?"

"What?" His forehead puckered in confusion.

"What if Amelia will not have you?" she repeated, a plan forming swiftly in her mind. She knew Amelia was wildly in love with Charles and would never entertain Justin's offer. Therefore, she reasoned, she would have little to risk should he approach her. She tilted her head back and met his burning gaze. "Would you force her to accept?"

110

"Of course not," Justin said, his frown increasing at her bold challenge. He had been so certain of Amanda's capitulation that it never occurred to him that he might actually have to offer for Amelia, or that if he did offer, the chit would refuse him.

"But what if she does?" Amanda persisted, her confidence increasing with each passing second. "I have already made it clear that *I* don't want you; how will you do your precious duty then?"

"Blast it, Amanda, I won't leave you and your family to starve!" Justin administered a small shake. He should have known better than to think the hellcat would make it easy on him, he thought furiously. She was more adept than Wellington for slipping in and out of tight spots.

"You won't have to," Amanda almost crowed with delight at the look of frustration on his handsome face. "For I have a counter-proposal to offer you."

He pulled his head back and regarded her through narrowed eyes. "What is it?" he asked, making no attempt to mask his skepticism.

"If Amelia refuses to become your wife, I will accept any financial arrangements you decide to settle upon us," she said, giving him her most magnanimous smile. "I will even allow you to act as the younger children's guardian if that is your wish."

"And if she accepts?" Justin asked, surprised by her offer. He thought he'd have to threaten to marry Belinda next and could scarcely believe she was being so reasonable.

"Then the same conditions would apply, I suppose, except that you would be Amelia's husband," Amanda said, dismissing the matter with an easy smile. "Have we an agreement?"

111

Justin weighed her offer, then said, "Not quite. When Amelia becomes my wife, then I will become responsible for all of you. Not just financially responsible," he added when she opened her mouth to agree, "but physically responsible as well. You and the others would come and live with us in our house, and I would become your guardian. *All* of you; is it agreed?"

"Really, sir, I am six and twenty, and—"

"Is it agreed?"

Amanda capitulated with an impatient sigh. "Oh, very well," she said, pulling free of his hold and offering him a slender hand. "It is agreed." She knew she should feel some guilt for the shameless way she had cozened him, but she didn't. The haughty devil deserved to be gulled for his arrogant assumption that any female was his for the asking. She only wished she might be there to see his expression when Amelia sweetly rejected his proposal.

Amelia was busy tying together the last of her sachets when something made her glance up toward the door. Her dark blue eyes widened at the sight of Colonel Stockton standing in the doorway of the dining room, his handsome face set in stern lines. When she realized he was moving forward to join her, she felt a warm wave of embarrassment wash over her.

"Good-good evening, Colonel," she stammered, wishing Amanda would hurry back from the kitchen where she had gone to fetch some more spices. This was the first time she had ever been alone with the colonel, and her usual shyness was compounded by maidenly reticence.

"Good evening, Miss Amelia." Justin gave the lovely blonde an appreciative smile. Since storming out of the

112

parlor some two hours earlier, he had had a great deal of time to consider the bargain he had struck with Amanda, and the more he considered it, the more determined he became to carry out his end of it.

Amelia might be years too young for a man with his jaded tastes, but he didn't see that he had any other choice. To win the control he considered vital, he would have to marry her. She was not his first choice but as he had never expected to marry for love, he supposed it really didn't signify. At least with her there would be no doubt as to who was in control, he thought, walking forward to stand beside her chair.

"What are you making?" he asked, reaching out a tanned hand to pick up one of the tiny bundles. He raised it to his nose, his eyes closing as he inhaled the enticing fragrance of a gentle May morning. He could detect the softness of lavender, mixed with the sweet smell of grass, and the heady aroma of a newly opened rose. In his mind he could feel the warmth of the sun on his face and hear the melodic chirping of a lark in a willow tree.

"Sachets," Amelia replied shyly, wondering at his intense expression. "They are gifts for the maids."

The images in Justin's mind dissolved at the sound of Amelia's voice, and he gave a convulsive start. "They're lovely," he said, his voice gruff as he returned the sachet to the pile on the table.

"Amelia," he began, feeling an awkwardness he hadn't known with Amanda, "there is something of import I need to ask you."

"Certainly, Colonel," she replied, dimples appearing in her cheeks as she gave him another smile. Poor man, she thought with a flash of sympathy which came easily to one of her gentle nature. It was easy to see something was distressing him. "What is it?"

"Before I begin, I should tell you that I have already discussed this with your sister," he said, deciding to be as brief and as blunt as possible. Considering the mess he had made of it with Amanda, he thought it best to keep matters as clear as possible without prevarication. "I have explained to her that I am aware of your family's . . . precarious financial position, and that as it is more or less my fault, I am determined to set things right for all of you."

"Oh, you mustn't think that, dearest sir!" Amelia exclaimed, her eyes filling with tears at the thought of the colonel holding himself to blame for Daniel's death. "What happened was God's will, and we must accept it as such and rely on His goodness to offer us succor. We don't blame you for what happened."

"That is what your sister said," Justin murmured, his mouth lifting in a slight smile, "but as I told her, it doesn't matter what you feel. *I* hold myself to blame, and I mean to set things right. But to do that I will need your help."

"My help?" She appeared genuinely confused.

"Yes." He could feel his heart pounding in his chest and realized this was going to be harder than he thought. What made it worse was that he wasn't afraid she would say no; he was terrified she would say yes. But there was nothing he could do about that now. He had committed himself to a specific course of action, and he would achieve the objective he had set for himself, regardless of the cost. Setting his troubling doubts aside, he straightened his shoulders and met her shy blue eyes.

"Amelia, will you marry me?"

She paled, staring at him as if he had run mad. "I-I

beg your pardon, Colonel," she stammered, casting a nervous glance toward the door and estimating her odds of reaching it safely.

He caught the direction of her gaze and smiled grimly. "You needn't look so fearful, Miss Amelia, I am in perfect control of my faculties."

"I didn't mean to imply otherwise, sir," she answered, her dainty chin coming up in a gesture that was strongly reminiscent of her sister. "But you must own this is all rather unexpected. We scarce know one another."

"That is so," he agreed, pleased to see she was behaving so reasonably. "And if I were offering you a love-match, your reticence would be understandable. However, that is not what I am offering."

She didn't pretend not to understand him. In light of his earlier remarks, his meaning was all too obvious. She raised her chin a notch higher, her heart pounding with trepidation as she faced him. "What are you offering, then?" she queried, steeling herself for his reply.

"A marriage of convenience." His clipped response verified her worst fears.

Amelia flinched, but other than clenching her hands tightly, she gave no indication of her inner turmoil. She thought of Charles, of the life they had planned to share, and then she thought of Amanda and the others. As Colonel Stockton had so succinctly put it, their situation was desperate, and she did not see how they could survive without assistance. Charles would do what he could, she knew, but he was hardly in a position to support her entire family. How could she ever know a moment's joy, knowing her happiness had been purchased at their expense?

Justin watched her through narrowed eyes, attempting

115

to gage her response. Instead of flinging his offer back in his face as Amanda had done, she actually seemed to be giving the matter careful consideration, and that gave him heart. He knew a wrong word or gesture on his part could tip the scales against him, but he was nonetheless determined to be honest with her.

"I don't want you to misunderstand me," he said, taking her hand gently in his and forcing her to meet his eyes. "This will be a real marriage, in every meaning of the word. I am past the age where I ought to be giving some thought to an heir, especially as my elder brother seems in no hurry to marry, and this seems the most sensible way of going about it. I shall honor and respect you, Amelia, and I give you my word I will never do anything to cause you to regret the terms of our marriage."

"What-what are the terms?" Amelia asked, her voice trembling slightly.

"If you agree to become my wife, I shall provide a home for your family and yourself," he said, expounding on the offer he had already made to Amanda. "The boys will go to school, and if they so choose, I shall purchase them a commission in the army. I shall also bestow a dowry on Belinda and Amanda, so that they might make a good marriage. None of you will ever lack for anything; that much I can promise you."

"That is very generous of you, sir." Amelia's heart sank to her toes at his words.

"Thank you, but it is no less than I intend to do regardless of your answer."

"What do you mean?"

"I mean that even if you decide that we will not suit, I still intend providing for your family," he answered bluntly, resisting the impulse to keep the truth from her.

"Amanda and I have agreed that should you refuse, I will become guardian to you and the others. I will provide financial assistance and any other aid I deem fit to see that you are all well cared for."

Amelia swallowed painfully, watching the dreams she had had since childhood fading away. "And if I accept?"

"We will become a family," Justin replied, his lips relaxing in a gentle smile. "We'll retire to my country estate, and there live out our days. It will be a good life, Amelia, and I swear on my honor I will do my best to make you happy. Now what is your answer? Will you marry me?"

Chapter Eight

Amanda scrambled to her feet, her eyes widening with shock as she stared at her younger sister. "You did *what?*" she gasped, praying she hadn't heard aright.

"I-I accepted Colonel Stockton's proposal," Amelia stammered, shooting her a troubled frown. She'd been expecting a warm hug of congratulations, and was more than a little puzzled by Amanda's reaction. "You did know he meant to ask me?" she queried anxiously, wondering if she'd misunderstood the colonel.

"Yes, but it never occurred to me you would accept," Amanda muttered, brushing back a lock of dark red hair from her cheek as she sat back down.

"Well, of course I accepted," Amelia answered, genuinely mystified. "We must live somewhere, and if the colonel is willing to support us, I don't see that I have any other choice."

"Is that what he told you? That if you didn't marry him we would all be thrown in debtor's prison?" Amanda demanded, her temper flaring to life. She might have known the wretch would pull something like this, playing on dear Amelia's love for her family in order to get his way. Oh, just wait until she got him alone, she vowed, her eyes darkening with plans for revenge. She would make him rue the day he had dared cross swords with her!

"Oh, no, Amanda!" Amelia seemed quite shocked by her sister's allegation. "He made it quite clear that regardless of my answer he should always have a care for us! It was all my idea to accept, I promise you."

"But why?" Amanda wailed, struggling to comprehend the younger girl's actions. "If he didn't bully you, why did you accept?"

Amelia was silent, searching for the right words to explain that which even she didn't fully understand herself. "I admire the colonel," she said at last, her voice firm as she met Amanda's troubled gaze. "He swears he will make me a good husband, and I believe him. This is what I want, Amanda."

"But what about Charles?" Amanda asked, realizing that Amelia seemed determined to go through with this insane marriage. "Don't you love him?"

Amelia turned away, her eyes misting at the mention of her beloved. "I shall always love Charles," she said quietly "but it changes nothing. I am marrying Colonel Stockton, and that is the end of it."

Amanda blinked at the firmness in Amelia's voice. She was so accustomed to the younger girl's sweetly obedient nature that it had never occurred to her she might have a will of her own. The realization was faintly unsettling, and Amanda made one last effort to change her sister's mind.

"Does Justin—Colonel Stockton know about Charles?" she asked, silently praying that his sense of honor would prevent him from taking another man's chosen bride.

"No"—Amelia whirled around to face her—"and you aren't to tell him either. I mean it," she added at her sister's incredulous stare. "I don't want him to know . . .

ever. Promise me you won't tell him."

"But—"

"No." Amelia shook her head, her blond curls brushing against her shoulders. "It would only upset him, and in the end what good would it do? We have discussed this at great length, and I am certain I am doing the right thing. It is all for the best, Amanda," she added, holding out her hand in silent supplication. "Please believe that and wish us happy."

Amanda's fingers shook as they closed around her sister's hand. "Very well, dearest," she said, making no effort to wipe away the tears flowing down her cheeks, "if that is what you wish. You and Colonel Stockton both have my heartiest best wishes. Although I take leave to warn you that if he does anything to cause you a moment's pain, he shall have *me* to answer to!"

"He already knows that," Amelia responded with a warm laugh, throwing herself into her sister's embrace. "He says it is the very thing to keep him firmly in the traces! Now, let us go and tell the others. I can't wait to see Jeremey's expression when he learns the colonel is soon to be his brother!"

"Our brother? I say, sir, that is beyond wonderful!"

Jeremey's reaction was all that Amelia had hoped for as he leapt to his feet, pumping Justin's hand with obvious enthusiasm.

"Aye, that it is," Joss seconded, his blue eyes bright with excitement as he followed his brother's lead. "Although it seems a dashed shame you have to get leg-shackled in order to do it. Not that Amelia ain't a capital female," he added, belatedly realizing he may have given offense.

Justin's lips twitched, but other than the twinkle in his eyes, he gave no other indication that he was amused by the lad's reaction. "Thank you, Joss," he said, reaching out a hand to ruffle his hair. "As it happens, I also consider her to be a . . . capital female." And he sent the pretty blonde standing beside him a warm smile.

It was early Monday morning, and at Amelia's request they had made their announcement over breakfast. He would have preferred waiting for a more auspicious occasion, but she had been gently adamant, insisting that the sooner the others were told of their pending marriage the sooner they could become adjusted to the fact. As he was feeling particularly benevolent, he had agreed, and now that the deed was done, he had to admit he felt better. The boys, at least, seemed delighted to have him in the family. Which was more than could be said of his soon-to-be sister-in-law he thought, shooting Amanda a thoughtful frown.

He'd spent most of last evening in his sitting room, waiting for her imperious summons. He was certain she would kick up a dust at her sister's acceptance and had been prepared to use every argument at his disposal to persuade her to accept the match. When it became obvious she wasn't going to send for him, he had toyed with the idea of going down and confronting her himself, but unfortunately he'd given Amelia his word not to interfere.

"Congratulations, Colonel." Stephen was standing before him, shyly offering him his hand. "I know this marriage would have made Daniel very happy."

"It is kind of you to say so, Stephen," he said, gravely accepting the youth's hand. "That is what I like to think."

"When are you posting the banns?" Jeremey asked, displaying a heretofore hidden streak of practicality. "It takes

121

a month, you know."

The banns! Amanda brightened as inspiration dawned. Of course! Charles would be certain to learn of Amelia's pending marriage once the banns were posted in the village church, and when he did, he would come riding directly to Lawrence Hall to demand an explanation. And once he did that, Justin would in all honor have to retract his offer! She was busily plotting how she would handle the young officer when she heard Justin say, "Actually, we are to be married by Special License in St. George's Cathedral, London. I have written my brother requesting that he handle the matter for me."

"St. George's!" Amanda exclaimed, dismayed at the thought of her scheme dying a premature death. "But, Amelia, you can't possibly want to be married in that drafty old pile of stones!"

Amelia, who was shocked to hear one of the loveliest churches in all of England described so disparagingly, said, "Justin and I have already discussed this, Amanda, and we have decided that it will be better for all if the ceremony takes place in the city, and as quickly as it can be arranged."

"Better for some, maybe," Amanda muttered, then blushed at Justin's dark look. She knew he was waiting for her to make some kind of scene, and she was determined not to oblige him. At least not until she had figured some way of putting a halt to this nonsense, she amended, hastily pinning a bland smile to her lips. But even as she raised her glass of sherry in a toast to the betrothed couple, her mind was spinning with plans.

The staff reacted to the news of the engagement with mixed emotions. On the one hand they seemed genuinely pleased for Amelia and Justin, but on the other they were obviously apprehensive about their own futures.

Justin sensed as much, and after accepting Linsley's congratulations, he took Amanda aside and quietly asked her if there were any servants she wished to take with her when they removed to his country estate.

"Isn't that something you ought to be asking of Amelia?" she asked, frowning up at him as she considered his question. "After all, she is to be mistress of your establishment."

"Yes, but you are mistress here, and you are most familiar with their abilities," he replied, wishing that just once Amanda would do as he asked without quibbling. "Also, I was hoping you would agree to instruct Amelia as to her new duties. You are an excellent household manager."

"Thank you, sir." Amanda wasn't taken in by either the compliment or the fawning smile that accompanied it. "But as it happens, I have already instructed Amelia in the domestic arts. I'm sure you'll not find her wanting."

"I'm sure I shan't, either, but that still doesn't answer my question!" Justin snapped, resisting the urge to give her a good shake. He'd never met a more argumentative person in his life, and he questioned his ability to share his home with her with anything approaching tranquility. Thank God she'd had the good sense to refuse him, he thought, struggling to control his temper. Lord only knew what would have happened had they actually been forced to marry.

A sharp retort rose to Amanda's lips, but she managed not to utter it. She knew Justin was being more than generous, and she was instantly ashamed by her childish baiting of him. "All of them, I should think," she said after a thoughtful pause. "I'm sure Aunt will be bringing her own staff with her when she takes possession."

"See to it, then," he instructed, grateful that for whatever reason, she had decided to cooperate. "Any servant who wishes to do so may come with us, and I will guarantee them a position."

"Will there be anything else?" Amanda asked, deciding it might be prudent to ignore the authoritative tone in his voice. She could see her brothers and sisters out of the corner of her eye and knew they were probably waiting for her and Justin to come to blows.

"For now." Like Amanda, Justin was aware of the others' amused scrutiny, and he was no more anxious than she to provide them with entertainment. He turned to go, only to be stopped by Belinda, who ran up to his side.

"You're not leaving, are you?" she asked, gazing up at him with wide, blue eyes.

"I was considering it, yes," he replied bending down to give her blond curls a playful tug. "Why? Do you want to show me another of your dolls?" Since recovering from his illness, he'd been introduced to a number of her precious dolls, and despite the twins' obvious disgust, he'd made a great show of being impressed.

"Oh, no!" She shook her head solemnly. "But the pudding is ready, and you have to take your turn stirring it. Otherwise how will your wish ever come true?"

The twins added their pleas to hers, and Justin soon found himself in the tiny kitchen, waiting for his turn at stirring the thick, fruit-laden concoction. He'd heard of the ancient custom, of course, but this was the first time he had ever taken part in it. His father had had little patience with such tomfoolery, he recalled bitterly, his hand closing over the handle of the wooden spoon.

"Here." Belinda folded her tiny hand over his, guiding his movements. "Stir it three times and make a wish. And wish for something very special," she cautioned with a quick frown, " 'cause it's Christmas, and you can only have one Christmas wish a year."

Justin smiled down at her, feeling a faint twinge of regret that he'd missed out on something so magical. Had he ever believed in Christmas wishes, he wondered, then answered his own question with a heavy sigh. Never. "Very well," he said, pushing the melancholy thoughts from his mind and doing as he was instructed. "I wish—"

"You're not s'posed to say it out loud!" Belinda was clearly scandalized by such a breach of etiquette. "You're s'posed to whisper it in your mind, that way only God and Father Christmas will hear you."

"My apologies, Belinda," he murmured, his eyes flicking toward Amanda, who was standing quietly beside the little girl. His smile widened at the defiance he saw shimmering in her dark eyes, and in that moment he made his wish silently entreating any deity who might be listening for patience in taming the shrew who was soon to become his sister-in-law.

Two days later Justin was sitting in the library examining the accounts when Linsley entered bearing a letter on a silver tray. "For you, Colonel," he said, bowing as he proffered the tray. "It arrived in this morning's post. I believe it is from your brother, the duke."

Justin glanced up with interest. "Is it?" he asked, reaching for the letter with some surprise. It had been only a few days since he'd written to Edward advising him of his plans, and he was amazed that he'd received a reply so quickly, Evidently the mails had improved since the last time he was in England, he mused, using his thumb to break the wax circlet sealing the letter.

The missive was indeed from Edward, and according

to the date scribbled in the upper corner, he must have written it immediately upon receiving his letter. It was written in his usual, florid style, and Justin found himself smiling as he struggled to decipher the atrocious handwriting.

My dear Justin, (it began)

Congratulations and best wishes to you and your bride! Now that you have done your brotherly duty and seen to the succession, I shall at long last be free of all those tiresome debs and simpering chits that clutter up London during the Season. Most obliging of you, I must say!

I've spoken with Aunt Letty, and she insists upon your fiancée and her brood putting up at her place until the pair of you are properly fired off. You, of course, shall billet with me, and once the deed is done you may move into Dover House. The old barn has been sitting empty a donkey's age, and I fear it will require a spot of work before it is habitable. Hope you have the blunt, brother mine, as I daresay it will cost you a pretty penny to set things right again.

On that note, I am hoping you will see your way clear to advancing me a bit of pocket money. I've sunk my funds into some intriguing investments and must wait until they pay off, as I am assured they will. It needn't be much; a hundred pounds or so will do fine.

It was signed simply, *Edward*, and Justin had to smile at his brother's lack of formality. He knew such casualness had little to do with false modesty. It was merely that there were times when Edward forgot he was the duke, and when he did remember, he was usually too preoccupied to bother with the pomp and ceremony attached to his rank.

"You really should have been the duke," he'd once told Justin, grimacing as he dressed to attend the opening of House of Lords. "I daresay you'd be much better at it. Wouldn't care to exchange places, I suppose?"

Justin reminded him that as he was a major in the army, exchanging places might prove somewhat dangerous, and Edward had good-naturedly agreed that he was probably right. They had then gone their separate ways, and Justin had forgotten all about the matter . . . until now.

As much as he loved his brother, the plain truth was that he *would* have made a better duke, he thought, frowning as he tapped the letter against the edge of the table. For one thing he had a much better grasp of the land and its people than did Edward and for another he would never have gambled away his inheritance to such an extent that he was forced to borrow against his capital. Whatever could his brother have been thinking?

"Is there some problem, Colonel?" Linsley asked nervously, noting Justin's grim expression with dismay. "I trust it isn't bad news?"

"What?" Justin asked, his frown vanishing as he glanced up at the elderly butler. "Oh, no, Linsley, thank you. Everything is fine. My brother was just offering me his congratulations, that is all."

"Very well, sir," Linsley replied, executing another bow as he turned and left the room. He knew the lad was being less than truthful with him and sent up a silent prayer that whatever the problem was, it would not prove to be insurmountable. The good Lord knew they'd had enough of those of late, he thought, making a mental note to drop a flea in Miss Lawrence's ear. If she even suspected something was amiss with the colonel, she'd soon nag the truth out of him, or he didn't know his mistress.

In the library Justin was pacing restlessly, trying to decide what he should do about Edward and his foolish investments. It wasn't that he begrudged his brother the money. Indeed, he was only too happy to lend Edward whatever amount was required, but that didn't mean he meant to sit quietly by while the Stonebridge fortune was being frittered away.

He would lend Edward the money, he decided, resuming his seat and picking up the quill lying discarded on the cluttered surface of the desk. But he would add a proviso that Edward refrain from any future investments. He might be a younger son, he thought with a sudden flash of resentment, but he still had some rights. In the event he and Amelia were blessed with a son, the estate and title would then pass to him, and when it did, Justin was determined that it be fully intact. With that thought in mind, he dipped the quill's tip into the silver inkwell and began scribbling a letter to his solicitor.

He had almost completed the letter when his concentration was shattered by the sounds of excited laughter and shouting drifting up from the entryway. At first he tried ignoring the disruptive noise, but in the end he admitted defeat and tossed down his pen with an impatient oath. Surging to his feet, he stomped over to the door and flung it open, his jaw set with anger as he stalked out into the hallway.

"What in Hades is going on down there?" he roared, bending over the upper railing to glare down at the others. "Can't a man even write a letter in—what the devil is that?"

Amanda glanced up from the huge log she and the others had dragged in from the courtyard, her cheeks flushed with exertion and merriment. The sight of Justin glowering at them like a disapproving papa made her eyes dance with amusement, and it was all she could do not to burst into outright laughter.

"It's a yule log," she called, brushing back a strand of hair that had fallen across her mouth. "Well, don't just stand there," she added when he made no move to assist them. "This dratted thing is heavy! Come help us.' "

Justin's cheeks flushed at her teasing challenge, and he belatedly hurried down the wide stairs to join them. Even with his assistance it took them almost ten minutes to drag the log into the dining room, and another fifteen to wedge it into the ancient stone fireplace.

"I'll go get the ashen faggots!" Joss cried, jumping up and down with excitement. "And the first wish is going to be mine!"

"Is not!" Jeremey protested, then rushed after his brother, the sound of their squabbling voices echoing after them.

"Aren't you being a trifle premature?" Justin asked, his earlier anger forgotten as he turned to smile at Amanda. In deference to the cold weather, she was swathed from head to foot in an ancient brown redingote, a woolen scarf wrapped around her throat for added warmth, and he thought she looked delightful. Amelia was also wearing a redingote, he noted, but hers was a far more fashionable color of celestial blue, and a blue felt hat decorated with swansdown added to her charming appearance.

"It's never too early to start celebrating," Amanda replied as she began fumbling with her scarf. She had taken off her gloves at one point, and her fingers were clumsy with cold. She was about to ask Amelia for help when he stepped up to her and gently brushed her hands aside, his agile fingers making short work of the knotted scarf.

"I suspected that is what you'd say." His warm breath feathered across her cheeks as he bent his dark head closer to hers. "It makes me wonder what else you have in store for me."

"Ah, sir, that would be telling," Amanda replied with a forced lightness, wishing he would finish untying her scarf and be done with it. His touch was having the oddest effect upon her sensibilities, and only the knowledge that he would find her nervousness amusing kept her from moving away from him.

"Really?" he drawled, the corners of his mouth curving in a wry smile as he lifted his eyes to meet hers. "That sounds suspiciously like a challenge to me, Amanda."

Fortunately for Amanda's peace of mind, the twins, bearing the burning remnant of last year's yule log, burst into the room sparing her the necessity of answering Justin's provocative remark. The next several minutes were devoted to the ritual of lighting the log that would burn through the rest of the holiday season, and singing the familiar carols. Justin's deep voice blended with the others in perfect harmony, and they sang several songs before the twins grew restive and announced they had had enough of celebrating.

Following the singing, they trooped into the parlor, falling upon the tea Mrs. Hatcher had prepared for them like so many starving wolves. While he enjoyed the freshly baked pastries, Justin listened to the lively conversation flowing around him, his sense of contentment increasing with each passing second. So this was what it meant to be a part of a family, he mused, watching the twins' antics with amused indulgence. He'd never felt so comfortable before, so—his mind searched for the right word—so accepted, and he found himself wanting more.

For most of his life he'd been the outsider looking in; ignored by his father because he wasn't the heir, and then dismissed by the London hostesses because as a second son he would only inherit a modest living and an obscure title. The only place he'd ever felt valued was in the army, and now that the wars were ending, he knew that even that would soon be denied him. If he wanted a place in this world, he would have to create it himself, and that was precisely what he intended to do.

"Aren't you, sir?" Jeremey's words shattered Justin's revery, and he looked up in surprise to find the twelve-year-old studying him with a hopeful expression.

"Er . . . aren't I what, Jeremey?" he asked, sending the lad an apologetic smile. "I fear I wasn't attending."

"Aren't you taking us into Godstone in your carriage," Jeremey prodded, his voice pitched at its most wheedling. "You did say you would, Colonel."

"Justin," he corrected automatically, amused at the lad's attempts to maneuver him. As he recalled, he'd mentioned the possibility of taking the boys into the village but no definite plans had been made. He glanced from Jeremey's face to Joss's worshipful countenance and surrendered to the inevitable. "And you are quite right, I did promise the family a ride in my coach." He turned next to Amanda, his eyebrows raised inquiringly. "Will tomorrow be all right with you, ma'am?"

"That will be fine, sir, thank you," she said, sending both her younger brothers a suspicious frown. She knew them well enough to suspect they had wheedled the invitation from Justin, and she vowed to have a private word with them at the first opportunity. Justin might be marrying Amelia to give them all a home, she thought, returning her gaze to her plate, but that didn't mean they could abuse his generosity. She would make it quite clear

131

to the twins that they weren't to ask for anything ever again.

"That sounds wonderful, Justin, when shall we be leaving?" Amelia asked, shyly reaching out to touch his hand. Since they were now officially engaged, Amanda had sat them beside each other, and Amelia was gradually accustoming herself to his presence. He wasn't her dearest Charles, of course, but he was very nice. Given time, she was confident she would eventually come to care for him.

"After breakfast?" he suggested, his eyes flicking once more in Amanda's direction. "We could leave first thing in the morning and then make a day of it. I am sure you ladies must have a great deal of shopping to do."

Amanda's first inclination was to refuse, but after giving the matter some thought, she nodded her head. "All right. There are several things I need to buy, now that you mention it, and I am sure the boys will welcome a chance to see the shop windows."

"Can we have luncheon at the inn?" Belinda asked, wiggling on her chair in anticipation. "Oh, please say that we might; they have the loveliest cream buns!"

"I don't know, dearest," Amanda answered with a thoughtful frown. "The prices at the inn are excessively high, and—"

"If that is what you want, imp, then that is what we shall do," Justin interrupted, smiling at Belinda even as he sent Amanda a warning look. "We can even have our tea there before starting home if you like."

"Really, Justin," Amanda protested, annoyed by his high-handed tactics, "there is no need for such largesse. We do not expect you to spoil us all so shamelessly merely because you are to marry Amelia!"

"Nonsense." He overrode her objections with a cool

smile. " 'Tis Christmas; what better time to spoil one's family? Besides"—his smile widened to become a devilish grin—"I adore cream buns."

Amanda knew when she had been bested and sullenly surrendered the field to her more able opponent. "Very well, Colonel," she said, using his title in a deliberate attempt to annoy him, "the inn for luncheon it shall be. You are too good to us."

"It is my pleasure, Amanda." Justin inclined his head, his amber eyes sparkling in silent acknowledgement of her attempted set-down. "You must know how much I enjoy doing things for my new family. In fact, I am quite looking forward to our shopping expedition on the morrow. I've never really shopped for Christmas before, and you must take pity on a poor bachelor and show me how it is done."

While the rest of the family exclaimed happily over his offer, Amanda had to content herself with shooting daggers at him. The beast, she fumed, stabbing savagely at the crumbs remaining on her plate. He had done that deliberately! There was no way now she could instruct the others to refuse his presents without appearing the most selfish creature alive.

After the meal was finished, she lingered by the door, intending to let him know of her displeasure in no uncertain terms. Unfortunately for her, he had anticipated such an action and had placed a restraining hand on Amelia's arm.

"Don't rush off just yet," he said, favoring her with his most intimate smile. "I was hoping you might agree to walk about the gardens with me. With your sister's permission, of course," he added, turning an innocent face to a silently fuming Amanda. "I trust you have no objection, ma'am?"

Amanda had several objections, as he well knew but she was helpless to utter a single one of them. Sending Justin a look that promised retribution she said, "Certainly I have no objections, Justin. Amelia is your fiancée, and it is only natural that you should wish time alone with her. I only ask that you not stay out of doors overly long, as she is prone to colds."

"Oh, Amanda" — Amelia gave a pretty pout — "must you always be so sensible?"

Amanda's eyes met Justin's. "Always, my love," she said, her words a veiled threat. "It is part of my feminine charm. Enjoy your outing, and mind you take Belinda with you. I'm sure she'll prove a more than adequate chaperone for you." She inclined her head to them both and then departed, her mind already active with plans for revenge.

Chapter Nine

The morning dawned cold and clear, with a brisk northerly wind blowing from the sea. Despite the heavy snowfall of the past few weeks, the roads were surprisingly clear, and it took them less than an hour to reach the tiny village of Godstone. Many of the shops had yet to open, and after glancing around the tiny square, Justin announced they would retire to the inn and wait for the town to come to life.

"This isn't necessary," Amanda protested as the opulently appointed carriage turned down the cobblestoned street leading to the town's best inn. "We can wait in the carriage until the shops open."

"Nonsense," Justin replied, his tone genial but determined. He'd already decided that the best way to handle Amanda was to ignore her fiery temper and do as he pleased. "We have no idea how long that will take, and we wouldn't want the youngsters to become chilled . . . would we?"

Amanda bit her lip, holding back a sharp retort with an effort. After spending much of yesterday afternoon plotting how to avenge herself, she'd decided that the only way to handle Justin was to smile sweetly at his orders, however high-handed they might be, and then to do precisely as she had always done.

"You are quite right, Justin," she said, gritting her teeth as she gave him her most docile smile. "I wouldn't wish the younger ones to fall ill so close to the holidays."

The twins' ire at being referred to as "the younger ones" vanished shortly after the usually surly proprietor escorted them into his best parlor. Helping themselves to the buns and hot chocolate, they vacillated between stuffing their faces and eagerly exploring their new domain.

"I say, Justin," Joss exclaimed, wide-eyed as he peered about the room, "this is much nicer than sitting in some drafty old carriage! I think I shall like having you for a brother."

"Jocelyn Richard Blanchford!" Amanda exclaimed, blushing for her younger brother's unrepentant greed. "How can you say such things!"

"Well, it's the truth," he replied, his bottom lip protruding in a familiar pout. "Whenever we've come to the inn before, Mr. Peasey always gives us the parlor off the taproom, and you have to ask him twice to fetch us our tea."

"And it was never as nice as this," Jeremey added, loyally supporting his twin.

Not wishing to be excluded from the conversation, Amelia and Stephen began eagerly recounting some of their encounters with the difficult innkeeper. Even Belinda joined in, reminding Amanda of the time Mr. Peasey had kept them sitting in the smoky common room while he prepared a basket for them.

"You remember, Mandy," she said, delicately licking the icing from her fingers, "he was ever so rude to us. You went all red in the face, and I was sure you were going to pop!"

Amanda recalled the incident all too well; it had occurred less than a month after Daniel had been posted to the Peninsula. Mr. Peasey had taken her roughly aside, showing her a fistful of Daniel's bills and demanding to know when he could expect payment. She'd eventually settled the debts, but it was obvious the odious man still bore her a grudge.

"I remember, poppet." She laughed, leaning forward to wipe Belinda's mouth with her napkin. "I also remember the way you had those cakes gobbled down before we were halfway home."

The conversation soon turned to other topics, and Mr. Peasey was soon forgotten. But if the others were willing to let the matter drop, Justin was not. Something was definitely amiss, and unless he was much mistaken, he was fairly certain it involved money. Doubtlessly Amanda was indebted to him, and the fellow was pressing her for payment. Well let him try, he thought, his eyes taking on a dangerous gleam. He would make it obvious to Mr. Peasey and the other shopkeepers as well that the Lawrences and Blanchfords were now under his protection, and any slight of them would not be tolerated.

He'd also inform the tradesfolk to forward any outstanding bills to him. Now that he and Amelia were officially betrothed, it was only fitting that he assume responsibility for their debts, although he doubted Amanda would agree with him. In fact, given the lengths she'd been willing to go to, to avoid such a fate, he'd count himself fortunate if she didn't screech like a scalded cat and then box his ears! Not that he'd let that stop him, of course. He'd just have to take care that she never learned of it until it was too late.

The rest of the hour passed pleasingly enough, and soon it was time to go. While Amelia was busy putting on Belinda's coat and mittens, Justin pulled Amanda to one side of the parlor.

"I thought I would take the lads about while you and the other ladies go to the dressmakers'," he said, giving her a guileless smile. "Provided I have your approval, that is."

"You have more than my approval, sir, you have my undying gratitude," she replied with a light laugh, her eyes flashing to the corner where the twins and Stephen were pulling on their coats and arguing among themselves. "I must own I was at my wit's end wondering what I would do with them. They are not the most patient of souls and tend to make a shamble of things if I keep them waiting overly long."

"A male failing, I am sad to say," he replied, his eyes dancing merrily as he studied her upturned face. "Until a man reaches a certain age, he would rather be tied to the rack than venture inside a modiste's shop."

"And after he reaches that age?" she teased, feeling greatly daring.

"Then he endures it . . . or tries to," Justin admitted with a gruff laugh. "But I should not be admitting to such things to you, else I may find myself accompanying you to every tiresome little dress shop in the village."

"I wouldn't dream of taking such shameless advantage of your good nature," Amanda assured him, a soft smile touching her lips at the image of a resigned Justin following her and Amelia from shop to shop, all but hidden by a mound of parcels and hatboxes. "Besides, we shall only be going as far as Mrs. Whistler's, and perhaps to Mrs. Garthwaite's if there is time. Amelia ordered a new bonnet, and it should be ready by now."

Justin made a mental note of the names, hiding his interest behind a pained expression. "And the shoemakers' as well, I'll warrant," he added with a heavy sigh. "I have never known a woman yet who could resist looking at slippers and the like."

Amanda's smile widened at his resigned countenance. "Now that you mention it, Belinda could use a new pair of shoes for Christmas," she said, placing a thoughtful finger on her lips. "And Mr. Pettiwitte did say he had some lovely kid the last time I saw him. Perhaps we should pay him a visit as well," and she cast him a teasing look.

"Please, ma'am, no more, I pray you," Justin said, holding up his hands in mock surrender. "Only tell me what time the boys and I should meet you ladies back here."

"One o'clock," Amanda decided, doing some quick calculations in her head. "And you needn't think that you menfolk will be free to hang about the town and fall in with bad company, either," she scolded, digging into her reticule and extracting a list which she then handed to Justin. "Both the twins' and Stephen's wardrobes are in sad want of refurbishing, and I shall expect you to see to the matter for me. Take them to the tailor's shop and see that they are properly rigged out, I will not have them arriving in London looking no better than rag-pickers."

Justin studied the short list and stuck it in his pocket. "Aye, sir!" he said, executing a sharp salute. "Have you any further orders for me, sir?"

Amanda's lips twitched in an effort not to laugh. This was the first time she had ever seen Justin in such a playful mood, and she found the spectacle most delightful. A pity he didn't relax more often, she thought, tilting back her head to smile up at him. He really was quite charming when he smiled like that. . . .

"Don't let the twins out of your sight for any reason," he cautioned, giving herself a mental shake. "If you think Napoleon capable of creating havoc the moment your back is turned, he is nothing compared to what those two can do once they put their minds to it."

"I shall watch them like a hawk," he promised, fixing both boys with a stern eye. "Although I think I can vouchsafe their good behavior. We have already had a talk about the necessity for following orders. Haven't we?" His brows lowered in a threatening scowl.

"Yes, Justin!" they chorused, looking so angelical that Amanda burst into delighted laughter.

"Now I am doubly suspicious, sir! Never mind watching the scoundrels; you'd best chain them to your side!"

"Oh, I think we understand each other," Justin drawled, his tone warm as he reached out to tuck a strand of red hair beneath Amanda's bonnet. "A pity we have not yet reached such a cordial meeting of minds."

The touch of his hand as well as the intimacy of his words made Amanda's heart flutter uncomfortably, and her cheeks were delicately flushed as she turned to where Amelia was waiting for her. "Really, Amelia," she complained, forcing a light note into her voice, "I protest. You simply must do something about this fiancée of yours; he is growing even more arrogant than ever! Surely you don't mean to allow him to continue like this?"

"But of course I do, dearest," Amelia responded, pleased to see that her sister and Justin had finally reached some kind of truce. "He is to be my husband, after all, and 'tis only proper that he should be the one in command."

"Thank you, Amelia." Justin sent her an approving smile. "Spoken as befits a proper bride. Now, we had best be off if we are to accomplish our mission. Amanda, ladies, we shall see you at one o'clock, and mind you don't be late, for we shan't wait for you," and with that he turned and ushered the boys from the room, calling out orders and issuing commands as the door swung closed behind him.

Amanda was pleased to note he had left the carriage at

140

their disposal, although she wasn't surprised. Despite his uncertain temper, Justin was first and foremost a gentleman, and she knew the boys couldn't do better for a pattern card on which to model themselves. She said as much to Amelia, and the younger girl nodded her head in agreement.

"Yes, Justin is very nice," she said, her expression thoughtful as she fingered a length of blue silk the fat seamstress had spread out before her. "I am sure he will make me an admirable husband. I only wish. . . ."

"Wish what?" Amanda asked when her sister's voice trailed off.

"Nothing." Amelia shrugged her shoulders. "I'm merely being foolish." She handed the material back to Mrs. Whistler, a set smile pinned to her lips. "This is lovely, Mrs. Whistler; I believe I shall order a gown, after all. Now, have you any patterns to show us? Something in the new style, perhaps?"

The heavy-set seamstress heaved herself to her feet, muttering beneath her breath as she padded toward her workroom, a chattering Belinda trailing after her. The moment the door had closed behind them, Amanda whirled around to face Amelia.

"All right, what is wrong? And don't try telling me 'tis nothing, because *I* know better." Her eyes moved over Amelia's pale features. "Has this anything to do with Charles?" she asked in a flash of understanding.

"This is his favorite color, you know," Amelia said in answer to her question. "He loved seeing me in it. He said it made me look like an angel." Her voice broke on the last word, and she turned her head away, but not before Amanda saw the shimmer of tears in her eyes.

The sight of her sister so obviously distressed made Amanda's heart clench with pain. She'd been against this insane marriage from the start, she reminded herself fiercely, fighting against her own tears. If Amelia was now beginning to have second thoughts, then she would do all that she could to put an end to this nonsense once and for all.

"Amelia." She reached out and laid a comforting hand on Amelia's arm, forcing her to meet her compassionate gaze. "Are you certain you want to go through with this? It's not too late to call things off. I could go to Justin and—"

"No!" Amelia interrupted sharply. "No," she repeated, her voice softening at the concern in Amanda's eyes. "I told you, I've given this a great deal of thought, and I am certain we are doing the right thing. As you say, Justin is a good, honorable man, and I know we shall have a good marriage."

"But—"

"Don't scowl so, dearest." Amelia gave a shaky laugh, enfolding her sister in a quick embrace. "Haven't you always told me I ought to know my own mind?"

"Yes, but I never thought the day would come when you would hurl those words back in my face," Amanda admitted gruffly, her eyes searching Amelia's. "You're sure?" she asked at last.

"I was never more certain of anything in all my life," Amelia squeezed Amanda's hand gently. "Now, do stop hounding me about it, else I will think that it's you who's had the change of heart."

"What do you mean?"

"Only that I've seen those languishing glances you have been casting Justin's way when you think no one's watching," Amelia continued, breaking into soft laughter at the expression on her sister's face. "You seem to be most taken with him. Are you certain *you* wouldn't rather be his

142

bride? As you say, it's not too late to call things off."

"Don't be ridiculous," Amanda replied, flushing at Amanda's playful teasing. "I'd as soon be wed to the duke of Clarence than marry that overbearing bully! I just wanted to know that you were happy."

"I am, delightfully so," Amelia assured her with another laugh. "And I don't want you to fret; it will all turn out for the best, you'll see." She glanced up at the door as Mrs. Whistler and Belinda came hurrying toward them.

"There you are, love," Amelia said, holding out her hand to Belinda. "Come and help me choose my gown. Only mind that it's in the first stare of fashion," she warned as the little girl joined her on the settee. "Once we are in London we must take care not to appear like country bumpkins. Now, what do you think of this?" And she turned her sisters' attention to the pattern book in her hands, effectively ending the conversation.

"But, Justin, why can't I have an orange waistcoat?" Jeremey wailed, raising tearful eyes to Justin's face. "Squire's oldest boy wears one, and he's all the crack!"

"I don't care if he's a tulip of the ton," Justin shot back, thrusting an impatient hand through his dark hair and making yet another attempt to hang on to his temper. "I told you I wasn't buying you one of those demmed things, and I meant it. We'll hear no more of the matter."

Jeremey gave a loud sniff and turned his back on his idol, clearly put out by such an unreasonable attitude. While he and his twin returned to perusing the fashion magazines offered by the long-suffering tailor, Justin sought refuge in his brandy, silently wondering how the devil things had managed to get so out of hand. He'd once commanded an entire battalion, he reminded himself grimly, taking a restorative sip of the indifferent liquor. How the devil was it he couldn't even control two half-grown schoolboys?

At first things had gone just as he'd planned. With Stephen acting as his guide, he'd visited the milliner's, the dressmakers', and the shoemaker, carefully explaining to each proprietor that Miss Lawrence's and Miss Amelia's bills were to be forwarded to his London solicitor for payment. He'd even taken the precaution of ordering them to make up a complete wardrobe for Amanda, knowing instinctively that she wouldn't buy herself so much as a lace handkerchief. That done he had then led the boys to the tailor's shop, and it was there his carefully laid plans unravelled.

The twins, excited by their first visit to a "real gentleman's shop," became completely unmanageable, pulling down bolts of material from shelves and tearing through stacks of pattern books in their eagerness to order the most outlandish outfits they could find. Justin had said no to gaudily striped trousers, pink and green waistcoats, and a vile, puce-colored jacket, the shoulders of which were so fully stuffed as to give the wearer the appearance of a hunchback, and his patience was all but at an end.

Even the normally staid Stephen had fallen in love with a greatcoat that contained no less than seven capes and was pestering him for it. "Please, Colonel," he pleaded, clutching the illustration to his chest. "No one else in my forum has anything half so grand, and I'd be the envy of all the lads if I came back with this!"

Justin hesitated, recalling an incident from his own boyhood when he had longed for an ivory-topped cane. The other boys had all had them, and he'd wanted more than anything to be like them. His father had refused to even consider his request, calling it vain and frivolous. But then Edward had paid him an unexpected visit, accidentally leaving his own cane behind when he left. Justin had dutifully, written him, reminding him of it, but Edward had simply sent back word that Justin might as well keep the damned thing as he had no further use for it. He'd felt like the cock of the walk for the rest of the term. . . .

"It does look rather grand," he relented, giving the lad a warm smile. "And at least with all those capes we wouldn't need to worry about you catching a cold. All right, you may have the wretched thing."

While Stephen was stuttering out his thanks, Joss and Jeremey set up an immediate protest, demanding that they should receive equal consideration. Finally Justin had had all that he could endure and put his foot firmly down.

"We shall ask your sister," he said, not feeling one ounce of shame at laying the responsibility at that hoyden's feet. "If she doesn't mind you looking like a lot of man-milliners, then I suppose I might be persuaded to pay for them."

"We might as well forget it, then." Joss gave a tragic sigh and returned the pattern book he'd been pawing through to its shelf. "She's a girl."

"Yes" — Jeremey nodded sagely — "they don't understand how it is with us men. Ah well, maybe next year . . ." and he quietly submitted to the tailor's measuring tape.

When the tailor had finished measuring the boys, he showed Justin several sketches for what he termed a proper wardrobe for the young gentlemen, and he waved a hand in agreement. He knew he'd probably end up replacing everything once they were in London, but at the moment he was too exhausted to care. The drive across the Peninsula hadn't left him feeling half this drained, and he wondered if he still had a touch of the fever. Certainly that was a more acceptable explanation than was the possibility he couldn't keep up with two twelve-year-olds and a bookish schoolboy.

A glance at his pocket watch showed it to be a quarter before one, and he began rounding up his charges. They were less than three streets from the inn, but knowing the twins as he now did, he knew he'd best leave at once if he hoped to arrive on time. It turned out he was right, and it was a little after the appointed time before they came spilling into the private parlor, the twins so covered with snow that it took Amanda a few seconds before she could identify them as her brothers.

"What on earth happened to you?" she demanded, pulling Jeremey out of his coat and tossing it over the back of a chair. "You look as if you jumped headfirst into a snowbank!"

"He did," Justin grumbled, performing a similar service on Joss. "And then this little imp jumped in after him. We were more than ten minutes in digging them out."

"You should have seen it, Mandy!" Stephen exclaimed, his eyes shining with excitement. "At first all we could see was the very bottoms of their boots, and when they stopped wiggling, we was certain they were dead. The drayman who helped us free them said as much, and all the old ladies watching fainted dead away. It was grand, wasn't it, Colonel?"

"Grand," Justin answered with a grim smile, recalling his horror at the thought the twins could have been smothered in the thick snow. When they'd finally succeeded in extracting them, he'd been torn between giving them a sound thrashing and hugging them to his chest. His hands still shook at the memory.

Amanda saw the betraying tremor, and a smile of understanding softened her lips. She longed to say something comforting, but knew Justin would not thank her for calling attention to what he would surely consider a weakness. Instead she turned to Amelia, who was busy handing out hot cups of chocolate and gentle admonishments to the others.

"While you are busy warming up these scamps, I believe I shall go and have a word with Mr. Peasey. He must have some extra blankets somewhere in this inn," Amanda said.

"I'll go with you," Justin said, recalling the conversation of that morning. He'd already spoken sharply to the innkeeper about his treatment of Amanda, and he wanted to be certain the message had been understood.

"No, you're almost as badly chilled as the boys," she said, sending him a stern frown. "This won't take but a few minutes, I assure you."

"But—" Justin began, only to find himself addressing thin air. For a moment he was strongly tempted to go storming after her, but in the end he decided against it. He knew such an action would be certain to infuriate her, and as he was more interested in keeping the peace than in exercising his male prerogatives, he thought it best to let the matter drop.

Besides, he admitted, limping toward the chair, the chit was right. He *was* frozen to the very marrow of his bones, and the prospect of sitting before the crackling fire was too tempting to resist. But later he intended to have a word with his independent-minded sister-in-law. He would make it clear that he was now in command of the family, and if there was any fighting to be done, then he would be the one to do it.

Amanda returned within a few minutes, followed by a maid bearing a large pile of blankets. After making sure the boys were properly wrapped, she turned her attention

147

to Justin, bearing down on him with such determination that he raised his hands in mock surrender.

"Peace, madam!" he exclaimed, his eyes dancing merrily. "You'll get no quarrel from me, I promise you."

Amanda flushed at his teasing words. "See that I do not," she muttered, her manner brusque as she settled the blanket about his broad shoulders. "I vow, there are times when you show no more sense than do the twins!"

He grabbed her hand as she turned away, anchoring her to his side. "Aren't you going to tuck me in?" he drawled, his tone deliberately challenging as he smiled up at her.

"I shall leave that happy task to Amelia," she retorted, trying not to smile as she snatched back her hand. She knew he was trying to provoke her, but rather than taking offense as she once would have done, she was secretly delighted. He was usually so prim and rigid in his behavior that it was rather reassuring to see that he could misbehave on occasion.

Luncheon was a pleasant meal, with everyone excitedly bragging of their morning's purchases. Justin noted Amanda remained silent, and was smugly pleased that he had anticipated her actions. He couldn't wait to see her expression when the wardrobe he had ordered was delivered at the house.

It was as they were lingering over dessert and discussing what they would do that afternoon that he realized he hadn't bought any Christmas presents for the family. He was about to demand Amanda accompany him when he had a sudden change of heart. Perhaps it might be better if Amelia went with him, he thought, flicking a speculative glance at his fiancée. Since their engagement had been announced, they'd spent almost no time at all alone together, and he decided it was time to remedy the situation.

"Amelia," he began, catching her soft blue eyes as she glanced up at him, "do you think I might prevail upon you to show me about the town? This is my first visit to Godstone and I am looking forward to seeing more of it."

"Oh." Amelia appeared momentarily nonplussed by his request; but she recovered quickly, and there was no faulting the sweet smile she flashed him. "Of course, Justin, that would be delightful. Is there anything of particular interest you would like to see?"

"Wherever," he replied with an indifferent roll of his shoulders. "I shall leave that up to you, my dear."

"Are you sure you wouldn't rather have us show you about?" Jeremey offered, leaning toward Justin in a confidential manner. "She'll only want to take you to all those boring old monuments and such. *We'll* take you to the cockfights!"

"I'm not even going to ask how you know about such places," Amanda said before Justin could answer. "Something tells me I am better off not knowing. In the meanwhile, I think it best that Amelia act as Justin's guide."

"Why?" Jeremey whined.

"Because, you little ninnyhammer, she is his fiancée," Stephen said, lording it over his younger brother with a smug superiority. "And engaged couples often want to be alone together."

"I don't see why." Joss was quick to pick up the cudgels in his brother's defense. "Cockfights are much more interesting than any dusty old monuments!"

"I want to go!" Belinda said, setting down her spoon and casting Justin a hopeful smile. "I love monaments!"

Justin glanced from one child's face to another, wondering vaguely how he was going to extract himself from this contretemps. He turned to Amanda. "Help," he implored in obvious desperation.

"Belinda, Joss, Jeremey, that is quite enough," she said, her stern voice at odds with her sparkling eyes. "If Justin wants to go about with Amelia, then we shall let them. The rest of us have more than enough errands to keep us occupied until it is time to go. Don't forget we still have to call on the vicar."

This pronouncement was greeted with groans, but her brothers knew her too well to protest. While they were busy commiserating with each other, Justin leaned forward to cover Amanda's hand with his own.

"My thanks for your able rescue, ma'am," he said, his expression warm as he regarded her. "I haven't felt so harassed since I was cut off from my unit by a platoon of French Hussars."

"You're welcome, sir," she replied, laughing at his apt analogy. "Only mind you and Amelia aren't gone overly long. I don't trust the looks of that sky, and I want to get home before it starts snowing again."

"All right. Actually, I only wanted to do some shopping for the children. Is there anything particular you think they would like?"

"Anything noisy, dangerous, or gaudy will suit the twins," she said, well aware of her younger brothers' tastes. "Although for my sake, I ask that you not buy anything too noisy or dangerous, et cetera. And as for Stephen, he is rather fond of books and anything of a scientific nature."

"Chemical kits?" he asked, arching his brows over his eyes.

"Only if you don't value your skin. If he doesn't blow us all to kingdom come, then the twins would be certain to steal the kit the moment our backs are turned and do it for him."

150

"A horrifying probability. Well, what of Belinda? A doll, I suppose?"

"Or a new ball," Amanda said, after giving the matter some thought. "The twins threw her old one down the well. And you might want to buy her some paints and paper. It is time she began her art lessons."

Justin frowned. "Is that all?"

"Why, yes." She was surprised by his question. "We seldom exchange more than one or two presents and most of them are homemade. You mustn't think you need to spoil us," she added, shooting him an anxious look. "We don't expect it."

"Perhaps not," he replied, unexpectedly stung by her words. "But perhaps I need to spoil you." He threw down his napkin and rose to his feet, holding out his hand for Amelia.

"Come, Amelia," he commanded, his tone harsher than the one he usually used with her, "it is time we were going. There is much we need to do." He cast Amanda a cold look. "Shall we meet back here or at the vicar's?"

"The vicar's," she answered quietly, aware she had offended him. "Even though the wedding is to be held in London, you must still seek his blessing. He christened Amelia, and he would be deeply hurt if we were not to advise him of your plans."

"And of course you would never wish to hurt anyone," he replied bitterly. "Very well, the vicar's it shall be. We'll meet you there at four o'clock," and with that he guided Amelia from the room, leaving Amanda to stare after him.

"Well, he certainly was up in the boughs about something," Stephen said, turning a confused look on Amanda. "What on earth was that all about?"

"I am sure I do not know," she sniffed, taking refuge in

151

her cup of luke-warm tea. "Colonel Stockton is rather high in the instep at times, and I suppose we must accustom ourselves to his ill-temper."

"Really? I've always found him to be extremely pleasant," Stephen replied with a thoughtful frown. "You don't suppose his leg is hurting him, do you? I noticed him limping earlier."

Amanda had also noted the limp, and she'd meant to scold him for over-taxing his strength. After all, it hadn't been so very long ago that he'd been bedridden with the fever. She opened her mouth, about to agree with Stephen's diagnosis, when her innate sense of honesty stopped her.

"No," she admitted with a heavy sigh, "Justin's leg may well be troubling him, but that isn't what upset him."

"What did?"

"I fear I may have offended him," she said, her slender fingers playing with the handle of her tea cup. "He wanted to buy some Christmas presents, and I told him he mustn't think he needs to spoil us."

"I see." Stephen looked grave. "No wonder he was so angry. You must have hurt his feelings."

"What do you mean?" Amanda demanded, annoyed at being taken to task by her younger brother. "I didn't say he couldn't buy anything, I just said, he shouldn't buy out the toy shop!"

"Yes, but you remember what he said yesterday," he continued in a gentle tone. "He's never shopped for Christmas presents before, and he only wanted to do it right. You even promised to help, remember?"

Amanda did, and her sense of shame deepened. She shouldn't have been so stiff-necked, she realized unhappily. Justin was rich as a nabob, and if buying the children presents brought him happiness, then who was she to deny him? It certainly wouldn't hurt him, and heaven knew the children could use a bit of pleasure in their lives. The financial difficulties of past few years had left little room for extravagances such as toys or candy.

Very well, she decided, her eyes sparkling with resolve, she would do it. In the interest of family harmony she would swallow her pride, and the next time Justin offered something, she would accept it with a gracious smile. Pleased with the way she had resolved the crisis, she began making plans on how to keep the twins entertained until it was time to meet Justin and Amelia.

 *Chapter Ten*

"Please, Justin, won't you slow down? I can scarce keep up with you!" Amelia gasped, her hand tightening on Justin's arm as they hurried down the ice-coated street. Her feet slipped on the slick cobblestones, and she tugged frantically at his sleeve. "Justin! I'm going to fall!"

Justin heard the fright in her voice and halted, his breath coming out in cloudy puffs as he turned to face her. "I'm sorry, Amelia," he apologized, feeling faintly embarrassed for having taken his temper out on her. He straightened her bonnet and stared down into her pale face. "Are you all right?"

"Yes," she replied softly, searching his set expression, "but would you mind telling me why you are in such a hurry? Surely you can't be that anxious to see our village?" She cast a teasing look around them.

Justin had the good grace to flush. "No," he admitted, his mouth relaxing in a smile. "It is just that sister of yours; she has a most regrettable effect upon my temper. I swear I have never met a more obstreperous female in all my life!"

"Oh, dear, that does sound rather serious," Amelia murmured, amusement evident in her blue eyes. "I take it you quarreled?"

That was all it took to unleash Justin's resentment. "You

154

may call having one's innocent offer to buy Christmas presents hurled back in one's face 'a quarrel,' " he snarled, his mouth tightening in anger, "but I call it out and out rudeness! That minx dared accuse me of trying to buy my way into the family!"

Amelia's amusement vanished at once. "Amanda accused you of . . . of that?" she gasped, her gloved hand fluttering to her chest.

"As good as," he replied, his cheeks darkening with fury. "I wanted to buy each of the children a little something for Christmas, and she informed me, very pointedly, that as you only exchanged one or two presents each year, I mustn't think I need spoil you. Spoil!" His eyes flashed contemptuously. "And all I wanted to do was to make Christmas Eve a little nicer for the younger ones. That's what Christmas is for, isn't it?"

"Of course it is," Amelia replied stoutly, appalled by her elder sister's behavior. She loved Amanda dearly, but there were times, such as now, when she could have happily boxed her ears. She knew that beneath Justin's fury he was genuinely hurt by Amanda's actions, and she was determined to set things right. After all, Justin was soon to be her husband, and her first loyalty must lie with him.

"Of course that is what Christmas is for," she repeated, her small chin coming up in a rare show of temper. "And I know the boys would adore anything you bought them! You are going to be their brother and their guardian; it is your right to buy them whatever you like!"

Justin was faintly surprised by Amelia's reaction — surprised and more than a little pleased. He thought her a very sweet, lovely girl, but there was no denying he also found her a trifle boring. It seemed regrettable to him that one sister had been cursed with the temperament of a Billingsgate fishwife while the other was as biddable as a sheep. Such a scenario might work well in Shakespeare, he thought, his eyes bright with amusement, but in real life it made things damned uncomfortable.

"What about Amanda?" he asked, enjoying the play of emotions across Amelia's face. "May I also purchase her a present?"

"You may buy her whatever you desire," she said, dismissing her sister's opinion in the matter with an airy wave of her hand. "Although I don't see why you should want to. As poorly as she has behaved, she deserves to find nothing in her Christmas stocking but a lump of coal!"

He threw back his head and laughed, drawing interested stares from passersby. "Then a lump of coal it shall be," he said, feeling years younger. He'd never even exchanged presents with Edward before, and suddenly he couldn't wait to partake of the joyous tradition that had been a part of the holidays since the very beginning of Christianity. He grabbed Amelia's hand and began dragging her toward the nearest shop, this time taking care that she didn't slip.

"Come, my dear," he told her, flashing her a boyish grin, "we have a great deal of shopping to be done!"

They spent the next three hours moving from shop to shop while Justin spent a small fortune on every bright and shiny object that caught his eye. Amelia was secretly shocked at the reckless abandon with which he spent money, but she didn't have the heart to stop him. He was so obviously enjoying himself, and she knew the children would adore their presents.

They had just left the bookshop and were about to stop at the milliner's when Amelia heard a familiar voice calling her name.

She whirled around, her heart leaping into her throat at the sight of the tall young man wearing the scarlet uniform of the Twelfth Regiment rushing toward her. Charles!

"Amelia, sweetest." Captain Charles Maxfield gave an exuberant laugh, his strong arms stealing about Amelia as he

156

lifted her off her feet and swung her in a small circle. "I couldn't believe it when I saw you walking down the street!" he continued, smiling down at her. "How did you know I had managed to get leave for the holidays? It was supposed to be a secret."

"Charles," Amelia murmured brokenly, tears filling her eyes at the sight of his beloved face. This was the moment she had been longing for, the moment she had been dreading above all others. She was aware that Justin was standing beside her, obviously waiting to be introduced, and for a few agonizing seconds, she was certain the pain of what she must do would surely kill her. Drawing a deep breath, she stepped back from the man she loved and turned to her fiancé.

"Justin, I should like to introduce you to my oldest neighbor, Captain Charles Maxfield," she began, praying that her voice did not betray the anguish she was feeling. "Charles allow me to make you known to Colonel Justin Stockton of the Light Infantry."

"Daniel's commanding officer?" Charles exclaimed, his gray eyes widening as they took in the silent man standing beside Amelia. "I've heard much of you and the brilliant way your battalion performed at Vitoria. It is a pleasure to meet you sir!" He thrust out a hand in greeting.

"Captain Maxfield." Justin accepted the young officer's hand, his eyes narrowing as they flicked between him and Amelia. He sensed there was more between the two than simple neighborliness, but he was uncertain what it was.

"I'm so dreadfully sorry about Daniel." Charles was gazing down at Amelia, feeling faintly puzzled by her odd behavior. "He was a capital fellow. I would have attended his funeral if there had been time but. . ." He shrugged his shoulders helplessly, unable to say anything else.

"I understand," Amelia said, giving his arm a reassuring squeeze. She felt Justin shift beside her and knew she had to speak before her courage deserted her completely. "Colonel Stockton was there," she said, her words tumbling out of her lips in an incoherent flow. "He has been so good to us, so kind. I do not know what we would have done without him."

Charles felt the first stirring of unease. "Indeed?" he asked studying the older man with growing interest.

"Yes." Amelia moistened her lips. "In-in fact you may be the first to wish us happy, Charles. I have accepted the colonel's proposal of marriage. We are to be married by Special License in London."

For a moment Charles could only stare at her, too stunned to feel anything. "I beg your pardon?" he asked weakly, shaking his head as if to clear it.

"Amelia has kindly consented to be my bride," Justin said, realizing now the reason for the odd undercurrents about him. The young puppy obviously had a crush on Amelia, and she was trying to let him down as gently as possible. He silently applauded her sensitivity and was anxious to aid her in any way he could. Judging from the poleaxed way Maxfield was staring at them, the news had hit him hard.

"We were about to join the others at the vicar's," he said, laying a proprietary arm about Amelia. "You are more than welcome to join us. I'm sure they would enjoy seeing Daniel's friend again."

Charles turned to Amelia, his silver-colored eyes bright with fury. *"Daniel's* friend?" he ground out, his hands balling into fists at his side. "Is that how you explained me to him?"

"Charles, please," Amelia began, tears escaping from her eyes and wending their way down her chilled face. "You don't understand—"

"Oh, I understand," he interrupted, his tone dripping with venom. "I understand perfectly! A wealthy lord, even if he is only a second son, is infinitely preferable to a half-pay captain, isn't he?"

158

"Watch your tongue, puppy," Justin warned softly, the sympathy he felt for the younger man only stretching so far. "I should hate to have to call out a fellow officer, but make no doubt that I will if you say much more."

"Have no fear, Lord Stockton I know well my place," Charles said, his smile bitter. "Rest assured that I have nothing left to say to your *fiancée*," and he turned and stormed away, his shoulders held stiff with pride.

"Are you all right?" Justin asked as soon as the other man had disappeared. "He didn't upset you, did he?"

"Take me to my sister," Amelia pleaded, making no attempt to wipe the tears from her cheeks. "Please, Justin, take me to my sister!"

Fearing she would burst into sobs, or worse still, swoon, Justin quickly commandeered the first private coach he could see, explaining to the startled occupants that it was an emergency. The journey was accomplished in a matter of minutes, and the carriage had barely stopped before Amelia leapt out, running toward the ivy-covered rectory as if it were the only sanctuary left in the world.

"Amanda! Oh, Amanda, it's Charles!" she wailed, dashing into the small study where the maid indicated the others were waiting.

Amanda, who had been politely listening to the sermon the vicar intended reading at the Christmas Eve service, had barely had time to rise to her feet before Amelia threw herself into her arms, sobbing as if her heart would break.

"Darling, what is it?" she asked, her arms closing protectively about the younger girl. "What about Charles? Has something happened?" Only one possibility occurred to her, and it was too dreadful to even contemplate. "He's not dead, is he?"

"No!" Amelia shook her head wildly. "He's here, in God-stone, and he—oh, Amanda!" She began sobbing anew.

Amanda understood at once, and her heart went out to

her sister. Poor Amelia, she thought, lovingly stroking her thick blond curls. How dreadful it must have been to be confronted by the man you loved while betrothed to another. She was searching for the right words to comfort her when Justin walked into the study, his expression growing even grimmer at the sight of his fiancée in Amanda's arms.

"Is she all right?" he asked, moving to stand beside them. "She encountered your old neighbor in the street, and I fear the rascal upset her."

"Charles isn't a rascal," Amanda protested, shooting him an annoyed scowl. "He's—"

"Please, Amanda," Amelia interrupted, raising her tear-stained face from Amanda's shoulder and sending her an imploring look. "Just take me home. I—I have the headache!"

"But—" Amanda began, and then abandoned the effort. It was obvious Amelia was genuinely distraught, and in light of the promise she had made earlier, what was there left she could say? Suppressing a weary sigh, she turned to the vicar, who was regarding them with his usual look of vague inquiry.

"My apologies, Reverend Smythe, but I believe it would be best if we left now," she said with an apologetic smile. "Amelia is prone to headaches, you know, and I must get her home."

"Of course, of course." The elderly man bobbed his head in understanding. "Poor wee thing. Doubtlessly seeing young Maxfield was an unpleasant reminder of her dear brother."

"Yes"—Amanda grabbed on to the explanation as if it were a lifeline—"that is precisely it. Daniel and Charles were the best of friends, and even spoke of enlisting together. It must have been a great shock seeing him again. Now, if you'll excuse me, I want to get Amelia settled in the coach. Come dearest," and she guided the still-sobbing girl from the room.

Justin only paused long enough to thank the vicar for his help and accept his blessing, and then he was hurrying after the others. He climbed in beside them, glancing around in surprise when he noticed the younger members of the family were nowhere to be seen.

"Where are Belinda and the boys?" he asked, settling his shoulders against the plush, golden velvet squabs. "Surely you're not leaving them behind?"

"No, tempting as though that thought might be," Amanda said, pausing in her ministrations long enough to cast him a reassuring smile. "There was a skating party on the village pond, and the squire's wife promised to see them safely home."

"I see," he said, a slight frown puckering his brow as he glanced out at the threatening skies. He thought the weather too uncertain for such frivolity, but at the moment he was more concerned with Amanda.

She had finally stopped crying and was curled into the corner of the coach, a plaid blanket tucked warmly about her. Her eyes were closed, and her blond head was once again resting on Amanda's shoulder. Quizzing her was clearly out of the question, at least for the moment, although he had no intention of letting the matter drop. There was clearly something going on here, and all of his instincts told him Amanda probably knew what it was. His instincts also told him that she would doubtlessly die sooner than tell him what it was.

"How did your shopping go?" Amanda asked as the carriage slowly made its way home. "I didn't notice you had any packages with you."

"I am having them delivered," Justin replied, accepting the conversational gambit for what it was . . . a diversionary tactic. "You'll be happy to know I didn't buy Stephen any dangerous chemical sets, although I did find a book on ballooning I thought he might find interesting."

"Yes, it is a hobby of his," she agreed, relieved to see that he was going to be pleasant about things. Given the state of her nerves, she didn't think she was up to spinning tales.

"We'll have to take care that the twins don't get their hands on it," he continued, folding his arms across his chest and watching her through half-closed eyes. "Else I shudder to think of what they might do."

"It doesn't bear thinking of," she agreed once again, her lips curving in a gentle smile. "They would probably try launching one of their own, and heaven only knows where they might land."

"Have they always been so . . . exuberant?" He chose the word with delicate care.

"So incorrigible, do you mean?" She wasn't taken in by his attempts at diplomacy. "Always. Jeremey is the main instigator, although Joss is usually not far behind. And they are utterly fearless. When they were less than six they disappeared over night, and searchers found them in the woods. They were looking for Indians."

"That would have been about the time your mother and stepfather died, wouldn't it?"

She glanced up at him. "About then, yes," she said, amazed that he had remembered the details of her parents' deaths. "The accident happened in April, and this happened that summer. Did Daniel tell you about it?"

Justin hesitated, wondering if he should tell her the truth, that he had only met her brother the night before his death. He knew she and the others assumed he and Daniel had been bosom beaus, and he'd never bothered correcting that impression. At first he'd been too ill, and later he'd decided it was more prudent to remain silent. His demand to assume responsibility for the family was based on his obligation to Daniel, and if they were to learn how shaky that claim was . . . he refused to consider what Amanda's reac-

162

tion would be.

"He mentioned it," he said, keeping his answer deliberately vague. "He also mentioned your stepfather gamed. Is that why you're in such financial difficulty?"

Amanda glared at him, resenting his sharpness. "Partially," she agreed coolly, "although I will thank you not to mention it to the others. They have few enough memories of their father as it is, and I wouldn't want those memories tainted."

"You're a very good sister," he said suddenly, tilting his head to one side as he continued studying her. "Have you always taken care of them?"

"Always," she admitted, her dark brown eyes taking on a soft glow. "Mother was never very strong, and the care of the children just naturally fell to me. One of my first memories is of holding Daniel and trying to get him to drink milk from a cup. I couldn't have been more than three or four." She shook her head at the memory and then fixed him with an interested look.

"What of you? I know you have an older brother, Edward, but have you any other brothers? Or any sisters?"

The light that had been warming Justin's golden eyes faded completely, leaving them flat and cold. "No," he said, his voice unconsciously hard. "There was just Edward, the heir, and me, the second son."

"I see," she said, detecting the bitterness in his voice. She'd noticed it once or twice before on those rare occasions when he spoke of his past. In fact, she realized with something akin to shock, he seldom mentioned anything of a personal nature. Outside of knowing that he was an officer and a lord, she knew almost nothing of him, and she was suddenly anxious to rectify that lack of knowledge. If he was to be her brother-in-law, then it behooved her to learn as much about him as she could.

"What sort of older brother was Edward," she asked, settling into a more comfortable position. "Was he a perfect monster to you at times? Or did he treat you with pompous superiority, the way Daniel occasionally treated the twins?"

The question caught Justin unawares. "Edward was very good to me," he blurted out in surprise. "He always remembered my birthday, and he came to visit me at school at least once each term."

"Then, he's a great deal older than you?"

"No, less than ten years actually." He frowned at her question. "Why?"

"I'm not sure," Amanda admitted candidly. "It is just that I realize how very little we know of you, and I was curious. You seldom speak of yourself, you know," and she gave him a look that was frankly speculative.

Her scrutiny made Justin uncomfortable, and he shifted on the padded seat. "There is nothing to say," he muttered, wishing she would change the conversation. "My life is not unlike other men of my rank and station."

"Yes, but as you are the first man of your station I have ever met, I fear I am woefully ignorant on the subject," she replied, hoping to cajole him into a better humor. "You are as exotic to me as a Bedouin chief, and I am consumed with curiosity."

A reluctant smile relaxed his mouth. "What is it you want to know?" he asked.

"Everything," she replied eagerly, clasping her hands together as she leaned forward. "I know you went to Eton; were you a good student?"

"Am I to take it from the avid gleam in your eyes that you are hoping to hear I barely squeaked my way through?" he teased, temporarily forgetting about Maxfield and Amelia. "Well, I hate to disappoint you, ma'am, but the truth of the matter is I was a superlative student, both at Eton and later on at Oxford. In fact, had it not been decided that I would go into the army, I might have gone on to be a don. I've always been fascinated with Shakespeare."

She puzzled over his answer. "What do you mean had it not been decided,' " she asked. "Didn't you want to go into the army?"

"That is the family tradition," Justin replied stonily, some of his goodwill vanishing as memories washed over him. "The second son always goes into the army. It is the way it has always been done."

"But is it what you wanted?" Amanda pressed, scooting closer until her knee was brushing his. She felt as if she was close to finally understanding the man behind the haughty air and clipped commands, and she wasn't about to back away now.

"It was my duty," he answered, feeling cornered and disliking the sensation. "I was born knowing Stonebridge would never be mine, and that all that was expected of me was that I stay out of trouble, marry well if at all possible, and die bravely when my country required it of me!"

Amanda sat back, stunned by his blunt reply and the bitterness she saw burning in his eyes. "You can't believe that," she managed at last. "That's dreadful!"

"It is the way it is," he told her coldly, "and yes, I believe it—every word of it. My father devoted the last few years of his life making certain I understood that reality in no uncertain terms. He had the heir he craved, and I was no more to him than an afterthought, a disappointing afterthought at that."

"But surely your mother would never have allowed such a thing—"

"My mother died when I was barely old enough to remember her," he said harshly, the long-forgotten pain welling up inside him. "Not that it would have changed things even if she had lived. I told you, it is the way things are done in my class."

"And you intend to raise your children the same way?"

Amanda demanded incredulously. "That is ridiculous!"

Justin jerked his head back as if she had struck him. Until now, he'd never given the idea of children more than a passing thought. To be sure the possibility of heirs was one of his main reasons for marrying, especially as Edward had made it obvious he had no intention whatsoever of taking a bride. And he had told Amelia he wanted children of his own, he remembered, flicking the peacefully sleeping girl a somewhat stunned look. But until this very moment, he'd never even considered how they would be raised.

Did he want one of his sons to be reared as he'd been? To feel useless and redundant because he'd had the misfortune to be born second rather than first? Did he really want his son to lie awake at night in some damned boarding school crying for a home that would never truly be his?

"No, by God, I do not!" he thundered, his jaw flexing with suppressed fury. "I'll never raise a child of mine that way!"

Amelia jerked at the sound of his voice, her eyes fluttering open as she glanced around her. "Are we home yet?" she asked, rubbing fretfully at her head. "I am so tired!"

"Soon, love," Amanda soothed, reaching out a hand to brush a damp strand of hair back from her sister's flushed cheeks. She'd been so engrossed in her conversation with Justin that she had completely forgotten about Amelia, an oversight that left her badly shaken.

She'd begun quizzing Justin more out of a desire to distract him from the subject of Charles than anything, although the more he spoke, the more interested she became in his answers. He was an enigma, she mused, murmuring soft reassurances to the exhausted girl. He could be so cold and haughty one moment, and then gentle and teasing the next. Much of his commanding ways she put down to his military training; now she wondered how much was due to the burdens of command and how much was due to his sterile childhood.

No wonder he knew nothing about Christmas, she thought, her sense of shame over this morning's row increasing. He'd probably spent his holidays alone at school, or isolated in a country house with a cold and distant father who barely tolerated his existence. He'd even admitted he hadn't much experience buying presents, and she had all but thrown those presents back in his face.

Well, that would have to change, she decided, noting they had arrived at the house. Christmas Eve was in two days time, and between now and then, she would work doubly hard to get along with Justin. Not only would she accept the presents he had bought the children, but she would actively encourage him to join in the family festivities. Perhaps she'd even enlist his help in putting up the *tannenbaum* and in putting on the pageant that had been part of Lawrence Hall tradition since her great-grandfather's day. She'd been considering dropping the tradition this year in light of Daniel's death, but now she would go ahead with it as planned.

Justin was much taller than either Daniel or her stepfather, although she was sure her father's costume would fit him, and with any luck the red beard he'd worn as Henry the Eighth hadn't been totally consumed by mice . . . or worse. Yes, she thought, her excitement growing as plans began taking shape in her head, she would do it. In between the *tannenbaum*, the pageant, and the little surprise she and Mrs. Hatcher had arranged for Christmas morning, this would be the best Christmas Justin had ever known. And if it wasn't—her smile grew wide—if it wasn't, she would eat old Henry's moth-eaten beard!

Chapter Eleven

Amanda took Amelia directly to her rooms, dismissing the hovering maid as she assisted her sister into bed. "Would you like some tea, darling?" she asked solicitously, alarmed by Amelia's pallor. The poor dear was prone to migraines, and once she contracted one, she could be ill for days.

"No." Amelia's head moved restlessly on the pillow. "I would just like to be alone now, if you please."

"Very well, if that is your wish," Amanda said quietly, rising to her feet and turning toward the door. She and Amelia had always been so close, and she could not help but be hurt by her sister's withdrawal. "I'll just—"

"No, wait!" Amelia sat up in the bed, tears sparkling in her eyes as she held out a hand to Amanda. "Don't go!"

Amanda glanced over her shoulder at the panic in the other girl's voice. "Yes, love?" she asked, wondering if she ought to ring for some of Mrs. Hatcher's laudanum.

"Do . . . do you think you might do something for me?" Amelia stammered, nervously pleating the bedsheet with her fingers.

"Certainly," Amanda said, resuming her chair beside Amelia's bed. "What is it you wish done?"

"Would you write a letter to Charles for me?"

Amanda blinked at the whispered request. "I thought you'd already written him," she replied, recalling Amelia had said, something about it shortly after accepting Justin's proposal.

"I didn't know what to say!" she cried, wiping ineffectually at her tears. "I couldn't tell him the truth, that I am marrying Justin for money. Nor could I bring myself to let him think I had fallen in love. That would have been too cruel."

"Well, what would you have me do?" Amanda demanded, eyeing her in frustration. "If I can't tell him the honest truth, then what is there left to say? I refuse to lie for you."

Amelia's chin came up at that. "I wouldn't expect you to," she said in a surprisingly regal tone. "I . . . I just want you to see him, to explain that I am only doing what I think best. He has always admired you; I am sure you could make him listen."

Amanda hesitated, torn between her desire to help her sister and a reluctance to interfere any more than she already had. "I don't know Amelia," she said, nibbling thoughtfully on her bottom lip. "This is really between you and Charles. Perhaps it might be better if you—"

"No! No, I could not!" she cried in genuine anguish. "I love him so much; I think it would destroy me if I were to see that look of contempt in his eyes again. Please Amanda. . . ."

In the light of her sister's distress, there was no way Amanda could refuse her. "All right, dearest," she said, laying a restraining hand on Amelia's shoulder and easing her back against the pillows. "I promise I shall write him at once. Now, I want you to close your eyes and sleep. You'll feel better once you have rested."

Amanda sat by the bed until she was certain Amelia was asleep, and then she quietly left the room. She closed the door behind her and turned around, a soft gasp escaping from her when she collided with a broad, male chest. Strong arms closed about her at once, anchoring her struggling form to him.

"Justin! For heaven's sake, what are you doing here?" she

demanded, pushing ineffectually against his chest. "You scared me out of my wits!"

"I wanted to see how Amelia was doing," he said, amused by her attempts to free herself. "How is she?"

"She is asleep," Amanda snapped, glaring up into his dark face. She knew it was useless to struggle as he was much stronger than she, and she refused to humble herself by begging him to let her go.

"What was wrong with her?" he asked, feeling in no particular rush to release his fiesty captive. He was surprised by how tiny she was. She was such a tyrant that he had somehow formed the impression that she was physically formidable as well, and yet the top of her head barely brushed his nose. All it would take to kiss her would be to tilt his head just so. . . . He released her at once, his arms dropping to his sides as he stepped back from her.

"A migraine," she replied, grateful for her release but annoyed by the feeling of breathlessness she was experiencing at his nearness. She tried telling herself it was guilt for the shabby way she had treated him, but she knew that was only part of the truth. She refused to dwell on what the rest of the truth might be.

"You're sure that's all it is?" he asked, frowning as he fell into step beside her. He was also experiencing some disquieting emotions, although he was man enough to know what they meant.

"Well, the scene with Charles certainly didn't help matters," Amanda continued, wishing he would just go away. Not that he would, of course. Given Justin's heavy sense of responsibility, she knew he wouldn't leave until he received satisfactory answers to his questions. If she wanted to be shed of him, she would have to find some way of telling him just enough to placate him, but stopping short of the actual truth.

"I know you said she was upset because of Maxfield's friendship with Daniel," he said, his hand cupping her elbow

170

as he guided her down the staircase. "But I sense there is much more to the story than that. Is the puppy in love with her?"

Amanda missed her step and would have fallen had it not been for Justin's firm grip on her. She recovered immediately and shot a look of burning resentment. "Sir," she began, acutely aware of the danger of the conversation, "I know Amelia is your fiancée, but that doesn't give you the right to—"

"Yes," he interrupted, dragging her into the parlor and closing the door behind her. "It does. If another man is enamored of my fiancée then I most assuredly have the right to know. Now, I am asking you, is Maxfield in love with Amelia?"

Oh, Lord, was there ever such a tangle as this? Amanda wondered glumly, crossing the room to stand before the fireplace. She couldn't tell Justin the truth without breaking her word to Amelia, and the idea of lying to him was strangely distasteful. There had to be some way, she thought, frowning at her reflection in the gilded mirror.

"I am not privy to Charles' feelings," she said slowly, picking each word with painstaking care, "but I think I can safely tell you that he has always had something of a crush on her. We all grew up together, and he was forever following her about."

"And how does she feel about him?" Justin asked, folding his arms across his chest as he leaned against the door. He accepted Amanda's story so far, although he could not help but think there was something she wasn't telling him. "Does she return his regard?"

"In a manner of speaking," she admitted hesitantly. "But there was never a formal declaration between them. She is fond of him, certainly, but she is not engaged to him."

"That isn't what I asked, Amanda," he chided softly, studying her averted face with soft eyes. "I asked if her emotions were engaged. Are they?"

"Only in that she is deeply fond of Charles and that she cares very much what happens to him." Amanda mentally threw up her hands in surrender and turned to face him. "She is aware of his feelings for her, and it distresses her that your engagement has caused him pain; but that is all I am prepared to say. If you want to know anything else, you must ask Amelia."

Justin digested her reply in silence before slowly nodding his head. "All right," he said, his eyes steady as they met hers. "I will accept your explanation . . . for now. But if Maxfield causes Amelia any more *distress*," he emphasized the word mockingly, "then he will have to deal with me. I will not have her plagued by the fellow."

"I'm sure that won't be a problem," Amanda said, almost melting with relief. "As he is in the army, we seldom see him these days. Now, if you will excuse me, I must go and have a word with Mrs. Hatcher. The children should be arriving home soon, and they are certain to be famished." And with that she scuttled past him, fleeing toward the relative safety of the kitchens.

The twins and the others returned from their skating party shortly before dinner, and the sound of their excited laughter drew Amelia from her sickroom. Following dinner the whole family retired to the parlor to spend a quiet evening before the fire. They had been enjoying one of Mrs. Radcliffe's tamer offerings, but in light of her earlier conversation with Justin, Amanda decided on a change in the evening's entertainment.

"Shakespeare!" Stephen exclaimed, wrinkling his nose in obvious disgust. "Oh Amanda, must we? I am on holiday!"

"Yes, we must, you shameless philistine," she retorted, lovingly mussing his blond hair. "A strong knowledge of our country's greatest writer is an estimable trait in a young man, and one I think you would do well to acquire. Be-

172

sides"—her eyes flicked in Justin's direction—"he happens to be the colonel's favorite author."

Three pairs of horrified blue eyes were clapped on Justin. "You like Shakespeare?" Jeremey demanded, distressed that his hero should have such feet of clay.

"Very much so. In fact, I consider him to be the greatest writer who ever lived," Justin said, delighting in the conversation. The twins were a source of increasing pleasure for him, and he was looking forward to guiding them into manhood. If they managed to escape the gallows, he thought they would do rather well.

"But he wrote poetry *and* love stories," Joss added his protests to those of his brother. "You can not like all that romantic nonsense . . . can you?" He studied Justin with decided suspicion, his sulky pout leaving no doubt as to his opinion of that particular form of literature.

"I not only can, Joss I do," Justin said firmly. "But if it relieves your mind, Shakespeare wrote more than poetry and love stories. Have you never heard of *Macbeth* or *Julius Caesar?*"

"I can assure you, sir, I have done my best to expose these ruffians to the classics, but as you can see, it was all for naught. They hold that anything even remotely of cultural interest is something to be avoided at all costs," Amanda replied, defending herself with a rueful shake of her head. She knew he was enjoying the exchange with the boys, and it relieved her to see he was not offended by the uninhibited way they joined in the conversation. She would not have their bright, inquisitive natures smothered by the conventions of society.

"Then, perhaps 'tis time we remedied that," Justin said, rising to his feet and exiting the room. He returned a few minutes later, a worn, leather book cradled in his big hands. "I think you will like this," he told the boys, settling back in his chair. "It's about one of England's greatest warrior-kings, Henry the Fifth." He flipped open the book and began reading, his deep, resonant voice washing over his listeners.

"O for a Muse of fire, that would ascend the brightest heaven of invention: A kingdom for a stage, princes to act, and monachs to behold the swelling scene . . ."

Amanda sat quietly, her head bent over her needlework as she listened to the play unfolding. What a domestic picture they must make, she thought, her lips curving in a gentle smile. Justin, looking every inch the country squire in his jacket of green kerseymere and buff pantaloons, and Amelia sitting tranquilly at his side in a simple gown of dark blue wool. The boys were spread out before the fire, their chins cupped in their hands as they hung on to Justin's every word. Belinda had already gone to bed, but she found it easy to imagine the little girl curled on Justin's lap, her thumb in her mouth as she cuddled against his chest. . . .

Where did she fit in with this charming scene, she wondered, an unexpected pain jabbing at her heart. Certainly she would make her home with them, at least until the children were safely raised, but what about afterward? Once Justin and Amelia were married and their own children began arriving, what would become of her?

Unbidden, the image of Aunt Elizabeth rose to taunt her. Was that to be her fate? Was she destined to spend her young years caring for everyone else, only to end her life alone and embittered? The realization was strangely disquieting, especially because she knew it could well happen. Her family needed her now, but when that need was gone, where was she to go?

"Amanda?" Amelia laid a gentle hand on Amanda's arm, frowning at the frozen look on her sister's face. "Is everything all right, dearest?"

"What?" Amanda gave a sudden start, a dark flush stealing across her cheeks when she realized everyone was staring at her.

"Is everything all right?" Amelia repeated. "You've been sitting there gazing off into space for the past five minutes."

"I was merely picturing Henry's court," Amanda replied quickly, feeling a slight twinge of guilt for having lied. "What a very interesting place it must have been, although I can not imagine why he was so foolish as to listen to those advisers of his. Imagine going to war over something as silly as tennis balls! How very like a man," and she cast Justin a challenging look.

"If you expect me to protest your specious reasoning, ma'am, I fear I must disappoint you," he drawled, tilting his head back against the chair as he regarded her. He knew she hadn't been giving Shakespeare a single thought, but as he didn't know what had brought that look of pain to her face, there was nothing he could do but play her game.

"Meaning?" She arched her eyebrows at him.

"Meaning, ma'am, that ultimately all reasons for going to war are declared foolish by succeeding generations. Posterity is seldom kind to warriors."

His answer shocked Amanda, as she had been expecting a lighthearted reply to her sally. She gazed at him for a long moment and then glanced uncomfortably away. "An interesting observation, Colonel, and one I should be happy to debate with you at another time. As for now, the hour is late, and 'tis time the boys were asleep. Joss, Jeremey, go to your rooms."

As expected they sent up a loud chorus of protests, which she sternly ignored. When they realized she was not to be moved, they turned to Justin.

"You won't read any more tonight, will you, Justin?" Joss asked, pausing by his chair.

"No," Justin promised, including both boys in his warm smile. "In fact, I shall mark the place where we stopped so that we might start again tomorrow evening. How's that?"

"Oh, capital, sir!" Jeremey answered, relieved. "Thank you." And they departed happily, their voices fading away as they hurried up the stairs to their rooms.

"I believe I shall also be retiring," Stephen volunteered as he rose to his feet. "Amanda, what time tomorrow do you wish to go to the farm?"

"Oh, before luncheon, I suppose" she said, laying a thoughtful finger on her lips. "Amelia has promised to take the boys out in the sleigh, so that should give us more than enough time to get the tree in the parlor before they get home."

"All right. I shall see you at breakfast, then." He nodded to both Amelia and Justin before quietly taking his leave.

"A tree?" Justin repeated, glancing at Amanda in confusion.

"An old family tradition from one of my Hessian ancestors," she explained, recalling her decision to include him in the festivities. "We cut down a small fir tree, bring it into the house, and decorate it with cookies and candles. Would you like to help?"

Justin was about to refuse when he felt Amelia's hand on his arm. "Please, Justin?" she asked, shyly raising her blue eyes to his. "The children do love it so."

"Very well," he relented, reluctant to disappoint the others. "Although I must say bringing a tree into one's house seems a rather odd sort of custom."

"No odder than hanging holly or greenery," Amanda retorted, although she was glad he had given his consent so easily. She'd been so certain at first that he was going to refuse.

"Touché." he laughed, inclining his head in acknowledgement. "But at least the holly and greenery serve a purpose. And the mistletoe," he added, his eyes flicking to the ball suspended from the doorway with a green velvet ribbon.

Amelia's cheeks flushed at this, and she scrambled hastily to her feet. "I-I beg you will excuse me, Justin," she stammered, backing away from him, "but I am tired now. Good night," and she fled as if from a fire.

176

"Good heavens, I never intended to frighten her," Justin said, staring after her with amazement. "I was merely making conversation."

"I am sure she knows that," Amanda answered, although she was equally as mystified. Amelia was modest and shy, but she was no ninnyhammer. What on earth could have come over her? She was going to be marrying Justin, for heaven's sake! How could she hope to make a good wife if the very thought of a kiss sent her into the vapors?

That very thought was occurring to Justin, and he found himself wondering if perhaps he might have made a mistake. A chaste bride was greatly to be desired, but one who shrank from intimacy was another thing altogether. He stirred uncomfortably in his chair, clearing his throat before he addressed Amanda.

"Amanda have you ever . . . er . . . that is to say, did your mother ever talk to Amelia about . . . about things?"

Had the matter not been so serious, Amanda would have laughed to see the cool, self-possessed Justin hemming and hawing like an embarrassed schoolboy. But as it was, she could only feel for his concern, and appreciate the delicacy with which he approached the subject.

"My mother had a talk with me when I was a child," she said, recalling that stilted conversation with her mother. "Daniel and I caught one of the maids with the footman, and poor mama had no choice but to explain matters to us or leave us to draw our own conclusions." She didn't add that she'd already had a fair understanding of what was what from having observed the animals in her father's stable.

"And you . . . explained things to Amelia?"

"Of course," she said simply, staring at him in surprise. "Daniel performed the same service with Stephen, and would have done the same with the twins had he lived." She shot him a mischievous smile as a sudden thought occurred to her. "I can only suppose that task will fall to you now that you are to be their guardian."

"God forbid," he muttered with considerable feeling. "I think I would rather face a crack troop of Napoleon's finest!"

"As you are so fond of Shakespeare, sir, I should like to quote him by saying *"Uneasy lies the head that wears the crown,"* or in your case, the mantle of parental responsibility. As you can see, 'tis not an easy task."

"No," he said, abruptly serious, "but you have done an excellent job of it. You are to be congratulated, Amanda. You have raised a fine family."

She flushed, embarrassed as much by his steady regard as by his soft words of praise. "Thank you," she said, lowering her eyes to the mending still lying in her lap. "It . . . it hasn't always been easy, you know. I am fortunate the children are all so loving, else I don't know how we would have fared."

"You have done a wonderful job," he repeated, his eyes catching and reflecting the red and golden glow of the fire as he leaned forward to gaze at her. "I can see your influence in Amelia and each of the other children as well. Even Daniel. He was the kind of man he was because of you, and you are to be commended."

"That . . . that is very kind of you, Justin" she said, putting down the slow warmth washing through her as modesty.

" 'Tis the truth." Justin's voice was soft. "I know we do not always see eye to eye, Amanda, but please don't think it is because I have found any fault in you. I admire and respect you very much."

"And I you." Amanda's reply was equally as soft as she raised her eyes to meet his. "Although I had reservations at the beginning, I . . . I am glad that you are marrying Amelia. She could not hope for a better, more honorable man."

Justin dipped his head in acknowledgement of her compliment, his expression growing thoughtful as he took in her appearance. She was dressed in a gown of brown merino, trimmed at the collar with ivory-colored lace, and in the glowing dance of shadow and firelight, her burnished hair shone like polished copper. Her velvet-brown eyes were deep pools of moonlight and mystery shimmering in the oval perfection of her face, and gazing into their ebony depths, he felt his senses stirring in response to her quiet beauty.

The carnal nature of his thoughts brought him abruptly to his feet. "If we are to be up early tomorrow, then perhaps it would be best if I retired now," he said, walking purposefully toward the door. "Good night, Amanda," and he left, determined to put as much distance as possible between Amanda and himself.

"I mean it, Stephen." Amanda's voice was stern as she fixed her sternest gaze on her brother's flushed cheeks. "You aren't to stir from this bed today, and that is final!"

"Don't fuss so, Mandy; it's just a little cold," the teenager protested, wiping his nose with the sleeve of his nightrobe and trying his best to look indifferent. Not an easy task considering how wretched he felt.

Amanda, however, was not swayed by his braggadocio. From the moment she'd been summoned to her brother's room by the concerned maid, she'd known she'd have her work cut out for her. But after almost losing Stephen to the influenza last spring, she wasn't about to risk his health over something as inconsequential as a tree. There had to be something she could say that would convince the wretch to stay in his rooms, she thought, tapping her foot impatiently.

"Very well, Stephen, if you are certain you are up to it," she said, as inspiration dawned. "Although I do hope you are right. It would be a shame if Colonel Stockton were made to suffer for your folly."

"Justin?" Stephen blew his nose vigorously before casting a bleary eye at his sister. "What about him?"

"You know he has only just recovered from the fever and is still quite weak," she began casually, not wishing to overplay her hand. "Catching a cold now is certain to do him no good, but if you are insistent upon going . . ." she allowed her voice to trail off meaningfully.

Stephen shifted restlessly in his bed. "Perhaps he won't catch it," he said, plucking at the crocheted spread covering him.

"Perhaps, although given the inclement weather we have been having, I shouldn't be too surprised. There is nothing like this cold, wet snow to settle a heavy cold in one's chest."

"Oh," Stephen replied quietly, his expression growing increasingly glum as he considered his options. For a gentleman of honor such as he hoped to be, there seemed to be only one course open to him. He raised his head and met his sister's gaze.

"I expect it would be better if I didn't go," he said, determined not to let his disappointment show. "It wouldn't do to infect our guest."

"Indeed, I can think of fewer actions less uncivil," Amanda agreed, pleased that Stephen had chosen to do the proper thing. "Now, I want you keep to your bed and try to get some sleep," she instructed, backing slowly toward the door. "It also wouldn't hurt you to drink some beef tea, and some of the special tisane that Mrs. Hatcher has prepared for you."

"Ugh!" Stephen's nose wrinkled in remembrance of the pungent brew. "Oh, Mandy, must I?"

"You must if you want to celebrate Christmas Eve with the family," she said, opening the door and turning around. "I will not have you infecting—oh!" She let out a startled exclamation and whirled around to stare up at the man she had just collided with. "Justin!"

"Amanda." Justin grinned down into her flushed face, noting with amusement that he had managed to startle her yet again. Did the minx never look where she was going, he wondered with a sudden flash of fond exasperation. His eyes flicked over her head to where Stephen was lying, and the laughter faded from his eyes.

"I hear you're not feeling quite the thing, old man," he said, gently setting Amanda to one side as he advanced toward the bed. "Glad to see that you're doing the sensible thing and remaining in bed. Colds can be the very devil."

Stephen preened at the words of praise from his idol. "I do feel rather muzzy-headed sir," he replied, admitting to an infirmity he had just vehemently denied.

"I can imagine." Justin nodded his head in understanding and then snapped his fingers. "Tell you what; I'll have my man mix you up a batch of the Spanish cough medicine he made for me last time I was ill. It will have you on your pins in no time at all."

"Oh, sir!" The teenaged boy looked ecstatic at the very prospect. "Thank you!"

Amanda shifted from one foot to the other. She appreciated Justin's actions in setting Stephen at ease, but was not at all certain she wanted the boy dosed with heathenish potions.

"Justin," she began, stepping closer to Stephen's side, "I don't think this is a very good—"

"Think nothing of it, my boy," Justin interrupted, wisely ignoring Amanda's protests. He clamped an arm about her waist and began dragging her backward, ignoring her futile attempts to free herself. "Happy to be of service. Now, mind that you get well, or I shall be most displeased with you." And he closed the door behind them.

Once in the hallway Amanda was able to pull free, her hands on her hips as she glared up at Justin. "*Spanish* cough medicine?" she repeated, her lips quivering as she fought back a smile.

"Cinnamon, sugar water, and just enough brandy to give it character," he answered with a low chuckle. "And you needn't look so outraged, ma'am. It's not nearly half so potent as that devil's brew the twins poured down my throat, and at least Stephen is awake and able to defend himself. Besides the medicine *will* help him."

"I know," Amanda said, as they made their way down the main staircase and into the dining room where the cook had held breakfast. She waited until they had been seated and served with steaming cups of tea before continuing, "I suppose you must think me horribly over-protective," she said, studying him over the rim of her cup, "but we nearly lost him last year, and he is still susceptible to inflammation of the chest."

Justin gave a sympathetic nod. "That is what the maid told me when she said, Stephen was ill" he said, reaching out to cover her hand with his own. "I can understand your wanting to protect him at any cost. I even understand your hinting I was some sniveling invalid who must be protected from every draft," he added, his eyes sparkling with laughter at her guilty start.

"You're not angry?" she asked, scarcely believing her good fortune.

"How could I be?" The twinkle in his light-brown eyes grew more pronounced as he continued smiling at her. "I am a soldier; I can appreciate the need for covert strategy, and you, my dear, are a master of the art. Should you ever decide to cut your delightful hair and exchange your petticoats for a uniform, I know a general or two who could make use of your rather devious turn of mind."

"Thank you, sir . . . I think," Amanda replied with a gurgle of appreciative laughter. She cocked her head to one side and regarded him through playfully narrowed eyes. "Why is it that with you I am never sure if I have been complimented . . . or insulted?"

He gave another chuckle and picked up his cup. "I am sure I don't know what you mean, ma'am. But while you are deciding, let us finish our meal. It is already grown shockingly late, and we will have to hurry if you want this tree of yours secured in the parlor by luncheon."

 *Chapter Twelve*

After a hearty breakfast of beefsteak and kippers, Amanda and Justin set off to fetch the family's tree. In honor of the occasion, the grooms harnessed Justin's team of high-stepping bays to the ancient coach, and in no time at all they were whisking across the snow-covered countryside. They hadn't travelled very far when Justin turned to Amanda, disapproval obvious in the hard set of his jaw.

"I still say we should have brought one of the maids or grooms along with us," he said his hands tightening on the reins. "It's not proper for us to go about unescorted."

"Don't be silly," she replied with a soft laugh, determined not to let his priggish notions overset her. "We are soon to be brother and sister. I don't see how even the biggest prude alive could possibly object to so innocent an outing. Besides," she added as an afterthought, "it is much too cold for the servants to be out."

Justin considered her answer for a moment, and then gave a reluctant chuckle. For some reason her reply struck him as decidedly amusing, and his dark mood vanished in a twinkling. "I see," he said sending her a wicked grin, "you hesitate exposing your staff to the elements, yet you have no such compunctions with me. What of my delicate constitution? I am only just recovered from the fever, you know."

Amanda was so shocked at his teasing banter that she could think of no reply. She stared at him, her velvet-brown eyes wide, and then she started laughing. "Wretch!" she said, giving his arm a friendly punch with her gloved fist. "You know perfectly well what I mean."

"I greatly fear that I do, hoyden," he shot back, his grin widening. "I vow, I have never met anyone so independent, or who possessed such little regard for the proprieties."

"And I have never met anyone who was so insufferably high in the instep," she replied in much the same spirit. "It is no wonder we are so often at daggers drawn."

"That is so," he agreed and was surprisingly content with the knowledge. They soon fell into a companionable silence, each enjoying the quiet beauty of the day. Although the sky was still overcast, the sun could occasionally be glimpsed, and its soft rays set the ice and snow to sparkling like diamond dust. Justin fell to daydreaming, quietly comparing this Christmas season to last year's.

He had been on the Peninsula, shivering in the mud and the rain along with his men. Victory had never seemed so distant, and he'd found himself wondering if he would ever know anything but death and war. Had anyone told him then that next Christmas would find him in England, betrothed and about to take on a huge family, he would have thought them quite mad. Yet, here he was. The realization made him shake his head in wonder at the vagaries of fate.

Amanda was also lost in memory of other Christmases. After her parents' death, she and Daniel had always picked out the tree together. Last year had been the first time she'd had to do so alone, and this year she was accompanied by Justin. How odd life could be, she mused with a sad smile, reaching up to brush back a strand of hair that the wind had blown across her face. It made her wonder what next Christmas would have in store for her.

They reached the small farm where they would be purchasing the tree in less than half an hour's time. The farm's holdings included some fine woods not enclosed by the local squire, and after paying what seemed to Amanda an exorbitant price, they began hiking through the deep snow to reach the stand of firs the taciturn farmer had indicated with a wave of his grubby hand.

"It is because you are with me," she grumbled, hitching up the voluminous folds of her heavy cloak as she floundered through a snowbank. "He would never have charged me half so much if he hadn't spotted those gold fobs of yours."

"You should have bargained with him," he answered cheerfully, his breath coming out in cloudy puffs as he shot her a teasing glance over his shoulder. "Now, stop complaining, and let us get your tree and be on our way. 'Tis damnably cold out here."

Amanda muttered a few choice words beneath her breath, her eyes resting on Justin's back with evil intent as they continued their trek. The thought of planting a snowball directly between those broad shoulderblades was almost irresistible, but she managed to control her impulses. But one of these days. . . . Her lips curled in delight at the thought.

"So this is a *tannenbaum*," Justin said, arching his eyebrows as he glanced from Amanda to the drooping fir she had selected from the other trees standing like sullen sentinels in the deep snow. "You'll forgive me if I fail to be impressed. Wouldn't it be kinder to leave the poor thing here?"

"Fie, sir, have you no imagination?" Amanda laughed, leaning forward to brush handfuls of snow from the heavily laden branches. "Only picture how it will look sparkling with decorations and blazing with the light of dozens of candles. It is a sight you'll not soon forget."

"To be sure, the spectacle of a burning bush in one's parlor is certain to leave a lasting impression," he replied wryly, trying and failing to conjure up an image to match her colorful description. "Which reminds me; just how safe is this tradition of yours? Trees and open flames would seem a dangerous mix."

"Considering my family has observed this custom for the past fifty years with but one serious incident, I am sure you need not fear for your safety," she said, shaking her head at his stolid practicality.

"One?"

"The twins."

"Ah." He nodded in understanding. "Well, now that I have been reassured . . . somewhat, I suppose we had best be at it." He took out the small hatchet the farmer had given him and waved her back. "Stand aside, ma'am, this is men's work."

Amanda gave him an indignant scowl. "What do you mean men's work?" she demanded, whirling around to face him. "I have often chopped down our trees! Surely you don't think me *that* helpless!"

He sent her a look that spoke volumes. "I think, Amanda, that you are a lady, and as a gentleman I am not about to let you exert yourself while I am here. Now, please stand aside so that I can chop down this blasted tree before we both freeze to death."

She stepped back with a loud sniff, her displeasure growing at the short work he made of cutting down the tree. Insufferable beast, she thought, her eyes flicking from his unprotected back to the snow piled at her feet. Without pausing to consider her actions, she bent and scooped up a handful of snow packing it into a tight ball. Taking careful aim she sent her missile hurtling toward her target.

Whup!

The snowball hit with unexpected force, causing Justin to stagger as he dropped the hatchet. He spun around, glancing about for his assailant, and took another snowball directly in the face. Seeing Amanda taking aim for a third shot, he hunched his shoulders and rushed toward her, a wicked grin making his intentions all too obvious.

At the sight of her victim turned aggressor, Amanda

dropped her snowball, a shriek of laughter bursting from her lips as she turned to flee. She didn't make it very far before Justin brought her down with a tackle.

"Monster!" she cried, laughing as she fought to free herself from beneath his oppressive weight. "Let me up!"

"So that you can ambush me again? I think not, ma'am," he replied, barely winded as he grinned down at her. "A soldier must guard his flank, you know."

"Well, it's no less than you deserve," Amanda informed him, still giggling. "Hinting that I am such a milk and water miss that I can't be trusted to chop down a simple tree! Now, kindly let me up; this ground is cold."

"Is it?" he asked, his tone teasing. "Perhaps that is something you should have considered before attacking me. Did you not think I would retaliate?" And he settled his weight more evenly over her, his strong thighs brushing against hers as he pressed her deeper into the snow.

Amanda's smile vanished at the intimate touch. She was suddenly aware of Justin in a way that made the blood run wild in her veins. She could smell the spicy scent of the cologne he favored and feel the warmth of his hard body seeping into hers. A strange hunger stole over her, and in that moment she wanted nothing more than to feel his mouth seeking hers in an urgent kiss. In the next moment she was struggling frantically.

"Let me up! Curse you, Justin, let me up this minute!"

Justin moved away at once, a deep flush of horror mixed with shameful desire coloring his dark cheeks. He turned away, grateful his thick greatcoat hid the physical evidence of his reaction to Amanda. My God, what sort of rutting beast was he, he wondered, fighting for control. One moment he'd been playing with Amanda as if the pair of them were no more than schoolchildren, and in a heartbeat he was lusting after her like a stag in heat.

He heard the snow crunching as Amanda rose to her feet, and he closed his eyes, steeling himself to hear her angry accusations.

"I suppose we should be on our way," Amanda said, amazed she could sound so calm when she was silently dying of anguish. "The others will be wondering what has become of us."

Justin stiffened, scarcely believing the evidence of his own ears. He would have sworn he'd seen the flash of feminine awareness in the midnight depths of Amanda's eyes, and he couldn't understand how she could be so calm now. Surely she wasn't such an innocent that she didn't know what had just passed between them, he thought, risking a quick glance at her stiff features.

"Yes, it is late," he agreed, unable to detect anything other than embarrassment on her averted face. He supposed he should be grateful it was not disgust he saw there; his actions had hardly been those of a gentleman. He bent down and picked up the five-foot tree as if it were no more than a shrub. "Let's go," he said, his deep voice husky with unslaked passion and regret.

"Excuse me, Miss Amelia," Linsley paused at the door to the schoolroom, his lined face set with worry. "I was wondering if I might have a word with you. In private," he added, casting a significant look at the younger members of the family.

Amelia glanced at once toward the twins, relieved to see them so engrossed in their Christmas project that she felt she wouldn't be risking catastrophe by leaving them unattended for a moment. Belinda was sitting quietly beside her, painstakingly stitching some handkerchiefs for presents, and she knew she could be trusted to behave. "Of course, Linsley," she said, setting her own needlework aside as she rose to her feet and followed the elderly butler out into the hallway.

"You'll forgive me for taking you away from the children," he began, all but wringing his hands, "but there is a visitor downstairs, and he refuses to leave until he has spoken with you."

Amelia's heart gave a convulsive leap. "Who-who is it?" she stammered, her cheeks paling and flushing by turns.

"Captain Maxfield." Linsley's words confirmed her deepest fear . . . and her most secret hope. "He doesn't appear to be foxed, but I have never seen him in such a state. Should I have the footmen show him out?" He cast her a worried look.

"No!" Her command was instinctive. "No," she repeated more softly. "I . . . I will see him. Please ask him to wait for me in the library."

"Very well, Miss Amelia, I will tell him at once," he said, relieved the awkward matter had been taken out of his hands. He disliked the notion of throwing out the young soldier — whom he'd known since the lad was in short pants — but neither had he wished to anger the colonel. This way, should there be any fuss, he would be innocent of any wrongdoing. Pleased with the clever way he'd managed things, he hurried off to obey Miss Amelia's instructions.

Amelia rushed into her room and changed from her comfortable day dress into one of her newer gowns of mulberry velvet, accented at the throat and cuffs with falls of cream-colored lace. She paused long enough to thread a ribbon of the same color through her thick hair, and then rushed down to where Charles was waiting.

"Amelia." He stumbled to his feet, his gray eyes devouring her as she walked hesitantly toward him. "How-how are you feeling?" And then he blushed for his foolish question.

The sight of the uncomfortable flush staining his cheeks made Amelia's heart swell with love. How much more she preferred Charles' uncertainty to Justin's wealth of self-assurance, she thought her eyes filling with tears. Charles was more like her, shy and somewhat hesitant, while Justin always seemed to know precisely what he was about. Charles would always understand her reluctance to put herself forward, but she doubted Justin ever would. She shook her head at the traitorous direction of her thoughts and settled quickly onto one of the striped chairs set before the fireplace.

"I am well, Charles, thank you," she said, praying for the strength to get through his visit without crumbling. "You have just missed Amanda. She and-and Justin have gone to fetch our tree."

"I know," Charles replied, awkwardly returning to his chair, "Linsley told me. I rather got the impression he didn't approve of my being here without your *fiancé* being present."

Amelia flinched at the inflection in his voice. "Yes, well—"

"Blast it, Amelia, how could you have done it?" He was on his feet again, his hands balled into fists as he loomed over her. "If you were in such dire financial straits, why didn't you come to me? How could you sell yourself to a-a stranger?"

"You know why!" she cried brokenly, tears streaming down her cheeks as she gazed up into his face. "Amanda told me she'd written you. . . ."

"Oh, yes, she wrote to me." Charles made a heroic effort to regain mastery over his emotions. "She told me all about Colonel Stockton's offer of a marriage of convenience and that you felt you must accept. But that still doesn't explain *why*. I thought you loved me!"

"I did! I do!" She rose to her feet, her hands held out in supplication. "Oh, Charles, don't you see? There was nothing else to be done! Daniel was dead and Aunt Elizabeth was about to evict us from our home. How could I secure my own happiness at the expense of my family's future?"

Charles turned away, mentally calling himself a brute for the tears in Amelia's beautiful eyes. He laid his arms on the oak mantlepiece, staring down into the flames with unseeing eyes. "I know, I know," he said, his voice ragged. "You are so good, so loving; you would never put your happiness before another's. It is just that I love you so much, and the thought of you as another man's wife is killing me."

"It is the same with me," she said, coming up behind him and laying a gentle hand on his arm. "But there is nothing else to be done."

"Could Amanda not marry him?" Charles didn't trust himself to turn around. "They are more of an age, anyway."

"Yes, but much too alike in temperament, I think. They are forever quarrelling."

A rueful smile relaxed the lines of anguish bracketing Charles' mouth. "Aye, I can see how that might be," he agreed softly. "Amanda can be as stubborn as the devil, and Colonel Stockton is not one to show any quarter. It would make for a most uncomfortable marriage."

"That is what she said when she cried off," Amelia said, happy that he seemed to be accepting her marriage. "She said they would never suit."

"When-when is the marriage to be?" Charles' knuckles turned white as he gripped the mantle.

"Shortly after we arrive in London," she replied with all the enthusiasm of one discussing her funeral arrangements. "Justin is handling the matter for us. He has a Special License, and says we will be married from St. George's."

"I see," Charles said, painfully accepting the reality of the situation. "Well, then, I suppose there is nothing else left to do but wish you happy."

"N-no." Tears pooled in Amelia's eyes at the realization she would most likely never see Charles again. It was abruptly too much to bear, and she knew then that she could not endure it. She had to see him, at least once more, or she would never know true happiness for the rest of her life. Gathering her meager courage in both hands, she said, "Will-will you come to Christmas dinner? You and your family?"

He gave her a startled look over his shoulder. "I hardly think that a good idea, considering," he said, swinging around to face her. "My parents know about your engagement, and—"

"Please, Charles!" she interrupted abandoning all pride as she grasped his hand in hers. "I must see you! I must! For one more Christmas at least. Please?"

Charles felt his own eyes fill with tears, and for a moment he feared disgracing himself. "Ah, my love, what you ask of me," he murmured brokenly, his hand shaking as he reached out to caress her cheek. "Very well; for Christmas dinner, then. When will you be leaving for London?"

"Two days afterward. Justin is arranging for us to all travel down together while the servants follow with our things."

"He is good to you?" The words were forced out between clenched teeth, but Charles felt he had to know.

"He is a perfect gentleman," Amelia replied with gentle honesty.

"Good." Charles gave a jerky nod. "But if he ever hurts you, Amelia I swear to heaven I shall kill him." And with that he turned and left, fearing he would loose all semblance of honor if he remained.

Smuggling the tree into the parlor was much easier than Amanda had anticipated, mostly because the twins were too busy with their Christmas project to make mischief. After instructing the maids to finish bringing down the rest of the ornaments, Amanda went up to her room to rest and change for luncheon. She'd barely closed the door behind her when Amelia rushed in, fresh tears welling in her eyes.

"Oh, Amanda, it is beyond all enduring!" she cried, and then threw herself into her sister's arms.

"Amelia, dearest, what is it?" Amanda asked, freeing herself from Amelia's stranglehold and gazing down at her with gentle concern. Had she not just peeked in on Stephen to see him sleeping quietly, she would have been fearing the worst.

"It is Charles," Amelia sobbed, laying her head on Amanda's shoulder. "He came here to see me, and—oh, Amanda!" She launched into a tearful account of the morning's events.

"I don't see how I can endure marrying Justin when I love Charles as I do," she concluded delicately blowing her nose into the handkerchief Amanda had pressed into her hands. "I was certain that I could but now . . ." and more tears flowed down her flushed cheeks.

Amanda continued patting her sister's back, murmuring comforting phrases and feeling like the most wicked sister alive. This was her fault, every bit of it, she realized with mounting unhappiness. If she had accepted Justin's offer in the first place, it need never have come to this. But it was too late now, wasn't it?

Amelia looked up to see the dark look on her sister's face and gave her another hug. "Don't worry dearest," she said, her voice hoarse from her stormy weeping. "I'll do what I must. I-I won't let everyone down, I promise."

"Hush, darling," Amanda murmured, feeling even worse a witch than ever . . . if such a thing were possible. "You must know I would never have you do anything that is abhorrent to you. If you don't want to marry Justin, then naturally we will think of something else."

"Wh-what?"

"Well, once we explain about Charles, I am sure Justin will do the gentlemanly thing and—"

"No!" Amelia interrupted. "You promised me you wouldn't tell him, remember?"

"But darling, if you are so unhappy, what other choice have we?" Amanda asked, doing her best to reason with her overwrought sister. "Justin isn't such an ogre, you know. He'd understand."

"I can't." Amelia was adamant. "Justin has already been so kind to us, I-I simply can not throw him over like that."

"But if you can not bring yourself to love Justin, surely it would be better to tell him so now," Amanda said in a final attempt to reason with Amelia. "There is more to a marriage than an exchange of vows, you know. Have you considered that?"

"You must know that I have." Amelia's cheeks grew rosy at the intimate nature of the conversation. "But I-I am determined to do my duty."

Unbidden, the memory of last night and this morning rose to taunt Amanda. Despite her chastity, she wasn't wholly ignorant of what went on in a marriage bed, and she somehow doubted that Justin would be long content with a wife who merely "did her duty." He was a man of strong passions, and he deserved a wife who would satisfy those passions wholeheartedly.

"Now I have upset you," Amelia sniffed, dabbing at her eyes. "Pray, pay me no heed. I-I will be fine. It was just the shock of seeing Charles."

"Yes, and you will be seeing him again in less than two days' time," Amanda reminded her bluntly. "Are you certain you are up to it?"

"Oh, yes," Amelia answered with another delicate sniff. "I-I must be strong, for Charles' sake, as well as mine. It will be the last time we see each other."

"Amelia—"

"No, I have already said far more than I should," Amelia said, rising to her feet and shaking out her wrinkled skirts. "Please, Amanda, say no more of this, I beg you."

"Very well, dearest." Faced with such an appeal, there was naught Amanda could do but agree. "If this is what you want. . . ."

"It is." Amelia's voice was surprisingly firm as she met her sister's troubled gaze. "Now, tell me all about the tree you and Justin picked out for us. Is it as large as the one Grandmama had the year before Mama married Mr. Blanchford?" And she firmly guided the conversation to more mundane topics.

Christmas Eve day was filled with secret excitement as each family member busied him or herself with final preparations for the big day. The twins were holed up in the schoolroom, still hard at work on their mysterious project, while Belinda laboriously wrapped the presents she had made for everyone. Even Stephen worked in his sickbed, and Amelia oversaw all with the loving patience Amanda had come to rely on.

By mid-afternoon the younger children had retired upstairs

to "rest," leaving the adults free to decorate the tree. Although he was openly skeptical at first, Justin soon entered into the spirit of the thing and his height was greatly appreciated as he set the angel on the very top of the tree. "It looks like something out of a dream," he said, stepping back to admire his handiwork. "I don't know when I have seen anything lovelier!"

"Wait until you see it with the candles all lit," Amelia said softly, giving him her shy smile. "It will make you believe in all sorts of wonderful, magical things."

"I already do," he replied with a laugh, amazed to find it was so. In the sennight since he had first come to Lawrence Hall with his sad news, it seemed his whole life had undergone some wondrous change. He had never felt happier, more at peace with himself, and he knew much of the reason for that happiness lay with his new-found family. No longer was he the odd man out; he was a viable, important member of the family, accepted for who he was rather than condemned for what he was not.

"I remember my first tree," Amanda mused, tying another cookie to a branch. "I was scarce more than five years old, and I thought it the most glorious sight in all the world. It seemed so tall and bright, and Papa lifted me up to touch the angel." Her expression grew dreamy.

Justin stared down at her, touched by the sudden vulnerability reflected in her soft mouth and wistful eyes. He was so used to seeing her face animated with laughter and challenge, and more often than not, sheer temper, that he sometimes forgot how very lovely she was. His eyes rested on her moist, delicate lips, and he was suddenly reminded of the passion he'd longed to taste there yesterday morning when they'd lain in each others arms. . . .

He turned his back with an impatient curse, furious with himself for his inability to control his thoughts. He may not love Amelia, he admitted savagely, but that didn't mean he should so dishonor her or himself with thoughts of her sister. Amanda had made it more than obvious in refusing his suit that she was completely uninterested in him as a man, and the sooner he put this inexplicable hunger from his mind, the better they would all be. But oh, God, he thought, unable to keep a sensual shiver from running through him, she had felt so sweet lying beneath him.

". . . the services," Amelia concluded, giving Justin a questioning look. "Don't you agree?"

He gave a guilty start aware she had been speaking to him. "I'm sorry, my dear," he said with an apologetic smile, "but I fear I was so lost in admiration of our tree that I wasn't attending. What did you say?"

"Only that I thought it would be better to wait until after church before we show the children the tree," Amelia repeated dutifully, not seeming to note his distracted state. "Otherwise we will never get them to sit quietly through services."

"Especially the twins," he agreed with alacrity. "The mind spins at the very thought of those two gallowsbait growing restive. But what of Stephen? Will he be well enough to join us?" Although he addressed his question to Amanda, he was careful not to look too closely at her lest she read his mind and guess the true nature of his thoughts.

"If we take care that he doesn't become chilled on the journey there and back, I see no reason why he shouldn't accompany us," she answered quietly, wondering at his glib tone. "We'll attend the early service and then come back for dinner and the tree lighting. With any luck the children should all be safely in bed no later than ten o'clock."

"Yes, and that will give Father Christmas more than enough time to be about his business," Amelia added, shooting Justin a teasing smile.

Justin took her meaning at once. "If you are expecting me to come down one of these chimneys, ma'am, I fear you are in for a long wait indeed. I have a horror of cramped, sooty places."

Amelia giggled, tossing her blond curls over her shoulder as she exchanged smiles with Amanda. "I only hope you don't

196

have an equal horror of beards, m'lord, else I fear Amanda's plans for tomorrow may go sadly astray."

"Oh?" He gave Amanda a speculative look, enjoying the lighthearted banter. "And pray, what does she mean by that?"

"Nothing." Amanda did her best to look innocent. She'd already decided that the only way she could get Justin to participate in the pageant was to spring it on him at the last minute. That way, she reasoned, he couldn't possibly refuse.

Justin wasn't fooled by her evasive answer, although he didn't pursue the matter any further. Knowing the minx as he did, he figured he'd know what was afoot soon enough. In the meanwhile, there was still the rest of the day to enjoy, and he found himself looking forward to the evening's festivities every bit as eagerly as the twins.

The coach bearing the presents and other items Justin had ordered arrived just as the family was sitting down to tea. After making sure the presents were safely hidden, he called the others into the drawing room where he began handing out boxes amidst much laughter and good-natured teasing. The twins and Stephen tore excitedly into the boxes, scattering paper about as they exclaimed over each piece of clothing. Even Belinda and Amelia joined in the fun, lifting up their new dresses and bonnets with every indication of enjoyment.

Amanda sat off to one side, a smile of pleasure lighting her face at her family's obvious happiness. It had been so long since any of them had indulged in new clothes, she thought, nodding her head in approval of Stephen's new greatcoat. Perhaps with careful savings she might be able to take them all shopping once they were in London.

"For you, ma'am." Justin was standing in front of her, holding out a box to her.

"But I didn't order anything," she said, her brows wrinkling as she took the box from him. "Mrs. Whistler must have made some kind of . . ." her voice broke off at the sight of the dress nestled in a pile of tissue paper. "Oh!" she exclaimed, holding it up for closer inspection, "it's exquisite!"

Fashioned out of shimmering chocolate-colored velvet and trimmed with almond lace, the gown was the most beautiful thing she had ever seen. The skirts were full and deeply flared, while the bodice was modestly cut in a heart-shape that Amanda knew would be flattering to her tall, slender build. She glanced up from the dress to meet Justin's eyes.

"I knew you would not buy anything for yourself," he said quietly, pleased that the modiste had followed his instructions so well, "and I wanted you to have something special."

"Justin, I-I don't know what to say," she stammered, clenching the soft material between her fingers as she quickly lowered her eyes. Part of her wanted to reject the stunning gown out of pride while the rest of her ached to accept it. Not just to preserve the family peace, she realized with a flash of insight, but because she was loathe to hurt him again.

"Say that you will accept it," Justin replied, his gaze resting on her bent head. He'd been expecting a royal battle over the gown and the other items he had bought her, and he could scarcely believe she was being so calm. "Consider it my present to you," he added by way of final persuasion.

She stroked the lustrous fabric with a shaking finger as pride and emotion warred within her. "All right," she said at last, her eyes suspiciously bright as she glanced up at him again. "Thank you, Justin. 'Tis a lovely gift."

"You are welcome," he said, a relieved smile breaking across his face. "May I hope that you will wear it tonight?"

"Oh, I'd thought to keep it for tomorrow," she answered with a slight frown. "But if you wish, I suppose I could wear it tonight as well."

Justin thought of the other gowns he'd ordered for her that the maids had already carried up to her rooms and decided that now was probably not the time to mention them. She'd learn of them soon enough, he reasoned, and to paraphrase the poets: Discretion was occasionally the better part of valor.

"It would please me very much," he said, flashing her a warm smile. "Just as it will please me to see the others all rigged out in their finery. After all" — his sherry-brown eyes took on an innocent sparkle — " 'tis Christmas Eve."

Chapter Thirteen

"You are a devil," Amanda announced some three hours later as the carriage made its way down the snowy lane toward home. "And I hope you are properly ashamed of yourself."

Justin leaned back against his seat, folding his arms beneath his greatcoat as he considered Amanda's laughing admonishment. "Indeed, ma'am?" he said, feigning innocence. "I'm sure I have no notion what you might mean."

Amanda's eyes sparkled with rueful amusement. "You know perfectly well what I mean," she retorted, grateful the others were too involved in their own conversations to pay her and Justin any mind. "*One* dress might be considered a gift, but an entire wardrobe. . . ?" She shook her head at him.

"I would scarcely call a handful of gowns and a few fripperies a wardrobe," he corrected, his smile growing more pronounced at her mock-fierce expression. "Am I to take it my small gift has somehow displeased you?"

"I am furious," she assured him, albeit with a chuckle. "But as I know you meant well, I am resolved to put the matter behind me. Besides" — she stroked the luxurious fur wrap that had been waiting in the carriage for her — "you heard the vicar's sermon; in this holiday season it is required of us to forgive each person their shortcomings."

"That is most noble of you, Miss Lawrence." He inclined his

head graciously. "Thank you."

"You are welcome." She mimicked his gesture and then turned to gaze out the window. Although it was well after nightfall, the brilliance of the fallen snow made it almost as bright as daylight, and she had no trouble picking out familiar landmarks as they rumbled past. How beautiful it was, she mused, snuggling deeper beneath her wrap, and in the light of such beauty, she found it impossible to remain angry about anything. And she *had* been angry, she thought, recalling her amazement when she'd walked into her room to find her maid unpacking a veritable mountain of boxes.

Her first reaction had been to go storming back downstairs and demand that Justin return the purchases post haste. She was about to do just that when she suddenly remembered the look on his face when he had offered her the first gown. He'd looked hopeful, she recalled, hopeful and a little frightened, as if he was afraid she would reject his present. Then she remembered her conversation with Stephen, and she knew then that no matter the price to her pride, she would accept his overwhelming gift.

Later, as she sat in her family's pew listening to the vicar talking of Christ's birth and the gifts of the Magi, she was glad she had behaved as she had. Reverend Smythe was right, she decided; Christmas was a time of joy and good fellowship, and it was past time she put aside her foolish pride. They were a family now, and she would no longer fight Justin out of simple stubbornness.

Justin sat in his corner of the carriage listening to the children's chatter half-attentively as he mulled over Amanda's behavior. He was both surprised and gratified by her good-natured acceptance of his gifts. It would have made things decidedly awkward had she refused them, and he could only be grateful she had decided to be cooperative . . . for a change. He smiled in sudden pleasure at the thought of her in some of the gowns he'd selected. The emerald satin would be particularly suitable for tomorrow morning, he mused, especially if she wore her wonderful hair down with a green velvet ribbon wending its way through her fiery curls.

"Are you feeling tired, sir?" Amelia laid a shy hand on his, shattering his thoughts. "You are rather quiet."

"No." He turned his head toward her, smiling at her question. "I was just thinking about tomorrow, that is all. I can not think of the last time I was so impatient for a day to arrive."

Amelia nodded her head in agreement. She, too, was also looking forward to the morrow, although not for the same reason as he was, of course. She'd caught a glimpse of Charles as they were leaving the church, and she trembled at the thought of seeing him again. Oh, God, she thought, her eyes suddenly misting with tears, however was she to survive the rest of her life without Charles?

"Is this your first Christmas without Daniel?" he asked, seeing the sparkle of tears in her eyes and misinterpreting their cause.

"No." She realized what he was thinking, but made no effort to correct him. "He-he sailed for the Peninsula last year shortly before the holidays. But we have you now, so it will not seem quite so lonely." And she flashed him a quick smile.

He accepted her explanation with a reassuring pat and then returned his gaze to the window. Why couldn't Amanda be as open and honest as her sister, he wondered, noting they had turned up the lane leading to the manor house. Amelia was sweet and well-behaved, and he need never wonder what she was thinking. Just the sort of bride he had always wanted . . . or so he tried telling himself.

"Oh, Justin!" Belinda's eyes were wide with awe as she gazed up at the candle-lit tree. "It's beautiful!"

"Do you really think so?" Justin asked, smiling with pleasure at the young girl's exuberant praise. In keeping with the family's tradition, as the eldest person there he'd led the youngest family member into the parlor, giving Belinda the first glimpse of the spectacular tree. Amanda had been right, he realized, stealing another glance at the *tannenbaum,* the tree was a sight he'd not soon forget.

"Oh, yes," Belinda said, tugging on Justin's hand as she guided him farther into the parlor. "It's the bestest tree I've ever seen!"

The twins soon came rushing in, adding their words of praise to Belinda's. "Not that *we* believe in that Father Christmas rot," Joss hastened to explain to Justin. "We just pretend to for Belinda's sake. Girls like that sort of thing," and he nodded his head wisely.

"Not just girls," Justin said, a dim memory stirring in his mind. "I can recall hanging my stocking by the chimney in the hopes of getting a sovereign."

"Did you get one?" Jeremey crowded closer, his eyes wide at the thought of such largesse.

"No," Justin admitted with a shrug, remembering how stealthily Edward had crept into the nursery to leave a small gift tucked in the stocking. "But I did get an orange and a whistle."

"Oh." These were the sorts of presents both boys could identify with, and they soon lost interest.

The rest of the evening was spent singing carols and enjoying the delightful repast Mrs. Hatcher had prepared for them. The children were wound up as tightly as clocks, and when Amanda sternly ordered them into bed, they set up a hue and a cry.

"But Amanda, it ain't even nine o'clock yet!" Jeremey wailed, his bottom lip thrusting forward in an angry pout. "Belinda just went up, and you know we get to stay up an hour past her. You can't send us to bed now!"

"Oh, yes she can, lad," Justin spoke before Amanda could open her mouth. "She is your commanding officer, you know, and you must obey her. I have told you this before."

"Females can't be officers," Joss said, cautiously defying his idol. "They can't even be foot soldiers!"

"I was speaking figuratively." Justin was wise to the twins now and would not be swayed. "Besides, you are usually abed at half-past eight, so she has already granted you a favor by letting you stay up late. Say your good-byes and go to bed."

"What about Henry?" Jeremey asked in a last desperate appeal. "It is just before a big battle, and you promised you would finish reading it to us."

"Later."

The twins exchanged bitter glances, knowing that when an adult said "later" in that tone of voice, it was time to stage a retreat. Dragging their heels, they said their good nights, their muttered complaints audible as they closed the door behind them.

Stephen stayed up another half hour, trying to hide his pleasure at being invited to join the adults in a glass of champagne. After taking his first swallow, he set the glass down with a sigh.

"What's wrong, lad? Don't you care for the taste?" Justin asked, noting his disappointed expression with amusement. "You'll soon grow to like it, I promise you."

"It isn't that, sir," Stephen replied with another sigh. "It's just that . . . well . . . it didn't tickle."

"Tickle?" Amanda set her own glass down and moved closer.

Stephen nodded. "I heard some of the older boys in my forum talking, and they said champagne is supposed to tickle your nose when you drink it. This didn't tickle. Maybe it's not real champagne." He picked up the glass, studying it with suspicion.

"It's real enough, Stephen," Justin said, managing not to crack so much as a smile. "And on occasion champagne bubbles do tickle one's nose, but not always. This is still excellent wine, however," and he drained the contents of his glass in a single swallow.

Stephen followed suit, his face screwing up at the sharp taste. "If you say so, Justin," he said, setting his glass back down. "But I think I shall prefer sherry."

After he had gone upstairs, the three adults set out the presents, laughing and visiting comfortably with each other. Justin seemed genuinely touched when he saw the presents the children had made for him, and Amanda was glad they had thought to include him in the celebration. She set the package of gloves she had made for him on top of the pile and was surprised when he snatched it up and began examining it like a curious child.

"Stockings?" he guessed, tipping his head to one side as if trying to make up his mind. "Or a scarf, perhaps?"

"Brat." She was laughing as she snatched it back. "You aren't supposed to peek at your presents until Christmas morning."

"Yes, but that won't be for another hour and a half," he protested, imitating Joss's pout. "Can't I have even one peek?"

"No." Amanda returned the present to the pile. "And if you persist you'll find naught but a lump of coal in your stocking!"

Justin was about to reply in kind when something caught his eye. Glancing up he saw a sprig of waxenlike berries with bright green leaves, and a slow smile spread across his face. "So, you believe in following traditions, do you," he drawled, moving to stand beside her.

"Yes," she replied warily, not trusting the gleam in his tawny-colored eyes.

"*All* of them?"

"All of them," she affirmed, albeit reluctantly. "May I ask why you seem so curious about the matter?"

In answer he simply pointed upward, and the sight of the mistletoe dangling from the main beam brought a rosy blush to her cheeks.

"He has you now, Amanda!" Amelia laughed, delighting in Amanda's discomfiture. "You must kiss him; you must!"

Amanda's color grew more pronounced. "Really, Amelia, the wretch is your fiancé; *you* kiss him!"

Amelia's blond curls danced around her shoulders as she

shook her head. "Oh, no, 'tis you he caught beneath the mistletoe," she reminded her with every indication of enjoyment. It wasn't often she saw her formidable sister so flustered, and she was determined to derive what pleasure she could from the experience.

"Traitor." Amanda turned to face Justin, who was regarding her with a maddeningly superior smirk on his face. "Oh, very well, then," she muttered ungraciously, "let's get it over with." And she steeled herself as if for a blow.

"Such enthusiasm," he murmured, eyes dancing with laughter as he drew her against him. His hands cupped her shoulders, and the jest he was about to utter withered on his lips as he gazed down into the velvet softness of her eyes. Suddenly his reasons for starting this foolish game disappeared, and he began responding to her in a way he had never intended.

As if possessed of their own will, his hands slid slowly up her neck, his thumbs supporting the gentle curve of her jaw. His fingers were nestled beneath the thick coil of her hair, and for a brief moment he wondered what it would feel like to bury his hands in the glowing, copper strands. The delicate scent of roses teased his nostrils as did the enticing warmth of her slender body held so close to his. He closed his eyes as desire, hot and sweet, threatened to overwhelm his sanity.

Amanda was lost in a maelstrom of her own emotions, trembling with a hunger she dared not name. She was burningly aware of Justin's strong masculinity and her own melting response to it. For the briefest of moments she longed for the kind of kiss no gentleman would ever give a lady—a kiss she herself could only imagine. But in the end sanity prevailed, and she stepped back from him, breaking the sensuous spell that had ensnared them both in its silken coils.

"Well, sir?" she challenged, purposefully infusing a teasing note into her tremulous voice. "What are you waiting for? I've much left to do, and I can not wait all night for you. Kiss me or kindly let me go."

Justin's hands curled into tight fists. He was aware of what she was attempting to do, and he was grateful for it. "Ever the tyrant, aren't you?" he replied with a light laugh, then bent and deposited the lightest of kisses on her cheek. "There," he said, drawing back, "and from now on, mind where you stand."

"Oh, I will," she promised fervently. "I will."

"Happy Christmas, Justin, Happy Christmas!"

The twin's voices, loud with their customary exuberance, rang in Justin's ears, bringing him rudely awake. He groaned loudly and prayed he was still dreaming. He'd just fallen asleep, he reminded himself, snuggling deeper beneath the down comforter. It couldn't possibly be morning.

"Justin aren't you *ever* getting up? It's almost eight o'clock!" He recognized Joss's insistent wail seconds before the twins landed on the bed beside him, all but knocking him onto the floor.

"Mandy says we wasn't to wake you," Jeremey continued, unconcerned that he had just violated that stern admonishment. "But you was already awake . . . wasn't you?" He bounced up and down.

"I am now," Justin said, surrendering to the inevitable as he raised one bleary eye to study the twins. The room was still quite dark and he gave them both a suspicious look. "And just how close to eight of the morning is it?" he asked, not bothering to hide a huge yawn.

"A quarter until seven," Joss supplied, struggling valiantly for a guileless expression. "But we wanted to be the first to wish you Happy Christmas, so it's not the same thing as waking you."

Six forty-five; Justin bit back an oath as he closed his eyes again. The last time he looked at the stately clock on the mantle it had been a quarter after three. No wonder he felt as if he'd only just closed his eyes! Perhaps if he offered them no encouragement, the twins would leave, he thought hopefully, inching the blankets over his head.

"Aren't you hungry?" Joss shouted, bending over to insure Justin could hear him. "Cook's got breakfast waiting."

Justin didn't bother holding back his next oath, although he did temper it somewhat. He opened his eyes and met the twins' eager looks. "You're not going to leave, are you?" he asked resignedly.

"Well" — Jeremey shifted uneasily — "Mandy did say we couldn't open the presents from you 'til you was there. And since you did give us ever so many things, it could take a long time. . . ."

"And what with the pageant for the villagers this afternoon, we really shouldn't dally," Joss concluded when Jeremey's eloquence failed him. "It wouldn't be right to open them in front of the townsfolk, you know," he added in a reproving tone.

"No, I suppose it would not." Justin was amused by the twins' mendacity, despite his exhaustion. He'd often gone on forced marches and then into battle with little or no sleep, he reminded himself as he threw back his bedcovers. Ignoring their excited chatter, he pulled on his robe and was about to ring for his valet when something stayed his hand.

"Pageant?" he asked, swinging around to face them.

Jeremey nodded. "We always have a pageant," he said in a proud tone. "It's about King Henry — the fat one and not your Henry — and about how he granted the first Lawrence title to this house." He cocked his head to one side and studied Justin. "Course you won't need so much padding as Daniel, but I think you'll make a dashed fine king."

"I will?" The reason for Amelia's jest was suddenly readily apparent.

"Oh, yes," Joss seconded his brother's words of praise. "And you're almost as old as him too; we won't need to draw wrinkles on you! Oh, this is going to be a wonderful Christmas!" And he clapped his hands in eager anticipation of the day that lay shining before him.

The exchange of presents occupied the better part of the morning, as each present had to be dutifully admired by each family member. As Amanda predicted, Stephen was delighted by his book on ballooning, although both Amanda and Justin were careful that the twins didn't get too close a look at it. The doll he had selected for Belinda was quickly set up as her "bestest doll," and he was deeply touched by the shy kiss she pressed on him, along with the packet of crudely hemmed handkerchiefs. Amelia had given him a lovely charcoal sketch of the family which he promised to have framed, and Amanda's gift of gloves was highly praised. Exhausted by all the merriment, he was about to settle back with a cup of chocolate when the twins suddenly appeared carrying a huge box between the two of them.

"For you, Justin," Jeremey said, puffing slightly as he stepped back. "We made it for you all by ourselves!"

"Yes," Joss added, preening with self-importance, "and it was all my idea!"

"Thank you, gentlemen, I am most deeply touched," Justin replied, giving the package a cautious poke. Knowing the twins, the package could contain anything from some sort of explosive device to heaven only knew what else. He glanced up and saw both Amelia and Amanda watching him with varying degrees of curiosity. "I may need help opening this," he said, directing his statement to Amanda. "Any volunteers?"

"Oh, not me." She gave him a quick smile. "I am needed in the kitchen to check on final preparations for our meal. Amelia is your fiancée; she will help you."

"Coward." Amelia gave a delighted laugh, but moved forward gracefully to kneel beside Justin's chair. The action reassured him somewhat, as he knew Amanda would never intentionally place her sister in any danger, and within a matter of moments, they had the package ripped open. He extracted the large piece of metal, with strips of leather crudely hammered to the sides, and examined it in silence.

"It's a piece of armor," Joss explained, noting Justin's perplexed expression. "And there's a sword, too," he said, diving into the box and emerging with a length of metal which he began waving about. "See?"

Justin took the crude weapon from him before he could do any harm, his fingers shaking as he turned the sword over in his hand.

"We was worried you might have to go back into battle," Jeremey said, uncertain as to the gift's reception. "When you was reading us about Henry's soldiers and their armor, we thought it might protect you. . . . Do you like it?"

Justin had to swallow twice before he could answer. "I like it very much," he said, his voice husky with the tears that burned in his eyes. "Thank you." He glanced back up at Joss. "You were right lad. This is going to be a wonderful Christmas."

As the villagers and other invited guests would be arriving in late afternoon, the family ate their holiday meal shortly before midday. They had just finished with the fish course when Linsley appeared in the doorway leading into the kitchen. "We are ready, Miss Lawrence," he intoned in his most impressive accents.

"Thank you, Linsley," she said, turning to Justin with a set smile. "When you mentioned you had studied at Oxford, my lord, I was reminded of a ceremony my father once mentioned as being part of that school's holiday tradition. When I was no more than Belinda's age we even celebrated it ourselves, and so now in honor of your visit here, we should like to observe it again. Stephen?" She glanced at the schoolboy expectantly.

The lad, resplendent in his new finery, stumbled to his feet, clutching the lapels of his first dinner jacket as he began:

Caput apri defero
Reddens laudes Domino

210

The boar's head in hand bring I.
With garlands gay and rosemary.
I pray you, all sing merrily
Qui estis in concivivio.

The last note had scarcely died when the footman appeared carrying a large silver platter on which the boar's head was displayed, a wreath of rosemary draped rakishly on its head and a lemon stuck squarely in its mouth. He solemnly carried it twice about the room before setting it down in front of Justin with a low bow.

"Oh, I say that was infamous!" Joss exclaimed, his blue eyes shining with delight. "I'm going to Oxford if that's the sort of thing one gets to do!"

"Me too," Jeremey said, then cast the boar's head an uneasy look. "Er . . . do we actually have to eat it?" he asked worriedly.

"No," Amanda assured him, although she was certain the servants would suffer from no such scruples. "We are having goose, remember?"

Justin remained silent, staring down at the platter and struggling manfully to swallow the lump that had lodged in his throat. He hadn't the heart to tell Amanda that he'd never participated in the ritual himself, although, of course, he had heard of it. The thought that she should have gone to such trouble for him was quite touching, and it was several seconds before he could trust himself to look at her.

"Thank you," he said, his eyes glowing as he gave her a smile that was not as steady as he would have liked. "I shan't ever forget this. You have all been so good to me."

The rest of the meal passed in a merry fashion as everyone joined in the festivities. The *pièce d'résistance* was the plum pudding, presented in all its flaming glory by a beaming Linsley. After devouring the traditional delicacy, the other family members rushed upstairs to slip into their costumes, leaving an uneasy Amanda alone with Justin.

"Er . . . Justin, about this afternoon's pageant" she began, nervously fingering her napkin. "There is something I've neglected to tell you."

"Oh?" he asked coolly, secretly delighted to see her squirm.

"Yes." She moistened her lips, unable to meet his gaze. " 'Tis the custom at each pageant to present a small play about how Lawrence Hall came to be in my family's possession. It was a gift from Henry the Eighth, you know."

"Was it? I had no idea."

She cringed at his polite tones, feeling like the worst hypocrite alive. Perhaps she should have said something earlier, rather than springing it on him like this, she thought, casting him a worried look from beneath her lashes. The knowing grin on his face brought her head snapping back up.

"You beast!" she exclaimed, tossing her napkin at him with a rueful laugh. "You've known all along, haven't you?"

"Not all along," he admitted, catching the napkin one-handed. "But Amelia's hint last night was rather difficult to miss, and then this morning the twins told me how happy they were that I am to play Henry. I wouldn't need nearly so much padding as Daniel, they said, nor would it prove necessary to draw wrinkles on my face as I already had them."

Amanda covered her burning cheeks with her hands. "Brothers!" she muttered in a strangled voice.

"Yes, they are a trying lot, aren't they?" Justin agreed, but if the smile on his face was any indication, it was not a situation he found displeasing.

Damn but this wig was uncomfortable, Justin thought, tugging impatiently at the stiff arrangement of horsehair and felt. And the red beard Amanda and the twins insisted he don for his part in the play was certainly the most insidious instrument of torture ever devised. He cast a quick glance about him to make sure no one was looking and then slipped into the parlor, hoping for a few moments respite from the crowds.

Much to his relief it was deserted, and he wasted no time in pulling off the offending wig. He was about to do the same with the beard when he heard the doorknob rattling behind him.

Not another damned villager offering his thanks, he thought with a sudden flash of irritation. He'd already spent the better part of the afternoon playing the congenial host, and his store of patience was at an end. Without pausing to consider his actions, he quickly secreted himself behind the faded velvet drapes, hoping that whoever it was would have the good sense to leave upon seeing the room was vacant.

"There's no one inside," he heard a familiar male voice say as the door was carefully shut. "We can talk in here."

"Oh, Charles, I really do not think this is a good idea." Justin stiffened as he recognized Amelia's hesitant tones. "What if someone should see us?"

"They won't," Charles replied, "and even if they did, what can they say? There is nothing wrong with a man taking his leave of a neighbor. Not even your haughty fiancé could object."

The haughty fiancé took seriously leave with this and was about to make his displeasure known when something stayed him. Perhaps it was the caution that had been won so hard on the battlefields, or perhaps it was vulgar curiosity, but whatever its cause, Justin was suddenly reluctant to reveal himself to the two young people. It was obvious they were unaware of his presence, and he realized that if he but waited, he would finally have the answer to the question he had posed to Amanda on their return from the village. Calling on the skills learned in combat, he forced himself to stand perfectly still, listening with increasing grimness as the little drama unfolded before him.

"I-I wish you would not call him that," Amelia said, her eyes filling with unhappy tears as she glanced away from Charles' face. "He has been so very good to us."

"I know." Charles' smile grew bitter. "He is a fine gentleman and a commendable officer, but that doesn't mean I hold the fellow in any particular esteem. How can I, when he is about to marry the woman I love?"

Amelia's heart thrilled to his words, only to break seconds later as she considered the impossibility of their situation. "Please, dearest, I would that you not speak of . . . of what can not be," she said, turning back to gaze up at him. He looked so handsome and yet so stern in his regimentals, and she knew that she would carry his image to her grave.

"Then, why did you ask me to come today?" he demanded angrily, crossing to take her into his arms. "Damn it all, Amelia, what game is it that you are playing? I thought that you loved me, but —"

"I do love you!" she interrupted, abandoning all propriety as she flung her arms around him. "And I'm playing no game. I-I had to see you one last time, even if it was only from a distance." Her fingers gently explored the planes of his face as if committing them to memory. "I needed to know that you will be all right, that-that you will be happy."

He captured her hand in his and pressed it to his lips. "Happy? Never that, my love. You are my heart, and a man can not live without his heart. Oh I shall survive," he added as her blue eyes grew wide with fear, "I shall exist, after some fashion. But I will never truly be alive again."

"Nor will I," Amelia admitted, brushing her fingers against his warm mouth. She thought there was no pain left to feel, but she was wrong. The agony she was feeling was almost unendurable, but she knew that she would endure it somehow. She had to. For her family's sake if nothing else.

"I would sell my soul to kiss you again," Charles said, his voice shaking with emotion. "But I will not. If I can not have my heart, I will have my honor." He stepped back, his hard body trembling visibly at the effort it cost him. "Come, my love. 'tis time I escorted you back. Your fiancé is certain to be looking for you."

Amelia could only stare up at him, overwhelmed by the love

that she felt. For a moment she wished Charles was not so decent, but she quickly dismissed the thought as unworthy. Charles' honor and innate goodness were two of the reasons she loved him, and she would not change a single thing about him. Making a futile attempt to wipe the tears from her cheeks, she accepted the arm he offered her.

"You are right, Charles," she said, drawing on his strength. "It is time we were going back," and she accepted his escort from the room, her blond head held high with determination.

The moment the door had shut, Justin stepped out from his hiding place. "Damn it to blazes!" he exclaimed, his eyes flashing with fury. "Just wait until I get my hands on that minx!" He stormed out of the room, a look on his face that would have sent the most battle-hardened men in his command scurrying for cover.

 *Chapter Fourteen*

Lord, would this afternoon never end, Amanda thought, forcing a polite smile to her lips as she listened to the loquacious wife of a neighbor prattling on about past Christmases. Shifting to one side, she cast a furtive glance at the clock on the mantle, noting glumly that it was barely three o'clock. That meant she would have another hour of this tedium to endure before she could begin hinting her guests home. She sighed in resignation, hiding a yawn behind the fan she had affected as part of her costume and doing her best to look attentive.

"The year after my Reginald was born, now *that* was a Christmas not to be forgotten." Mrs. Hurbert sighed gustily, pausing in her conversation long enough to pop another cream cake in her mouth. "It had been snowing since the first week of December, and the roads were so clogged with snow that I was certain Mr. Hurbert would never make it home for the holiday. He was in the Army, you know, and had just returned from fighting those tiresome Colonials. I know they style themselves Americans nowadays, but I still think—"

"A word with you, Miss Lawrence." Justin's voice cut through Mrs. Hurbert's rambling discourse seconds before his lean fingers curved about Amanda's elbow. "Now."

Amanda glanced up, startled as much by his icy voice and

bruising grip as by his appearance. He had changed out of his costume and he was wearing an evening jacket and silk breeches. It was so like the day of Daniel's memorial that she was about to make some jest, an impulse that quickly died when she saw his hard expression. Something was clearly amiss, and whatever it was, her instincts warned her that it boded ill for her. But that didn't mean she would endure him treating her like a disobedient child, she decided, surreptitiously freeing her arm from his grip.

"Of course, Justin," she replied, her sweet smile not reaching her snapping eyes. "Mrs. Hurbert, if you will pray excuse—" She got no further as Justin dragged her off with such force that the toes of her slippers barely touched the ground.

"Really, sir!" she protested, renewing her struggles to be freed. "What on earth ails you? If you think I will countenance such churlish behavior, you—"

"Silent!" he snapped, his jaw clenched with fury. "You'll have time enough later to defend yourself; but for now I want some answers, and you, madam, will provide them." He frogmarched her into the parlor he had only just vacated, shoving her none too gently into the striped chair.

"Now," he began, looming over her, his eyes almost golden with the force of his emotions, "I have asked you this once before, and I'm asking you again; but this time, I want the truth." He drew a quick breath and then fixed her in a compelling glare. "Is Amelia in love with Maxfield?"

"Really, sir," Amanda began, praying she could somehow divert him, "this is hardly a matter you ought to be discussing with me. Amelia—"

"Is she?"

She flinched at the harshness in his voice and knew she could no longer lie to him. Clutching her hands together to hide their trembling, she managed to meet his gaze. "Yes," she said quietly, "she is."

The curses that burst from his lips would have set a lesser woman to swooning, but Amanda was made of sterner stuff.

Besides, she admitted with a flash of honesty, Justin was entitled to his fury.

"Why the devil was I not told?" he demanded as he paced up and down the parlor like a caged lion. "You must know I had no idea her affections were engaged when I proposed to her."

The guilt Amanda had been experiencing for her part in the deception vanished at his cutting tone. "I wasn't aware that ordering a young lady to marry you constituted an offer in form," she said, her chin coming up defiantly as she met Justin glare for glare.

He brushed aside her challenge with an impatient wave of his hand. "Cut line, hellcat, for I haven't time to brangle with you now. Just the truth, if you please. Why was I not told?"

Amanda shrugged her shoulders, her defiance dying in the light of his determination to have the truth. "It was Amelia's decision," she answered levelly, fixing her eyes on the gaily decorated tree. "You had told her quite plainly what her duty was, and for all her flightiness, Amelia's sense of duty is quite strong. Once you offered to provide a real home for us all, there was no doubt what her answer would be."

"I also offered to provide for you, regardless," he reminded her curtly, "so kindly do not paint me as the villain of this piece. Had she refused me and given her reason why, I would have kept my word to you."

"I know that!" Amanda leapt to her feet, her hands clenching at her sides. "I made certain that is what she *would* do, given her feelings for Charles. But I hadn't reckoned on her sense of obligation . . . oh! What does it matter? What's done is done."

"Perhaps not."

She blinked at his oblique remark. "What is that supposed to mean?" she demanded, shooting him a bitter look. "And why the sudden concern for Amelia's feelings? Surely you didn't think she was in love with you? You have already made it quite plain that you don't hold with such fustian!"

"Nor do I, but that doesn't mean I would relish the thought

of my wife in love with another man," Justin answered coolly, laying his arm across the mantle and studying her through narrowed eyes. "No man who counts himself such would endure so untenable a situation."

Amanda rose immediately to her sister's defense. "If you are implying that Amelia would betray either herself or her sacred vows, then you are sadly mistaken! She would never—"

"There are many ways to be cuckolded, Amanda," Justin said, his chin coming up with pride. "I'll not have my bride lying in bed and enduring my touch while she dreams of her lover."

Amanda's cheeks darkened at such frank talk. "Perhaps that is something you should have thought of before setting out to buy a bride," she muttered, feeling sadly pressed. "The state of Amelia's heart never occurred to you before you offered, so I fail to see why it should concern you now."

"Because it does!" he shouted, completely out of patience with her. He crossed the room and pulled her out of her chair, administering a gentle shake. "My God, Amanda, do you think me such a monster that I would force Amelia—or any other woman for that matter—to marry me if I even suspected her heart had already been pledged to another?"

Despite her annoyance at being handled so summarily, Amanda could not find it in her heart to remain angry with him. "No," she said, her voice soft as she gazed into his eyes, "I know you would not. And—and I am sorry I wasn't honest with you from the start. I can see now that I was wrong."

Justin was stunned by her contrite confession. "You are?"

She nodded miserably. "I wanted to tell you, but Amelia grew hysterical at the very suggestion. She knew your honor wouldn't permit you to pay your addresses to another man's fiancée, and so she swore me to secrecy. I'm sorry."

He released her and made his way back to his post before the fire. "Well, at least 'tis not too late to right the wrong," he said, after taking a few moments to gather his thoughts. "Things might be dashed awkward for a while, but between the pair of us, I think we have the brass to rub our way through the gossip. And naturally after we are married no one will dare—"

"*What?*" Amanda stumbled to her feet, wondering if her hearing had failed her. "What are you talking about? I thought it was agreed we would not suit!"

"We haven't killed each other yet," he reminded her, feeling surprisingly lighthearted. "I think we might actually deal rather well together."

"Well, I do not!" She scowled up at him. "And what of your promise to provide for us if Amelia refused you? Have you forgotten about that?"

"Not at all. But she didn't refuse me, did she?"

Something in the silky menace of his voice set Amanda's heart to racing. "What-what do you mean by that?" she asked, slowly lowering herself to her chair.

"Merely that I am determined to do my duty by Daniel, even if it means breaking Amelia's heart by forcing her into a marriage she does not want," Justin said, his own heart pounding with trepidation. He knew he was doing the right thing; every instinct he possessed was screaming as much; but he was also well aware that if he blundered this now, it was doubtful he would get another chance. He'd gambled once on Amanda's sense of loyalty to her sister, and he had lost. If he was wrong. . . .

"But you just said you didn't want an unwilling bride," Amanda protested, a feeling of inevitability stealing over her. She knew what was coming next as surely as if the words had already been spoken, and she was pitched into a storm of conflicting emotions.

"Nor do I, but I can not see that I have any choice in the matter. To honor my obligation to Daniel, I must marry one of you, regardless of who gets hurt. If you will not marry me, then I will marry Amelia. It is your decision."

"But I don't wish to marry you either!" Amanda cried, angrily dashing the tears from her eyes. "Nor do you wish to marry me!"

Justin gave a careless shrug. "That may as be, but again I do not see that either of us has a choice. My mind is set on this course, Amanda, and I will not be deterred. Now will you marry me or must I hold Amelia to her promise?"

"You are hateful!"

"Perhaps."

"I shall never forgive you!"

"Undoubtedly." He smiled at her passionate declaration. "But this way, at least, we'll only be destroying two lives instead of four."

Amanda ignored his unwonted levity. "My family will remain with me," she insisted, knowing the die had already been cast. "I refuse to sit alone in the country rusticating while you're off in London!"

"You may have Belinda and the twins with you until it's time for them to join Stephen at Exeter," he agreed, taking care to hide his satisfaction. "That has already been arranged. And naturally once our own children are born, you'll be too busy with them to worry about . . . er. . . rusticating." He smiled at the word.

Amanda paled and then blushed. "Our ch-children?" she stammered in alarm.

The devil reappeared in his eyes. "Of course children. I thought I'd made it plain when I offered for Amelia that I intend this to be a marriage in every sense of the word. Why else would a man shackle himself to a wife, but for the begetting of heirs? Legitimate heirs, that is," he added outrageously.

"I would want to call my son Daniel." It was the only thing she could think of to say, and the moment she said it, Amanda knew she had effectively committed herself to this farce.

"Our second son you may call what you please," he agreed pleasantly, accepting her declaration for what it was. "But our first son will bear my name. Should we have a daughter I would that we name her Elizabeth Marie, after my mother. Agreed?" And he held out his hand to her.

Amanda stared down at the well-shaped limb with something akin to horror. In her mind she could already hear the prison door clanging shut behind her, and yet as he had said, what other choice was there? "Agreed," she said softly, her icy fingers closing around his warm ones.

"Good." He carried her hand to his lips for a brief salute before stepping back. "Now, all that remains is informing your family of the change in brides."

"Amelia!" Amanda gasped, clapping her hand over her mouth and regarding him with dismay. "She will know what I am doing and refuse to play along!"

"I've already thought about that," Justin said, pleased he had anticipated her objection, "and I believe I have the perfect solution."

"What is it?" She didn't trust his wolfish smile by so much as an inch.

"Well, if you and I were to be caught in a . . . shall we say, compromising situation, then she would have no choice but to acquiesce to our plans, n'cest pas?"

"Justin!" Amanda's color returned tenfold. "If you think I mean to put myself beyond the pale, then you are quite mistaken! What of the children?"

"What of them?" His rounded eyes were too innocent to be convincing. "I was thinking of letting ourselves be caught exchanging a less than innocent kiss; that is all. What were you thinking of?"

"Never mind," she muttered, wondering what she was letting herself in for by agreeing to his outlandish terms. "When?"

"When what?"

"When do you wish to be caught exchanging this less than innocent kiss?" she expounded impatiently. "It will have to be quite soon as we are to leave for London in less than two days' time. Unless you want to wait until we are there?" she added, trying to hide her horror at the thought of the gossip that would be bandied about.

"Good God, no." His heartfelt reply reassured her somewhat. "We must be firmly engaged long before we arrive."

"Well, then when?" She placed both hands on her hips and shot him an aggrieved look.

Justin grinned at her. In the Tudor-styled gown of black velvet, with her glorious hair falling across her shoulders, Amanda looked very much as he imagined Good Queen Bess might have looked: haughty, defiant, and passionate. Most decidedly passionate, he mused, his eyes resting thoughtfully on her sulky mouth. He heard a noise just outside the door and pulled her into his arms, his eyes sparkling with merriment as he gazed down into her startled eyes.

"Why, now, my sweet," he drawled, his mouth descending on hers in a burning kiss.

At the first touch of his firm lips against hers, Amanda stiffened in automatic rejection, but Justin would have none of her missish ways. His arm tightened around her narrow waist, lifting her more firmly against him as he sought to deepen the kiss.

Amanda gasped at the intimate touch, of his tongue seeking hers, innocently giving Justin the entry he wanted. She had never imagined a kiss like this, and she was helpless to resist the feelings that were rioting inside her. Her hands moved from his shoulders to slip about his neck, her fingertips revelling in the softness of his dark hair. She could feel the warmth of his body through the heavy velvet and pressed herself even closer, wanting more. Wanting something she could not put into words. . . .

"Amanda!" A startled gasp shattered the sensual haze filling Amanda's head, and she turned to find Amelia and Stephen standing in the doorway, their faces wearing identical looks of shock and disbelief.

Amanda blinked rapidly, trying to still the swift beating of her heart. "I . . . Amelia, 'tis not what you think," she began automatically, and then shot Justin a helpless look.

"We will discuss this later," Justin said, suddenly grateful for the costume's padding. "In the meanwhile, I think I can count upon your good sense not to make mention of this to any of our guests."

"B-but you were kissing her," Amelia stammered a weak protest, still staring at her sister in obvious confusion.

"I said we will discuss this later," Justin repeated, infusing his voice with steely command. He had finally regained control of his senses and was anxious to put all of this farce behind him. The sooner he severed his engagement to Amelia, the sooner he and Amanda could be wed, a circumstance he found himself anticipating with increasing hunger. If the heated kiss they had just exchanged was any indication, marriage to his little hellcat was going to prove most satisfactory. Most satisfactory indeed.

"In love?" Amelia exclaimed, her eyes flicking from Justin's controlled expression to Amanda's averted face. "But how can this be? I thought the two of you could barely tolerate each other!"

"That is what we thought too," Justin replied, giving Amanda a loving smile. "But all of that changed last night; did it not, my sweet?"

She winced at the endearment, silently wishing the floor would open up and swallow her. Justin had given her no warning of his intentions, and she was almost as shocked as Stephen and Amelia when he declared himself passionately in love with her and pleaded with Amelia to release him from their engagement. She was agreeable to their being forced into marriage, but to attempt to carry this thing off as a love match . . . whatever could the wretch have been thinking?

"Amanda, aren't you going to answer Justin's question?" Stephen's voice was surprisingly deep as he gazed solemnly at her. He had insisted upon being included in the interview, a courtesy Justin had wisely granted him.

"Er . . . yes, last night we finally recognized our true feelings for each other," she stammered shooting her "beloved" a sickly smile. "We are mad for each other."

There was an awkward silence in the room as Stephen and Amelia exchanged uneasy looks. "This is bound to cause a scandal," he said at last, shifting restlessly in his chair. "I do not like that my sisters should be made the object of unpleasant talk."

"Nor do I," Justin returned, impressed by the lad's maturity. "That is why I propose Amanda and I marry immediately upon our arrival in London. The sooner we are wed, the less damage such gossip can cause. My engagement to Amelia is not widely known, and if anyone should say anything, we can always hint that they are mistaken about the names."

There was another uncomfortable silence, and then suddenly Amelia was laughing. "I knew it!" she exclaimed leaping to her feet and rushing to her sister's side to envelop her in a fond hug. "Dearest Amanda! Did I not always say you were better suited to Justin than I?"

"So you did, my love," Amanda agreed, hating that she should deceive her sister so. Unfortunately she could see no other choice but to follow Justin's lead. As abhorrent as she found such prevaricating, it was obvious her family was delighted. She could not bear that they should ever learn the *real* reason for the sudden change of brides. Blinking back her tears, she turned her head to study Justin.

"Although I still say he is insufferably high in the instep," she added in what she hoped was a loving voice.

"And you are a shrew without equal," he answered with a wide grin, "so I would say that we are well-suited. Do you not agree, Stephen?"

"Yes, my lord," Stephen agreed with alacrity, silently relieved things had worked themselves out so nicely. He'd had visions of being forced to challenge the colonel to a duel, a rather daunting prospect for a fifteen-year-old lad who'd only shot at rabbits to date. He should have known his hero would not fail him, he thought, giving Justin an admiring look.

"Well, what is to be done now?" Amelia asked, returning to sit beside her brother. "I gather we will be leaving in two days' time as planned?"

"Actually, I thought to leave sooner; tomorrow in fact," Justin surprised them all by saying. "We will pack up just enough to see us on the journey, and the servants can see to the rest."

"But what about our neighbors?" Amanda protested, thinking of Amelia and Charles. "They already know of your engagement to Amelia. Should they not be told?"

Justin's broad shoulders moved in an elegant shrug. "Let them read about it in the *Times*," he said indifferently. "It really does not matter as we shan't be returning. But speaking of your neighbors puts me in mind of Daniel's friend . . . what was his name again?"

"M-Maxfield," Amelia replied, blushing at the mention of his name. "Charles Maxfield."

"Ah, yes." Justin nodded thoughtfully. "He is with the Twelveth Regiment, is he not?"

"Y-yes."

"I wonder if he would be agreeable to accompanying us to London. These are uncertain times, and I should welcome his escort." He gave Amelia an innocent look. "Do you think you might send him a note? I would normally write him myself, but with so much to be done, I fear I shan't have the time."

Amelia's eyes glowed at the joy it would give her to write such a missive. "I'll send it at once," she said, rising quickly to her feet. "Do you think one of the footmen might take it right away?"

"I'm sure something can be arranged," Amanda assured her quietly. At least some good would come of this, she thought, studying Amelia's ecstatic expression. She couldn't remember the last time she'd seen her sister looking so happy.

Amelia left almost at once, and Stephen, displaying his new-found maturity, soon followed. When they were alone, Amanda turned to Justin. "Neatly done, my lord," she said with a half-smile. "It never occurred to me you meant ours to be a lovematch, and I must own I was somewhat taken aback. Couldn't you have given me some inkling of what you were planning?"

" 'He travels swiftest who travels alone,' " Justin intoned, although his light brown eyes were bright with mischief. "Besides, I'd only just thought of it myself. You must admit it worked; neither of them suspect a thing."

"That is so," she admitted, wondering if she should protest the fact he was still sitting beside her on the settee. The memory of the kiss they'd exchanged earlier was uppermost in her mind, and it was all she could do not to blush like a schoolgirl.

"Are you sure you want to leave on the morrow?" she asked, shifting slightly away from him. "I don't think you understand the logistics involved in relocating a family of seven."

"It can't be any more difficult than taking an army across the Peninsula," he said, hiding his amusement at her subtle move. "If I managed that, I think I can survive a trip to London. And as I said, we'll only be taking our clothes and very little else. The servants can see to the rest of it."

Amanda considered his words and then shook her head. "I think it might be better if we kept to our original schedule," she said decisively. "Even if we're only taking our clothes, there is still much to be done. I must see to the packing, and meet with Mrs. Hatcher and—"

"Amanda" he interrupted, laying a gentle hand on her arm, "I think there is something we should make clear from the start."

"What is that?" His careful tones warned her that what he was about to say was serious, and that she was certain not to like it.

"I know you're accustomed to making all the decisions where your family is concerned, and you've done an admirable job so far. However, there can be but one commander in any enterprise, and I think for all our sakes it would be best if it is agreed that *I* am that commander. Do you not agree?"

Amanda blinked at him in surprise. "But running the

household has always been the woman's responsibility," she protested. "Surely you do not expect me to relinquish everything to you?"

"Not everything, but certainly I expect you to obey me when I make a simple request," he replied bluntly. "I have my reasons for leaving tomorrow, and all I desire in return is that you be ready. Is that too much to ask?"

Put that way, her actions did seem churlish, Amanda admitted, shooting him a resentful glare. Looking at him now she thought how easy it would be to brush aside his protests as unimportant; that is, until one saw the hardness shimmering just beneath his handsome exterior. The years of command in life or death situations had clearly left their stamp on him, and suddenly the reasons for her defiance seemed foolish.

"No," she said, glancing away from him to study the bright dance of the flames, "if that is what you want." She rose to her feet with a weary sigh and turned toward the door.

"Wait." Justin caught her hand staying her. "Where are you going?"

"To pack," she replied perplexed. "I told you, there is much left to be done."

"And I told you, let the servants see to it," he replied, using his hold on her hand to pull her down beside him. "I'm not yet done talking to you."

"Indeed?" She couldn't help but be amused at his arrogant tone. "And pray, sir, what other orders do you have for me? Do you wish to inspect the troops before we move out? Or perhaps you'd like to have us march about the house a time or two? We are, of course, yours to command."

"Brat." Justin's lips curved in a delighted smile as he reached up to brush back a lock of hair that had fallen across her cheeks. "Actually, I wanted to talk to you about London."

"What about it?" She tried not to blush at his touch.

"I told you that you and your family will be staying with my aunt, Lady Lettita Varonne," he continued, aware of the effect he was having on his bride. "She is the dowager countess of

Rayburne, and she's an absolute lioness of society. She'll be arranging your and Amelia's coming out once you have been properly introduced."

"Introduced!" Amanda exclaimed, dismayed at the thought of the expense such an undertaking would entail. "But surely there is no need for that! You-you are not in the social whirl . . . are you?" She looked at him askance, for such a possibility hadn't occurred to her.

"As a second son?" He shook his head bitterly. "No. But Edward has made it plain that he doesn't mean to marry, and with his death, either I or my son will inherit the title. Because of that I must plan ahead. I want my son—our son—to have all the advantages, and that means assuring him a proper place in society."

"I-I hadn't thought of it like that," she said, much struck by the notion of her future son. What would he look like, she wondered. Would he have Justin's dark hair and sherry-colored eyes, or would he be more like her in appearance? Perhaps he would be an interesting blend of them both. The very thought brought a warm glow to her eyes.

A son, she mused dreamily. Ever since her parents' deaths she'd put all thoughts of having her own family firmly on the shelf. She'd convinced herself that it was unimportant, that she was content with her life the way it was. But now she knew she'd only been deluding herself. She *did* want a child, very much. But not just any child, she admitted with growing awareness. She wanted Justin's child.

 *Chapter Fifteen*

They set out early the next morning with the best wishes of the staff ringing in their ears. Justin and Amanda travelled in his carriage, ably chaperoned by Stephen and Joss, while Amelia and Charles and the other children followed in the Lawrence's coach. The younger couple was now formally engaged, and a glum Jeremey predicted they'd spend the greater part of the trip "billing and cooing," as he put it.

A suspicious Joss asked if Amanda and Justin meant to behave in a similarly reprehensible fashion and Justin replied languidly, "We might lad. After all, we are engaged."

"Well, if that is what one must do, then I shall never get engaged!" Joss retorted, his nose wrinkling in distaste. He was silent a few seconds, and then he turned to Amanda. "What about you?" he demanded, his tone faintly accusing. "I never knew you liked that sort of thing."

Amanda blushed scarlet, aware of Justin's obvious amusement. "That is not the sort of question a gentleman asks a lady, Jocelyn," she informed him in her severest tones, "and I will thank you not to ask it again."

Joss grumbled beneath his breath at the reprimand, but fortunately for Amanda's equanimity, he didn't pursue the matter. They had travelled a little farther before Justin took pity and turned to face her.

"I suppose I should tell you something about where you'll be staying," he said his tone carefully neutral. "You know you'll be staying with Lady Varonne?"

"Yes," Amanda replied, grateful for the diversion. "I believe you said she is your aunt?"

"My mother's youngest sister," he answered with a nod. "She's a delightful widgeon who managed to snare an earl almost thirty years her senior. He passed away after less than twelve years of marriage leaving her a very young and very wealthy widow."

Amanda gave a start of surprise. She'd been expecting a formidable dragon with gray hair and a disapproving air, someone like Aunt Elizabeth, and since first hearing of the dowager countess she knew a stirring of hope. "How old is her ladyship?" she asked, her brown eyes sparkling with interest. "Or is that an indelicate question?"

"Doubtlessly Aunt would think so," he replied with a low chuckle. "She is quite vain about her appearance and has been known to stretch the truth a trifle. But in answer to your question, I believe her to be forty-two. I was still at Eton when she married Lord Rayburne, and he has been dead at least twelve years by my reckoning."

"And she has never remarried?" Amanda was intrigued.

"No." Justin's lips curled at the thought of his flighty aunt. "Her husband left her well-provided for, so she need not marry unless she chooses to. From what I have gathered, she rather enjoys her widowhood and the freedom that it brings."

"Has she any children?"

"A boy, thankfully. Elliott must be almost nineteen now, and the last I heard, he had been booted out of Oxford and Cambridge both. Edward delights in the scamp, although God only knows why."

"Will he be in residence?" she asked worriedly, thinking that a "scamp" was the last person she would want around the twins. Lord knew they didn't need any more encouragement to misbehave.

"I think it likely, as his mama won't spring for him to set up his own establishment. But you needn't worry," he added, his eyes flicking in Joss's direction. "It's doubtful he should want to hang about the youngsters, but to be safe, I mean to drop a discreet word of warning in his ear. As I am one of his trustees, I'm sure we may rely on him to behave."

Amanda flashed him a warm smile, grateful but not at all surprised that he had been able to read her mind. Despite the many differences between them, they were amazingly alike, a fact that boded well for their future. She would hate to spend the rest of her life trapped in constant acrimony.

The thought of their coming marriage brought a worried scowl to her face. She'd spent most of last night vacillating between fury over Justin's cool machinations, and concern about the kind of wife she would make. She'd never given society a single thought, and she was honest enough to admit that she found the prospect of a London season more than a little daunting. What did she know of the *ton*, she brooded, sinking lower in her seat. She would consider herself fortunate if she and Amelia weren't laughed right out of town for the country mice they were.

She cast Justin a surreptitious look, studying his handsome, aristocratic face with increasing unhappiness. She'd grown so accustomed to thinking of him strictly by his military title that she'd forgotten about this other aspect of his character. Although not the duke himself, he was still a lord, and his place in society would be assured. As his wife, she would be expected to partake in the social round, and she found the thought of failing him completely unacceptable. In the next moment, however, her pride came quickly to her aid.

Why should she fail? she thought, her chin coming up with renewed determination. Her blood may not be so blue as Justin's, but she was still a member of the gentry. Her family could trace its roots back to the Tudors, and more than one of her ancestors had distinguished themselves in Parliament. As for society, well, how much more different could it be than what she was used to? Admittedly London was much larger than Godstone, but she had managed quite nicely there.

Her eyes began sparkling with sudden excitement as she warmed to the thought. She'd never backed down from a single challenge in her life, and she was not about to do so now. She would take on society, she decided with a cool nod, and she would win. And if any of those high-born lords or ladies thought to make her feel like a country bumpkin, she would make them rue the day they were born. She settled back in her seat with a contented sigh, her sense of excitement increasing with each passing mile.

The journey to London took less than three days, and with the exception of the twins attempting to sneak aboard a mailcoach, it passed without incident. They arrived in London to find the city in the grips of a terrible chill, and they wasted no time in driving directly to Lady Varonne's town house. One look at the Palladian-styled mansion with its elegant columns and portico, and Amanda's heart sank to the toes of her new boots. All of the doubts and uncertainties that had been plaguing her rose up in a giant wave, and she whirled around to face Justin.

"This is all a terrible mistake," she blurted out, her cheeks paling with distress. "We can't possibly stay *here!*"

Justin, who had just handed Belinda over to a waiting footman, turned to Amanda, his eyebrows lifting in surprise. "I agree that Wimpole Street isn't exactly the heights of fashion," he said slowly, more than a little taken aback by her declaration. "But it is more than respectable, I promise you. Besides, we needn't stay here very long. Once we are married, we'll be living in my house on Hanover Square."

"I didn't mean it like that!" Amanda's cheeks now blazed with color at the very thought Justin should take her for such a snob. "I-I just meant . . ." and her voice trailed off as she sought the words to explain her trepidations.

"Well whatever you meant, it will have to wait," Justin replied brusquely, stepping forward to take her arm. "It's too damned cold out here to stand around debating the matter. Let's go." And he guided her into the house.

The next few minutes were a blur to Amanda. Amelia and the children stayed long enough to make their bows to their hostess, and then they went upstairs, leaving Amanda alone to face the countess, who was staring at her with undisguised interest.

"So you are Justin's fiancée," she said, her vague brown eyes moving over Amanda. "How odd. I thought Edward said your name was Amelia."

"Well, actually"—Amanda shot Justin a beseeching look—"Amelia is my—"

"That silly boy never gets anything right," Lady Lettita interrupted, shaking her blond head impatiently. "Ah well, at least the notice hasn't been posted in the *Times,* otherwise I shudder to think of the talk it would cause. How old are you?"

The sudden shift in conversation made Amanda blink in surprise. "I am six and twenty your ladyship, but—"

"That old? Heavens, I had no notion you were so long in the tooth! And please do call me Lady Lettita, if you will. Your ladyship sounds so *ancient*, don't you agree? Almost as bad as being referred to as a dowager. I heard that awful Lady Jersey call me that at Almacks, and I quite longed to cut her dead. But that is old Sal for you, indiscreet as an opera singer. Would you like some tea? I know I am famished."

Faced with such a flood of words, it was all Amanda could do not to laugh out loud. Justin had warned her his aunt was a widgeon, but he had neglected to tell her she was as talkative as a magpie. She sent him a reproving look before turning to the other woman.

"Tea sounds fine, Lady Lettita," she said with a warm smile. "We haven't eaten since our last stop and—"

"Is that your natural haircolor?" Lady Lettita asked, cocking her head to one side as she studied Amanda. "Of course it is, for I can see you are far too well-bred to resort to dying your hair. We were all so worried when Justin announced he was marrying. I mean, he had been abroad for so *long*, and heaven only knows what sort of foreign thing he might have foisted off on us. Of course, Edward did assure us he was marrying a perfectly respectable miss from Surrey. But then, he also told us that your name was Amelia, and that you were just nineteen. Not that I mean to be hard on him, mind. He can't help it, being a man. Well, if you are hungry, I had best be about getting you some tea. Pray make yourselves comfortable. I will be back shortly," and she walked out of the door, still talking.

There was a moment of blessed silence, and then

235

Amanda and Justin were both laughing. "My word, is she always so talkative?" Amanda asked, settling back in the cream and rose settee and spreading out the skirts of her gold velvet travelling gown.

"Always," Justin assured her, cautiously leaning back against one of the tiny gilded chairs that dotted the opulent parlor. The room had been redone since the last time he had visited, and he found the lavish rococo style to be excessive. He hastily revised his plans to have Aunt Letty assist Amanda in redecorating Dover House.

"And before you ask," he added as Amanda opened her mouth to speak, "no, she did not talk her husband to death. His lordship died quite properly of the grippe. Although"—his amber-flecked eyes took on a wicked sparkle—" 'twas said it was the tantalizing prospect of eternal peace that finally carried him off."

"Justin!" Amanda was both shocked and delighted by his outrageous remark. "What a terrible thing to say!"

"Then, why are you laughing?"

"I'm not!" she denied, her lips quivering with the effort not to smile. In the end it was more than she could endure, and she gave in to the laughter bubbling up inside her. "You are a wretch," she accused, once she had regained a modicum of control. "I think Elliott is the least of our worries where the twins are concerned."

"If you are accusing me of being an improper influence on those two, then 'tis a charge I must deny. It is they who have influenced me," Justin said, equally delighted. He was not usually given to light talk—Old Sobersides, Edward had once called him—and he found it both fascinating and provocative to sit and exchange witticisms with his future bride.

"That is so," she agreed, tilting her head back and shooting him an unconsciously challenging smile. "I seem to recall thinking what a dreadful prig you were when first we met. How nice to see that there is some hope for you yet."

Before he could reply to this interesting sally, Lady Lettita returned and soon took control of the conversation. Over the lavish tea that followed, she outlined her plans for both Amelia's and Amanda's coming out, blithely ignoring the latter's increasingly vociferous objections.

"Well, of course you will be presented at Court!" she exclaimed when Amanda finally managed to get a word in edgewise. "What else has Prinny to do, I ask you? Even his oldest flirts are cutting him dead these days."

"But we are in mourning!" Amanda protested, not for the first time. "It will not do for us to be presented at such a time."

"Naturally you are in mourning," Lady Lettita said, glowering at Amanda with marked impatience. "*Everyone* is in mourning. Those the French haven't killed off the pox has. I have already spoken to Ladies Jersey and Hertford, and they have assured me there will be no problem at all with your being presented at Court, although naturally you must not waltz. You do waltz?" Here she shot Amanda a suspicious frown.

"I do not desire that my wife should waltz," Justin interrupted, deciding the time had come to rescue his beleaguered fiancée. "And I am sure Captain Maxfield feels the same about Amelia."

"Oh, pray, Justin, don't be so horribly *gothic*," Lady Lettita retorted with a shudder. "You can not expect your wife to live in your pocket; it is simply not done in our world. Next I suppose you'll want to drape her in Quaker's robes, not showing so much as an ankle or a bit of shoulder."

"Naturally I would expect my wife to dress in a respect-

237

able fashion," Justin answered, his good humor wavering slightly. He'd forgotten how very stubborn his aunt could be beneath her pile of artfully arranged curls.

"There's a man for you," Lady Lettita turned her shoulder on Justin. "As if one could utter fashion and respectable in the same breath! But never you fret, my dear. I have arranged for you to see my modiste, and she'll soon have you up to scratch." She gave Amanda a cursory look that spoke volumes.

Amanda glanced down at her new travelling dress in bewilderment. She'd thought the garment bang up to the nines, and Lady Letitta's comment drove home how very much she had to learn. Had it been left to her, she would have politely consigned her loquacious hostess to the devil, but she was not the only one involved. She turned to Justin with a worried look.

"My lord, do you think I —" she began hesitantly, only to be interrupted by Lady Lettita.

"My heavens, child, never ask a *husband* for permission to shop! If it was up to those wretches, we poor women would be reduced to wearing rags! No, you must trust my judgement on this. Now, tomorrow we will go directly to Madame Chiennette's and throw ourselves on her tender mercies. New Year's Eve is almost upon us, and we must look sharp if you are to appear properly gowned." She turned back to Justin. "When is the wedding?"

"I'll have to talk to Edward," Justin replied, abandoning the field to his aunt. "Although I hope it will be soon. I've already arranged for a Special License."

"We'll say two weeks, then," she turned back to a wide-eyed Amanda. "Naturally I will buy your trousseau; as Justin's only female relation, 'tis my right. How fortunate your hair is red; it will look perfectly lovely streaming down your back. You will set the *ton* on its ears. Now,

238

about your sister, I know she is already betrothed, but I know the most *charming* viscount . . ," and she rattled on until Amanda's mind went quite numb.

It was almost two o'clock before Justin was able to take his leave. After promising Lady Lettita that he and Edward would return for dinner, he dragged Amanda from the parlor, insisting he needed to bid the rest of the family *adieu*. Once they were out of earshot, he turned to her with a cheeky grin.

"My apologies for abandoning you to the enemy, ma'am," he said, reaching out a tanned finger to lightly caress her cheek. "If there was any respectable way for me to remain, believe me, I would do so."

"Oh, I believe you sir . . . almost," Amanda replied, willing herself not to blush. Except for that passionate kiss on Christmas Day, he hadn't touched her in anything approaching a personal manner. Of course, the children had been in almost constant attendance, and the rigors of travel were hardly conducive for lovemaking. But still. . . . Her color deepened at the direction of her thoughts, and she shifted shyly away.

"Almost?" Justin drawled, fascinated by the rosy blush stealing across Amanda's cheeks.

"Well, I am sure I would believe you completely were it not for the relieved look in your eyes," she answered in a rallying tone, praying he hadn't noticed her discomfiture. "But you needn't think you are leaving me totally without defense. I am sure the twins will provide the necessary firepower should I have need of it."

"I'm sure they shall," he replied smiling at her quick wit. "And knowing Aunt as I do, you may rest assured that you will have need of all the . . . er . . . firepower they can muster. Now, let us go check on our troublesome brats," he said, leading her up to the nursery. "They have been out of sight for almost three hours, and I shudder to think of the mischief they may have already fallen into."

After leaving Lady Lettita's, Justin went directly to Edward's house on Grovesnor Square. The butler who took his greatcoat and hat was a relic from his father's days, and Justin politely exchanged greetings with him before going in search of his brother. He found him in his study, his dark head bent over his account books.

"Edward!" he exclaimed, moving forward unabashedly to take his brother in a fond embrace. Evidently the easy affection of the Lawrence household was having a salutary effect upon him, he decided, his lips quirking in a rueful smile as he stepped back. "It is good to see you!"

"So I gathered," Edward, Sixth Duke of Stonebridge, replied with an answering smile, his brown eyes bright with affection as he studied his younger brother's face. His slender hand trembled as he lightly touched the angry scar on Justin's cheek. "A small token from one of your Spanish ladies?"

"More like a Spanish partisan," Justin said, shrugging aside the memory of the ambush that had almost taken his eye. "But what of you? How have you been? You must tell me all." And he led Edward to one of the large chairs set before the crackling fire.

"Not much to tell, old boy," Edward said, helping himself to the contents of the cellarette with his customary indifference to custom. "Society's a dashed bore, and the House of Lords is even worse. If it weren't for my little investments, would have succumbed to the *ennui* eons ago."

"Your little investments?" Justin repeated, remembering his plans to discuss Edward's finances with him.

Oh, this and that." Edward waved his snifter of brandy,

about indifferently. "A fellow ought to have a passion, you know."

"But a rather expensive passion, don't you think?" Justin pressed, thinking of the large fortune Edward must have already lost. The money was his to do with as he pleased, of course, but Justin's more cautious nature cried out at such a waste.

"All passions are expensive, dear boy; I should have thought you already knew that." Edward gave his brother a judicious look. "And at least with my passion, I needn't worry that she will betray me, or run off with the family silver!"

"How much have you lost?" Justin decided to cut to the heart of the matter, praying he wouldn't offend Edward's sensibilities.

He needn't have feared, for Edward tilted his head back and gave a merry laugh. "No more than I can afford, little brother," he said, giving Justin a fond look. "Why? Did you think I would lose your inheritance before I was even half in my grave?"

"Edward, I never meant to imply that—"

"Oh, don't fret, Justin," Edward laughed, shaking his head at his brother's look of consternation. "I was only twigging you! Of course I wouldn't do anything so foolish as to risk your inheritance! Especially after you have nobly sacrificed yourself on the altar of matrimony," he added with a teasing grin. "I can not tell you how much I appreciate the gesture. Things were getting decidedly uncomfortable there for a while."

"What do you mean?" Justin asked, grateful Edward hadn't taken offense.

"Lady Deidre Howell." Edward grimaced slightly. "The newest reigning beauty whose comely appearance is only surpassed by her avarice. She has already gone through

241

her late husband's fortune and is said to be on the catch for another. She was stalking me like one of those great jungle cats one reads about, but thankfully news of your betrothal cooled her ardor, especially when I made it obvious that I was deeding everything over to you. Up until then, you see she was certain I would *have* to marry, if only to see to the succession." He gave Justin a cheeky wink. "She was the second person I told about your coming nuptials. Aunt was most incensed, I can tell you."

"Who was the first?" Justin smiled to think of his aunt's fury at not being apprised of the situation.

"My solicitor, Henry Teale. You did say I was to contact him for you."

"Henry Teale?" Justin frowned in confusion. "I thought Sir Alec Creshton was your solicitor."

Edward shook his head. "Old Creshton popped off last year," he said. "I was certain I wrote you about it; it was dashed amusing, you know. The old goat had sneaked his latest doxy into his house, and when he died in the . . . er . . . heat of battle one might say, the silly creature screeched the house down. Are you quite sure I didn't write you?"

"Quite sure," Justin replied firmly. "Blast it, I have been sending all my correspondence to Creshton's office. . . ."

"Oh, if that's all that's bothering you, you may relax." Edward poured more brandy into his glass. "Teale took over old Creshton's practice last August, and has been running it ever since. He's a very good solicitor too, even if he is a trifle stuffy. The two of you ought to get along quite well, though." He raised his glass in a mocking toast. "He is almost as stern in his notions as you are!"

"Thank you." Justin inclined his head coolly, although his eyes gleamed with laughter. "Have you arranged for the church?"

"Teale is seeing to it. I told him I wanted you safely leg-shackled before you changed your mind . . . again."

Justin flushed at his brother's unspoken question. "I can explain about that," he began, leaning forward intently.

"No need, old boy." Edward waved his explanation aside. "I'm such an infamous clothhead that everyone took it for granted that I made a hash of the information you sent me. Think nothing of it."

"What about Teale? He knows the truth."

"He's your solicitor," Edward reminded him with a careless shrug. "Regardless of his feelings in the matter, I think you may count upon his discretion. After all, he is a Cit, and if he was to gossip about you, then you may be very sure he would lose each and every one of those highborn clients he has been at such pains to cultivate. But enough of that prosy fellow." He set his glass down and looked at Justin expectantly. "When am I to be introduced to Amelia?"

"Amanda," Justin corrected with a quick smile. "Her name is Amanda."

"You see? I told you I can never get anything right."

"I've promised Aunt Letty we would dine with her this evening; you can meet Amanda and the rest of the family then. Unless you have other plans?"

"Nothing I can't cancel," Edward said with a negligent shrug. "Family first, don't you know. Besides, I must admit I'm most eager to make the twins' acquaintance. If even half of what you've written of them is true, then I think it may be prudent to get on their good side as quickly as I can."

At Edward's insistence, Stephen and the twins were allowed to join the adults for dinner, a circumstance that

243

wasn't at all pleasing to Lady Lettita's pimply-faced son. He spent most of the meal with his nose buried in his mama's best brandy, and Amanda wasn't the least bit disappointed when he took his leave. His departure lightened the atmosphere considerably, and her first night in London passed quite pleasantly.

All too soon it was time for Justin and Edward to leave, and while Edward was busy flirting with his aunt, Justin took Amanda to one side.

"Have you made plans for tomorrow afternoon? Will you and the children be going out?" he asked, his eyes moving over her appreciatively. She was wearing one of the gowns he'd purchased in Godstone, and he thought the gold satin dress to be particularly flattering with her coloring.

"We might, although much will depend upon the weather," she replied, doing her best to ignore his warm look. "If it is as cold out as it was today, I think we'll stay indoors."

"That will probably be wisest," he agreed with a nod. "In fact, why don't you wait until I can go with you? I know London quite well, and I should love showing it to you."

"I'm sure the others would like that very much." Amanda's heart raced at the thought of spending even more time in Justin's company. "Although I daresay the twins will be chomping at the bit to be out. They've already drawn up a formidable itinerary."

"The waxworks?"

"And Gentleman Jackson's salon, and a list of gaming hells that would put a rake to the blush," she admitted with a laugh. "Why do you ask? Is there somewhere you wish to go?"

"I thought we might visit Dover House and check on

the preparations," he ans ered, grinning at the thought of the twins turned loose in one of London's gambling dens. "I will be at my solicitor's for the better part of the morning, but we could go afterward, say after lunch?"

"That will be fine," she said, doing some swift calculations. Lady Lettita had said something about going to the modiste's but she wouldn't let that stop her. "Will you be dining with us?"

"No." He shook h1s head regretfully. "I have some other business to attend to, and I've no idea when I shall be free. Amanda?"

"Yes?" She heard the intimate note that had crept into his deep voice and cast him a curious look.

"I'm pleased the others are looking forward to my company," he said, his strong hands cupping her shoulders and drawing her slowly to him. "But what of you? Would *you* like to spend the day with me?"

She met his steady golden gaze, her heart pounding with an emotion she dared not name. "Yes," she said softly, "I would like that very much."

"Good." Justin dipped his head to brush a warm kiss against her lips. "Until tomorrow then, my love."

 *Chapter Sixteen*

The next morning dawned even colder, and both Justin and Edward were shivering as they were escorted into Mr. Teale's office. The solicitor was a tall, cadaverously thin man, whose receding hairline and watery blue eyes gave him the appearance of a country cleric. But once he began talking, there was no mistaking his profession.

"I must say I find your coming nuptials to be most troubling, m'lord; most troubling, indeed," he said, peering at Justin over the rim of his spectacles. "Am I to understand that your bride, a Miss . . ." he consulted his notes, "a Miss Lawrence is an orphan with less than three hundred pounds per anum and no bridal portion to speak of?"

"Yes," Justin's voice had an edge to it that would have warned a more astute man. "May I ask how this concerns you?"

Mr. Teale's beaklike nose twitched in annoyance. "I am your elder brother's solicitor," he reminded Justin with a sniff. "It is my duty to insure that His Grace's interests are protected."

"I fail to see how my marrying Amanda can possibly endanger Edward," Justin said coldly. The little lawyer's audacity infuriated him, and it was all he could do to answer his insinuating questions in a civil manner.

"You are the second son," Mr. Teale continued in a reproving voice, "and as such you are obliged to make an alliance that will strengthen the family's coffers, not weaken them. Miss Lawrence has neither the breeding nor the fortune to make this marriage anything other than a *mesálliance,* and I urge you to reconsider before it is too late."

Edward took one look at his brother's face and gave a light laugh. "Oh, cut line, Teale," he said, hoping to forestall the violence he saw flashing in Justin's eyes. "This is surely much ado about nothing. Let my brother marry the chit if that is his wish. And you wrong her to say she brings nothing to the marriage. She brings her whole family, and a more delightful group of assets I have yet to meet."

"Yes, three young boys who will require schooling, and two girls to be provided with dowries," Mr. Teale said, his lips pursing with disapproval. "You may call them "assets," Your Grace, but I can not. There is the succession to be thought of—"

Justin surged to his feet, his patience at an end. "What you choose to call my *family* is of little interest to me," he snarled with deadly fury. "I sent you a list of instructions, Teale, and all I require from you is that you carry them out. Should that prove too difficult, there are other lawyers in London."

Mr. Teale's pallid face grew red with angry embarrassment. He picked up another pile of papers and began leafing through them. "In regards to your country house, I have written your manager, and he assures me all is in readiness," he said, not raising his eyes from the document. "Also, you are now the fifth Viscount Marston, and in addition to the property mentioned above, you have several holdings in Kent. Your annual income from these properties is slightly over ten thousand pounds. Not a large amount, but more than enough to keep you in style."

"And the church?" Justin had returned to his chair, but he

was still far from mollified.

"As you mentioned no specific date in your first letter, I have been unable to secure St. George's," Mr. Teale replied in prim tones. "Might I suggest one of the other churches? St. Michael's is quite lovely and better suited for . . ." he paused delicately, "smaller weddings."

"St. George's," Justin answered in a voice of steely command. "All my ancestors were married there, and I don't mean to be the exception. As for the date, the afternoon of January tenth will be fine. See to it."

"But, my lord, that gives me less than a fortnight! You can not expect me to—"

"See to it," Justin repeated, pleased to see the other man so discomfitted. "As I have already said, you are not the only lawyer in London. Unless you wish to seek one out, you will do as you are instructed. Am I understood?"

Henry Teale's face darkened. "You are understood," he said tonelessly.

Justin and Edward quickly departed, and once they were in their coach, Justin confronted his brother. "How the devil can you stomach that sanctimonious little worm?" he demanded furiously. "I vow, I came that close to snapping his scrawny neck!"

"So I noticed," Edward replied, unperturbed by Justin's show of temper. "But I did warn you he was rather nice in his notions."

"He's an insufferable prig, and I've half a notion to take my trade elsewhere!" Justin snapped, hunching his shoulders against the cold. "How dare he presume to pass judgement on Amanda?" He was silent for a few moments, and then cast Edward a worried look as a sudden thought occurred to him. "You don't agree with him, do you?"

"Me?" Edward gave a soft chuckle. "Good God, no. I have said that I approve of your choice, and I am dashed grateful for it. Since your engagement was announced, the matchmaking mamas have washed their hands of me."

Justin knew Edward was attempting to divert him, and he was oddly touched. He pushed aside his anger with the solicitor and shot Edward a teasing grin. "Really? And what of your avaricious widow? Has she also washed her hands of you?"

"Yes, may God be praised," Edward intoned piously. "And speaking of Lady Deidre, you will have the dubious honor of making her acquaintance. She and Aunt are bosom beaus and she will be attending the party."

"Will she?" Justin asked, not really interested. Instead he was thinking of Amanda and wondering what she would be wearing. He hoped it would be the dress she'd worn Christmas night. The deep green velvet made her hair glow like burnished copper, and the memory of the kiss they had shared that night made his heart race with excitement. He'd been delighted, to discover that her passion was every bit as strong as her temper, and his body grew heavy in anticipation of his wedding night.

Teale was a bloodless fool, he decided turning his head to study the slow stream of carriages flowing past them. A blind man could see Amanda was the perfect bride for him. They were well-matched in every way, and he could not wait to claim her as his wife.

If Amanda thought the bitter cold would discourage Lady Lettita from dragging her to the dressmaker's, she was soon disappointed. The countess simply sent her carriage for the plump little modiste, and Amanda spent the better part of the morning standing in resigned silence as the two women squabbled over each piece of fabric that was pinned to her.

"No, no, no, not this insipid blue," Lady Lettita snapped, tossing the square of satin to the ground. "My niece is an original, and that is how she must be dressed! Look at her coloring; only the most brilliant shades of green and turquoise will do."

249

"But I am in mourning," Amanda protested, although she doubted it would do much good. Her hostess had already made her opinion of the subject quite obvious.

"Mourning?" The dressmaker looked up with interest.

"My brother," Amanda explained, grateful that someone had some respect for the departed. "He fell in battle some months ago and—"

The little woman broke into a spate of incomprehensible French, flinging swatches of fabric about the room until she pulled out a piece of shimmering black silk. *"Viola!"* she exclaimed, holding the material up to Amanda's face. "She will wear only black, *comprehende?* Black and white; so simple and yet so chic. And we will dress her hair so." She pulled Amanda's hair down from its stern arrangement, gathering up a fistful of copper-colored curls and holding it to one side. "With a single rose nestled at her crown, hmm? She will be—how do you say—a diamond of the first water."

"Madame, Lady Lettita, this is all very interesting, but I—"

"No, not a diamond," Lady Lettita interrupted, ignoring Amanda's indignant protest, "a pearl. A rare and perfect pearl. The Stonebridge family has an extensive collection of pearls, and she has the perfect coloring to carry them off. Do you not agree, madame?"

"Really, your ladyship, I must protest," Amanda said in her sternest voice. "I appreciate your kindness, but I have no need of a new wardrobe. Furthermore, I refuse to be talked about as if I had no more sense than a chair!"

"Your ladyship is quite right; I shall begin my work at once," Madame Chiennette said, taking her cue from the countess. She saw no reason why she should pay any attention to the younger lady's complaints, especially when it was likely to cost her a generous bonus.

"I suppose it's too much to expect a gown to be made up by the morrow." Lady Lettita sighed, giving the other woman a meaningful look. "Although I'm sure Miss Lawrence's brother-in-law the Duke of Stonebridge, would be most grateful. . . ."

The thought of such largesse was enough to insure anything. There were several customers who were behind on their bills, and as far as Madame was concerned, they could wait. "The impossible is my specialty, m'lady," the dressmaker announced with Gallic flare. "I shall have a selection of gowns made up *toute suite*. You have my word on it."

After the dressmaker departed, Amanda turned on her hostess, her eyes gleaming with a martial light. It was not her nature to be so docile, and she decided the time had come to set down her foot. "Lady Lettita," she began, choosing her words carefully, "it is very kind of you to trouble yourself with this—"

"Heavens, child, you needn't thank me," Lady Lettita gave her hand a fond pat. "It is my pleasure, I assure you. You're going to be my niece, and unless that dolt Edward takes a bride, which, my dear, I sincerely doubt, then you will be the next duchess of Stonebridge. Naturally I wish to see that you do the rank proud."

Amanda's angry protestations died on her lips. The duchess of Stonebridge, she thought, a feeling of sick horror washing over her. Justin had said he would be inheriting the title upon Edward's death, but until this very moment, she never thought of what that would mean to her. She would be a duchess, she realized dully, a lady of high rank and fashion, and the very notion chilled her to the marrow of her bones.

"Well, why are you just standing there?" Lady Lettita glared at her. "We have much left to do, and no time for dawdling! Now, don't tell Justin, but there is a dancing master I know, a most delightful Comte, and there is no one like him for teaching ladies to waltz. Perhaps we might arrange something. . . ," and she guided a silent Amanda from the room, plans and talk spilling from her in gay abandon.

Justin arrived just as the family was finishing luncheon. The twins waylaid him at the door, and after promising to take them out the moment the weather improved, he and Amanda set out for Hanover Square.

"How was your morning?" he asked, tucking the fur robe securely about her. "I gather you and Aunt were unable to visit the modiste?"

"Not precisely," Amanda replied with a sulky pout and went on to tell him of the morning's events, including an indignant description of the wardrobe the countess had selected for her.

"It's not that funny!" she exclaimed when he threw back his head in laughter. "I doubt you'd think it so amusing if you had to go about looking like a chess set, and that is precisely what will happen if those two have their way!"

"I am sorry," Justin apologized, still chuckling. "It is just that I am having a hard time envisioning you standing there in docile silence while Aunt ordered you about. God knows I have never had any success at it." He cast her a teasing look.

"That is because you're always so quick to take up the cudgels," she grumbled, ignoring his provocative challenge. "Lady Varonne doesn't argue. She simply keeps talking until the other person either gives in or runs screaming from the room."

"Ah, so that is her secret," Justin said, nodding his head thoughtfully. "I must remember that. In the meanwhile, humor her. Once we're married you can order up more gowns."

Amanda turned to gaze at him in dismay. "But what of the expense?" she cried, her frugal nature decrying such extravagance. "She must have ordered a dozen new gowns! And what of the dresses you bought me in Godstone? I haven't worn even a third of them!"

"Save them. They'll do nicely when we visit the country." Justin dismissed the matter with an indifferent shrug. "You can order whatever you like; I can afford it."

Amanda said nothing, falling into a troubled silence as she turned to gaze out the window. For the second time that day, she was reminded of how drastically her life would change once she and Justin were married. She'd spent the greater portion of her life mired in genteel poverty, and the thought of unlimited wealth was intimidating. How could she ever hope to be the sophisticated sort of wife Justin would require?

Justin was also troubled with thoughts of the future. After dropping Edward at his bank, he'd gone to Whitehall to visit an old friend who was now posted with the Foreign Office. George had been delighted to see him and over a glass of brandy, they discussed the course of the war. At the end of the discussion, George surprised him by offering to put his name in for a new command. A few short weeks ago he'd have accepted the offer and its accompanying promotion without hesitation, but things were different now. The thought depressed him even as it pleased him.

Dover House sat just off Hanover Square, its mullioned windows gleaming dully in the gray winter sunlight. Its exterior was lovely but unpretentious, and it in no way prepared Amanda for what lay inside.

"Justin, it is beautiful!" she gasped, her eyes growing wide as she gazed about the marbled foyer. "I've never seen anything half so elegant!"

"It is lovely," he agreed quietly, more entranced by the wonder on Amanda's face than by the opulence of his surroundings. "I'm glad that you approve."

"How could I not," she murmured, her eyes going from the Chippendale table, to the gilded mirror, to the crystal chandelier hanging above them. A beautifully carved staircase wended its way to the upper floors and Amanda's heart sank as she recognized Adam's impeccable work. She was to mistress of all this?

With the butler and housekeeper in attendance, they set

out to tour their new home. Away from the foyer, the house's appearance changed drastically, and Justin's displeasure grew at the signs of neglect that were so clearly evident. He'd been in the house several times as a young man, and he was furious that his elderly cousin had allowed the house to deteriorate to such a state. His critical eye noted where several *object d' art* had been removed, and where the expensive carpets he remembered had been replaced by shabby thread-bare rugs.

Amanda also noted the house's state but rather than being dismayed, she was secretly relieved. This was something she could do something about, and her spirits lightened as she made mental notes of the repairs she would make. They paused in one of the rooms that had been used as a study, and the general neglect in evidence made Justin's lips tighten in annoyance.

"I'm afraid the old gentleman was a bit odd in his last years," Mrs. Landsbury, the housekeeper, apologized, wringing her hands nervously. "He'd not let any of the maids in here, and after he died, things were so confused we didn't know what to keep and what to toss away. His Grace said to shut it up and leave it be."

Justin ran a finger over a pile of dusty papers. "How nice to see that you followed his instructions so thoroughly," he said, wiping his hand on his handkerchief. "Are the other rooms this bad?"

The butler and housekeeper exchanged uneasy looks. "Most of the upper floor, I fear," the butler, Tavers, replied, bravely facing Justin. "The roof has several holes in it, and there has been a great deal of water damage. Also, it has been many years since the chimneys were last cleaned and most of the fireplaces are all but useless they smoke so badly."

Justin bit back an angry curse. He'd been expecting some dust and the like, but never anything like this. He cast a resentful look about the room. How the devil could he bring

254

his family to this—this hovel?

"What about the bedrooms?" Amanda asked, ignoring Justin's black temper. "Are they habitable?"

"Oh, yes, miss," Mrs. Landsbury turned to her gratefully. "The master suite will be fine with a bit of cleaning, and the other rooms are only a little damp. It's the top floor that is so bad."

"Where have you and the other servants been sleeping?"

"The east wing, Miss Lawrence," Tavers answered her question. "And as to servants, I fear there are only six of us. After Sir Gillian's death, Mr. Teale, the solicitor, had me turn the others off. He said 'twas wasteful to keep them on."

"Well, perhaps it will be for the best," Amanda said, noting Justin's narrowing eyes with annoyance. "I'll be bringing several of my own servants up from the country, and we'll need to find positions for them all. In the meanwhile, you might want to hire some temporary staff to help you set the house to rights. I'm not sure when we'll be moving in, but—"

"January tenth," Justin interrupted, deciding it was time to reassert his control of the situation. "At least, that is when we shall be marrying. Since we won't be taking a bridal journey, we'll doubtlessly come directly here following the ceremony."

Amanda paled, then flushed deeply. This was the first she'd heard that a definite date for the wedding had been set. "January tenth?" she repeated, turning to him with raised eyebrows.

"If that meets with your approval," he muttered, the tips of his ears going red. He hadn't meant to blurt out the news in quite so tactless a manner.

"That will be fine," she answered, seeing no polite way she could object. How very like Justin to arrange all and then casually inform her of his plans, she thought with a rueful shake of her head. She supposed she should protest such high-handed behavior, but it would doubtlessly be a waste of time. And if they were to move into the house in a little over a sennight, there wasn't a moment to be wasted.

"Why don't you show us the bedrooms, Mrs. Landsbury?" she asked, giving the housekeeper a polite smile. "We'll only be needing three, perhaps four rooms, and you needn't worry that they be grand. We're not particular, I promise you."

They spent the next hour examining the bedrooms and suites that occupied the second floor. As Tavers had warned him, there was a great deal of water damage, and Justin pronounced several of the rooms unacceptable. In the end they had selected four rooms for the children and a large suite for their own use. That done, they returned to the parlor for tea.

"I'm sorry, Amanda," Justin said the moment they were alone. "I had no idea things were so bad! Edward wrote me that the house would require repairs, but. . . ." He shrugged helplessly and flung himself on the faded Sheraton chair.

"It doesn't signify," Amanda replied, handing him his cup of tea. "The house is quite lovely, and I'm sure it will be fine with a bit of work. Besides"—her lips quirked in a rueful smile—"it's no worse than what we are used to at home."

"Perhaps, but at least at Lawrence Hall you had a decent roof over your head," he grumbled, refusing to be mollified. If he accepted George's offer, then he'd be leaving England in a little over a month, and he disliked the notion of leaving Amanda to cope with all the repairs alone. There was the house in the country, of course, but still . . . .

"That's because it never rained while you were there," she told him with a reminiscent laugh. "Believe me, there are times when it is wetter inside than out!"

Justin gave an unintelligible grunt. One of the reasons he admired Amanda was because of her quick mind, to say nothing of the brave way she coped with adversity. Perhaps it wouldn't be so bad after all, he brooded, taking a thoughtful sip of tea. At least now she wouldn't need to worry about money. He would take care to see that she was well provided for.

Amanda was aware of Justin's distracted state, and it troubled her. He could be pompous at times, and even a bit of a prig, but she'd never seen him act as petulantly as he had while touring the house. He'd behaved just like one of the twins when denied their way, and she wondered if he was beginning to have second thoughts. The realization was almost too painful to be borne.

"Amanda," Justin began, deciding it was time to make a clean breast of it, "there is something I need to discuss with you. Something that will affect both our futures."

"I . . . I see," she said, her heart clenching with unexpected pain. Her teacup rattled in her hand and she set it down. She had been expecting this from the moment he'd made his altruistic offer. Now there was naught she could do but sit stoically and listen to him sever the tenuous ties that bound them. "Go on."

Justin cleared his throat nervously. "As you know, Napoleon is all but finished on the continent," he said, unable to meet her dark gaze. "We drove him from Spain, and now his own people have demanded his abdication. One might think our job is done, but in truth, it is only just beginning."

Amanda hid her surprise. Whatever she'd been expecting, it wasn't a political discussion. "Really?" she managed weakly, wondering what he was hinting at. "Why is that?"

"Napoleon has left chaos in his wake," he said recalling George's persuasive arguments, "and the governments he helped overthrow will require a great deal of aid in restoring their countries. England . . . all the allies are most desirous to see that this is done with as little bloodshed as possible."

"Well, thank heavens for that," Amanda said, thinking of Daniel and the thousands of other young lives sacrificed to Napoleon's insane thirst for power.

"Yes." Justin was grateful she was taking the news so well.

"At any rate, our government wishes to see that the transition of power is accomplished quickly, and to that end they are sending men to those countries to assist the leaders. Men who have some knowledge of the land, its people and its customs."

"That makes sense."

"I have been offered such a post."

It took a few seconds for his stark declaration to sink in, and when it did, Amanda could only stare at him in confusion. "I beg your pardon?"

"I have been offered such a post," he repeated frowning at her puzzled look. "I spoke with an old friend of mine, Lord George Bramwell, and he seems to think I would make an excellent liaison between London and Madrid. I speak the language fluently, and I know many of the most influential families. He says he is certain he can have me appointed as the provost marshal of the area, and—"

"You're going to be a diplomat?" Amanda demanded, torn between shock and relief. She had braced herself to hear his plea for freedom, but this was something else entirely.

"Good God, no," he said quickly. "The post would be a military one. I would be in charge of the occupying forces and help oversee the orderly transition of power. Things are rather sticky in Spain just now, and a strong military presence is needed to keep the peace. As I am experienced in dealing with the Spanish, I am the most logical choice, and George thinks I should receive the appointment with little or no trouble."

Amanda sat back in her chair. "But-but what of us? Our marriage?" she asked weakly. "Unless I will be accompanying you?" She gave him an uncertain look.

He shook his head decisively. "No. As I said, things are somewhat uncertain in Spain, and I won't put you in danger. There is no reason why this should change our wedding plans. Even if I am offered the post, I should only be gone a few months—a year at the most. Once I have completed my mission, we can retire to the countryside."

Amanda's shock was slowly giving way to fury. "Don't you think you might have consulted me before accepting this post?" she asked, her hands clenching tightly in her lap. "You must admit this changes things between us."

Justin's brows snapped together in a formidable frown. He was unused to having his every command questioned, and he found her obstinacy infuriating. "I don't see how," he answered in his coldest tones. "Our reasons for marrying remain the same. You need help in caring for your family, and I have need of a wife to insure the succession. What has my accepting a post to Spain to do with all of that?"

"Only that I should think it rather hard for you to insure anything when you will be hundreds of miles away!" Amanda retorted, her fury overcoming her modesty. "How can we be a true man and wife if you mean to be gone half the time?"

"Is that all that worries you?" He gave her a look that made her burn with something other than anger. "You need have no fears on that score, my sweet. After all, we'll have almost a month together before I shall be leaving."

Amanda blushed scarlet with mortification. "You have a rather high opinion of yourself, sir!" she said, feeling decidedly harassed.

"Perhaps," he drawled, his eyes dancing with mischief as he smiled at her. "But I shall leave it to you to decide if that opinion is warranted. On the morning after our marriage, you must let me know if I have lived up to your expectations."

"Oh! You are insufferable!" Amanda exclaimed, stumbling to her feet. "You are no gentleman to say such things to me!"

Justin also rose, his amusement vanishing at the flare of temper he saw in her eyes. "I may be no gentleman," he answered, his voice deliberately provocative, "but I will be

your husband. That much hasn't changed. You are my fiancée, Amanda, and within the sennight you will be my
wife. Whether circumstances force us to live together or
apart, I expect you to honor the bargain we have struck. For
better or worse, we are bound together. Remember that."

 *Chapter Seventeen*

The next evening Amanda stood before her mirror, turning this way and that as she studied her reflection. "Are you quite certain this gown will do?" she asked Amelia as she ran a nervous hand down the front of the bodice. "You don't think it too daring?"

The gown had been delivered that afternoon, a note from Madame Chiennette pinned to the box. Fashioned out of the sheerest black silk Amanda had ever seen, the simply cut gown was completely unadorned except for the white satin rosettes scattered across the filmy skirts. The daring neckline left her shoulders and arms bare, exposing the soft swell of her breasts to what seemed a shocking degree.

"Oh, no," Amelia said in answer to her question. "I think it most stylish, and I love your hair! That rose is just the thing to set off your hair and eyes."

Amanda touched the black silk rose the maid had spent a full hour pinning into place. Her hair had been gathered to one side in an artful swirl, with only a few curls escaping to trail down her neck. It wasn't quite the elegant coiffure Madame had envisioned, but it was far more flattering than her usual chignon.

"I suppose you're right," she said at last, deciding she'd

fussed over her appearance long enough. Turning from the mirror, she smiled at her sister. "You're certainly looking lovely, darling. Is that one of the gowns Justin bought you?"

"Yes," Amelia fingered the celestial-blue silk, her expression growing dreamy. "Do you think Charles will like it?"

"He'll love it as he loves you," Amanda assured her, giving the modest gown with its heart-shaped bodice and belled skirts an approving look. "Now I suppose it's time we checked on the twins. I only hope they haven't tied their bedsheets together and slipped out the window. You know how unhappy they were not to be included in the festivities."

"It would have been difficult to miss," Amelia replied, smiling as she remembered the dust her brothers had kicked up upon being informed they wouldn't be allowed at the party.

They found the twins languishing in their room, their faces wearing expressions of such mistreatment that it was all Amanda could do not to burst out laughing.

"Are you *quite* certain we can't come?" Jeremey asked, hoping his sister had experienced a change of heart. "We will be ever so good."

"We'll even let the old ladies pinch our cheeks and call us their darling boys," Joss offered, prepared to make the ultimate sacrifice.

"That is very noble of you." Amanda's lips quivered as she held back a smile. "But as I've explained, this is Lady Rayburne's house, and it is her right to invite whomever she pleases. And no sulking, or I won't let you join us when Justin takes us out to see the sights," she added, raising an admonishing finger when she saw two bottom lips thrusting out.

The pouts disappeared as if by magic. "Do you think he'll take us to see the catch-me-who-can?" Joss asked, his tone so diffident as to be automatically suspect.

"And the Frost Fair?" Jeremey added hopefully. "You needn't buy us anything; we just want to look."

"Oh, very well, you shameless beggars," Amanda capitulated with a laugh. "But first you must ask Justin. If he is agreeable, then I have no objection."

"It'll be all right, then," Joss said with smug satisfaction. "He's a man. He understands how it is with us."

"I don't know about you," Amanda said as she and Amelia made their way down the stairs, "but I have the strongest suspicion we have been properly gulled."

"I fear you're right," Amelia agreed, and then gave a shiver of anticipation. "Oh, Amanda, aren't you excited? Our very first London ball! I vow, I am all a-tremble!"

"They are only people, Amelia." Amanda firmly suppressed her own anxieties. This would be her first introduction to Justin's world, and for a moment it was all she could do not to pick up her skirts and scamper back to the safety of her room. Then she remembered what Justin said about giving their son a place in the Fashionable World. What sort of place would he have with a mother who couldn't even face thirty or forty people without trembling like the greenest girl?

"Come, Amelia," she said, lifting her chin with determination, "let us go and greet our guests." And she swept down the stairs before her courage could desert her.

"Ah, here's your little bride now," Lady Lettita said, cutting into Justin's conversation with her usual disregard for polite behavior. "How very lovely she looks."

Justin, who had been enjoying a reunion with an old comrade-in-arms, glanced casually over his shoulders, his eyes going wide at the sight of Amanda. Compared to the other ladies present, he knew she couldn't be termed a beauty, but that was something a man could easily forget when he saw her glorious hair curling about her creamy shoulders. That those shoulders were bared by the daring cut of her gown hadn't escaped his notice, and his jaw hardened with possessive fury.

Amanda spied Justin the moment she and Amelia entered the crowded drawing room. He was standing by the fireplace, deep in conversation with a gray-haired man whose proud carriage and tragically empty sleeve was mute evidence of his profession. For a moment she was unable to resist the opportunity of studying Justin, and a soft smile touched her lips as she admired his handsome form.

It was the first time she had seen him in the strict formal wear demanded in London, and the sight of his broad shoulders straining against the black velvet of his jacket made her heart race in admiration. His cravat was tied in a simple but stylish arrangement, and his hair was brushed back from his tanned forehead, adding to the aura of masculinity that radiated from him. She thought he was by far the most attractive man in the room, and she knew an oddly feminine sense of satisfaction that he was her fiancé.

"Hello, my dears!" Lady Lettita trilled as the girls joined them. She gave them both an airy kiss above their cheeks before drawing back to smile at Amelia. "You look like a veritable angel, my dear," she told the younger girl. "Your fiancé—and really, dearest, I had no idea he was so handsome—is right over there talking to Lord Greenton. *Listening* to him, actually, for he is the most infamous gabbler. Do you go and fetch him; I'm sure he will thank you for it."

After Amelia went to rescue Charles, the countess turned her attention to Amanda. "And you, my sweet, are simply exquisite. I must remember to send Madame a note, thanking her for her Herculean efforts on our behalf. I vow, one could hear the masculine hearts shattering as you walked past. Isn't that so, Justin?"

"I wouldn't know, ma'am," Justin said, taking Amanda's hand in his and carrying it to his lips. "I was too busy listening to my own heart break. You look beautiful, my love."

"Thank you, sir," she returned, her cheeks warming at the look in his eyes. To cover her embarrassment, she turned to the older man standing quietly to one side. Justin was quick to take the hint and performed the necessary introductions.

"Allow me to make you known to an old friend, Sir Everett Howard, my first commander on the Peninsula. Sir Howard my fiancèe, Miss Amanda Lawrence."

"Miss Lawrence." The old soldier bowed over her hand, his dark eyes studying her with approval. "It is a pleasure to meet you. Stockton is demmed lucky to have found such a charming bride."

Amanda blushed with pretty pleasure and stammered a reply. Lady Lettita, never one to let a moment of silence slip into a conversation, began pointing out her guests to Amanda, revealing their vices and virtues with happy indiscretion. The dinner bell finally sounded, and she turned to Justin, holding out her arm to him commandingly.

"Come, Colonel, you may escort me into the dining room. That scapegrace brother of yours is late as usual, so you may have the honor. No dawdling, now, I am sure we are all famished!"

As guest of honor, Justin sat at Lady Lettita's left, while Amanda was seated directly across from him at the countess's right. Any hopes he'd had of exchanging more than a few words with her were quickly dashed when his dinner partner, a stunning brunette with eyes the color of costly emeralds, began speaking, her determination to fix his interest more than obvious.

"So, you're dearest Edward's brother," Lady Deidre Howell purred, eyeing Justin with predatory intent. "I've heard him speak of you so often, I feel as if I've known you forever."

"Your ladyship is too kind," Justin drawled, returning her bold appraisal with sardonic amusement. He wondered if she was foolish enough to think him so blinded by her appeal that he couldn't guess the true reason behind her heavy-handed flirting. If so, she was sadly mistaken. Even without Edward's warning, he had no trouble recognizing a scheming fortune hunter when he saw one.

As if sensing his indifference, she leaned forward to lay her hand over his, her fingers lightly caressing his tanned flesh. "Oh, please, don't be so depressingly formal! You must call me Deidre, or else I won't feel free to call you Justin," she chided, expertly shrugging her shoulders so that her already shockingly cut gown of green silk slid even lower, exposing the white swell of her breasts.

"Very well, ma'am," he replied, taking a perverse delight in vexing her. "Although I trust you will forgive me if I am a trifle formal in my manners. As a colonel in his majesty's army, I tend to be somewhat rigid on occasion. Amanda is forever taking me to task about it."

At the mention of his fiancée, Lady Deidre's slender shoulders stiffened perceptibly, and the look she shot Amanda was filled with resentment. "Ah yes, the little bride," she said, raising her glass of champagne to her lips. "How charming she looks. But did I hear you call her Amanda? How odd. I would have sworn he said her name was Amelia."

"Amelia is her sister," Justin responded, remembering Edward had mentioned telling Lady Deidre of his engagement. "I'm afraid my letter to Edward wasn't as clear as it should have been."

"Mmmm," Lady Deidre murmured, glancing from Amanda to Justin. "But wouldn't it make an interesting *on-dit* if it turned out you were engaged first to one sister, and then the other? The gossip-mongers would adore so juicy a tidbit."

Justin's sense of amusement vanished at the threat implied in the woman's drawling tone. "I don't know about an interesting *on-dit*," he said, making no attempt to hide his icy displeasure, "but it would make a dangerous one. I wouldn't want to be the person caught uttering it."

For a moment Lady Deidre's cheeks paled with fright, but she was quick to mask her expression. "Oh, pooh, Justin," she said, managing a credible laugh. "You mustn't be so disapproving! All of society gossips; it is the very staff of life to us."

"Perhaps," he agreed, his voice still edged with warning, "and so long as it is not my wife they are wagging their tongues about, they may say what they will. But if I hear even a breath of gossip attached to Amanda's name, you may be very sure that I will act fast to protect what is mine."

Lady Deidre gave another laugh. "I fear your fiancée has the right of it, my lord," she said, seeking refuge in her wine. "You are in sad want of civilizing, and I wish her joy in the attempt."

Justin glanced at Amanda's animated features as she sat listening to her dinner partner. She looked so alive to him, her beauty so vital and real that it made Lady Deidre's ample charms seem tawdry in comparison. "Aye," he said softly, his mouth curling in a knowing smile as he thought of their coming wedding. "And a true joy it will be."

Following the sumptuous meal, Lady Rayburne led the ladies into the drawing room while the gentlemen lingered over their brandy and cigars. After making sure Amelia was settled with a young lady close to her own age, Amanda made her way to the corner where her hostess was holding court. "Are you feeling better, my lady?" she asked, her eyes lingering on the countess's sulky mouth. "I'm quite sure His Grace meant no offense."

"No offense!" the countess exclaimed, fanning her cheeks with unladylike vigor. "No offense when he tells me he was late because he completely forgot my dinner party? And pray, Miss Lawrence, how can such a slight be anything *but* offensive?"

That was so, Amanda admitted, wishing that Edward

had been a little less forthcoming with his hostess when he had finally made his appearance. He'd arrived just as the servants were removing the fish course, and after making his apologies to the countess, he'd commandeered the chair next to Amanda, regaling the other guests with the details of his latest investment.

"Steam power!" Lady Rayburne cried, her ire increasing at the memory of the duke's long-winded conversation. "Have you ever heard of a more ridiculous notion in all your days? And to go on and on about it as he did . . . ! Well, duke or no duke, that is the last time I shall ask him to dine with me. At least until he can think of a more suitable topic of conversation," she added grudgingly.

"Yes, Edward can be a trial," Lady Deidre agreed with a knowing laugh, her eyes flicking over Amanda. "Tell us, my dear, is his brother just as prosy? He was my partner at dinner, and I must say I found him quite delightful."

So I noticed, Amanda thought, her brown eyes narrowing at the memory of the other woman clinging to Justin's arm. Although her experience of society was limited, she wasn't so green that she hadn't guessed the true stamp of the lady's character.

"I have always found Justin's conversation to be most stimulating, my lady," she replied with a regal tilt of her chin. "As I have found Edward's."

Lady Deidre's lips thinned at the subtle set-down. "Yes, but coming from the country as you do, I daresay you are unaccustomed to polite conversation," she said with a condescending smile. "You must look to acquiring some town bronze, my dear, else you risk being taken for a bumpkin."

Amanda's cheeks grew warm. The viscountess's catty remarks cut all the deeper because she greatly feared they contained an element of truth. Listening to and observing the other guests tonight had made her realize just how much she had to learn, and not for the first time she found herself questioning her ability to learn it.

The gentlemen returned, and several of the guests, including Lady Deidre, left to attend other parties. The viscountess's departure lightened the atmosphere considerably, and Amanda began enjoying herself. Amelia and Charles were sitting with another young couple, and watching them she couldn't help but be moved by the love that radiated from them like a soft, golden light.

"They look happy together," Justin commented, handing her a glass of champagne as he joined her on the settee. "Maxfield's a good lad; he'll make her a good husband . . . especially if he knows what is good for him."

Amanda hid a quick smile. "You sound just like an overly-protective papa," she teased, lifting the sparkling wine to her lips. "I shudder to think of what you'll be like when Belinda makes her bows."

"To say nothing of our daughter," he replied, accepting her gentle ribbing with a surprising feeling of complacency. He'd never given the matter of a daughter much thought, but now he found he was rather taken with the idea.

At the insistence of some of the ladies, the dinner party adjourned to the ballroom for some informal dancing. Edward gallantly offered his services as a musician, and Justin led Amanda out onto the polished floor for the opening dance. "Do you know this is the first time we have danced together," he said, his hand tightening about hers as he guided her through the intricate steps of the polonaise. "You dance very well."

"Thank you, sir," she returned, hiding her nervousness as she concentrated on keeping time with the stately music. She'd never considered herself particularly graceful, but Justin's smooth movements were easy to follow. After they made their second turn about the floor without a misstep she risked sending him a pleased smile.

"You're also most accomplished," she teased, her cheeks gently flushed with exertion. "But then, I have heard it said that Wellington chooses his officers as much for their dancing skills as for their prowess as fighters."

"Vicious lies spread by his detractors," Justin assured her, expertly moving to the other side of her. "We were much too busy chasing the French to bother with such nonsense, I promise you. Besides, with whom would we have danced? Each other?"

The image of battle-hardened soldiers capering about in time to martial music made Amanda laugh out loud, and she brought her foot down on top of Justin's. "Now see what you have made me do?" she scolded, although she was enjoying herself too much to care.

When their dance had ended, she was quickly besieged by partners, including Edward, who'd been replaced at the pianoforte by an elderly lady who played with more passion than skill.

"Sorry I was late to your party," he said, leading her over to a corner of the room where a liveried footman was waiting with glasses of chilled punch. "I'd planned to leave early but. . . ." He shrugged his shoulders in a gesture that was oddly reminiscent of Justin.

"Think nothing of it, Your Grace," she answered soothingly. "I am only glad that you were able to come."

"Wouldn't have missed it for the world." He dabbed at his face with a rumpled handkerchief. "Justin's m'brother after all, and I want to know that he is happy. He's not had it easy, you know. Our father was a dashed cold fish who barely tolerated him."

Amanda was shocked by the duke's candor. "I . . . I thought as much," she began cautiously, hoping she wasn't betraying Justin's trust. "It's not so much as what he has said as . . . as . . ."

"As the way he is," Edward finished for her, his expression rather solemn as he studied her. "I know. That is why I'm so relieved he is marrying someone like you. I've never seen him so relaxed as he is with you."

Amanda's cheeks grew rosy with pleasure. Her feelings

for Justin were still too confusing to bear close scrutiny, but she was fond of him, and more than anything she wanted him happy with the bargain they had struck.

"May I ask you a question?"

"Of course, Your Grace." She glanced up at him curiously. "What is it?"

"Edward," he corrected, shaking his head at her. "I have told you, I prefer that you call me Edward."

"What is it, Edward?"

"Would it matter to you if Justin was rich? I mean . . . rich as a nabob or some such thing? Would you love him the better for it?"

"Of course not!" she exclaimed, feeling slightly indignant. "My feelings for Justin have nothing to do with the depths of his pockets! Besides," she added with a flash of her blunt honesty, "you must know that Justin is already far wealthier than I."

Edward nodded. "I know he is marrying you so that he might care for you and your family," he said with equal bluntness. "And I know that he had to blackmail you into accepting his offer. I just want to know that you care for him above the material goods he can provide for you and the others. Do you?"

There was no need to search her heart for the answer. "Yes," she said quietly, "I care very, very much."

To her surprise Edward pressed a warm kiss to her cheek. "Then all will be fine," he said, drawing back to give her a gentle smile. "So long as I know Justin has someone to care for him, I shall be more than content," and with that he tucked her hand in his arm, guiding her back to the corner where Justin stood waiting for them.

Justin watched them approaching, his face carefully blank of emotion. In light of the gossip he'd been hearing, he was grateful Edward was being so singular in his attentions to Amanda. His brother's approval would prove invaluable if they were to carry this thing off with any degree of success, he thought, his eyes narrowing with carefully controlled fury. The sooner society accepted his marriage to Amanda, the sooner all this talk and speculation would end.

"Now, Justin, you needn't look so threatening," Edward said, his eyes twinkling as he smiled at his younger brother. "I have returned your fiancée to you, safe and sound. Do say you won't be calling me to account; you must know I am a wretched shot."

Justin's expression relaxed at Edward's gentle teasing. "I suppose I might be persuaded to overlook it this time, providing you don't repeat the offense," he replied, placing a hand on Amanda's arm and drawing her firmly to his side.

Midnight came and went amidst the pealing of bells and much laughter. The countess had more champagne brought out and called upon Justin to make a toast.

"To my fiancée," he said, holding up his glass to Amanda, "may this be but the first of many New Year's we shall share together." They clinked their glasses together and drank a solemn toast, and then with the crowd looking on, he bent his head and brushed a warm kiss across her mouth.

Following a midnight buffet there was more dancing, and Amanda had another dance with Edward. He escorted her back to Justin and then took his leave, claiming the press of business. After he'd gone, Justin turned to her with a slow smile.

"So, what do you think of my elder brother?" he asked in a seductive whisper, his eyes taking in her flushed appearance with smug appreciation.

"He is wonderful," she whispered back, enjoying his warm perusal. She'd had several glasses of champagne, and a heady sense of daring filled her. She tilted back her head and sent a challenging smile. "It is easy to see where you get your charm, sir, although 'twould seem His Grace has received the lion's share of that particular commodity."

"Really?" He was delighted by her reply. "In that case, perhaps we ought to excuse ourselves from the company for a few minutes until I have raised your estimation of me."

She gave a soft laugh, her eyes taking on a wicked sparkle. "It would take more than a few minutes to accomplish that, Colonel Stockton," she informed him airily, and then turned her pretty shoulder on him. "Now, do behave, I wish to enjoy the music."

Justin hesitated, weighing his options with the sureness of a commander trained in battle. On the one hand Amanda was a lady, and as a gentleman he was honor-bound to protect her reputation. But on the other hand, the saucy minx was his fiancée, and certainly that entitled him to a few privileges. Reaching a swift decision, he grabbed her hand and pulled her out of the room, ignoring her laughing protests.

"You are always dragging me off," she complained once he had closed the library door behind them. "Hasn't it ever occurred to you to ask my permission first?"

He pushed himself away from the door, the gleam in his eyes growing more pronounced as he slowly advanced on her. "Indeed," he murmured, his voice husky with passion. "And pray what would your answer be if I were to say, 'Please, Amanda, would you come with me so that I might steal a kiss from you?' "

"I-I should tell you no," she stammered, some of her courage deserting her when his hands cupped her face. She remembered standing beneath the mistletoe with him on Christmas Eve, trembling in anticipation of his kiss. Then she'd been bound by convention, unable to respond to her sister's fiancé. But he was *her* fiance now, she thought dizzily, her eyes fluttering shut as he bent his head closer to hers.

"Then, perhaps it's just as well I didn't ask," he said, and then took her mouth in a demanding kiss.

At the first touch of his firm lips against hers, Amanda's shyness turned to desire, and she gave herself to the excitement burning inside her. Justin felt her hesitancy melting, and it goaded him to further boldness. He'd been torturing himself with memories of her taste, and now he was determined to drink his fill.

"Ah, Amanda, but you go to my head," he muttered, sliding his mouth down her neck to seek the scented hollow at the base of her throat. "You're more potent than the most expensive brandy, sweeter than honey. . . ." He nipped playfully at her shoulder.

"Justin!" She arched against him, trembling at the emotions that tore through her. She'd never known such wildness, and she wanted more. Casting all reserve aside, she pressed herself against him, revelling in the shudder that shook his hard frame. Justin's hand cupped her full breast, his thumb teasing the nipple until she was certain she would go mad.

This time when his mouth returned to hers, she boldly opened her lips, welcoming his tongue as it surged inside. Justin groaned at her boldness and the raw sound increased her pleasure. It excited her on some fundamental level that she could have such an effect upon Justin, and she sought to increase that effect. Her hands slid into the thickness of his hair, but when she would have held him closer, he stepped back, his breath coming out in ragged gasps as he stared down at her through passion-glazed eyes.

"We have to stop," he managed, his voice rough with unslaked passion. "We're not husband and wife . . . yet."

She flushed as much from embarrassment as from anticipation of the passionate promise in his voice. She ran a nervous tongue over her lips, her color deepening when she tasted him there. "I — Justin, I don't know what to say," she stammered, unable to meet his gaze. "This has never happened to me before."

"I know." His smile was rueful. "I wasn't expecting it either, but I will not pretend to be disappointed. It will be good between us, Amanda, that much I can promise you."

She wasn't certain how to answer that, and so she re-

274

mained silent. The rest of the evening passed in a vague haze, and it was only when she was alone in her bed that she allowed herself to relive that burning kiss. Her heart beat furiously in her chest at the memory, and it was then that she finally faced the hard and painful truth. She was in love with Justin.

Chapter Eighteen

The notice announcing Amanda's engagement appeared in Tuesday's paper, and by the following afternoon, she was inundated with invitations, most of which came from people she'd never met. She was mulling over the problem of how to begin answering all of the letters when the door to her sitting room opened and Lady Rayburne came bustling in chattering excitedly.

"My dear, I have just heard the *silliest* rumor," she said, her satin skirts rustling as she settled on the chair facing Amanda. "It's all a perfect hum, of course, and I pray that you will pay it no mind. Although the fact that the *ton* are already gossiping about you is sure to be a good sign. You must know they wouldn't waste their breath on a *nobody*."

"What rumor, my lady?" Amanda asked, wisely ignoring three quarters of the countess's rambling discourse. She'd already learned it was the only way to make any sense of her conversation.

"Well, the rumor that Justin is planning to run off and act as the governor-general of Madrid!" Lady Lettita exclaimed, shooting Amanda an impatient look. "Lady Milmount is putting it about that he has accepted a position with the Admiralty and will be sailing for Spain within the fortnight. Naturally *I* told her it was utter nonsense! How could he even consider such a thing when the pair of you ain't even properly leg-shackled as yet?"

Amanda swallowed a painful lump. She'd been so distracted with her love for Justin that she hadn't given his leaving much thought. Not that she'd completely forgotten about it, of course, but neither had she allowed herself to dwell on it. Hearing Lady Lettita's shocked response made her realize how the rest of society would view his leaving. So much for their passing this off as a lovematch, she thought with an unhappy sigh.

"Actually, Lady Lettita," she began, shifting nervously on her chair, "the offer came from Whitehall, not the Admiralty, and he is to be appointed provost marshal of the region."

"Then, it is *true?*"

"Yes, and a very great honor it is, too," Amanda said brightly, determined to put on as good a face as possible. "Justin says the government is sending only the most qualified of men, and the fact he is even being considered is bound to further his career. Why, it could even mean a promotion to general, and—"

"Don't be ridiculous!" Lady Lettita interrupted with a haughty sniff. "Military ranks are as common as coal dust! And what use has he for a career? He is Stonebridge's heir, to say nothing of his own title."

"What title?" Amanda demanded in a perplexed tone.

"The Viscount Marston," Lady Lettita gaped at her. "Never say that dolt hasn't even told you, you are to be a viscountess?"

Amanda shook her head. "It must have slipped his mind," she murmured weakly.

"Hmph!" The countess gave another loud sniff. "Only a man would forget to tell his bride he is bestowing a coronet on her," she grumbled, looking thoroughly disgusted.

"But that is neither here nor there. The fact remains, my dear, that you simply can not allow Justin to take this post. Only think of the tattle it will cause when it becomes known he *deserted* you on your wedding night!"

"It won't be on our wedding night, nor is he 'deserting' me," Amanda said, leaping to Justin's defense. "And as for my allowing him to leave, what else is there to be done? He will be my husband, and the decision is naturally his."

The look the older woman sent her spoke volumes. "You are young, Amanda, else you wouldn't utter such moonshine," she said wisely. "Really, I thought you much more clever than that. Of course you could get him to change his mind."

"How?"

"By any number of methods. Tears, threats, the vapors." She ticked them off on her bejeweled fingers. "Or if all else fails, you can always resort to the one method of persuasion guaranteed to make any man see the sweet light of reason."

"What is that?" Amanda asked, her brow wrinkling in concentration.

"Lovemaking."

"Lady Rayburne!"

"Oh, for heaven's sake, Amanda, don't be so missish!" Lady Lettita scowled at her. "We both know you're no green girl without knowledge of the world. You know perfectly well that men are possessed of certain base appetites."

"Certainly I am aware of the . . . the physical side of marriage," she stammered, her cheeks growing red at the memory of the impassioned kiss she had exchanged with Justin. The very memory of it made her tremble. Apparently men weren't the only ones afflicted with such appetites, she thought, struggling to hide her agitation.

"Well, there you are," Lady Lettita said, folding her

hands and beaming benevolently at Amanda. "You have only to deny Justin the delights of the marriage bed, and he'll turn up sweet as you please. How do you think *I* kept Rayburne in line all those years?"

Amanda's flush increased at the candid confession. "I don't think that would work with Justin," she mumbled, fervently wishing there was some way to end the frank conversation.

"Ah" — the countess nodded sagaciously — "like that, is it? Well, I can't say that I blame you. Justin is a devilishly attractive man. I can understand your not wanting to deny him his conjugal rights."

"Lady Lettita, I fear you are intruding upon my—"

"Of course, the other trick you might try is to keep him so pleased he can't bear the thought of leaving you," Lady Lettita said thoughtfully. "That is also quite effective. And probably a great deal safer. A young, healthy man like Justin would only seek a mistress if you barred your door to—"

"Lady Rayburne." This time it was Amanda who interrupted, her teeth set with annoyance. "This is between Justin and myself, and I will thank you to keep out of it. I appreciate your advice, but this is something that we must be allowed to resolve *on our own.*"

Lady Lettita's bottom lip thrust out in a pretty pout. "I was only trying to help," she said in injured tones. "You have no mother to advise you, and as you are my guest, I thought it my duty to render what aid I could. Naturally, if I have offended you, you have my most humble apologies, and my assurances that I shan't impose upon you again."

Amanda was strongly tempted to applaud the performance, but she knew it would doubtlessly offend her hostess beyond all bearing. "Don't be absurd," she soothed, giving the older woman's hand a fond pat. "Of course I appreciate all you have done for me. In fact, I was about to go in search of you when you came in. I find myself in something of a dilemma and was hoping you might be so kind as to advise me."

"About what?" Lady Rayburne brightened at once.

Amanda indicated the pile of invitations on her desk. "What am I to do about all these? There must be dozens of them, and there is no way I can attend even half of these affairs, to say nothing of returning their hospitality."

"Goose!" The countess shook her head at her. "They don't really expect you to *attend;* they merely wanted to invite you. But you are right; you will be expected to hold some kind of function to establish your reputation as a hostess." She laid a finger on her lips as she considered the matter.

"I have it! You shall have a tea party! It is the perfect sort of occasion for a young bride to try her wings."

That made sense to Amanda, and she nodded her head in agreement. "Yes, that would be nice," she said slowly. "Once I am settled in Dover House, I can—"

"Oh, no, you can't wait *that* long!" The countess exclaimed in horrified tones. "You must have one immediately! No later than next week if at all possible."

"But I am being married in less than six days, and the house is nowhere near completion," Amanda protested, remembering the state of the house the last time she had seen it.

Lady Rayburne gave a long-suffering sigh. "Then, you may have it here," she said in the tones of one explaining things to a slow-witted child. "In fact, it would probably be for the best. It would show you have the approval of Justin's family. Now, what about the guest list? Is there anyone you wish to invite?"

Amanda thought of Aunt Elizabeth. She didn't really want her querulous relation there, but she could see no polite way of snubbing her. "My aunt, Mrs. Elizabeth Herrick, lives in London," she said, hoping the dour woman was so angry with her she would refuse the invitation. "But other than her, I can think of no one else. Perhaps I could go through these invitations and—"

"Oh, no, child!" Lady Rayburne shook her head in disapproval. "You must leave this to me. As this will be your first official party, every care must be taken that only the *best* people are included, the *crème de la crème* of society."

"I have given other parties, you know," Amanda grumbled, an incipient feeling of pique stirring in her breast. "In Surrey I often gave dinner parties for our friends and neighbors."

"Really, Amanda," the countess returned archly, "one can not compare a country do with a London affair. It is an altogether different thing."

"If you say so, my lady." Amanda mentally tossed up her hands in surrender. "I shall leave it all in your capable hands. Thank you for your kind assistance; I appreciate your help."

"You're more than welcome, my dear." Lady Lettita dipped her head regally. "But really, 'tis no trouble. It's only a tea party, after all. What could possibly go wrong?"

True to his word, Justin arrived the following morning to take the family on the promised tour of London. Amelia was off with Charles visiting his aunt, but the twins' exuberance more than made up for her absence. To their great delight, Edward accompanied them, but when Amanda tried expressing her gratitude, Justin gave a negligent shrug.

"Actually, it was Edward's idea," he said, brushing her hands aside so that he could finish tying the ribbons of her bonnet beneath her chin. "It seems he's also been wanting to see the catch-me-who-can. We'll have to keep a sharp eye on him so that he doesn't help the twins steal the wretched thing."

After viewing the latest mechanical wonder to delight London, the children eschewed the more cultural aspects of the city, opting instead for the delights of Ackerman's Repository. Edward was unable to join them, but promised he would accompany them on the trip to the Frost Fair which was scheduled for the next week. When they reached the sprawling establishment on Strand Street, Justin gave each child a handful of shillings, admonishing them to be back within the hour. When they'd gone scampering off to spend the unexpected windfall, he turned to Amanda with a wide grin.

"I'll bet you thought I was going to give them each a sovereign," he teased. She'd been so quiet during the tour that he wondered if she was sickening after something.

"Not at all, although I'm surprised Edward didn't give them anything," she said, wincing when she remembered how she'd once accused him of attempting to buy the children's affection.

"Actually, he slipped them something when you weren't looking," he replied with a conspiratorial wink. "Nothing extravagant, mind, only a few pounds. I told him you wouldn't approve if he was *too* generous."

"You make me sound like an ogress," she complained, pausing to examine a length of striped French silk. It was just what she was looking for to recover the chairs at Dover House, and she made a note of the price. "Edward will think me a terrible person."

"Not at all. He approves wholeheartedly of the way you are raising the boys," Justin said as they made their way down the spacious aisles. "He admits our father spoiled him shamelessly, and that it was almost his undoing. But he warns me that he means to exercise his rights as a favorite uncle to indulge them on occasion."

Amanda hid her surprise at his off-handed remarks. This was the first time she'd heard him mention his father without a note of bitterness in his voice. Given what Edward had told her and what she'd already deduced, she knew his childhood hadn't been a happy one, and she was glad he was finally coming to terms with his painful past. She loved him so much that she couldn't bear to think of how cruelly he had been rejected, and she was determined that he would never know such pain again.

Following the unexpected shopping spree, Justin ordered the coachman to take them to Dover House so that the children could see their new home. While they were off choosing their bedrooms, Amanda and Justin walked through the rest of the house, inspecting the repairs that were underway. The chimney sweeps had arrived and were hard at work cleaning the many fireplaces while a dozen or more maids scurried about dusting and polishing.

"Do you really think it will be ready on time?" Justin asked, his expression forbidding as they made their way toward the back of the house. "I've seen sacked towns in better condition."

Amanda laughed at his analogy. "Really, Justin, don't you think you are doing it a shade too brown?" she teased, flashing him a bright smile. "I'll own it's a trifle messy, but—"

A loud crash from abovestairs disrupted her conversation, followed by a series of other crashes, angry curses, and the sound of running feet. She and Justin raced out into the hall when they saw Belinda tearing down the stairs, Stephen and Joss hot on her heels.

"Justin! Justin!" she wailed, running toward him with her arms outstretched and tears streaming down her face. He caught her easily, cradling her against his broad chest and gazing down at her worriedly.

"What is it, sweet?" he asked, running a gentle hand over her tousled blond curls. "What's wrong?"

"T-that man!" She sobbed, her chubby arms clinging to his neck. "That bad man!"

"What bad man?" he demanded, his eyes narrowing with dangerous fury.

"The chimney sweep," Stephen gasped, his chest rising and falling as he gasped for breath. "There's a kitten stuck up the chimney, and he was going to burn it!"

"Me and Jeremey told him to stop," Joss interjected, his small face set with anger, "and he called us guttersnipes and told us to mind our own business!"

"Oh, did he?" Amanda said, her chin coming up and her velvet-brown eyes sparkling in outrage. "Well, we shall just see about that!" She started purposefully toward the stairs.

"Amanda, let me deal with this," Justin instructed, giving Belinda a quick kiss as he set her down. "I'll soon set the arrogant fellow to rights."

"No, Justin"—Amanda's foot was on the bottom step— "I'll handle—"

There was another crash, and then a very sooty boy, clutching an even sootier object in his arms, came rushing down the steps, a large, filthy man running after him. "Come back here, ye little devil!" he shouted, shaking a bony fist. "I'll teach ye to make a fool o' John Falkes!"

The soot-covered boy ran behind Amanda, the flash of his blue eyes the only clue to his identity. "Jeremey?" she gasped, swiveling her head so that she could study him. "Is that you?"

"I got it, Mandy, I got it!" Jeremey crowed holding out a pathetic bundle of fur and dirt for her inspection. "I climbed right up that old chimney and I got it! Even though *he* said I was too big." He cast the sweep a triumphant look.

"Ye're lucky ye didn't get caught, but tight," the sweep responded, his tone modifying somewhat in the presence of the adults. He snatched the cap from his greasy hair and bobbed his head uncertainly. "I meant the lad no harm," he said, keeping a wary eye on Justin, "but I gots to do me work, and they was plaguing me something fierce about that cat."

"It was crying." Belinda sniffed, wiping the tears from her eyes and glaring at the man. "And you were going to burn it!"

"Ain't much else to be done," he muttered, shuffling his feet awkwardly and refusing to meet the children's accusing eyes. "And flames is a whole lot more merciful than letting it starve. It's already half-dead, anyways."

"No it's not," Jeremey denied, clutching the kitten to his chest. "He's purring."

"Jeremey, that is quite enough," Justin said, deciding it was time to put an end to the ridiculous farce. "We shall discuss this later. And as for you"—here he cast the sweep a cold look—"you may return to your duties. And if you ever dare threaten a member of my family again, you shall have *me* to deal with. Do you understand?"

"Aye, me lord," the man grumbled sullenly, and then turned and stomped back up the steps, muttering curses beneath his breath.

The children quickly forgot about the sweep as they crowded around Jeremey. "Can I hold it?" Belinda asked, reaching out a tentative finger to stroke the animal's head.

"I don't think that is a good idea," Justin said, giving the kitten a wary look. "The creature is likely to be diseased, to say nothing of being infested with fleas. Why don't you give it to me and I will—"

"No!" Jeremey held the kitten closer, his expression frankly suspicious as he glared at Justin. "You'll destroy it!"

Justin didn't attempt to deny the charge. "Jeremey, it would be best for the animal. You really can't expect to keep it, you know."

"Why not?" Amanda asked, sending him a quelling look. "The children have had pets in the past, and they've always taken excellent care of them. I see no reason why we can't find some place for the poor thing."

"But I—"

"Please, Justin?" Twin pairs of blues eyes gazed up at him hopefully. "We won't ever ask for anything ever again!"

"You won't even have to take us to the Frost Fair," Stephen added earnestly "not unless you really want to."

"And we'll take the *bestest* care of him, truly we shall!" Belinda assured him with an angelic smile. "Please?"

Justin knew when he was outnumbered. "Oh, very well," he relented with a low chuckle, "but I shall expect you to keep your word. The first time you neglect Cinders, I shall ship him off to the country. Is that understood?"

"Cinders?" Amanda's wry question rose above the children's earnest assurances.

He shrugged helplessly. "What else would one call a cat rescued from a chimney?"

After feeding the starved animal a bowl of milk, the children took him back to the pantry to be bathed. Much to their distress, Justin adamantly refused to allow them to bring the kitten back to Upper Wimpole Street, explaining that Lady Lettita disliked animals.

"But he'll get lonely!" Belinda protested with an unhappy pout. "He'll cry and cry for us!"

"Cook has a nice, fat cat that will keep him company," Justin told her. "And it need only be for a few days. Remember we shall all be moving in next week."

286

The children allowed themselves to be mollified and were subdued on the return journey. After they reached Lady Lettita's, they all trooped upstairs to rest before dinner, leaving Amanda and Justin staring after them suspiciously. "You don't think they . . ." Justin's voice trailed off as he turned to grin at her. "They wouldn't. They couldn't."

"Joss and Jeremey?" Amanda gave him a rueful look. "Surely, sir, you jest. You must know they would dare anything. But if it's any consolation, I am almost certain I heard Cinders meowing as we were leaving."

"I shall cling to that thought," Justin said, his mobile mouth quirking in a smile. "I wasn't exaggerating when I said Aunt is afraid of cats. She has a positive terror of the things, and they make her sneeze in the bargain."

"Then, let us hope they keep it well-hidden," she returned, thinking how handsome he looked when he smiled. This was the first time they'd been alone in several days and she felt a shyness in his company she had never experienced before. Her love was so strong that she feared he would somehow guess her feelings.

"How is the tea party coming?" Justin asked, sensing her sudden shyness. "I heard Aunt say Lady Jersey will be attending; that is quite a coup, you know."

"I know." She managed another smile. "I only hope that between her and Lady Lettita the rest of us will be able to get a word in it sideways. You see? Even in the wilds of Surrey we have heard of "Silence" Jersey."

"Shrew." He gave in to the urge to touch her by brushing back a lock of hair that had fallen across her forehead. "I implore that you not repeat that in polite company; Old Sal isn't known for her sense of humor. And what do you mean the wilds of Surrey? Godstone is hardly the ends of the earth, you know."

Amanda said nothing, although she couldn't help but

remember some of the subtle snubs to which she had been subjected on the few occasions she and Justin had ventured out. Nothing was ever said in his presence, of course, but she knew she hadn't imagined the whispers and malicious laughter that followed in her wake. She had even heard a cutting remark about "the country bride," and the cruel words had cut her to the heart.

Since her arrival in London, it had occurred to her more and more how much Justin was giving up by marrying her. Whatever he thought of himself, it was obvious the rest of society looked upon him as a prime matrimonial catch, and Amanda knew he could have his pick of any bride. Not only was he handsome and well-born, but he was also a viscount; and when Edward died, he would be Duke of Stonebridge. Never mind that that sad event was doubtlessly years into the future, Amanda knew society well enough to know that many women would willingly wait decades for the chance to be called "Her Grace." And perhaps Justin could love one of those ladies. The thought was truly depressing.

"Amanda?" Justin placed his finger beneath her chin and tilted her face up to his. "Is there something wrong?" He asked, his worried eyes moving over her face. "You're rather quiet."

She gazed up at him, the words of love and longing all but choking her, she longed so to speak them. But knowing he could never return those feelings kept her mute; not for anything would she burden him with the knowledge of her feelings. She swallowed the sweet words and managed a shaky smile.

"In comparison to your aunt and Lady Jersey, do you mean?" she rallied bravely. "Actually, I was thinking about Aunt Elizabeth. I had a note from her this morning, accepting my invitation. She must have sent word the moment she received my letter."

Justin gave her a sharp look, not believing her explanation for a single moment. He was fairly certain he knew what was troubling her, but he was uncertain how to deal with it. He was only just coming to terms with his feelings for her, and until he had firmer control of his emotions, there was nothing he could say. He only knew that come what may, he would never let her go.

"If she proves too troublesome, feel free to dump a pot of tea over her head," he said, his fingers skimming the curve of her delicate lips. "I am certain no one would object."

"Especially if they knew her," Amanda agreed, her heart racing at his touch. "But I'll do my best to restrain myself."

"Do that." Justin lowered his head, knowing he'd go mad if he didn't kiss her again. The kiss was brief but filled with passion, and they were both breathing heavily when he finally drew back.

"Five days, Amanda," he said huskily, his thumb whisking over her trembling mouth. "Five days, and then there will be no stopping me. Until then I think it best that I keep my distance, for both our sakes. But once we are man and wife, we will talk. There is much I have been wanting to say to you," and with a final kiss, he turned and walked out of the door, leaving her staring after him.

By employing all her skill, Lady Lettita was able to arrange the tea party to take place two days before Amanda's nuptials. As befit a bride, Amanda was attired in a new tea gown of white muslin, the wide sleeves of which were trimmed with ribbons and ruchings of Belgian lace. The dress, while beautiful, was hardly practical and Amanda was shivering as she and Amelia made their way downstairs.

"I hope Lady Lettita has a fire going in the parlor," Amanda muttered, chafing her arms with her hands. "Or else I'm going to say to devil with fashion and put on my best woolen dress!"

"Don't do that," Amelia implored, also looking decidedly bridelike in a gown of pale blue lace. "If you get too cold, have one of the maids fetch the silk shawl Edward sent you. It's so very lovely."

"And as impractical as this dress," Amanda said, thinking of the brightly colored piece of blue Chinese silk covered with colorful embroidery that had arrived yesterday afternoon. The shawl accompanied the box of jewelry Justin had sent her, along with a note that said she was to wear the pear-shaped diamond as her engagement ring. The casual gesture had hurt, but she was grateful that he thought enough of her to bestow the costly gem upon her.

Lady Lettita was waiting in the parlor when they arrived, dabbing at her nose with a lace handkerchief. "How I wish this tiresome event was over," she said in a decidedly thick voice. "I have the most wretched cold, and my poor head is quite killing me. Ah well, allow me to say that you both look lovely. You are certain to be a success."

"Thank you, Lady Rayburne," Amanda said, a vague suspicion stirring in her mind. She was fairly certain the twins hadn't disobeyed Justin by smuggling Cinders into the house, but she wasn't completely convinced. Not that it would matter if they had. She had other things to worry about just now, not the least of which was Aunt Elizabeth, who was due to arrive any minute. But once the party was over, was determined to search their rooms, and if she found the kitten, then she would be quite firm with them.

The chiming of the bell announced the first arrival, and Amanda drew a quick breath. Pinning a polite smile to her lips, she took her place behind the huge silver teapot, praying that she would somehow survive the next few hours. Not that she really had anything to worry about, she assured herself anxiously. As Lady Lettita had said; this was only a tea party. What could possibly go wrong?

"Well, you've done rather well for yourself, I must say," Mrs. Herrick said, her tone as poisonous as her smile. "No wonder you turned down my kind offer when you had this planned all along. Congratulations, my dear, you are indeed your mother's child."

Amanda stiffened at the hateful words. She'd spent the last two hours enduring not only her aunt's snipes, but those of the beauteous Lady Deidre as well, and her patience was all but gone. Her fingers tightened around her teacup as she sought for control. Just fifteen more minutes, she thought. She could endure anything for fifteen minutes.

"You are too kind, Aunt Elizabeth," she returned coolly, refusing to allow the other woman to see her anger. "Would you care for more tea?"

"My, but we are the lady of the manor." Mrs. Herrick gave a bitter laugh. "Well, don't think you're fooling anyone with those fine airs, missy! You're naught but a scheming country wench who managed to trap an honorable man with your clever machinations! You and that simpering fool of a sister!"

The cup rattled in Amanda's hand, and she set it down. She would tolerate anything her aunt chose to say, but she drew the line when the hateful creature turned her venomous tongue on Amelia. She turned toward the woman, prepared to do battle.

"Listen to me, you hateful old—"

A maid let out a sudden shriek, and the sound of shattered china echoed in the opulent room. The startled guests glanced toward the doorway just as a small cat, a bonnet tied to its head, came streaking into the room. At the sight of the animal, several of the ladies began screeching, and Lady Letty jumped up on her chair, her skirts held up to her plump knees.

"A cat! A cat!" she screamed, doing a little dance on the embroidered cushion. "Kill it! Someone kill it!"

The cat raced around the room, leaping onto tables and sending plates of delicacies flying in every direction. Amanda tried catching the terrified creature, but she was hampered by her full skirts and succeeded only in upsetting the tea table.

"Help!" Lady Letty cried, and then gave a loud scream as her chair tipped backward, sending her tumbling to the ground.

The sight of their hostess in such distress was all it took to set the other ladies off, and soon screams and moans filled the air as the guests quickly succumbed to the vapors. By now the cat was crazed with fear, and its golden eyes darted frantically about for some means of escape. It saw Mrs. Herrick's tall, angular form and made a dash for her, scrambling up her dress as if she were a convenient tree.

Belinda came running into the room just then and added her cries to those of the other women. "Don't hurt Cinders! Don't hurt Cinders!" she called, rushing up to Mrs. Herrick, who was screaming and attempting to pull the cat from her head. She succeeded in pulling the animal off, but the cat's claws were dug deeply in her wig, and when the cat came loose, so did the wig.

The twins and Stephen, drawn by the riotous noise, arrived in time to see this amazing sight and collapsed upon the floor, holding their sides and roaring with laughter. Amanda was also laughing, but she managed to grab the cat, wresting the wig from its claws and handing it back to Aunt Elizabeth.

"Well!" the outraged woman snapped, her face purple with rage, "I have never, never been so insulted in all my life! You little baggage! Just see if I ever speak to you again!" She stormed out of the room, all but tripping over the boys, who were laying prostrate on the floor.

Mrs. Herrick's stormy departure signalled a mass exit, and soon all the women were gathering up their belongings and rushing from the house as if it were ablaze.

Only Lady Jersey paused at the doorway, her blue eyes bright with laughter as she said, "My dear, thank you for such an entertaining afternoon! I vow, I can not remember when I have enjoyed a tea party more. They are usually so depressing *dull!*"

"Lady Jersey." Amanda had regained sufficient control to know she was in serious jeopardy of becoming a social outcast. "Pray accept my apologies. I assure you nothing like this has ever happened to me before."

The countess waved her fat hand. "Please, Miss Lawrence, you needn't fret. I was thoroughly entertained! And don't worry that this shall reflect poorly upon you. Once it becomes known that I was thoroughly entranced by today's events, you may rest assured that crazed felines will become as popular at tea parties as macaroons! Good day to you." She brushed a kiss over Amanda's cheeks and walked out, still chuckling with delight.

The moment they were alone, Amanda whirled on her younger siblings, who were huddled together in a forlorn little group. "I want an explanation, and I want it now," she said, struggling to make her voice sufficiently stern. "Who brought Cinders into this house?"

The twins looked down, Stephen shuffled his feet, and Belinda gave a tearful sniff. "I did," she said at last, hanging her head. "Cinders was so sad, I couldn't leave her! And I didn't mean any harm." She cast a remorseful look over to the corner where a sobbing Lady Lettita was being helped to her feet by several footmen.

"I know you meant no harm, Belinda," Amelia reproached gently, "but you can see the trouble you have caused. Poor Lady —"

"What the hell has happened here?" A harsh masculine voice cut into her admonishments, and they turned to see Justin standing in the doorway, his hat and cane clutched in his hand.

Amanda opened her lips to explain when something stopped her. Justin was white, his mouth set with pain and his eyes glittering with a strange intensity. She took a step toward him, her hand reaching out instinctively to comfort him.

"Justin, what is it?" she asked urgently, her eyes moving over his face. "What has happened."

Justin stared at her, and then he was reaching for her, pulling her into an almost painfully tight embrace. "It is Edward," he said rawly, his eyes closing as anguish washed over him. "He is dead."

 *Chapter Nineteen*

Amanda froze in horrified disbelief. "Dead?"

He nodded, unable to speak. From the moment the footman had burst into his study with the terrible news, his one thought had been to find Amanda. He didn't question the impulse; he only acted on it, knowing that he had to be with her or go mad. Tears slid down his cheeks as he buried his face in her hair, clinging to her with all his might.

Behind her she heard Amelia gather up the children and guide them quietly from the room. Lady Lettita, her lively chatter stilled for once, also left, closing the door behind her. When they were alone, Justin raised his head to gaze down at her.

"It was his heart," he said, his voice raw with grief. "He'd evidently been ill for some time, but he never told anyone. His valet said he didn't want to be a bother."

Amanda choked back a tearful laugh. How very like Edward that was, she mused, silently weeping for the gentle, unassuming man who would have been her brother-in-law. She laid her hands on his cheeks, her own eyes bright with tears.

"I'm sorry, Justin," she whispered, knowing the words were hopelessly inadequate. "So very sorry."

Her words and the gentle stroke of her fingers was the healing balm he'd been seeking, and he continued holding her in a desperate grip. He wept not only for the loss of his brother, but for the loss of the love that they were just beginning to share. That was the worst part of all, he realized. He'd lost Edward just as he was finding him.

Amanda continued holding him, praying her love would be enough to ease his terrible pain. Finally she realized he had stopped crying and guided him over to the settee, gently pushing him down onto the plump cushions.

"Here," she said prying the cane and hat from his fingers, "let me take those. Would you like some brandy?"

He gazed up blankly for a few moments, and then nodded. When she returned with the brandy, he took the snifter from her hands and downed the contents in a single gulp, holding it out to her wordlessly. She refilled his glass and handed it to him, watching him through worried eyes as he downed it again.

"That's enough," she said, plucking the glass from his hand and setting it on the side table. She sat down beside him and captured his hand in a comforting grip. "Now, tell me what happened? I believe you said it was his heart?"

"Yes." He stared down at their joined hands, his thumb moving in a slow circle over the back of her hand. "He'd gone to his club to meet some friends, and he apparently collapsed. They sent for a physician, but there was nothing they could do. He died within the hour."

Her fingers tightened spasmodically, but she remained silent, knowing he needed to talk.

"Do you know, I have seen death a hundred times . . .

296

a thousand times," he said, staring unseeingly at the fireplace. "I thought I was accustomed to it, but I was wrong. First Daniel, and now Edward. . . ." He ducked his head, unable to go on. When he raised his eyes again, his face was devoid of all emotion.

"There are several arrangements to be made: the funeral, and matters pertaining to the succession. Also, his business affairs are certain to be in shambles. God knows how long it will take me to straighten them out."

"Is there anything I can do to help?" Amanda asked, aching to touch him but lacking the nerve.

"Actually," he said, raising his eyes from the fire to meet hers, "there is something you can do for me. The marriage will have to be postponed . . . just for a week or so until after the funeral. I hate to ask this of you, but—"

"I shall see to everything," she interrupted, forcing a smile to her shaking lips. "Will there be anything else?"

Her brisk efficiency startled him, but he was too numbed with grief to pursue the matter. "No, at least not for the moment," he said, rising wearily to his feet. He'd never felt more alone or frightened in his life, and he wanted her to take him in her arms and hold him safe. But a lifetime of rejection left him mute, unable to ask for the love he craved. He turned toward the door, retrieving his hat and cane from the side table.

"I'll be going now," he said, settling the hat on his head. "As I said, there is much to be done. I'm not sure when I shall return. Will you be all right?"

"I'll be fine," she assured him, blinking back tears at how completely he had masked his emotions. Once she would have been taken in by his facade of cool control, but now she could see the pain behind his seeming rigidity. She walked over to where he was standing and laid her hands on his arms, staying him.

"What of you?" she asked softly. "Will *you* be all right?"

He raised his hand and traced a gentle finger down her cheek. "I'll be fine," he echoed her words huskily, a feeling of inner peace diluting some of the impotent grief and rage that had been consuming him since learning of Edward's death. That that peace came from Amanda was something of which he was well-aware, and that knowledge was in his eyes as he turned and walked from the room.

After leaving his aunt's house, Justin went directly to Henry Teale's office. He was ushered in immediately, and one look at the solicitor's pinched expression told him that part of his mission, at least, was for naught. The lawyer had apparently already learned of Edward's death.

"Your Grace." Teale's first words confirmed his suspicions. "Pray accept my condolences on your sad loss."

"Thank you," Justin replied guardedly, taking the chair the solicitor indicated. "May I ask how you learned of my brother's death? I was only informed of it a few hours ago."

"A solicitor must have many sources if he is to be of benefit to his clients," Teale answered mendaciously. "But as it happens, another client of mine, a certain Lord B., was at the club when His Grace collapsed. As he knew I was also the duke's solicitor, he thought I should want to know and came directly to inform me."

Justin leaned back in his chair and folded his arms across his chest. "How much did you pay him?" he asked coldly.

"Your Grace!" Teale turned purple with indignation. "I must protest this attack upon my character! I—"

"How much did you pay him?" Justin was unmoved by the other man's protestations of innocence.

"Well, naturally I reimbursed Lord Benc—Lord B. for

298

the price of his hackney," Teale stammered, nervously shuffling the papers on his desk. "But as to anything else, I really am not at liberty to say. But I assure you, sir, that any amount I may have given him certainly in no way constitutes *payment*. Indeed, the very idea is an affront to that gentleman's honor . . . to say nothing of mine!"

Justin decided to let the matter drop for the moment. It really was of no consequence; he merely wanted to confirm that which he had suspected since first clapping eyes on the prissy little solicitor. "Then, if you know of Edward's death, you know why I am here."

"Yes, Your Grace." Teale picked up the first paper and began studying it. "And may I say that I am glad you are being so sensible about all this. I admit I had my doubts upon our first meeting, but I should have known you would not so neglect your duty to your family. Naturally, if you wish, some small financial arrangement may be settled on Miss Lawrence, but I don't think it necessary to be too—"

"What in Hades are you prattling about?"

Teale frowned at the interruption. "Ending your engagement to Miss Lawrence, of course," he said, his blue eyes cool with disapproval at such rough language. "You must see that a marriage between you simply will not do. Now"—he picked up a second piece of paper—"I have here a list of some of the most eligible ladies in the country, and I am sure that with very little effort we can affect an alliance that—Your Grace!" The words ended in a frightened squawk as he was hauled out of his chair by the front of his jacket.

"If you say one more word, I vow I will throttle you," Justin said, his voice filled with such menace that Teale stilled at once, regarding his captor through bulging eyes.

"But-but, my lord, Your Grace, I meant only to help,"

he gasped, his voice thin with fear. "You are the duke now, and you need a wife who—"

"How the hell do you know what I need?" Justin demanded, the thought of losing Amanda filling him with killing fury. She was his life, his world, and if he had to chose between her and his title, he knew what his choice would be. Oddly, the realization calmed him, and he released Teale so abruptly the smaller man fell back in his chair.

"You may consider whatever arrangement that existed between us at an end," he said, flexing his hands as he stepped back from the desk. "I wouldn't trust you to handle so much as the contents of a chamber pot!"

Teale licked his lips nervously. "Your Grace, please, this is all a dreadful misunderstanding," he said, his tone conciliatory. "You are distraught. I'm sure you don't mean—"

"Oh, I mean it, all right," Justin assured him silkily, his smile chilling Teale with its promise of violence. "I mean every word of it. And if you dare repeat such remarks to anyone else, you have my word that I will see you ruined. You will wish yourself dead before I am done with you, and then I will grant you that wish. Remember that, Teale," and he departed without another word.

The next twenty-four hours were among the bleakest Amanda had ever known. Edward's death shocked London, as did the news that rather than squandering his inheritance with his imprudent investments, he had more than quadrupled it. Instead of inheriting an almost bankrupt estate, Justin found himself the stunned heir of a fortune said to be in excess of half a million pounds.

With Lady Lettita's and Amelia's assistance, Amanda was able to cancel the wedding with a minimum of fuss, although there was little she could do about the gossip. Callers stopped by ostensibly to offer their condolences, but they seemed more interested in quizzing her than in paying their respects. One plump matron even went so far as to openly speculate what would become of Amanda now that Justin was a wealthy peer, and by day's end Amanda's head was pounding with pain.

On the morning of what was to have been her wedding day, she went down to breakfast to find another stack of cards waiting for her. She sipped her tea, picking through the pile disinterestedly until one card caught her eye. *Henry Teale,* she read, frowning as she turned it over. Wasn't that the name of Justin's solicitor? She had a vague memory of his mentioning the name.

The message written on the back was terse, requesting that she present herself in his office as soon as it was possible. The added request that she come alone raised her eyebrows, and she was frowning as she placed the card to one side.

"Anything wrong, dearest?" Amelia asked as she entered the dining room. "You look rather pensive. Is your poor head still bothering you?"

"What?" Amanda gazed up at her blankly, and then shook her head. "Oh, no, Amelia, I was just reading this." She held up the card for her sister's inspection. "It is from Justin's solicitor. He wishes to see me as quickly as possible and he asks that I come alone."

"Does he? How very odd." Amelia helped herself to the pot of fresh tea the footman had just set out. "Well, perhaps it has to do with the will. Charles said it could be months yet before everything is set to rights."

The thought of waiting months before marrying Justin was enough to effectively kill the little appetite Amanda had. She picked up the card again, tapping it on the table as she gazed off into space. "Perhaps I should go," she said reflectively. "He made it sound rather important, and I did promise Justin I would do all that I could to help him."

"Naturally you must do what you think is best." Amelia's smile was gentle as she regarded her sister. "But are you certain you wish to go today? Lady Rayburne said we are sure to be flooded with callers, and I'm sure you wouldn't want to miss them."

That was all the encouragement Amanda needed. "Oh, I'm sure I shouldn't be gone above an hour," she assured Amelia, studying the address printed on the card. She wasn't overly familiar with London, but she was certain Harley Street couldn't be far away. From what she had observed, the *ton* occupied a narrow section of the city, and its members seldom strayed beyond its narrowly defined borders.

"Well, if your certain that's what you want, I'm sure Lady Rayburne and I shall manage somehow," Amelia murmured, hiding a knowing smile. "And perhaps it would do you good to get out for a while. You're rather pale."

"Yes, a breath of fresh air does sound nice," Amanda agreed, her mind on her escape. Both ladies ignored the fact the cold continued unabated and that it had been snowing most of the morning. Amanda set her napkin down and made to rise from the table.

"Well, now that that is decided, I suppose I should be going," she said brightly. "Pray tell Lady Rayburne I—"

"You sit right back down, Amanda," Amelia interrupted, pointing her fork at her threateningly. "You're not going anywhere until you've had a decent breakfast."

Amanda was so shocked by her sister's stern order that she did as she was bid, dropping meekly onto her chair.

"That's better." Amelia nodded her blond head in approval before turning to the gaping footman. "My sister will have two boiled eggs and some ham," she instructed in confident tones. "And pray bring some more tea out as well, this pot is tepid." When he rushed to carry out her orders, she turned back to Amanda.

"That was easy. Perhaps being mistress of my own establishment won't be so very difficult after all. More toast, dearest?"

"Ah Miss Lawrence, how good of you to come," Mr. Teale said, his tone impeccably correct as he bowed over Amanda's hand. "I trust you had a pleasant journey?"

Amanda thought of her harrowing ride from Wimpole Street through thoroughfares rendered all but impassable by the thick snow. Only her stern sense of duty and the knowledge of what awaited her at home kept her going when common sense dictated she should abandon the effort.

"Quite pleasant, Mr. Teale" she replied, pulling the gloves from her hands as she settled on the chair he indicated. "Now, might I ask what this about? Your note said it was important."

"Yes, but first I must ask if you have paid your hackney driver. It wouldn't do to keep him waiting, you know."

Amanda paused in the act of removing her fur-lined cloak. "I came here by private coach," she said, not caring for the man's tone of voice. "Justin arranged for a carriage and driver to be placed at my disposal while we're staying with Lady Rayburne. But had I come by hack, I am more than capable of paying the driver myself," she added with a proud tilt of her chin.

"Of course, Miss Lawrence," he murmured soothingly

as he took his place behind the massive desk. "And I assure you, I meant no insult. It is just that being aware as I am of your financial situation, I was anxious that you not incur any unnecessary expenditures on my behalf."

Amanda's back stiffened perceptibly. "What do you mean, my financial situation?" she demanded, shooting him a suspicious frown.

He didn't reply at first, seeming more interested in polishing his glasses than in answering her. When they were clean enough for his satisfaction, he returned them to this thin nose and picked up a piece of paper from his desk. "According to Lord Stonebridge, your annual income is slightly over two hundred and fifty pounds. Is this figure correct?"

"Yes," Amanda answered hesitantly, wondering why Justin had seen fit to inform him of her lack of fortune. She knew a marriage agreement was customary among their class, but she could not like that the facts of her personal life had been laid out before the neat little man regarding her with smug superiority.

"And you bring no wedding portion nor any kind of inheritance to the marriage?"

"No, sir, I do not," she said, a faint note of defiance edging into her voice. "Might I ask what business this is of yours?"

He shuffled the papers in his hand, a thin smile touching his pursed lips. "Well, Miss Lawrence, you must own 'tis odd that such a wealthy and titled gentleman as Lord Stonebridge would seek such an alliance. Among the gentry it is customary that a man, or indeed a lady, marry a person of equal rank and fortune. One can not help but speculate as to the reasons behind so unusual a marriage, and so hasty a one. I believe you met a little over a fortnight ago?"

304

Amanda's cheeks reddened at his veiled accusation. "Justin was not the duke when I accepted his offer," she told him frostily. "And I resent what you are implying."

He held up a well-shaped hand. "Please, Miss Lawrence, I have no wish to offend. I am only attempting to fulfill my obligations to my client. Now, is it true that you and the present duke of Stonebridge met for the first time some three weeks ago?"

"Yes." Amanda saw no reason why she should deny the obvious. What the devil did he mean he was only attempting to fulfill his obligation to his client? she brooded. Had Justin asked him to speak to her? Her heart plummeted at the thought.

"And is it also true that he spent much of that time under your roof without benefit of a chaperone?"

Amanda's head came snapping up in suspicion. She knew Justin would never have told him such a thing, and she wondered what he was up to. "Considering that my entire family and staff were in constant attendance, I should think that I was more than adequately chaperoned," she informed him haughtily. "Again, I must ask how this matter concerns you?"

"You might consider a young lady barely out of the schoolroom and four young children "adequate" chaperones, but I fear not all of society would agree with you," Teale continued mockingly. "Lord Stonebridge is a gentleman, and if he thought he had compromised you, I daresay he would feel obliged to do the honorable thing. Is that what happened?"

For a moment the man's audacity left Amanda speechless with rage. He was actually accusing her of trapping Justin into marriage! She opened her mouth to administer a blistering retort when something made her hesitate. Again, she wondered what the solicitor was up to. If Justin had wanted him to end their engagement, wouldn't he have told him the real reasons behind it? Yes, Justin felt honor-bound to marry her, but not for the reason Mr. Teale was hinting at. What the devil was going on? She fixed him in a cold look.

"Did Justin ask you to speak to me?" she asked, knowing she would know the truth by how he answered. "Does he wish to end our engagement?"

"What do you mean Amanda's not here?" Justin demanded, eyeing his aunt with mounting frustration. "Where the devil is she?"

"Really, Justin, how would I know?" Lady Lettita responded in a sulky voice, frowning at him in obvious disapproval. "And kindly lower your voice. You are supposed to be in mourning."

Justin bit his tongue to hold back his temper. In the past two days he'd had less than six hours' sleep, and he was in no mood to put up with his frivolous aunt's foolishness. "Are you quite certain you don't know where she is?" he asked in a strained voice.

"All I know is that Amelia said she had a note and had to leave," Lady Lettita informed him with a long-suffering sigh. "She was gone when I came down for breakfast."

"Then, let me talk to Amelia," Justin said, his tone not as polite as it should have been.

"*She's* gone too!" The countess exclaimed, raising both hands in exasperation. "They've both shabbed off, leaving me alone with a parlorful of callers! What have I to say to all these people? I'm not even acquainted with half of them, and those I do know I can't abide! I take leave to tell you, Justin, that that solicitor of yours is a most inconsiderate fellow. Couldn't this emergency of his waited for a more appropriate occasion?"

"What solicitor?" Justin's ears pricked up in sudden interest.

Lady Lettita raised her eyes heavenward in a mute appeal for patience. "The man is your solicitor, Justin," she informed him in tones that made it obvious she doubted his mental acuity. "If you don't know his name, then how could I possibly know?"

Justin's face darkened as his aunt's words sank in. Teale! "That bastard!" he whispered, his voice hoarse with fury. "That bastard! I'll kill him!"

"Let me be certain that I understand you," Amanda said slowly, regarding Mr. Teale with carefully disguised loathing. "You are telling me that Justin feels that I have unjustly trapped him, and he is requesting that I release him from our engagement. Is that correct?"

"Yes, Miss Lawrence," Teale responded, scarcely believing that taking his revenge would prove to be so easy. "He regrets any inconvenience he has caused you, and begs that you will find it in your heart to forgive him."

"I see," she murmured, and indeed she did. For whatever reasons of his own, the solicitor had apparently taken it upon himself to end her and Justin's engagement. Thank heaven she loved Justin and had such faith in him, she thought, hiding a rueful smile, otherwise she might have been taken in by his farrago of nonsense.

"He also asks that you leave London immediately and make no attempt to ever see him again," Mr. Teale interjected. Success was almost at hand, he was certain of it, and he squirmed with eagerness to taste its sweetness.

"Yes, 'If 'tis done, then 'tis best done quickly,' " she agreed, quoting Shakespeare, tongue-in-cheek. A sudden thought occurred to her and her eyes began sparkling with delight. It was really rather wicked of her, but considering the trick he was attempting to pull on her, it was no less than he deserved. She folded her hands in her lap and flashed him a demure smile.

"Ten thousand pounds."

He frowned at her. "Miss Lawrence?"

"Ten thousand pounds," she repeated, naming the biggest sum she could think of. "That is what I want to end my engagement to the duke."

"But-but that is impossible! Preposterous! You can not be serious," Teale blustered, seeing his dreams shattering before his eyes.

"Why not?" Amanda took perverse delight in his horrified expression. "You've told me Justin is far too rich and powerful a man to shackle himself to a nobody like me, and I am in complete agreement. But that doesn't mean I intend coming out of this engagement empty-handed. I have my family to think of, you know." She batted her lashes at him coquettishly.

"But ten thousand pounds," Teale protested, his voice trailing off as he considered his options. Perhaps he could scrape together a few hundred pounds, just enough to satisfy the greedy bitch into leaving. It would be worth it if he succeeded in ending the engagement. He'd see how high and mighty Stonebridge was when he realized the woman he adored had sold him out, he thought, licking his lips in anticipation.

"For a start," Amanda said with a sugary smile, tiring of the charade. She'd only give him enough rope to hang himself, and then she would neatly cut him off. She also intended informing Justin of the man's perfidity. It was obvious he was not to be trusted.

Before Teale could respond to her new demand, the

sound of violently raised voices reached their ears, and then the door to the room was flung open as Justin pushed his way in past the protesting clerk.

"Justin!"

"Your Grace!"

Amanda and Teale both stumbled to their feet at Justin's appearance, their faces wearing identical expressions of disbelief. Justin barely spared Amanda a glance before stalking over to the desk and plucking a terrified Teale out of his chair. "I warned you," he snarled, shaking the solicitor as a terrier would a rat.

"Justin! Have you gone mad?" Amanda streaked around the desk, grabbing wildly at Justin's arm. "Put him down this instant!"

Justin tore his eyes from Teale's purpling features to glare at Amanda. "Damn it, Amanda," he gritted, his breath coming harshly between his clenched teeth, "you don't know the bloody nonsense this fool has been spouting. . . ."

"Oh, don't I? I've spent the past half-hour listening to it," she returned tugging determinedly at his powerful arm. "Blast it, Justin, I said put him down! You're choking him."

Justin's fingers released their murderous grip, and he stared down at her, a sick feeling of horror washing over him. "You can't believe him," he said, his voice shaking with fear. "Amanda, you can't believe I agree with him. . . ."

"Ah, but she does, Your Grace," Teale gloated, rubbing his aching throat and glaring at Justin with obvious malice. "Only if you wish to secure your freedom from her, it will cost you ten thousand pounds. That *is* the price you demanded, isn't it, Miss Lawrence?" His malevolent gaze was transferred to Amanda.

"Why, you odious little man!" She started forward, her own hands reaching for his throat. "You must have known I was only twigging you! How dare you say such things!"

Justin grabbed her by the skirts and hauled her backward. "You demanded money?" he asked harshly, his hands clamping on her shoulders as he whirled her around to face him. "From me?"

"From him!" Now it was Amanda who was swamped with a feeling of horror, but that horror was diluted by a fury that was greater than anything she had ever known. She tried to tamp it down, but it burned ever hotter, until her temper exploded out of control.

"All right, that is it!" she shrieked, pulling free from his hold and glowering up at him with her fists resting on her hips. "I have had enough! This was to have been my wedding day, the happiest day of my life, and what do I get instead? A trip through a blizzard that would have killed a lesser woman, and almost an entire hour listening to some mewling little twit spouting the biggest pack of lies it has ever been my misfortune to hear!"

"You insolent baggage—"

"And now you have the audacity to actually believe that I would take money for ending our engagement." Amanda ignored Teale's outburst, concentrating all of her fury on Justin. She'd crowded against him and was jabbing her finger at his chest. "How could you believe such a thing of me? *I* believed you were innocent at once. But then of course I love you, and I know you would never ever go back on your word! Apparently it is asking too much to assume you—"

"You love me?" Justin interrupted, his anger and disbelief giving way to incredible, joyous hope.

"Well, of course I do," she snapped, still glaring at him. "Although I am sure I must be mad to do so. You are the

310

most arrogant, overbearing, opinionated man I have ever met, and I—"

"Shut up, Amanda."

"I will not shut up! And furthermore you—" She got no further as Justin swept her up in his arms, his mouth claiming hers in a kiss of unrestrained passion and love. Her struggles ceased at once, and she flung her arms about his neck, returning his kiss for all she was worth.

"I love you, Amanda," he whispered between ardent kisses. "I love you more than anything in this world. Don't leave me, don't ever leave me, my darling."

"Never," she vowed fervently, cupping his strong face between her hands and gazing up at him with tear-filled eyes. "I wouldn't leave you now even if you ordered me to go."

"I would stop breathing before I would do that," he replied, his own eyes shining with a suspicious brightness. "I am everything that you say I am—pompous, overbearing, arrogant—but I love you, and I will go on loving you until the moment I die."

"I never said you were pompous," Amanda denied when they stopped kissing.

"Perhaps not this time," he agreed, his hands sliding down her neck to rest beneath the sweet curve of her breasts. "But I seem to recall hearing the accusation from you at some point in the past, and will be hearing it again in the future, I daresay," he added with a whimsical smile.

Amanda smiled weakly in response; then her smile vanished. "Justin"—she searched his face with solemn eyes—"are you *certain* this is what you want? Mr. Teale said things have changed, and-and he is right. You're not the same man you were when you first offered me marriage, and I wouldn't want you trapped by your promise. You must be certain I am the wife you want, the wife you need. I couldn't bear it if you came to regret your decision."

Her loving generosity touched Justin's heart, and he bent his head to give her a reassuring kiss. "You *are* the wife I need," he assured her softly. "And the woman I want above all others. You're right when you say I'm not the same man who first proposed to you; that man was cold inside, and dead to everything save a grim dedication to what he conceived of as his duty. You were right to refuse him, my love."

"But—"

"Inheriting Edward's title and fortune isn't what changed me," he continued softly, his fingers tracing the soft bow of her upper lip. "It is you who has changed me. You and your delightful family who took an angry, bitter soldier into your hearts and made him believe in the miracle of love."

They fell to kissing, lost to everything save each other. When they raised their heads, it was to find themselves quite alone, the open door mute testimony to the speed of Teale's flight. Justin glanced at it and smiled ruefully.

"It is good that he had the sense to leave," he said turning his head to grin at Amanda. "I probably would have killed him if I'd gotten my hands on him."

"Why bother?" Amanda's shoulders moved in a delicate shrug. "He is really of no consequence. Besides, if it hadn't been for him, it might have taken us weeks to declare our true feelings for each other."

"Would it?" Justin bestowed a playful peck on her nose. "For your information, ma'am I went to Aunt's house today with every intention of laying my heart at your feet."

"Really?" She was entranced by the very notion.

He nodded. "I woke up this morning thinking that this

was the day we were to be wed, and the realization it was not to be filled me with such despair that I thought I should go mad. It was then that I knew what I had to do." He stepped back from her and extracted an official-looking document from his pocket.

"What is this?" Her brows wrinkled as she took it from him.

"Our marriage license," he said, his blunt fingertip flicking the thick paper. "You will note the date."

"January tenth," she read, smiling in pleasure at the sight of her and Justin's names set down together.

"Today's date."

"I know."

"Amanda," Justin spoke succinctly, "this is our marriage license, with today's date on it. Don't you understand what that means?"

Comprehension dawned. "We can still be married?" she gasped, raising joy-filled eyes to his. "Today?"

He nodded again, grinning at her expression. "On the way to Aunt's I stopped at St. George's. The vicar is there, and he has agreed to marry us this afternoon — if you are willing," he added, with sudden diffidence. "I'll understand if you want to wait until we can arrange for your family to be present."

For a moment Amanda was strongly tempted to take him up on his generous offer, but only for a moment. "No." She shook her head decisively. "I would like having them, there but it really doesn't matter. So long as the minister is there I shall be more than content. Besides" — she cast him a teasing smile — "the twins would never forgive me. They have been longing to have you as their brother since the moment they clapped eyes on you."

He laughed, then grew serious. "There is just one more thing. About my appointment to Madrid —"

313

"You must do your duty," she interrupted, laying her head against his shoulder. "I understand now. I only protested before because I was afraid you'd find some charming señorita and fall madly in love with her."

"There was never a chance of that," he told her firmly. "Not since Christmas Eve when we stood beneath the mistletoe. I knew then that my feelings for you weren't those of a brother for a sister. Even if I hadn't learned about Amelia and Charles, I think I would have found some other excuse to end our engagement. But you have distracted me. What I was going to say is that I have decided to refuse the appointment. I'm not going to Madrid."

"You're not?" Amanda's voice quivered with joy.

"I'd decided to refuse it even before Edward's death. The military life is fine for an unmarried man, but a man with a wife and children has other responsibilities. I was going to tell you sooner but. . . ." He gave a sad shrug.

They both fell silent as they thought of Edward and his untimely death. Amanda slipped her arms around Justin in a loving embrace, silently vowing that she would help him survive the devastating loss of his beloved brother.

"I suppose we should be going," Justin said after a long silence had passed. "Teale is certain to return sooner or later, and it would probably be best if I was gone. I am still strongly tempted to make him pay for his machinations. Let's go home."

Amanda's heart swelled with love at the words. "Yes," she agreed softly "let's go home."

 *Epilogue*

Stonebridge Hall, Christmas Eve, 1814

"To the right. No, Justin, not my right, *your* right," Amanda directed from her nest of cushions on the settee. "Are you sure you were once in charge of placing the artillery? I vow, I've never seen anyone with a poorer sense of direction."

"That's because you're looking at it from the wrong angle," Justin replied, unperturbed by her hectoring tones. "Come up here and look at it."

"I'd love to, but a certain *arrogant* male I know would have my head if I dared attempt such a thing," she said with a roguish smile. "He is such a tyrant, you'd scarce believe it."

Justin cast a wry glance over his shoulder, his eyes resting possessively on his wife's gently rounded belly. "Oh, I'd believe it, all right," he drawled huskily. "Now, mind you stay there. I have something for you." He gave the angel's gossamer wings a final tug to set it in place and then climbed down the ladder the footman was holding for him.

"Wait until we've finished dinner before lighting the candles," he instructed. "I don't want any accidents."

"Yes, Your Grace," the young man responded, flicking the beautifully decorated tree an uncertain look. He'd never heard of anything so queer in all his days, but if it made his master and mistress happy, then he supposed he could learn to tolerate it. Besides, it was rather pretty.

When he'd gone, Justin settled on the cushions next to his wife, his arms stealing comfortably about her thickening waist. "Feeling better?" he asked, enjoying the feel of his child beneath his hands.

"Mmm," Amanda replied noncommittally, sighing as she leaned her head on his shoulder. "Where did you find such a large tree? It must have cost a fortune."

"In Northumberland, and yes, it did," Justin answered each of her questions in turn. "But the price will be well worth it. I can't wait to see the look on Belinda's face when she sees it."

"Yes, she'll doubtlessly declare it the *bestest* tree she has ever seen," Amanda agreed with a soft laugh at her younger sister's probable reaction to the ten-foot tree. "I'm only sorry I wasn't able to be of more help to you."

"I enjoyed it," Justin assured her, and was surprised to find it was so. Following their hasty marriage, they'd stayed in town long enough to see Amelia and Charles safely married off, and then they'd retired to the country. In the ten months since then, he'd flung himself wholeheartedly into the family life, and with each passing day his joy and love increased even more.

Amanda drew a deep breath as another pain knifed through her. The pains were getting closer together, and she knew it would soon be time to send for the doctor. But for the moment she was content to stay where she was, safe and warm in her husband's arms.

"What was that?"

"What?"

"That." Justin frowned as Amanda's stomach jerked beneath his cupped palms. "Is that the babe moving?"

"Yes," she said, gasping slightly. "I think he must be getting anxious for Christmas to get here."

"Well, he shall just have to wait." Justin moved his hand

in a soothing circle. "Meanwhile his papa has a present for his mama," and he handed her a small, gaily beribboned box. "Happy Christmas, Lady Stonebridge."

Her fingers trembled as she tore off the ribbons and scattered them about the settee. She fumbled a little with the lid of the white velvet box; but finally she was able to open it and the sight of the small pin nestled inside brought a soft gasp of pleasure to her lips. "Oh, Justin, it's beautiful!"

"Do you like it?" He sounded pleased.

"Like it? I adore it!" she exclaimed, lifting the pin from the box and turning it toward the firelight. Fashioned out of emeralds, the pin was a miniature fir tree, its tiny needles dusted with a coating of diamonds so that it glittered in the light. She'd never seen anything lovelier, and her eyes were sparkling with tears as she gazed up into her husband's face.

"It's the tree we saw in the woods last year, isn't it?" she asked, tears wending their way down her cheeks.

He nodded, ducking his head to brush her tears away with a gentle kiss. "That's when I first began loving you," he said simply. "I'd seen so much of death that I'd forgotten what it meant to be alive, but standing there with you in those snowy woods I found myself believing in the magic you talked about."

"Magic?" she asked touching his cheek with a gentle hand.

"Magic," he repeated, brushing back a strand of fiery hair that had fallen across her neck. "You and the children have filled my life with magic and wonder, and I can not thank you enough. I love you, Amanda."

"And I love you." She pressed a kiss on his throat, and then gasped again as another pain shot through her.

"Don't tell me that was the babe moving," Justin said, his tone anxious as he glowered down into her almost white face. "What is it?"

"That," Amanda answered, laughing and grimacing at the same time, "is my present to you, arriving slightly ahead of

317

schedule."

Justin's sherry-brown eyes grew wide with alarm. "Do you mean . . ." his voice trailed off. "Now?"

"Now," she agreed, clinging to his hand for support. "Do you think you could send one of the footmen for Dr. Prescott? I think I may have need of him in a few hours."

Justin shot up from the settee and dashed for the door, calling out orders in a commanding voice that had the servants scurrying about like startled ants. While the butler, two footmen, and the burly groom went in search of the doctor, Justin carried Amanda up to her room, roundly cursing her for not informing him of her condition sooner.

The next few hours passed in a blur for Amanda. Justin stayed at her side until an outraged Mrs. Hatcher and exasperated doctor finally ordered him out. After that things were decidedly foggy, but through the pain, Amanda thought of Justin, clinging to his love with increasing desperation. Finally, it was over, and her new-born son was placed in her arms.

"Edward Daniel," she murmured in an exhausted voice, blinking back weak tears. "I want him called Edward Daniel," and then she was asleep with the suddenness of a candle being extinguished.

The room was in semi-darkness when she next awoke. A single candle burned at her bedside table, and she could see Justin sleeping on the chair. The drapes had been left open, and the soft, white glow cast by the snow outside filled the room with an unearthly light. She lay there a few moments revelling in a feeling of loving contentment, and then she noticed Justin was awake and regarding her with glistening eyes.

"Happy Christmas, my love," he whispered, moving to kneel beside her. "How are you feeling?"

"Tired," she admitted, touching a hand to his wet cheeks. "But happy. And you?"

"Happy." He turned his head and placed a reverent kiss in